THE
WIDOW
OF THE
SOUTH

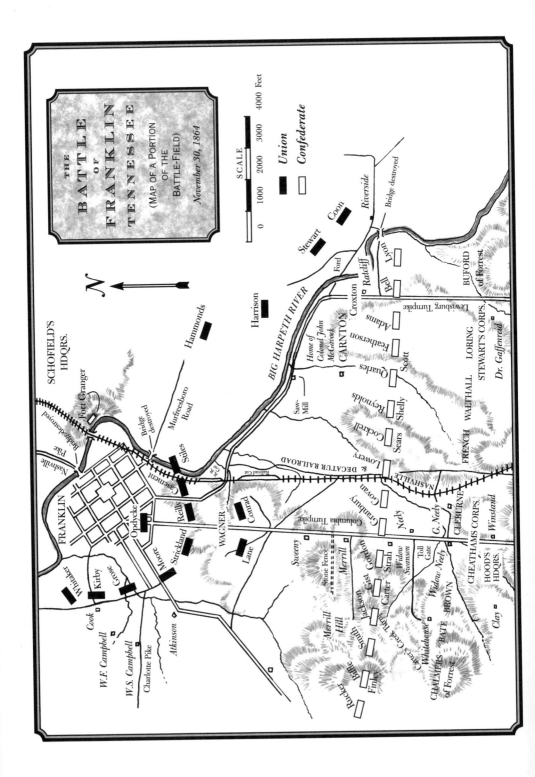

THE
BATTLE
OF
FRANKLIN
TENNESSEE

(MAP OF A PORTION
OF THE
BATTLE-FIELD)

November 30, 1864

SCALE

0   1000   2000   3000   4000 Feet

■ Union

□ Confederate

THE WIDOW

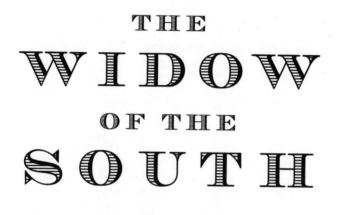

OF THE

SOUTH

ROBERT HICKS

WARNER BOOKS

NEW YORK   BOSTON

This book is a work of historical fiction. In order to give a sense of the times, names of real people or places as well as events have been included in the book. The story is imaginary, and the names of nonhistorical persons or events are the product of the author's imagination or are used fictitiously. Any resemblance of such nonhistorical persons or events to actual ones is purely coincidental.

Copyright © 2005 by Robert Hicks

Warner Books

Time Warner Book Group
1271 Avenue of the Americas, New York, NY 10020
Visit our Web site at www.twbookmark.com

Printed in the United States of America

First Edition: August 2005
10 9 8 7 6 5 4 3

Library of Congress Cataloging-in-Publication Data
Hicks, Robert
  The widow of the south / Robert Hicks. — 1st ed.
      p. cm.
  ISBN 0-446-50012-7— ISBN 0-446-57882-7 (lg. print)
  1. McGavock, Caroline E. Winder, 1829-1905—Fiction. 2. Tennessee—History—Civil War, 1861-1865—Casualties—Fiction. 3. Tennessee—History—Civil War, 1861-1865—Hospitals—Fiction. 4. Tennessee—History—Civil War, 1861-1865—Fiction. 5. Franklin, Battle of, Franklin, Tenn., 1864—Fiction. 6. Plantation owners' spouses—Fiction. 7. Williamson County, (Tenn.)—Fiction. 8. Plantation life—Fiction. 9. Cemeteries—Fiction. I. Title.
  PS3608.I287W53 2005
  811' .6—dc22

                                                                    2005010568

Book design and text composition by L&G McRee
Frontispiece map by Leo McRee

for
Tom Martin, Jr.
Semper Fidelis

PROLOGUE

1894

Down the rows of the dead they came. Neat, orderly rows of dead rebel boys who thirty years before had either dropped at the foot of earthen works a mile or so away or died on the floors of the big house overlooking the cemetery. Now there were stone markers, but for so many years there had been only wooden boards, weathered and warped, and tall posts proclaiming the numbers of the dead.

The two women knew the cemetery as they might have known the wrinkles on their faces or the pattern of repoussé on the coin silver. The white woman, dressed in worn black crinoline, carried a book tightly under her arm and periodically consulted it *just to make sure*. Her servant, a Creole, walked close by.

Over to their left, beyond the house, cedars and oaks sprouted, survivors of a once ancient grove. The Union had cut them down like a great whipping scythe. Carrie McGavock, the mistress of Carnton, keeper of the book of the dead, hardly thought of the grove anymore. The only grove that concerned her was the one beneath her feet, a grove of boys and men. She knew this was a ghastly thought, and yet it kept her from imagining bones and beetles and scraps of gray. It helped to think of her charges as constituting something monumental and not something in decay. She had seen enough of death and felt entitled to imagine herself as something other than an undertaker.

104 Killed at Franklin/Arkansas

A small boy ran along behind them at a distance, ducking between the grave markers and probably thinking he could elude her notice, but nothing eluded her in the graveyard, least of all clumsy, stumbling boys with Lord knows what jangling in their pockets. *Why must they always be following me?* she thought. *At least they're living and breathing and walking around, even if they* are *grubby and presumptuous.*

The boy was one of Carrie's adopted children, one of near two dozen orphans she'd taken in during the years since the war. Paul was his name, and he was only ten. Since arriving at Carnton almost a year before, he had developed the bad habit of pretending he was a Confederate scout and tracking Carrie and Mariah as they made their daily walk through the cemetery. It was as if something had been bred into him, Carrie thought, and he couldn't help acting out a role from a moment in time that had passed into memory decades before his birth. It was time to break him of that habit.

Carrie walked along slowly with Mariah eyeing her. Mariah knew she was up to something; she always knew. Mariah had been born knowing everything, Carrie reckoned, but she herself had needed to learn some things along the way.

When she had lulled Paul into thinking she wouldn't turn around, she looked over her shoulder and locked onto his eyes as he peered over a Texas marker, his yellow hair peppered with the twigs and leaves he imagined would disguise him. She pointed at him and opened the small brown book with the words "McGavock Cemetery" embossed in gold on its cover that she carried under her arm, the book in which she had recorded the names of the dead and their exact place in the earth, the book she carried with her at all times.

"I suppose we'll be needing to add another name to this book, Mariah."

"Reckon so."

"He spends so much time in the cemetery anyway."

"That's the truth, yes, ma'am."

"How do you spell his name again?"

"You know I ain't good with my letters, but I believe it's *P-A-* . . ."

Of course, this was too much for any little boy to stand, let alone a boy like Paul, whose desire to be around Carrie only barely exceeded his fear of the dead men in the ground.

"Please, ma'am, I ain't meant nothing by it."

"You *didn't* mean *anything* by it."

"Yes, ma'am. Not nothing."

Not nothing. *Can't fix everything,* she thought.

"But you spend so much time in here, Paul. I believe you'd like to spend more time if you could, and I can't think of a better way."

She took a pen out of her apron pocket and pretended to write in her book.

"You do, too," he said

"I do what?"

"Spend time in this place here. With the dead people."

For a moment Carrie felt the urge to defend herself. She had not felt the need to defend or justify herself for years. She had seen too much to have to explain anything to anyone. And yet the boy had a point.

"Come here, Paul."

The boy peeled his way around the grave marker slowly, expecting punishment, and walked heavy-footed up to Carrie's skirts before looking up at her through his messy bangs. She put her hand on his head and brushed his hair out of his eyes.

"I promise you'll never get your name in this book, if you promise to never come in here again."

"Yes, ma'am."

"You promise?"

"Yes, ma'am."

"All right, then."

"Now, take my name out of the book. Please, ma'am."

Mariah covered her mouth to keep from laughing, as she always did when she watched her mistress get sassed. Carrie would have laughed, too, but she couldn't risk the boy not taking her seriously. She wanted him never to come into that cemetery again, and if she could, she'd have made it so that he never went into any cemetery again and never heard of or saw a dead person the rest of his life. She'd done plenty of time with the dead, more than enough time to exempt the people she loved from morbidity.

"I will take your name out of this book when I see you running into that house to finish up your lessons. And if I ever catch . . ."

But Paul was already gone, running so fast his muddy leather boots slapped his rear as he went, leaving little marks.

Carrie watched him go and then turned to Mariah, whom she had once owned, a gift to her from her father. She *was* a gift, whatever the meaning and implications of that word. Mariah had been her tether to the earth when things had spun away, when Carrie wasn't sure if there remained a real and true life for her, and then when she wasn't sure if she wanted that life even if it existed. Things had been different once. She couldn't believe that she had ever been so . . . *what?* Weak? No, that wasn't it. She'd never been weak. She'd been buffeted and knocked down, like grass bent to the ground by the wind preceding a thunderstorm. She'd been slow to get up. But she did get up, eventually. There had been no choice. She was not afraid of much, and she especially wasn't afraid of God. Not anymore, not for a long time.

"Mariah, what do you see?"

A mockingbird chased a hawk across the width of the cemetery, diving and chattering at the black shadow until it was banished from whatever bit of territory the smaller bird claimed for its own.

"I see a mockingbird. And some of them yellow birds. Finches. Big old bird with claws, too."

Mariah looked past her mistress, across the field of tall grass.

424 Killed at Franklin/Mississippi

"You know that isn't what I mean."

Carrie could see the markers and the grass, and the iron fence ringing the graveyard. She could turn and see the back of her house and remember the beards on the dead generals laid out on the porch below and the keening of the wounded on the balcony above. She could see just fine. But there was more to seeing than that, she thought. It was either a failure of imagination or a slight by the Lord Himself, but in any case she could not see the things Mariah could see. Mariah could tell her about things that gave her comfort, and Carrie cared not a whit about how she came upon the knowledge.

She pointed at a grave marker in the Tennessee section. *MJM*, it read. In places, twigs leaned against the stones. She made a mental note to tell the yard boy about them.

"What about him? That one."

"Miss Carrie, please, ma'am. This ain't right."

Carrie stared hard at the seam of her dress, where the new thread of her latest mending stood out like a long dark cord against the faded black of her ankle-length dress. She hadn't known how to sew before the war, and she still wasn't very good at it. They would have to dye the whole thing soon.

"I would like to know about that man."

Mariah wasn't sure that what she saw in her mind was real, just the product of a fevered imagination, or maybe the work of the devil himself making her play games with the white woman whom she loved in a way she could not describe. Fragments of light and sound came to her when she let her mind drift, and the words Carrie craved formed on Mariah's lips unbidden. It was a thought-less exercise, a pastime to while away an afternoon. The thing she *did* know, the only thing she knew for sure, was that Carrie *believed*. Mariah could feel that on her.

"I don't know what to say, ma'am."

"Yes, you do. Don't play. We're too old for that. Tell me what you see when you stare into the earth right there. Don't hold back. I know when you're holding back."

Mariah closed her eyes and went silent, hoping Carrie would forget her little obsession and keep walking. But Carrie stayed put, so Mariah began to speak.

"There a man and a boy. It sunny. They ain't working, so maybe they just home from church."

"How old?"

"The man, he a man. Got a beard. Dark, strong. He ain't old or young. The boy, he just a little one, though he think he bigger. Maybe ten. He got a fishing pole in his hand. They going to catch fish."

"Is there a woman?"

"She dead."

"How do you know that?"

" 'Cause they going out fishing in they church clothes."

They walked past MJM and whatever he might have become. The air was thick, the grass was soft, and they moved so slowly they seemed to float. Another Tennessee summer, thick and grown over. Carrie was long used to the weather, but sometimes she missed the breezes of her home parish, the smell of wind off the water. There was nothing wet nearby but a little river, and that was almost a mile away. She'd learned to walk calmly and to look out for shade.

The mockingbird returned from the fight and perched nearby on a Missouri marker. The bird eyed them first from one eye and then the other, its long tail feathers pumping up and down. Carrie frowned. It was a ridiculous display coming from a bird so common and so obviously unfriendly. What if all the mockingbirds in the world just disappeared? Stranger things have happened, and she wouldn't miss them.

She and Mariah moved so lightly the grave markers seemed to march toward them.

130 Killed at Franklin/Missouri

The cemetery contained the remains of almost 1,500 of the 6,000 Confederate soldiers dead or wounded under General Hood's command in a few hours on November 30, 1864. On this very ground, men had formed up and marched off to fight. The men who remained now were the men who would never be returned home—men who were forgotten or from people too poor to fetch their remains or from people who were never told what became of their sons. Carrie had heard the nicknames: the Morgue of the South, the Temple of Dead Boys. Snide, she thought, but not unexpected. Cemeteries were rightly the province of governments and historical societies and ladies' patriotic aid organizations. It was an odd thing to keep a private cemetery so large without assistance or official sanction. Carrie knew this. She didn't much care. The war had come to her one day, suddenly and with an otherworldly insistence that wasn't the work of the sovereign God she thought she had known. Who else could understand that, except perhaps the dead men in her cemetery? She would not give up her little part of the war; she would not let the war invade and then disappear without a trace, as if there were no need for a reckoning, no way to atone for the great crime. She had long before determined to hold on to it by the tail.

Since the war she hadn't spent much time in the company of women other than Mariah. She rarely went into town for social engagements. Why would she want to attend any more commemorative tea parties thrown by ladies fighting over the legless officers who lent luster to their guest lists, ladies who ran when the Yankees came and lived off their poorer relatives while clutching their silver? She'd seen too much of them and of their endless reunions. They bored her.

No, she was inescapably the Widow of the South, the Keeper of the Book of the Dead. She would wear black until she died. This was who she was now. Let the gossips have their little parties and caress the folded sleeves of the armless. Let them blather on about the wisdom of the old ways and of the invincible resilience of the Southern people and of the glories of the war. She had more important things to do.

"We're going to need to clean this place up today, Mariah. Sweeping and raking is what's needed. We'll have to start at the far end and work back. And I'm not happy with the way that old obelisk is leaning, the one in the section of the unknown boys. We need to get a man up here to straighten that old thing out. Won't do for it to be looking like it was too old to stand up. And I'm not sure, but I think I've got some of the Texans misidentified in the book. You'd think I'd have it right by now, but nothing is ever done, not ever. And while we're at it . . ."

She heard him before she saw him. A small cough, followed by a louder, deeper cough that he tried to swallow back. She turned toward the house and there, in the path between the gravestones, stood an old man. A surprisingly old man. He was thin and pepper-haired, and his eyes were too dark for her to see where he was looking. They were set back too far in his head to distinguish them from the shadows. He stood up tall and held his old bowler in his hand. She could see him nervously massaging his knuckles under the hat, which caused a little halo of dust to rise up off the felt. He wore a long coat that was slightly too short and scuffed boots. His mouth was twisted up in what appeared to be a smirk, but which she knew was not. He watched her closely and walked toward her with the faintest hint of a limp, enough to make her heart break. The twisted and dried-out parts of him still contained just the memory of his old beauty—all the parts of him were still there, they'd just been used up. He stood before her, so close she could hear the air whistling in and out of him. She knew him immediately, as if he'd left only the day before.

"Why'd you scare that boy, Mrs. McGavock?"

"I love that boy."

"He one of yours?"

"Do I look like he could be my child?"

"I meant, is he your grandson or something? That's possible, ain't it?"

"No, he's not my grandson, just a stray off the street."

"Just a stray," the man repeated.

They paused and looked at each other, and Carrie felt angry that he'd come without warning. The feeling passed. She pushed a stray lock of hair behind her ear and squinted hard at him.

"I didn't mean to insinuate anything," she said.

"I reckon I ain't had anyone insinuate anything about me in a long time. I didn't take no offense."

"But none was meant."

The old man stopped and toed at the grass with his foot. He looked around at the grave markers like he had misplaced something. He started to sway a little, and Mariah moved quickly behind him, ready to steady him if she had to, but not willing to speak or acknowledge him. He spoke again.

"I thought we decided a long time ago that folks don't always know what they mean. Or what things mean, for that matter."

Carrie considered this. "I suppose we did."

The old man bent over in a fit of coughing, slapping at his breast pocket until he found an old handkerchief to spit into. Mariah bent over him with her hand on his back and looked up at Carrie like she'd just seen something she wished she hadn't. He stared at his handkerchief, snorted dismissively, and put it away, all the while bent over like he was catching his breath.

Carrie had the feeling that she was falling. How could he be like this? This was not the man she'd known, not the man she remembered. The air spun and hummed around her.

She walked to his side and took his chin in her hand, hard, and pulled until he was looking her in the eye. Mariah cried out and tried to stop her, but Carrie waved her off. She saw him fully for the first time and reached with her other hand to wipe rheumy tears from the corners of his eyes and to feel the loose drape of his skin over sharp cheekbones. He struggled to keep from coughing in her face.

"What's the matter with you, soldier?"

She let him go, and he slowly stood up straight. He held his bowler near his mouth, just in case.

"Well, I reckon I can guess, but I ain't seen anyone who could tell me straight. Can't afford such a person. I've been thinking that, after all these years, I might finally die and not know for sure what killed me. That makes me laugh some."

Carrie said nothing, and then: "If I were to guess from your past history, I would say you'll outlive us all."

"I once thought I was cursed that way, yes, ma'am. But no more. There ain't no more curses out there. My history don't mean nothing. Not anymore, thank God."

She could picture him as a younger man, lying bleeding on the floor of her parlor and then sitting up in one of the chairs of her husband's study, staring out the window. She remembered his nose and how sharp it was in profile, how the light seemed changed after passing over it. He was like a cameo; at least that's what her mind remembered. She'd become used to him quickly, and back then she thought he'd be there forever. Then he was gone. She closed her eyes.

"If you're going to die, there's a place for you here."

"That's what I meant to ask you about."

BOOK I

1

NOVEMBER 30, 1864: DAWN

That day in 1864 was unseasonably mild for late November. There had been a frost already, and the land lay fallow. The cotton, which lay white on the fields in early fall like the crashed remains of an exhausted wave, had been gathered and ginned and baled and shipped off for when it could be transported in safety, which was practically never. Most of it sat stacked near the gins, in warehouses, and in barns around town. But the fields looked healthy, and the houses weren't burned to the ground, and the barns weren't stripped of their joists and planking, and the nearby rail line, the Nashville & Decatur Railroad, still had all the pieces of its track.

Early that morning, long and twisting columns of butternut gray moved slowly up the three pikes that cut their way toward Franklin, Tennessee. They were miles away but closing fast. Bright metal flashed from within each column, like the glistening of a snake's scales. The locals later remembered that the thump of boots and bare feet upon the macadam rattled the windows of their houses. These were the Confederates, come to smash the Federals. They had been ridden hard. They wore raggedy homespun and crumpled felt slouch hats, and they were so skinny that no one—not even the Federals—blamed them for looting the dead of their food. It did not escape their notice that the land they were moving into had been spared the ravages of war, unlike Atlanta and the little towns of northern Alabama where they had lately been. There they had seen ghost towns and torched fields, houses that retained only the barest skeletal relation to their former selves. There they had seen what looked like the ruins of an ancient civilization.

Here they saw houses circled by groves of giant cedars and magnolias so beautiful they thought they would never see a thing so pretty again, and white board churches that inspired silent oaths of faith and devotion from even the lapsed and godless, promises of good works in exchange for survival. The meanest, most dissolute and liquored-up men looked on the land and wanted nothing more than the quiet, pious life they could lead in one of the houses along the side of the road, tending crops and riding to the little wooden churches with their plump wives and their cherub-faced children. Few such men ever lived such lives later on, if they survived, but it could be said that the imminence of death had inspired in even the hardest cases a momentary appreciation of anonymity and quiet.

The columns kept on, converging as the roads angled in. They seemed unstoppable, inexorable, churning on and on as if to chase down and devour the town itself. There would soon be no escape, but this was not something anyone in Franklin could know at dawn on November 30.

In the town another mass—this one of blue—swarmed and jittered upon the outskirts, scraping at the dirt with their shovels and picks and bayonets, felling trees and Osage orange hedges, building bulwarks and ramparts. These were the Federals, who had snuck by the Confederates the night before when they rightfully should have been beaten down and destroyed. Good-bye, Andersonville, *they had whispered to each other as they walked quietly up the pike past the Confederates at Spring Hill, invoking the name of the most feared*

Confederate prison. How could 21,000 men walk up a road within a few hundred yards of another 25,000 men and not be noticed? Better not to wonder, thought the men laboring at the ditches, their shirts torn off and their muscles glazed in dirt and sweat. Might jinx it.

And so the Federals, bone-tired, threw up even more defenses across the southern end of town, a crooked smile of trenches that ran across the bend in the river, from one side of town to the other, in the off chance that the rebels would put up a fight. The possibility was absurd, and after getting together a decent defensive position, many of the Federals wandered about the town in search of food and drink. Many of the Federal officers, that is. They found the natives friendly and hospitable. Or perhaps they were just worn down by the occupation and endless requisitions of the small Yankee garrison that had lived among them for two years while fortifying the town. In any case, the newcomers helped themselves to their stores and their whiskey. Don't mind if I do, they said, filling their canteens and propping their boots up on the railing of porches, watching their men dig and saw and hammer.

A little town, Franklin had its share of rambling two-story frame manses surrounding its square, and plenty of ancient oaks and maple trees with branches hiding little boys staring goggle-eyed and dumbstruck at the bluecoats, thousands more than they'd ever seen. Amid the sound of pickaxes and shouts drifting up toward the square, ladies sat on their porches moving backgammon pieces and wondered if they'd actually see a real battle now, the sort of thing they had read about in the Chattanooga Rebel, which published the clever little irreverent letters of one of the local boys off fighting somewhere to the south.

A hawk circling high above the land, floating on the thermals thrown into such disorder by the heat of the day, would have seen the stream of butternut gray gliding ever closer to the mob of blue, the glint of metal and the flash of bright flags, the gashes of newly turned dirt, the orderly streets and the regular gray roofs of Franklin. Whatever coincidence or divine intent had conspired to bring it about, Franklin was surrounded.

A squad stirred awake. They stoked fires grown cold overnight and watched them crack and spark before they remembered that the things they had to eat weren't worth cooking. Hickory nuts and sugarcane. One by one they abandoned their fires. They dried their rifles with their shirts and hoped they would fire when the time came. They were in no hurry for that time to come, but the sun kept rising. A few voices carried over the shuffling and groaning.

"What you gonna do with them oats? Give 'em here."

"Damn, boy, you look green. What's that smell?"

"Please, y'all, that blanket was from my mama."

"The hell you say. My oats. Mine."

"I don't know about this cut I gotcheer on my arm. It's got a smell to it."

"The blanket was from his mama! Well, somebody better give it over right quick, or Mama gonna whup his ass."

"There bugs in 'em oats, so what you care? Cough it up. You gonna die anyway."

"You got to see the doc about that, Harlon."

"He all infested, you ain't gone want it. Got the fleas or something, got that itch. Just give the boy his blanket."

"And you'll be a-dying right before me, I guarantee it. No oats for any of you. Get back."

"I ain't gone see the doc. Just as soon keep my arm."

"That's all right, I'll just get it back when you through with it. Don't go getting blood on it, now."

"All right, just a few, then. Gimme some crumbs."

"Better your arm than otherwise."

"When we're what with it? Speak up."

"Steal your own damn oats. Steal from Pendergrass."

"What's worse than losing an arm?"

"When you're through, when you're dead."

"Pendergrass is dead."

"Than otherwise dead."

The bright jingle of stirrups and bridles silenced them. Officers.

No sense calling attention to themselves. Silence could keep you alive sometimes, keep you from being volunteered for something stupid.

Hundreds of horsemen rode out of the Confederate camp as the sun rose behind the clouds. They were led by a tall man, hunched over in his saddle and unnaturally thin. The tall rider led them along the Columbia Pike, which ran hard by the army's night camp, and headed north toward Franklin. Many more of his horsemen rode toward the town on other roads. The cavalry was on the move.

In the dust of the macadam road the tall rider could make out the boot prints of 21,000 Union soldiers who had somehow passed that way undetected in the night, a turn of events so impossible it made him flinch every time his new mare stumbled over a caisson track. When fellow riders strayed too close, he pushed them off with one of his big, bony hands and warned them to watch the road and stay the hell away from him. He had no time for their god-awful horsemanship. He had no time, either, for the god-awful hills of middle Tennessee, with their hollows, draws, ridges, and points, all no doubt hiding Yankees lying in ambuscade.

When did that happen? When did the Yankees start lying in wait for him? He was the impossible fighter, not the stumbling Yankees, who were ever fat and lethargic in his unsettling night dreams. He worked miracles against long odds, he made General William T. Sherman afraid, he made fools of the enemy. Had he not been called a monster and a devil by the abolitionist newspapers? Yes, he had, and damn them for their ignorance. He was no monster, he thought. He just wanted victory worse than most men.

And yet it was undeniable that they had all been fooled in their sleep, even Major General Nathan Bedford Forrest. Whose fault was that? It was a question that couldn't really be answered, not right then, but the tall man was damned if he'd have the blame laid at his feet. Not ever. He was not in charge, not this time. He, Forrest, had never been beaten when he was in charge, which is a whole lot more than he could say for that cripple Hood. Let the commanding officer pull himself away from the fog of his precious laudanum and take the blame. Let Hood take it, and damn him to hell.

In four years he had never seen Southern land so unmolested. Tennessee had once been his home. Now look at it: Unionists and deserters and traitors everywhere. He wondered what deals had been struck to spare those fields. He'd been a businessman once, and he knew about deals. There was a time when he always got the better half of a deal on a slave, but no longer. That life was past him now, and that fact made him resentful.

He rode with the broad brim of his hat pulled over his face, shielding his sunken eyes and the cheekbones that seemed ready to burst through his sallow skin. He had boils and a cough. The years of battle had made him seem smaller, robbing his frame of its solidity and power and leaving behind a bony carcass that could only be roused by battle. Before Hood began his mad march into oblivion, Forrest had hoped to get some time to go back to Mississippi and recuperate. There was no time for that now. He rode on, swaying in his saddle and brooding.

Yes, he knew something about chasing Yankees. Get 'em skeered and then keep the skeer on 'em. How he wished those Yankees up there in Franklin were scared. He could work with fear. Hell, he had won whole battles with little more than the fear in the eyes of trembling Union commanders peering out between the cracks of their forts. But it would be a queer thing if those Yankees were scared much right then, he figured. It was his men who were riding into the unknown. Who's got the skeer on 'em now?

His staff wasn't much to look at. He'd had so many of them come and go he sometimes forgot their names. They were skeletal and bone-tired like Forrest, but they had a certain irrational hope that Forrest could not share. They were riding with Forrest, by God! Hero of Shiloh and Brice's Cross Roads! They had faith in him, and Forrest felt the burden of their faith. They could not see battlefields like he could; the strengths and weaknesses of the enemy were not as plain to them. He had come to resent that they could not read his mind and anticipate what he would do. This was unfair of him, but he could get wore out just like any man. Why do I got to do all the thinking all the time? *They were loyal, at least. He could say that for them.*

Up the pike they went, gray and ragged, picking their way over the footprints of the enemy. The road rolled gently and straight, bordered on each side by farmhouses and fields lying rich and fallow. Faces watched warily from farmhouse windows. Women used to run out of their homes in their bedclothes when we rode through, and now we get this. Shit. That pretty little bastard Jeff Davis should see this.

The whole world was queered, and Forrest no longer knew who loved him and who hated him. Well, that wasn't exactly true: he knew the Yankees hated him. And the niggers. They could be Yankees and niggers behind those windows, homegrown goddamn Yankees and runaways, for all he knew.

He stopped. He looked out at the farmland passing beside him, dormant brown humps rolling off as far as he could see. The remnants of old weeds poked out of the fields here and there and shook in the wind. He looked harder at the fields stretching out before him, and everything was familiar for a moment. He had almost forgotten that he'd been there before, right on that road. He'd fought there and won, way back almost two years before. He'd lost his favorite horse there, too, a big sorrel stallion named Roderick. Loyal and stupid. Wouldn't stay out of the fight, even when Forrest had sent him to the rear with a gunshot wound. Broke loose and went galloping around the battlefield until he took a bullet in his head while leaping over a hedge. Just looking for his master. There was no lesson in that, Forrest thought. It just was what it was.

They rode on. He expected to hear the sounds of cattle and chickens, the shouts of children, the creaking of wagons—but there were none. Except for the eyes peering out from the windows, everyone seemed to have vanished. They know a fight's comin'. *He spurred his horse on a little more. It wasn't far to Franklin, but it seemed an endless slog over the hills. Forrest didn't like how the road had begun to slope gently up toward the town, straight and unbroken by cover or protection. He called a halt, and his men's horses came skittering and snorting to a stop around him. He scanned the sunburned and dirty faces staring expectantly at him and asked if anyone knew this place.*

One man raised his hand while spitting out some tobacco and pulled his yellow hair out of his eyes. He'd been in Forrest's troop longer than most.

"My uncle lives around here, I been here before."

"Where is there a place I can see the town from without getting out from cover?"

Forrest trusted this man, who had once shot a Federal officer in the face before he could run Forrest through. He liked that kind of loyalty, the kind that saved his skin.

"There's a house off the Lewisburg Pike. Got two stories. McGavocks own it."

McGavock, McGavock. I know that name.

"Where is this house at?"

"I can take us there. There's woods, be easy to sneak up on it."

McGavock. I might have sold him slaves.

"Go on, then."

CARNTON

Mariah knew Carrie would not come greet the men. She closed the door behind her before walking heavily across the passage to the staircase, which she took down to the ground floor. If Confederates were coming, she decided, she must receive them at the front of the big house like proper folks. If she had to cover for her missus yet again, and this time with men who frightened her like the devils in one of her old dreams, she would use all the power of the house and whatever might still be dignified and imposing about it. Not much to go on, but still . . .

Sometimes she thought of herself as the mistress of the house. She planned the meals and directed what was left of the house staff. She had intercepted many visitors on the front brick walkway during the last two years, telling each of them that her mistress was not feeling well and could not rise to see them. Town people had quit coming to visit unless it was to transact business with Colonel John or Mariah, and she had heard there was some speculation about Carrie's health and the propriety of any household that would leave a nigger in charge. Hattie and Winder, Carrie's children, came hollering for Mariah to settle their disputes now, after encountering Carrie's closed and locked door all too often. It had come to this, finally: she sometimes forgot about Carrie, something that would never have happened when she was running around fetching food and sewing and books and mops and what all. When her mistress ran things. Sometimes now she would jump a little when she heard footsteps on the floor above her.

Mariah walked past the plaques of the "Masks of Tragedy" on the walls of the hallway and, now hurrying, across the worn-out floorcloth that led to the front doors, which she unlocked. She stepped out onto the portico. She held her hands clasped in front of her to keep them from shaking.

At the end of the front walkway a small group of riders had come to a halt, and between the rows of boxwoods and cedars that lined the front walk she could see a tall man unwind himself from the back of his horse and step to the ground. His movements seemed so languid she was surprised by how quickly he moved up the path. She wanted him to stay forever down by the gate. He walked bowlegged and loose, with his head down, and was upon her before she knew it. When he first noticed her, he made a gesture as if to take off his hat, but when he saw her fully, he left it on. Down by the gate one of the other gray men dismounted and held the horse of his leader in one bony hand.

"I need to use your back porch, second floor. I saw it on the way up here. Get your people so I can talk to 'em."

"Pardon me, sir, but Colonel McGavock's out, and Mrs. McGavock's a mite too sick to take visitors. She would be happy to receive you on another day, and she send her regrets."

He eyed her for a moment, as if he was trying to figure her out, and then he nodded. He knocked his boot against the bottom step of the landing, and clods of red mud fell into the path.

"I ain't a visitor. I am General Forrest, and I'ma use your house to reconnoiter awhile. Watch yourself."

With that, he strode up the stairs two at a time and tried to brush past Mariah, but she had already fallen back to the doorway.

"Please, sir, Colonel McGavock say no visitors or disturbances."

Forrest pulled up and clenched his fists for a moment before rocking back on his heels and nodding again. He seemed to be trying to remember something he had once known, maybe something he had been taught when he was a boy but had long since forgotten. He nodded and took a deep breath.

"Please tell your mistress I am right sorry she's sick and that I hope she gets well. I will do my damnedest to stay quiet, but I'm coming in. Get out of the way."

Mariah had made her attempt, and now she knew it was time to step aside. She remembered where she'd heard Forrest's name. Some of the town Negroes had been talking about him the last time she'd gone in to get supplies. *Forrest killed all them colored soldiers, throttled them right around the neck. He left not a one standing, and he put their heads on sticks all around the place. Fort Pillow it was. He the devil, no doubt. The Lord goin' to make him pay, yes.* This memory made him seem smaller to her, less human, and therefore more contemptible. She would not give him respect. She stood with her back to the wall as he strode into the house and trod hard across the diagonal squares of the floorcloth toward the stairs. Mariah saw his steps raise little dust balls.

"Is this the way up'n the top floor?"

"Yes."

"You let me know when *Colonel* McGavock gets back, hear?"

"Yes."

But Mariah followed him up the stairs. She would not let him out of her sight, not while Carrie was up there.

3

SERGEANT ZACHARIAH CASHWELL, 24TH ARKANSAS

We were marching up that pike, and everywhere you looked there were things cast off by the Yankees littering the sides of the road, and it was everything our officers could do to keep the young ones from ducking out of formation and snatching up something bright and useful-looking, like crows looking to decorate their nests. The old ones, like me, we knew better than to pick up anything, because you'd have to carry it, and we knew that our burden was heavy enough. But, hell, the Yankees had thrown away more than we'd laid our eyes on in months, maybe years. There were pocket Bibles and little writing desks, poker chips and love letters, euchre decks and nightshirts, canteens and pots of jam, and all kinds of fancy knives. It looked like a colossus had picked up a train full of things, from New York or one of those kinds of places, and dumped it all out to see what was what. And I'm just mentioning the things that you might want to pick up and keep. There was a lot more, besides. There were wagons left burning on the side of the road, crates of rotten and infested meat, horses and mules shot in their traces. I reckon those animals weren't moving fast enough, and you couldn't blame the Yankees for lightening their loads if they could, but it was a sorry sight. Even so, all that gear gladdened my heart because it seemed so desperate. They were *running*, by God. They were running from us, the 24th Arkansas, and all the rest of the brigades ahead of us and behind us. The columns stretched far as I could see when I wiped the sweat from my eyes and got a good look around. But mostly I just kept my head down and put my feet down, one in front of the other, the way I'd learned to do.

The officers rode up and down the column on their horses, saying all sorts of things to keep our spirits up. I'd learned that if you needed an officer to pick up your spirits, you were in sorry shape. But some of the younger boys listened, and they were heartened by it. The officers talked about the glory of the South and about how our women would be watching and how they would expect us to fight like Southern men—hard and without quitting. I wanted to say, *Until that bullet come for you*, but I didn't. Those officers were getting a whole lot of the men riled up for a fight, and I figured that was good no matter what else I had to say about it. Some of our boys had their homes around there, and you could just tell they were itching to get going. You had to hold them back, tell them to pace themselves, or else they'd start running and whooping and getting all lathered.

One big hoss in the company ahead, a man with a full beard and a neck like a hog's, started yelling for the band to give us a tune. He stomped his feet and rattled the bayonet he had at his side, and then some other of the boys did the same thing, and pretty soon we were all yelling at the band to play "The Bonnie Blue Flag," to give us a tune and be useful for once. The band even got a few notes off before one of the company commanders rode by, snatched up a trumpet, and threatened to beat them with it if he heard another note. That was funny to watch, and it was about as good a morale lifter as hearing "The Bonnie Blue Flag" straight through, on account of our band wasn't very accomplished.

The thing I kept thinking about was the nightshirts and the pots of jam, lying there on the roadside. They made me wonder whether we'd been fighting in the same war.

And then the order went out to get on line. They just up and stopped us, and I couldn't help running into the man ahead of me and getting a whiff of the sweat and stink rising up off his homespun shirt. The men quit jabbering, and then the thousands of us were moving to either side of the road, all bunched up at first but then thinning out as the line got longer and longer, like a ball of twine unwinding. There wasn't any stomping of the feet then, no bayonet rattling. We picked our way across the hills, some units stopping at the edge of a tree line, most of us out in the open. It took me a few moments to realize we were going to stop and fight right here, rather than chase the Yanks all the way to Nashville. It looked like a mighty long way to the Union lines, which were up on a rise. I could see men way up there in town tossing dirt around. The sunlight flashed off their shovels and picks, and sometimes it seemed like you could actually pick out the sound of their work a few seconds after you'd seen their tools go chunking into the dirt. It was so damn hot for late November. What had General Hood said when we crossed the river into Tennessee? *No more fighting on the enemy's terms.* I looked at those battlements up ahead over a mile distant, and I thought, *We must be the greatest army in the world if these are our terms.*

I'd been fighting for three years by then. I'd been shot once, and my left arm still didn't feel right. Sometimes I had a hard time lifting my rifle and keeping it steady. I thought about this and began flexing my arm to get it limbered up. We sat down in place and began the long wait.

It always seemed a long wait before the fight, no matter how long it took. Officers rode here and there conferring with one another, and then they'd come back and huddle with their sergeants, and word would come down about what was happening, and then they'd do it all over again and the word would change. This drove some of the men crazy every time. *Shit, let's just go,* they'd yell to no one in particular, and they'd jump up and pace around and kick a tree or something. Sometimes you didn't know what they meant by "go": fighting or running. I'm quite sure that both options crossed the minds of most men. It crossed my mind every time, and I'd been in a lot of fights and hadn't run yet.

Well, I hadn't run until everyone else was running. I had that rule.

The thing I'm about to say, you might not understand unless you've been in war. But in those moments before the fight, if you were a smart man, you'd figure out a way to convince yourself that it didn't matter to you if you lived or died. If you're safe in your house, with your children running around underfoot and with fields that need to be worked, it's an impossible way of thinking unless you're sick or touched in the head. Of course it mattered if you lived or died. But if you went into a battle caring what happened to you, you wouldn't be able to fight, even though you knew you were as likely to die as the next man whether you cared or not. There wasn't any logic to who got killed and who didn't, and it was better that your final thoughts not be of cowardice and regret. It was better not to care, and to let yourself be swept up in the rush of the men beside you, to drive forward into the smoke and fire with the knowledge that you had already beaten death. When you let yourself go like that, you could fight on and on.

Everyone had their own way of getting their mind right. We lingered there on the outskirts of Franklin, and I could see each of the men in my company going through their little rituals. There were two ways of getting ready. Most of the new men, unless they were unusually wise or strong-minded, went about tricking themselves into forgetting the possibility of death. One youngster in an almost clean uniform took a couple pieces of straw, stuck it in his hat, and began to loudly tell every joke he could remember to no one in particular, as if everything would be all right if he could keep laughing right up until the bullet got him. A few people were listening to him, but that wasn't really the point.

Listen here, I got another one. Three old men come courting a young lady, and she says, "What can I expect from a marriage to you?" And the first old man, he says, "I've got a big ol' . . ."

Other younger ones paced back and forth, hitting themselves in the chest, shaking their heads like bulls, and cursing. These were the ones who were trying to make themselves so angry and riled up that they'd run like they had blinders on and rush wherever someone pointed them without thinking about anything except throttling something or somebody. Some of these boys picked up rocks and threw them as hard as they could at the confused rabbits, squirrels, and coveys of quail flushed out of their hiding places by our noise. I caught one mountain boy with stringy auburn hair and no shoes punching and kicking at an old locust tree behind us, and I yanked him around and sat him down before he hurt himself.

Me and some of the other veterans, we had different ways. We'd all been in battle, and you couldn't go through such a thing more than a couple times without it becoming impossible to forget death. The boy I'd joined up with three years before, my best friend from Fayetteville, he'd gotten a minié ball through the eye at Atlanta. In my dreams I still see his pink round face thrown back on the ground, his mouth open and his crooked teeth bared, his straw-blond hair matted with blood. After that, I never forgot about death.

The way I prepared myself was to sit down on my pack, pick out a point on the horizon, and stare at it. This is what I did that day at Franklin. I stared and stared at what appeared to be a church steeple on the edge of the town, just at the limits of my vision, and I took stock of my place in the world. My father had died young, and my ma ran off when I was about ten. I didn't have a girl, I had no one to go back to. I was just a man, and even if I'd lived to be a hundred, I'd still be forgotten someday. Men die, that's how it is. I had lost my faith by then; otherwise, I guess I would have prayed for my safety, but I didn't. I took deep breaths, stared at that steeple, and convinced myself I didn't matter in this world. I was an ant, a speck of dust, a forgotten memory. I was insignificant like everyone else, and it was this insignificance that made me strong. If my life was insignificant and my death meaningless, then I was free of this world and I became the sole sovereign of my own world, a world in which one act of courage before death would be mine to keep forever. I could keep that from God.

When they called us up to get on line again, this time for keeps, I was ready. Men dusted themselves off, tightened their belts, and obsessively checked their cartridges and ammunition, just in case. I stood there, staring forward, silent, looking out over the rolling land, hearing the *pop pop pop* of pickets firing their first shots, and thinking I could almost see around the bend of the earth if I looked hard enough. It was so pretty. The hills were glowing and soft-looking, and I saw a couple of deer scatter out of the woods and leap across the fields as we moved out. I could have seen myself living in that little town in front of me, in a proper house, under a different set of circumstances and in a different lifetime. Before we stepped off, I thought, *I wonder why they chose this place for me to die.*

And that, finally, was my real strength: I knew I was going to die. I wasn't happy about it, but I felt relieved to know it.

4

CARRIE MCGAVOCK

I heard the muffled voices downstairs in the central passage and then the sound of hard boots on the creaky stairs. I could smell tobacco and sweat, a scent I imagined drifting off him and insinuating itself into the warp and weave of my house, disturbing my peace, throwing everything off kilter. What could possibly be so important? I turned back to Martha's dress and scrubbed until the threading began to fray.

We must endeavor to keep her cool, and her room darkened. Close the blinds, please.

The room felt suddenly hot and stale. There seemed to be no air; whatever air that remained seemed thin and fragile and musty. I stood up from the bed and crossed to the window that looked out over the front walk. The condensation had evaporated in the sun, which now loomed high over an unusually warm day. I could see out to the driveway and observed the men waiting with their horses. I began to drum the windowsill with my fingers, yawning. I yawned uncontrollably when I was nervous, one little yawn after another. It was an odd habit that had possessed me since childhood. It caused my hand to flutter mouthward whenever I felt myself growing agitated. I stared down at the horsemen and tried to project my thoughts toward them. *Go away.* I thought they might hear me, but they didn't. They looked scared, but I didn't trust my reckoning of things anymore. I would not credit them with fear.

I turned my back to the window and hurried toward the door, which I locked. I pressed my ear to it and felt the cool chalky paint against my cheek. What were they saying? I could barely hear.

Doctor, she won't move.

No. Something else. They were saying something about the war. The war, which had pulsed and droned all around me for so long and which had already leveled much of our ancient grove, cut down by slaves I hadn't recognized for reasons I couldn't fathom. There wasn't much about the mechanics of war I cared to understand. Even so, I couldn't help thinking that I was besieged, and I couldn't help hoping that the Southern army would come raise the occupation and drive the invaders out. My desire to be rescued was tempered by the paradox of its source, which was my abiding urge to be left alone. I wanted the Confederates to fight, just not *here.*

It hurts, Mama.

I heard the man shuffle through the bedroom next to Martha's, I heard the squeal and rattling of the big jib window being wrenched open, and then I heard the man step out onto the second floor of the porch. Mariah's soft, irregular steps followed behind him. I turned slowly from the door and stood staring at Martha's silk day dress, green and red plaid, so neatly laid out on the bed.

Our Father who art in heaven, hallowed be Thy name.

A new hole had appeared in the dress's hem. Time kept ticking on and on, pounding and pounding at my temples. The moths would not leave my little girl's things alone, always chewing and chewing and chewing. I could feel my pulse beating in my throat and my stomach twisting. I found it difficult to focus my eyes; everything seemed guarded by a gauzy shroud. I thought I might faint and looked around for a place to crumple.

We can only wait and see.

Without thinking I snatched up the dress as if the bed had stolen it from me. I walked to the closet, put the dress onto a hanger, and pushed on the closet door until it clicked shut. For a moment I could hear the clothes swishing back and forth before all went silent.

I went back to the door. They were out on the back porch. I held my breath and tried to shrink into the folds of my black crinoline. After a few minutes I heard a voice again, but this time the man seemed to be talking to himself, mumbling without reply in a voice that sounded rusty and agitated. I heard just a few words. *Lookout . . . order of battle . . . enfilade . . . skeer . . . wounded.* I wondered what kind of madman talked to himself like that.

> *Dear Mama,*
> *We have lost Martha, who has gone to be united with our Lord Jesus. I was with her to the end, and even as she lay dying she reached out and took my hand and told me that all would be well. I shouldn't worry, she said, our Savior would carry her home. Then she rose up from the bed a little, looked to heaven, smiled, and then fell back unto death. She was at peace, finally. She was so beautiful.*

He was mumbling about the war. The man had invaded my house because of the war. I had to see him, to know who would dare bring that filthy business into my house, even if he *was* a Confederate. I straightened my dress, smoothing out the wrinkles where my lap had been, and looked in the mirror. I refused to acknowledge the face looking out at me. I looked out the window again and noticed that most of the men had dismounted and one of them was walking fast up the path toward the house, presumably to join his commander. I went to the door, unlocked it, and walked out.

In the passage the sunbeams from my doorway seemed solid, and the glowing and swirling dust was as substantial as anything I could imagine. I passed out of the light into the brief darkness of the hall and then turned into the spare bedroom the man had just clomped through. Long glass curtains flapped slowly in the window, which was almost as large as a door. I was shocked to discover that the air outside smelled fresh and sweet. I walked to the window to spy on the man without being seen.

Around the corner of the windowpane a tall and sour-looking man bent over the porch rail, leaning his head out and staring at Franklin in the distance. He pursed cracked lips and rubbed his hand over greasy hair. Before him stretched many acres of grove and farmland, a rolling sea of brown punctuated by an occasional stand of trees, a little creek running into the little river. He held that position and was almost motionless. I thought he might fall over if he were not careful. He wore big black boots that bore the remnants of mud and macadam. He rocked back and forth. Behind him, so close I could almost touch her, stood Mariah.

The man's voice was startling.

"How big is this house?"

Too big, I thought. *Bigger than the whole world sometimes.*

"It got eight main rooms, some hallways, and the old wing where the family livin' now. The rest of us, we in those cabins over there."

She pointed at the lattice wall at the end of the porch. I looked about me as if I, too, were a stranger. Yellowing white linen still hung from every doorway and mirror, marking the death of the children who had once lived within. My children, so weak and pure and trusting. At night the drapes looked like ghosts, moving around in the drafts that broke through the walls and under the doors. Mariah had wanted to take them away years before, but I had forbidden her.

"They got water close by?"

I noticed how he referred to "they," as if Mariah didn't live here. There was something funny about the man, about the way he looked at Mariah through half-closed eyes. He looked like he was waiting for something to impress him, I thought, and that Mariah had somehow failed. I resented him and his people and wherever he came from. He looked like the kind of man who figured he knew everything about you, and about whom you could never know a thing, not really. I was afraid for Mariah.

I remembered a conversation I'd once had with her when we were children back in Louisiana, long before we'd come here. *My great-great-grandfather prayed for me a long time before I was born,* Mariah had said, *a long time before I was nigh on a thought in my mama's mind. And my mama, she already doing the same for my children, and I ain't even kissed a boy yet.* This was the way Mariah's family made sure that their children's children came into the world with the proper protection of God, Mariah said.

I had wondered aloud if my own grandparents had ever prayed for me like that. Mariah said that she had a hard time imagining those white people in the paintings on the wall of the house getting down on their knees and praying for someone who didn't even exist, who might not ever exist. I had known she was right. *Too impractical, too superstitious, too much like the niggers,* I heard them saying.

Now I wondered if this was the problem. Maybe I *had* been forgotten in prayer, and perhaps this explained why I became lost to the world. It wasn't as if I was the only one who had ever lost a child. Mariah was someone who believed she had been blessed by the long dead, so she was not fearful of men like the one standing in front of her, I knew. *Until I get the keys to the Kingdom, Lord, I ain't giving up,* Mariah liked to say.

I was more skeptical, and this had the odd effect, at that moment, of making me want to pray for Mariah.

"They's water nearby," Mariah was saying. "They's a cistern out the side door and a little creek nearby."

Mariah met my eyes, as if trying to tell me something, but I only stared at her and twisted my fingers in the billowing curtain.

"Do any of you know how to bind wounds?"

"They only a few of us left, but I do believe we know how to take care a bumps and cuts."

"Going to be a lot more than bumps and cuts, if I got this battlefield read right. What about Mrs. McGavock?"

"She indisposed."

"I mean, she know how to take care of wounds?"

"I reckon she's seen her share of blood."

The man chuckled, as if he was warming to her. "You a smart nigra, ain't you?"

"I's smart enough, thank you."

"You know what's coming today?"

"No."

"The whole goddamn Army of the Tennessee is comin', that's what. Where's Mrs. McGavock?"

"She not feeling well."

I knew that by repeating herself Mariah had meant to reprove the man, but even I could tell that this was a man on whom nothing was lost. His good humor disappeared. His eyes grew narrow and black.

"You're smart, but I'll still punch you in the mouth you keep talking like that. Mrs. McGavock's goin' to have to get out of that bed or wherever she is no matter what you think or what she want to do. When that army comes, I reckon there'll be dead and dying and wounded all over this goddamn town who'll need taking care of. And you goin' to do some of it."

I was about to reproach the man, but as I opened my mouth to speak, I noted that Mariah was not scared. She stood up straighter. Mariah could hold her own.

"Colonel McGavock will want to speak with you 'bout that, sir. May I get you something while you wait?"

Mariah motioned as if she was going to lead him off the porch and down to the sitting room. The man shook his head.

"I won't be waitin' on pretend colonels, nigra."

A voice behind me: "I was looking for General Forrest, ma'am."

I let out a little shriek and covered my mouth as I turned to face the man behind me, in the doorway of the spare bedroom. He was dirty like his commander, but his voice sounded Irish. He was also short, thin, and a little twitchy. He cleared his throat, dusted his pant legs with his slouch hat, and peered intently at me.

So that's who the man is, I thought. *A general.* There was nowhere to retreat, and so I stood up straight and struggled to smile, but yawned instead. I was so very nervous.

"The gentleman is out on the porch. Right through here."

"Thank you, ma'am."

The man walked past me, but General Forrest seemed to ignore him. He turned toward the window.

"Mrs. McGavock? I'd like a word with you, ma'am."

I had come to the window intending to confront the invader, but something about him and his voice had stopped me. He had cowed me. I hadn't realized how isolated I had become these last couple years, how few people had come to visit me, how thin my connection to the larger world had really become. Who was the pastor at the church now? I did not know. Whose boy was the latest among the dead? I did not know that, either. From this back porch I had sometimes watched funeral wagons move up the pike toward town, and the only thing that I could remember of them were the most primitive impressions—the shapes of the wheels, the tilt of the men's hats, the sound of the caisson crunching on the road, the color of the coffin laid out and polished like something they should all cherish. The faces . . . there were no faces. But there must have been faces! I could not recall a one.

This man stood before me now, and my mind emptied. I had no idea who he was or even what he was. He was a creature risen from swamps I'd never seen, molded by forces and events I could not name.

I had spent hours in John's office bent over his globe, tracing its lines and squiggles and unnatural shapes. I spent some time memorizing the points of my own boundaries—here is Natchez, Mobile, humpbacked Kentucky, and Wilmington. There is Nashville. I spent hours whispering to myself the names of places on the other side of the world and wondering how they had been named and how their lines had been drawn and what forces conspired to make them stay put. I wondered if they really did stay put and, if they didn't, why men bothered to draw them upon globes. I spent much time considering the border between Europe and Asia, which marked the boundary, apparently, between existence and nothingness. To the left, on the western side of "The Euxine (or Black Sea)," the map was full, dense with names rendered in a spidery typescript, and mountain ranges, and colors. Hungary, Moldavia, Little Tartary, The Krim, Dalmatia,

Gallipoli, Bagnaluk. To the east the map went white and flat, broken only by the words "Anatolia (or Asia Minor)." Could it be that there was really nothing there in Anatolia? It was an extraordinary idea, one that made me nervous in my stomach. I also thought it strange that the mapmakers couldn't decide what things were supposed to be called, and had decided not to choose. It had been difficult naming my own children, too.

General Forrest, standing before me now, was as alien as a platypus. Perhaps he was from Anatolia or one of those vast places on the globe labeled simply "Desert." What could I say to such a man? He looked like a skeleton, a tree, a gnarled piece of metal. Did he even speak my language?

It was too late to worry about such things.

"Yes. I am Mrs. McGavock."

I stepped out onto the porch and stood before him, my eyes clear and watery, my hands clasped before me.

He watched me closely, as if I might at any moment crumple into dust.

"Ma'am, my name is General Nathan Forrest. I'm sorry to make a fuss while you tryin' to rest, but it can't be helped. I wish to God it could. We's using your porch to inspect the field before the fighting begins. Goin' to be a fight around here later, no mistake. If I was guessin', I'd say the fighting ain't goin' to happen right here, but it goin' to be close by, maybe from around the river to the town. That's where the enemy has his works. There goin' to be men passing through this way, and the fighting may come this far."

"Why here?"

I surprised myself. I hadn't meant to engage the man in conversation, this General Forrest, but the idea had worked its way up and out of my mouth before I thought much about it. I looked past Forrest to my garden, where magpies were picking at stems and seeds with their black bills. I moved gently back a step, not wanting to have Forrest approach too close.

"This is where the Yankees at today. Tomorrow, maybe they'll be some other place. But today they right here."

"What do they want with us? It's such a little town."

"They probably don't want nothing. They want us to go away and die, I reckon. They goin' to be many men hurt today. We need a field hospital. Your house would work well."

I thought he was talking hypothetically, simply making an observation. I warmed to him. I liked the thought of someone else seeing something of value in our old crazy house.

"I suppose it would, General Forrest."

"Then you would agree."

Now I was confused.

"I'm sorry. I do believe I've misunderstood you."

Forrest's face set hard, and I saw color rise in his sharp cheeks.

"We may need your house for a hospital. I'm sorry to be in a hurry, ma'am, but I need to know if you'll agree, right now."

A hospital? This was no hospital. Every creaking floorboard, every repetition of curve and line in the wallpaper, every mildewy smell wafting down from the attic—they weren't to be disturbed. Couldn't he see that?

"I don't know how we could possibly be a hospital."

"Your floor and your roof make it possible, ma'am. Nice and comfortable in here."

I could not imagine what war would look like and what the wounded and dying would sound like. Where would we put them? *This place has never been a good hospital. Everything dies.* I knew this man on the porch was strong. I could see in the way he stood—straddle-legged and solid—that he wasn't used to being told no.

"Ma'am, I don't want to be rude. Your house is in a good spot. It's close enough to the battlefield, but it ain't too close. You can see it from miles off. If I decide so, it's goin' to be a hospital today, and we're goin' to send our wounded to this place. Now, I understand that your man ain't here and that this might be coming as a shock to you, so I will ride around to see if I can find us another house that might work for us. I will send word to you either way. But if I decide it's goin' to be your house, you got to get ready."

I wished I'd never come out of Martha's room. I wished I had locked the door and stayed behind it. How dare he come into my home and order me around? I looked straight into his eyes, trying to divine the meaning of this burden he was proposing to lift onto me. I saw a man who knew more than he was telling. His eyes pleaded while the rest of his body straightened to its full height and shaded me from the sun. I wondered why he even bothered to ask my permission.

"Then I suppose we will have to make do if it comes to that. I will tell my husband when he returns."

Forrest looked like he was going to say something else, but stopped.

"Expect a messenger from me shortly. Probably Lieutenant Cowan right there. If the hospital goin' to be at your house, then he will stay to help with arrangements and organization."

"As you wish."

I wondered what we would use for bandages, for supplies. *Surgery.*

5

NOVEMBER 30, 1864: MIDMORNING

Forrest had second thoughts. He worried about his plan for the woman and the nigra, fearing they might not be capable. He had no idea what exactly had happened to the woman shrouded in black standing there on the porch, but he knew that something was clinging to her and wringing her dry. He had seen such haunted faces in Mississippi, western Tennessee, Alabama, Georgia, widows and orphans chopping at the soil with broken hoes or running ahead of the invasion in their fancy carriages. Same face. There was a time when he'd brought relief to such people, or at least hope, and their faces had cracked open and smiled. But now he knew he only brought more fear. He had the stink of death on him, and it was too late to do anything about it. But this woman who stood in front of him, with her long, heavy bombazine dress and necklace of black beads and her large, clear eyes and chalky skin, with her cramped smile which suggested she expected the worst—this woman made him think of his own wife in Mississippi and how he had neglected her during the years of chasing Yankees. He wondered if she looked as worn out as this one, who couldn't be much older than thirty. He wanted to go home more than anything at that moment, to run away from such women. He swallowed that thought and tried to forget it. There was no running.

He removed his hat and nodded at the lieutenant as he passed toward the end of the porch to look at the battlefield. Take a look at that shit and come up with a plan, for once, *he thought. He glared at him and turned to the young woman. She made him wish he had a cleaner shirt.*

She resisted his plan for her house and tried to engage him in a conversation about war and battle. How many such conversations had he suffered through? Thousands maybe. He had no more time for it. He might someday have to flap his gums again about the war, but at the moment he was too busy fighting it. He'd already spent too much time at the house. There was something attractive about the place that had made him linger. In another time he might have stayed awhile, but who knew when such a thing would be possible again? He had to move on.

Lieutenant Cowan returned to stand by Forrest, visibly pale and wild-eyed. Forrest smiled the briefest smile, knowing what the man had seen and appreciating his discomfort. He had seen the Federal works and Fort Granger and the remains of a grove and cleared fields strewn at the feet of the battlements for miles around. Open country. His army might as well just shoot themselves, Forrest thought. The two of them walked off the porch, through the bedroom, down the stairs, and out the front door. It wasn't until they reached the horses that the lieutenant said a word.

"Damn."

The troop mounted up and rode off. They'd ridden for about a mile before Forrest turned to Cowan. He'd put his slouch hat back on, and this time it was pulled down so tight his eyes disappeared in the darkness. He talked low so the others wouldn't hear.

"Now, what I want you to do, Cowan, is ride out to Hood's head-quarters and get the word passed that this here house, Carnton or

whatever the hell they want to call it, that it's goin' to be a hospital. I reckon we goin' to need too many hospitals today, but this one'll get us started. Make sure they send out messengers with the word, don't just tell his shitheel staff. Then I want you to ride back to that house and tell the woman that General Forrest, upon much reckoning and reflecting and what all—you make it fancy—that General Forrest has decided that the house will be used as a field hospital for the good of the cause. You make sure that goddamn place is a hospital where a man can go to die comfortable. And if it ain't like that, I'ma come for you. You hear me?"

"Yes, sir."

"Now, git."

"Yes, sir."

All the while Cowan rode, and all the time he was talking with Hood's people, he wondered why Forrest had chosen to spare him for hospital duty. For surely they were going to die that day. The old man wants a nice comfortable hospital because he sees himself ending up there today, *Cowan thought. He mistrusted the motives of most men, but toward Forrest he could never muster too much animosity. The general had saved their necks any number of times, and they all owed him that. But Cowan simply liked Forrest, liked that the man could make every word out of his mouth sound homely, profound, and vaguely threatening all at once. He wouldn't begrudge Forrest a warm place to die. And he vowed never to forget that he himself had been spared, and by whom. Lieutenant Cowan was not a courageous man, and he did not care to be. He preferred to be alive, whatever the circumstances.*

When he returned to Carnton, he rode right up to the front door and dismounted his gray horse. He walked around the side of the house to take stock of the grounds—he knew they wouldn't be able to fit all the wounded and dying in the house—and around the back he saw a little dark-haired girl in a gingham dress playing with a hoop, which she rolled down the mowed walkway until it gained speed and got away from her, finally crashing into the tall, dead grass that sur-

rounded a little cemetery plot. He stopped. She was lovely and clean and happy. That is the most beautiful girl in the world, *Cowan* thought. *The girl drove off all memory of the whores he'd been with in Atlanta, all rouge and stink and sharp tongues.* Pure, pure, pure, *he* thought, *looking at the girl. And then he thought,* You're a sick bastard, *and walked past her to the back steps. The nigra servant was standing there, watching him. He called up to her.*

"I'd like to speak with Mrs. McGavock."

"I keep telling y'all she indisposed, and y'all don't listen. Now she asleep."

Cowan was afraid of nigger women; they always seemed like they knew something you didn't, and so he didn't rise to her bait.

"Well, then, will you please tell Mrs. McGavock that General Forrest sends his apologies and that he has regretfully concluded that this house is the only suitable structure for a hospital to serve the upcoming battle and that he trusts she will not be too inconvenienced by the intrusion."

"Inconvenienced?"

The Negress laughed through her nose. Cowan heard the girl banging on the hoop some distance behind him and thought he could hear the swish of her dress. The Negress just turned, walked back in the house, and left the door open. Cowan followed.

6

LIEUTENANT NATHAN STILES, 104TH OHIO

We were digging just as fast as we could with everything we had—bayonets, cups, picks, shovels. I was the commander of my company now, by virtue of the death of the three previous company commanders in the last three months—not much to commend the job, truth be told. But the outfit practically ran itself. You said dig, they dug. You only had to be in one fight to know what a beautiful thing a trench could be. The first minié ball whizzes by your head, and you're a digging man evermore. But we couldn't quite figure out why we were supposed to be digging so hard here. It didn't seem possible that we would fight. I climbed up on top of the cotton gin around which we were digging a trench line and looked out, and I couldn't see a thing—just open fields for two miles around and those rolling hills we'd stumbled over the night before. Who would fight here? I looked around and saw all the rest of the brigades and companies digging in just as hard as we were, and it looked mighty cozy on our side of things. My little piece of it was right there at the cotton gin, and between us Ohioans and the Indianans and the Illinoisans, we were wrapping a pretty good trench and battlement system right around it. We were a bulge in the line—the colonel called it a salient, but I didn't go to West Point and learn such fancy words, so it was just a bulge to me—and we were exposed on three sides instead of one. But it was pretty steep coming up the hill toward us, and out front some of the boys from Indiana were cutting down a big spiky hedge and dragging it into place at the bottom of the hill. No one was going to make it up that hill.

I was ready to sleep. Some of the other officers had already found places to rest, up on porches and even in some houses. Someone had found some whiskey, and more than a few men were taking their fill. I couldn't help thinking that there were rebs in those houses, even if they were hospitable and their women gracious, so I didn't trust them or their whiskey. I stayed out at the trench line and tried to boil up a cup of coffee. I saw a general stumble down the middle of town, his eyes on fire and spittle flying out of his mouth and sticking in his beard as he cursed a couple messengers about something I couldn't understand. Those men had come riding up from some units that were way out in front of us on the pike, down the hill a half mile or so. I squinted my eyes hard, and I could see those men out front frantically digging in just like us, maybe harder, like they'd seen something big and terrible. I heard a couple shots, but I didn't pay it much mind, which I would regret later. I couldn't figure why those men were out there, but then, I didn't always understand the stratagems of war, I just did what I was told. I told my men to keep digging, and burned my tongue on my coffee.

I will always remember an odd scene I witnessed a little while before the shots rang out and everything went to hell. I had walked back from the lines a few hundred yards, wandering in and out of occupied houses. I had decided that I actually could use some of that whiskey, but it was now scarce and I had no luck. I don't know how many pie-eyed, lolly-tongued men told me they were fresh out before I finally realized I wouldn't be finding any. I was about to turn back after rooting around in one more cellar, located below one of the larger houses just off the town square, when I heard loud voices out in front. There had been some socializing on the front porch, and now it sounded like there was a fight about to break out. It's odd to think, now, that at that moment just hours before the battle, I was excited to see a fist-fight. But I was.

I walked around the front, and what I saw was astounding: a young Confederate officer. *We have taken a prisoner,* I thought. But then it was apparent that he was no prisoner. He sat on his horse glaring down, red-faced and fiery as he tossed errant blond locks from his eyes and spit words down to an older civilian man. The soldier was disheveled like we'd come to expect rebs to look, but he didn't have that broke-down mien that made you think you were seeing a raggedness that was natural. This was a man used to better things, a better class of man. The Confederate and the old man were having a row, and I had a hard time keeping up with the words they flung at each other. I couldn't understand what he was doing there, but my fellow officers just looked on goggle-eyed. The old man was bareheaded and dressed in a severe black suit. His iron-gray hair blew about in the warm breeze, and he glared back at the young rebel. I wish I could remember everything they said, but all I really remember is this: the old man telling the younger one he was a fool, and the younger shouting back that the older man was a traitor consorting with the enemy.

At that, the lollygaggers on the porch finally got up their liquor courage, and one of the bigger men stepped down as if he would apprehend the man on the horse. But the old man held up his hand, which was big and flaky and rough like a farmer's.

"Gentlemen, this man is the only son of a widow," he said, which seemed to mollify our boys, because the men on the porch just sat back down and shook their heads.

I wanted to say, *I'm the only son of a widow, too,* because it was true and it hadn't kept me from being shot at yet, but among these men that phrase seemed to mean something. I expect they were Masons or some such. You never really know how men choose to associate themselves, and especially why, until it's too late to understand or to care.

They let that young rebel go, just like that. I watched him turn his fine chestnut mare around and trot off as if no one would dare stop him, which they didn't. I felt embarrassed to watch him, and I had a momentary urge to run up and apologize to him for being here, in this place that was so obviously his home. He rode well in the saddle, and that mare kept tossing her head back at him as if to urge him to go faster. They looked like they'd been together a long time. But he kept it slow, and I watched him peer into the windows of the occupied houses as he passed.

After he disappeared out of sight, the men on the porch tried to convince the old man in black to have one more drink with them.

"None of us getting any younger, Mr. Baylor, least of all this whiskey, thank God."

But he waved them off and bowed his head as if to look intently at his shoes. Then he shoved those big hands in his pockets and walked off, right past the corner of the house where I was standing. He didn't seem to notice me, and I almost asked him who the hell the rebel was to him, but his face was furrowed and twisted like something was trying to chew his skin right off, and I let it alone. Just when I thought he had passed, he took notice of me and turned for a moment, straightening the front of that black suit and looking at me curiously with the most unusual gray eyes.

"You're a smart boy," he said, and then he walked away.

I knew that I had witnessed something I'd rather not have seen.

I wandered back to my unit, suddenly despondent, and not just because I hadn't found a drink. The streets had become crowded while I was away. Wagons full of Negroes jostled with each other and with the finer carriages of white refugees who wouldn't make eye contact and wouldn't yield to the escaping slaves, though they were both fleeing before the same Confederate army. On every wagon hung a collection of pots and pans of varying sizes and conditions, which made quiet music against the wood as the wagons swayed. Slowly the flood of civilians ran toward the north end of town, where the bridge over the Harpeth River was being repaired and reinforced. With a little luck it would soon groan again under the weight of the refugees and the army's supply wagons. I could hear the distant shouts of quartermasters trying to keep order at the bridge, and I heard the splashes of people who could wait no longer to cross the water. There was singing. *We'll praise the Lord in heav'n above, roll, Jordan, roll.*

When I finally arrived back at the cotton gin, the digging had stopped and my men were standing on their toes at the edge of the entrenchment looking out across the fields that surrounded the town. They stood in various states of stupor and were quiet like they were afraid of being heard or singled out. One new man, Colbert, sat back from the others and was crying into his hat, but the others apparently didn't notice, they were so mesmerized. (Colbert, I would learn, had just received word of his infant son's death due to smallpox. He wasn't just a sniveler. Later he fought well and died quick.) One of our veterans, a short, bandy-legged German named Weiss, stood on top of the cotton gin with his head cocked and his one good eye squinting at something in our front. I joined him, climbing up on bales of cotton until I could get my arm up on the shingle roof and swing my legs over. Soon I stood beside him.

What I saw was the most beautiful thing I have ever seen, and I wished to never see it again. In the distance the entire Confederate Army of Tennessee stood on line. All of them. We'd been fighting out here in the west, in Alabama and Mississippi and Tennessee, always hemmed in by rivers and forests and tight little winding roads, and I had never thought about what thousands of men would look like if they stood out and faced us. But there they were. They shimmered in the distance, the warming air making them look wavy like a dream, something from another world. There were flags of all sorts snapping in the wind—the red and blue cross on their battle flag, the odd, faded blue and white flags of one of the divisions in the center. Sounds of brass bands, one playing "The Girl I Left Behind Me." I wanted them to stay there always, frozen in their splendor. An odd happiness possessed me then, and I can only explain it by saying that I had fought them so long and they had fought so hard I was proud to finally see them in their entirety. I was proud that such an army, a vibrating mass of butternut gray and sharp metal, screeching that strange wail of theirs, was arrayed against me and my men. I was proud that we were worthy of that. And though I knew that not one of them would hesitate to shoot me in the head as I stood there watching with Weiss, who was muttering curses in a strange tongue, I didn't take it personal. I wished it could all end right there and that the rebels could see themselves as I saw them at that moment. But such things never happen, and such sights are bound to disappear. And so they began to move.

Weiss put his hands to his head and mumbled to himself. "My God, they will fight us here, and they—they will be slaughtered. Butchered, like animals. Stupid, stupid."

Weiss cursed some more.

"It is not right, no, so stupid. I cannot fire my gun at sheep, no."

I told Weiss he must, and to get off the goddamned gin.

"I will not shoot sheep," he said again.

"Keep digging," I told him.

7

THE GRIFFIN HOMESTEAD

On Winstead Hill, a couple miles south of Franklin along the pike, two boys crouched in the weeds, watching.

Each had stuffed a ham biscuit in his pocket, not cured, but fresh meat off the pig that the Willises had killed not two weeks before. Ab Willis had water in a canteen made from a bull's bladder, which he claimed had once been the cherished possession of a slain Indian but which his friend Eli just happened to know had been bought off one of the traders that came through the country every once in a while. Eli had bought himself a little pocketknife from the trader with some of his egg money, and that's how he knew about the canteen. The old trader and his unusually young wife had kept dozens of the things piled up in the back of their wagon, and Eli had mistaken the canteens for a pile of fantastically large mushrooms. He played along with Ab's story, though. Ab was a good friend, if a little slow.

Ab had been the one to bring the news of the war that afternoon, pounding on the Griffins' door while Eli was finishing his midday dinner. Eli had been trying to convince his pa that the

steers didn't need to be moved that afternoon, and he was proposing that fishing wouldn't be such a bad way to spend some
time, when he heard Ab stumble up the steps to the front porch.

Pound pound pound. Ouch.

Ab had found the nail sticking out of the door. Eli was supposed
to have removed the nail last winter, but he'd forgotten, and then
he figured it didn't make any sense to take it out anyway. Mr.
Griffin came to the door, and Ab, always afraid of the old widower
with his baggy eye sockets and heavy, fat boots, could barely
squeak out his request to see Eli while sucking on his knuckle.

Eli Griffin's house was something more than a cabin, but just
barely. It stood several miles down the pike toward Columbia,
about a mile off the road in quiet woods. It had two floors and a
wood stove in the kitchen, where Becky cooked their meals.
Everything was gray, washed-wood, horizontal beaded poplar
boards on the inside, from floor to ceiling, but there was a small
stone fireplace at the opposite end of the room from the kitchen
stove, and they all—Eli, Becky, and their father, Joseph—thought
it was quite smart and cozy. They each had their own special chairs
drawn right up to the hearth. There were three bedrooms upstairs,
each with a plain-style rope bed covered with a corn husk mattress.
The Griffins didn't have anything hanging on the walls except for
a picture of George Washington that Eli had lifted from a farmhouse abandoned a few years before by their neighbors, and a
sketch of their mother that Becky had drawn when she was little.
It had been three years since Mrs. Griffin had died, and they still
prayed for her safe passage to paradise whenever they sat down to
eat at the table. She had never bothered to teach Becky her special recipes—probably because she hadn't figured on dying of the
cough—but Becky had made up a few of her own, and Eli never
thought to complain about the food.

When Eli came to the door, Ab told him loudly what he'd seen
earlier that morning: thousands and thousands of Confederates
marching up the pike with guns and sabers and all sorts of things
warlike. It looked like the end of the world, Ab said. Without a
word Mr. Griffin hurried out to move the cattle, forgetting that
he'd told Eli to do it, and Becky, who had also been listening while

she put away the dishes, disappeared upstairs to her bedroom. For the first time in recent memory Eli had been left alone. He didn't bother to wonder about it.

Guns! Men on horses! Ab handed him a biscuit, and they were off, out the front door and down the path that led to the Griffins' well, and then past the well. They ran fast and recklessly, howling and leaping around like they had been released from someplace stuffy and dark, where all anyone ever did was pray nothing would happen. Something was happening now, by heaven, it was.

They ran for a long time through the fields that lined the road, occasionally stopping to fondle things the soldiers had left strewn along the way. Eli picked up a bone-handled knife with notches on the hilt and stuck it in his pants. Ab held a jar of some sort of confection high above his head to see what the sun looked like when filtered through the glass, and then he threw it down against the road where it broke with a pop, spreading tendrils of peach jam in every direction. They wrestled over a pack of cards, and Eli won. Ab settled for a dented brass spyglass with a couple big scratches and a crack on the lens. Then they paused to catch their breath.

"Well, where are they? Thought you said there were thousands of 'em." Eli wondered if it had all been a figment of Ab's imagination, the litter on the side of the road notwithstanding.

"They gone up the road, probably to town by now. They's moving fast, faster than you can run, slug. I bet they taken the town by now, and we missed it because you too busy eating and not minding what's goin' on."

"You saying you didn't eat lunch, fatty?"

"I'm saying I don't eat lunch all leisure-like."

They wrestled some more, and then, without saying anything, they started running up the road toward town. Each had only the vaguest idea what they would find up there, which was the main reason they were so eager to see it for themselves. By fits and starts they spent the next couple of hours traveling the five miles to the foot of Breezy and Winstead hills, on the east and west sides of the pike, respectively. To the west they could see a number of people on top of Winstead Hill, men and women, who had gathered to watch whatever was about to happen. A few of the ladies sat in chairs that their husbands had brought in the buggies Eli and Ab found parked on the south side at the bottom of the hill. A couple dozen people milled around up there like they were at a party, and Eli and Ab climbed up to join them.

"Let's make like we're spies," Eli said.

"Hard to be a spy with all them people around. They catch you right quick."

"We'll sneak around 'em, jackass. They're right there on top of the hill, and they can't see us if we sneak around the side all the way to the front. We'll stay in the tall grass."

"I don't know, they look like they got a good view up there, and they right comfortable. I think there's a whole mess of them, if I ain't mistaken."

"We are well provisioned, Private Willis. Let's go."

They crawled crouched low and climbed halfway up the back side of the hill and then began making their way around the hill to the right. It was slow going. Eli kept insisting on using Ab's new spyglass to observe the people gathered on top of the hill. The crack in the lens cut everyone in half and made their heads gigantic and their legs tiny like a midget's. Eli giggled at them. They were like elves up there on that hill, strange little monsters.

After a half hour of wiggling around through the weeds, Eli and Ab found a position on the front of the hill, down from its crest and out of sight of the picnickers. What they saw in front of them was breathtaking and so foreign they just lay there without speaking.

Directly in front of them, and spreading out a mile each way, stood the army. The long gray line snaked on and on in each direction. They tried to count, but after a while they could swear they were seeing the same men over and over again, as if they were all the same man. They nibbled on their biscuits and took turns with the spyglass. The boys watched the Confederates spread themselves out along the line, some men mincing along on tender feet, others striding along like nothing had ever hurt them in their entire lives. One man stopped to relieve himself in the bushes at the bottom of the hill, and when the wind kicked up, Eli swore he could smell the wet odor of chicory and maybe a little coffee.

There were flags of all sorts whipping in the wind and tangling around the guidons. The flags were mere decorations, but the men looked like the whole world.

Ab was the first to break the silence. He shook his head a couple of times like he was going to say something and then thought better of it. He picked up the spyglass and looked for something he could understand.

"Look at that skinny man right over there. He looks like he's about to burn up and float away. Cooked up in that uniform of his. Like a sausage."

Ab pointed to a weedy, gangly private lost in his oversize uniform, barefoot and sweating. He was fiddling with a long rifle and trying to get his shirt off at the same time. Ab thought he saw a button go flying off into the grass.

"What kind of gun you reckon that is?"

Eli took the glass and looked at the thin man. He had bags under his eyes that seemed to jiggle some, and he looked a little scared. Eli felt sorry for him. He didn't know anything about the man's rifle, but he made something up.

"That right there is a Robert E. Lee rifle with special deluxe hawkeye sights. Kill a man at two miles. That soldier right there must be a right good shot. They don't give them rifles out to but a few. I bet he's one of the best shooters in the army."

"Never heard of that gun. Two miles? Damn."

"Shoots a thousand bullets without even getting a little warm, you know. *And* it's got a timbering attachment that cuts down trees big around as you. And you know that's big."

"Damn."

They were silent again. Eli watched the skinny soldier waddle off to get on line, and he let his mind wander. He wondered if Cotton, the only Confederate soldier he'd ever seen up close, was somewhere on that field. *I wish Becky were here to see this*, Eli thought. *Then maybe she'd understand.*

Ab trained the spyglass away from the Confederate lines forming in front of them and noticed that over on another hill, a mile or so distant and east of town, a Yankee artillery battery was limbering up. Men in blue were shoring up the trails of their three-inch rifled guns, others were piling up hundreds of shells for action. Still others were busy aiming the black, glistening, wrought-iron weapons toward the bottom of Winstead Hill. It all seemed so distant, so separate from his world, as if he were watching a fabulously intricate play.

The first shot from the artillery battery was long. The shot went into the air, and it began to whistle and wail as it descended in the last part of its ballistic arc. That sound finally made things clear for Ab. He had just enough time to throw himself to the ground and squirm into a little indentation in the dirt. But Eli raised himself to one knee to look around, curious to the end. The sharp-nosed shell buried itself in the dirt of the hill behind the Confederate line and forty yards in front of the boys' position. The shell was a few inches in the dirt before it exploded, a malfunction of the fuse that saved the boys from the ripping and buzzing shrapnel. But the *sound*. The percussion of the explosion shattered one of Eli's eardrums. The compressed air, fanning out in waves from the impact, lifted the boy up off his feet and threw him back ten yards. The last thing he noticed was how deep the sky appeared, endless and calm, before his head met the sharp edge of a limestone shelf barely peeking out of the soil.

CARNTON

A tall young black man on a mule picked his way among the old cobs and broken stalks of a hilly cornfield that lay a couple miles away from the McGavock house. He had spent the better part of the morning casting around the property, spurring Zack the mule to stumble along a little faster, and cursing when the beast looked back and bared his teeth. This was Theopolis, Mariah's nineteen-year-old son. When he finally spotted Colonel McGavock across the large cornfield winding wire around a fence post, he reined in old Zack and approached with some semblance of dignity and grace. For he was a young man who greatly prized dignity and grace, and it was for this reason that the Colonel liked him better than any slave he had ever owned.

Colonel John McGavock could barely see for all the sweat in his eyes, and so he didn't notice Theopolis until he and the mule were almost upon him. He noticed how Theopolis struggled to keep his face still, but the corners of the young man's mouth turned up slightly. The Colonel knew it amused Theopolis to see a white man laboring away in a suit.

"What are you laughing at, boy?"

"Ain't laughing at nothing, sir. That's a fine fence right there, sir."

John looked back at his work. The snake fence had begun to rot down there in the corner of the field where it got wet and muddy near the creek, and so he had cut down some young trees, stripped them of their bark, and lashed them together. The new pieces stuck out like parts of a giant jigsaw puzzle, glaring and white against the muted silver of the old fence pieces. Not bad.

"It's better than I would have thought. Now, why are you interrupting me?"

"I come to tell you they's men come to the house, men on horses and in uniforms."

"What kind of uniforms?"

This news worried John very much. He started to whistle for his horse, who was eating old corn shucks off in the distance.

"They gray uniforms. Secesh, I reckon."

"Confederate."

"Yes, sir."

John bit his lip and crossed his arms. "We're going to ride back and see what's going on. I'll lead."

John swung up onto his horse and took up the reins. McGavock looked much younger than his forty-odd years. His full beard was unsullied by even the smallest gray hair, and in the saddle he rode with his back unwaveringly straight. His eyes were a deep evening black, shot through with flecks of lighter brown. His three dead children had had the same eyes, but his two living ones did not. He was a sensitive enough man, and he had noticed and filed away that coincidence.

Since he'd sent most of his slaves south to escape capture, loaning them out to friends in Montgomery who were out of the way of the fighting, he himself had done most of the work required to keep the plantation running, and it had kept him fit. He liked to think he was running the plantation. But in his more thoughtful moments he admitted to himself that he was really just able to raise enough food to feed his household and keep a little money coming in. He hadn't even bothered to make a payment on the debt he owed on his land, and if not for the chaos of wartime, he surely would have already lost it through foreclosure. He'd resigned himself to simply holding on until the war ended, when he would be able to put the whole of his rolling farm into cultivation: the green sea of corn and tobacco and clover would return, the orchards would be groomed, and the Herefords and Shorthorns would be able to live well again. He was a colonel in name only, an honorific bestowed upon him when he bought uniforms and supplies for the Confederate company that mustered out of Franklin. The money he'd borrowed had gone to clothe and arm men, many of whom had been killed and buried in places far away from Franklin. That's where much of his debt was—moldering in the ground in graves already forgotten. To John McGavock the word *colonel* had come to mean "debtor."

They'd been riding in the general direction of the house for a few minutes when off to the left they saw something moving in the tree line. Horses.

John stopped to look harder. He saw a flash, then another flash, and then he heard the report of a repeater. He looked over at Theopolis, who had withdrawn under the shadow of his broad straw hat, as if he could disappear. When he looked back again, he saw a rider astride a piebald mare step out from the woods. From a half mile distant, John could see the man push his blue campaign hat back and scratch his forehead. He seemed to be trying to lock eyes with John.

At any other moment on any other day this encounter would not have troubled him very much. The Yankee presence in the county had become something he'd learned to tolerate, something that had evolved from a terror to a nuisance. He'd suffered their occasional inspections, their disrespect, their veiled taunts. He had even taken their meaningless loyalty oath, as had most everyone else in the county. He prayed for their defeat even as he accepted their occupation.

But today, if Theopolis was correct about what was happening back at the house, the presence of Yankees on his property posed a threat. If they were following him, and God knows why they would, he could not lead them back to a confrontation at his house. He had escaped the war thus far, and he would not have it unfold on his doorstep in front of his family.

He turned east, away from home, and began picking his way across the field.

"We is expected at the house." Theopolis's voice quavered.

John cut him off. "Be quiet, boy, and come on."

Out of the corner of his eye he saw three more men saunter out of the woods to join the first. John reckoned they were scouts. They looked like they'd been riding hard, not like the well-fed and content men who had manned the quiet garrison at Franklin. Their appearance foretold something new.

John and Theopolis managed to ride most of the way across the field, headed for another road that would take them across the creek and back toward town, before the scouts took up the chase and spurred their rides on, closing quickly. Just as John and Theopolis entered the woods, they heard gunfire. Three bullets whipped through the brush around them, one after the other. John dug his heels into his mare to make a run for the bridge. The limbs of young redbud saplings slapped at his face, raising welts.

But old Zack rushed for no man, damn the gunfire. Theopolis began to kick and punch the mule, but it was no good, and when John looked around, he realized he would have to turn back. He wrenched Zack's head around and came to a skidding, stumbling stop. Behind them he saw the scouts appear on the brink of the tree line and crash into the woods behind them. One lingered behind and raised his rifle.

"Get down," John yelled, and waved his hands at Theopolis, who began to slip off the mule on the side opposite their pursuers. A bullet slammed against old Zack's withers, and Theopolis could feel the vibration of lead against bone just as he fell to the ground and rolled into the brush. Zack screamed and turned on his rear legs, colliding with a tree and knocking himself to the ground. Blood splattered against the trunk of the tree and dotted the limbs above. He kicked twice with his rear legs, each time almost crushing Theopolis's skull. Theopolis scrambled off, ran to John, hollering for a leg up behind the saddle.

John knew they could not escape. He placed his boot in the center of Theopolis's chest just as Theopolis took hold of the horse, and shoved him violently to the ground, hoping that Theopolis would realize it was just for show and not hold it against him.

John watched the scouts make their way toward him. He sat tall in his saddle at first, but then he thought better of that posture and decided to slump a little, pretending that not even a Federal patrol could arouse him. He tried to keep his horse from fidgeting, with no luck. Zack's dying moments—the squeals and honks and thrashing—kept her on edge.

The man on the piebald horse reached the clearing first. He was short, paunchy, and bald, with a wild, long beard that was matted at the ends. He looked at once like a feedstore clerk and an avenging prophet. His eyes were a light blue, and they flashed from behind puffy crimson-veined cheeks. His men pulled into the clearing and gathered around him in an elaborate choreography of intimidation. They were younger than their master, and they were having various degrees of success with their beards.

"If you don't mind, would you kindly get off that horse, sir?"

He was solicitous, even deferential, to the tall middle-aged Tennessean he had captured at gunpoint: he was a comedian, and this was one of the reasons why his little band of scouts and cavalrymen stuck by him.

John waited a few prudent seconds before dismounting, trying to decide how quickly he could get down without seeming weak.

"Why did you chase us? We did nothing."

"Why did you run, if you'll pardon my prying?"

The other scouts chuckled and eyed each other.

"We thought you might be Confederates out foraging, or maybe bandits. It's hard to know who you're dealing with these days."

"We are not bandits, and we are not Confederates, as you can plainly see. Who the hell are you?"

John stared up, and the scout looked down, his chin lost in a confusion of beard. John decided to take the offensive.

"Why did you shoot my mule? That's a good animal, a hard worker. We were only passing through to town. I will want compensation."

"Your mule?"

"The animal should be shot to spare it any more pain, and as you can see, we have no guns. I insist that you complete what you started."

"*Your* mule? I don't think so."

John was momentarily flummoxed. "If you are suggesting that I have stolen this animal, sir, you are quite mistaken."

His words hung out there in the air between them.

The scout leaned back a little in his saddle.

"This here is Union country, whatever you think. And everything in it, that's Union, too. That mule? How many fields has it plowed these last four years? How many nasty rebels has it worked to feed? That animal there is a weapon of the enemy, and as such is the property of the U.S. of A."

Zack had collapsed into a pile, lying on one side, groaning from down deep in his throat. Bloody foam dribbled out of his mouth. John had never much liked Zack as a working animal. When he'd allow himself to be hitched up—which wasn't often—he had to be hitched up solo. He wouldn't work alongside another mule or horse, and there were a half dozen animals in John's barn with scars on their neck and withers to prove it. But he didn't mind being ridden, especially by Theopolis. Fancied himself a horse, John had always thought.

"Well, seeing as how this is your mule, sir, my original point still stands. Have one of your men shoot him."

The scout shook his head.

"I don't think so. I would need to get authorization, you see."

"Then I shall do it. Give me a gun."

"I am not in the practice of arming rebels. And if you harm that mule, there will be consequences, my rebel friend."

John let the insult pass by. He was overcome with remorse, the illogical feeling that he had betrayed old Zack and the conviction that every moment Zack suffered was a rebuke to John personally. He might not be roused to defend his honor before men, but the dumb beast had become his most eloquent accuser. He went to the tool bag hanging from the saddle and removed the sledgehammer he had used on the fence. He swung it a few times in a slow arc, trying to get it balanced perfectly.

The scout spit a stream of tobacco juice at John's feet.

"Think about what you're about to do, my friend. That there is government property."

He said this only halfheartedly. He and the other scouts appeared more interested in watching John than in stopping him. John toed some dirt over the pool of tobacco juice, crushed it to mud under his boot heel, and strode toward Zack.

The animal lay his head back and kept his eye on his master. He stopped trembling, as if he knew what was coming. John tried to decide on the best place to land the blow. On the forehead or the back of the head? On the ear? He wondered whether Zack felt lonely, then cringed and shook his head at the thought. When had he become so sentimental and stupid? He stood over Zack and tried to be as calm and reassuring as it was possible to be with a sledgehammer. The scouts grew silent, and Theopolis pulled back into the woods. John decided that Zack's temple held the most promise. He drew the hammer behind him and then raised it above his head. Zack exhaled and seemed to be trying to close his rheumy eyes.

When, after it was over, John turned back to his tormentor, the fat little scout had his repeater trained on him.

"You are now a criminal, besides being a coward and a reb. And you ain't much with a sledgehammer."

John felt certain he would be shot, and the prospect was not as frightening as he thought it would be. His stomach clenched and roiled, his heart raced, and the blood ran to his face. He clenched his teeth and frowned. He was ready.

But the little scout shrugged his shoulders as if bored, and then turned his horse back toward the opening in the tree line, back toward the field. His other scouts crashed about in the brush and dead tree limbs until they were lined up again, two by two. The little scout steered his horse to the side and waved the rest on through, ordering them to head south by the Columbia road. He turned back to John and tipped his hat.

"The fellow at your house, whom your nigger here has seen, is the bloody General Nathan Forrest. I'm sure you've heard of him. He's surely no gentleman, like you and me, *sir*. While you were out here playing in the woods, a battle has been convening all around this place. I'll wager you didn't even hear it coming. If I were you, I'd leave the mule for the crows and make for the house as quickly as you can. Good day, *sir*."

When the Federals had vanished from sight, John and Theopolis mounted up and took the man's advice.

9

THE GRIFFIN HOMESTEAD

Becky knew that Cotton was on that battlefield. She knew it like she had known he would come for her and that he would leave her and that he would die.

"'Cotton'? What kind of man would let himself be called Cotton?" Eli would ask. It wasn't a Christian name, that was certain.

Becky wouldn't tell Eli who Cotton was. She never let Cotton meet her father or let her father even see them together, and they never went courting in the open like proper folks.

Cotton brought Eli gifts—fresh apples, puzzles, drawings of generals cut from the newspaper—and he must have won him over, for Eli conspired with them to keep their relationship secret.

After Cotton had enlisted, she would steal away to her bedroom to write letters—hundreds of letters, by her reckoning. He fought at Chattanooga, he had been captured by the Yankees, he had escaped at great risk to his life and had walked alone back to Tennessee, where he joined up again: she knew this, but it seemed sometimes when she thought about him that she was telling herself a fairy tale about some other person, not Cotton. It was one of the strange effects of war that a man so handsome and lighthearted could be revealed by circumstance to be a warrior. Each night she sat curled like a sapling at her little dressing table, writing to him. He rarely responded to her. Worry had taken her up and squeezed life out of her. All the baby fat had left her, the line of her cheekbones cut hard across her face, deep grooves dug in the space between her eyes. She barely filled out her dresses anymore. Tears welled at the corners of her eyes where wrinkles had collected after eighteen hot summers squinting at pea vines and searching for wayward hens gone off to lay their eggs in secret places. He said he loved her. But it had been so long.

And then, just a few days before the Confederates came marching up the pike, Cotton had appeared again. He rode up to the house on his old horse, looking dusty and harassed in his Confederate uniform with the single row of brass buttons bunching up over his chest. He was taller and blonder than most and had a straight beautiful nose that looked like it had been chiseled by a Greek sculptor two thousand years before, kind blue eyes, and a long neck. He was not the most likely candidate for a war hero, Becky thought. When he dismounted, he looked grim. He was thinner, and his face frowned more quickly than it used to. He didn't see her immediately in the dimness of the house, and at first he stood straight with his chin cocked up as if he were about to give out commands, his eyes narrowed and unblinking. But then he saw Becky, and he slouched over, like he had just then remembered where he was. He looked relieved. He took Becky by the hand and walked her down to the neglected orchard.

In a clearing surrounded by apple trees all suffering at different stages of decline from cedar rust, they had stopped.

"It has been so long since you wrote," Cotton said.

Becky wasn't looking at him. She stared at the trees in front of her and stood very still.

"I don't know what to say anymore. There's nothing new here to write about, and I know I've bored you about my chores too many times."

"Nothing you write bores me. And boredom might be a nice

thing to experience every once in a while, besides. I long to be bored sometimes. So much marching and shooting, messengers whipping to and fro."

"So you're here because I haven't been writing you about the chickens?"

Cotton smiled. "I'm here because I love you."

That closed Becky's mouth right quick. She looked hard at Cotton for a moment, right straight into his eyes, and he held her gaze. Withstood it actually. She stared at him, and then she placed her right hand on his gray coat sleeve and ran her palm over the dirty yellow piping that twisted over and around his cuffs. Then she withdrew her hand quickly, like the sleeve had burned her.

She backed off a few steps and strolled over to a dead fallen tree at the edge of the clearing. She sat down for a few seconds and then spoke again.

"What are you doing here? Isn't there a war? I could have sworn there was a war, what with all the funerals they keep having up in town. Lots of people wearing black around here these days, but maybe that's just the fashion. Is it the fashion? Because I don't know a thing about fashion. Are they wearing it in Nashville? What do the girls at the Franklin Female Institute think? I surely wouldn't know."

Cotton walked closer to Becky but wouldn't sit down. She was mad, but her eyes were full of tears.

"Please calm down, darling."

"Oh piss."

Cotton seemed momentarily flummoxed by Becky's cursing. He stood and blinked at her for a moment and then ran his left hand through his hair a couple times, matting it against his head. Becky noticed how greasy it was.

"I am here because some of us local boys let off on French leave for a day to see family. The army is down in Columbia, and there was some time. You've got no cause to be angry with me."

Becky hardened where she sat. Her face twisted down and puckered. She stared up at Cotton. "I have much cause to be angry with you. How dare you tell me you love me when you know your father would rather cut off his own arm than see his son with a farm girl who smells like woodsmoke and chores?"

"I thought that was 'soap.' "

"I suppose you think that's funny."

Cotton slouched a little and looked at her out of the corner of his eye, like he was getting ready to be hit. "You know I love the way you smell. I've come riding up here past God knows how many Federals, out looking to skin someone like me, just so I could see you, so please don't hold my every word against me. I have been in the company of men for too long."

Becky fiddled with the hem of her dress. "By your own choice."

"What?"

"That you've been in the company of men for too long. It's by your own choice."

"There was no choice."

Becky rolled her eyes and twisted her dress into a little knot in her hand. "I will not be loved by any man with so little sense. I will not spend my time, my *life*, if that was ever a question, with a man who'd just as soon get his fat head shot off as come home."

Cotton was beaten. Whatever remained of his military bearing drained out of him, and he seemed to go limp, balanced precariously on his skinny legs like a dizzy man on stilts. He ran his hands through his hair over and over again. He dragged himself over to Becky's log and sat down on the opposite end, resting his elbows on his thighs. He watched the dirt like it was going to tell him something. A mockingbird berated him from its perch in an apple tree not ten feet away.

"I won't go back if that's what you ask me to do. I won't. I will stay here and hide out until it's all over, and pray that no one ever catches up to me and that my reputation isn't ruined."

"Curse your reputation."

Cotton cocked his head at her. "When did you get so mean, Rebecca Griffin? It's so easy for you to dismiss thought of my reputation. You know better than that, and yet you persist."

"It's because I have no reputation of my own, as you know."

"That is your own ignorance talking, and it isn't true."

She had turned to him, dropping the hem of her dress and placing her hands in her lap like she was in church. "I suppose I am supposed to love a man who thinks I am ignorant?"

"I don't think you're ignorant, Lord knows. I think you're being willfully ignorant and that you know what it would mean to desert, and that you also would not think nearly as much of me if I were the sort of fellow who left people to die, people who had put their trust in me. Who was it who gave me her first kiss when I went off to fight, and told me that she was proud? I don't recall your opposition to the *company of men* back then."

"First kiss? I don't remember my first kiss. There have been so many."

"Do not tease me."

"Look who has no sense of humor now."

Cotton rose up. "Give me your answer."

Becky leaned backward and felt suddenly frightened. Her eyes went wide and they glistened. A strand of her long brown hair had escaped the tight bun on the back of her head and fell against her forehead.

"My answer?"

"Shall I stay?"

Becky's mouth drew tight, and she bit down on her bottom lip. Cotton stood waiting, with his hands clasped behind him, his legs slightly apart, as if he were addressing troops at parade rest. Becky spoke first.

"You're a kind man. You're a good man. I've been unkind and awful."

"I will stay here forever if you ask."

Becky stood then and fiddled with her hands, trying to keep Cotton's gaze but failing. Tears began to run down her cheeks, but she wasn't the sort to sob.

"I can't ask that."

"You can. I promise. I'm sick of it, too."

"But I won't ask it."

Cotton crossed quickly and wrapped his arms around her. She buried her face in his bony chest and put her hands around his waist. They stood still. Then they kissed. And whether it was their first kiss or their second kiss or their thousandth, it was as if the embrace was their proper state. The mockingbird flew off.

Later they walked up to the porch where Cotton had tied off his horse, and stood looking at each other with weird, quizzical looks on their faces, as if they weren't sure what had just happened. Becky had not bothered to put her hair back in its bun but had tied it in a loose ponytail that swung to and fro across her back. Cotton had taken the time to put his uniform together again, and he looked unruffled and ready for war again.

Eli sat on the porch chewing a piece of straw, as if he were waiting for them.

"What's your real name, Cotton?"

Cotton reached up and touched the side of Becky's head and then reached over to take the reins of his horse.

"My full name, you mean, Eli?"

"Yes."

He mounted, and Becky went stock-still and closed her eyes. She sat down on the steps and stared at Cotton's horse, unwilling to look up at him.

"My full name is Cotton Gin, of course."

"That's your real name? Doesn't seem right."

Cotton paused to consider that idea and then just smiled at Eli.

"My horse has a stranger name."

"What?"

"Guidance."

"That's a name?"

"More like a hope."

He had nothing more to say. He looked down at Becky and nodded his head, trying to say something without speaking. Becky looked up only once, and when she caught Cotton's eye, she quickly looked down again, nodding herself. Then Cotton turned the horse's head down the path toward the pike and cantered off. When the sound of the horse's hooves became almost silent, Becky and Eli both looked up in time to see Cotton turn around and wave his hat before disappearing.

It was when he turned back and waved that Becky knew Cotton would die.

10

SERGEANT ZACHARIAH CASHWELL,
24TH ARKANSAS

I was in my reverie, having made my peace with death, but the thing that shook me out of it was how precisely the Yankees cut us down. We were in rifle range, holding our fire until we got close, when the Yankees opened up a volley that flashed out at us like sheet lightning, and the men in the ranks ahead of me fell so quickly they lay in neat rows like mown hay. There was nothing chaotic about it. You could draw a straight line from the end of every Yankee rifle to the flesh of every one of our dead. There had been no waste, no error, no uncertainty. They were all dead, a hundred dead or worse, in a second. Luck had not fiddled with the aim of a single Yankee rifleman, nor had it turned the flight of any bullet. It had been luck that kept us all alive these many months, and without it what did we have? We stepped between the crumpled rows of the fallen and kept moving.

After that first volley we reckoned we were going to make it pretty far. They seemed to hold their fire after seeing what they had done to us. I guess they figured they didn't have anything to worry about. So we got to hollering again, we got those flags up in the air, and we started to run. My lungs got to burning quick, it seemed so hot. The younger boys were trying to strip off their jackets and shirts, and some of us tried to tell them it was stupid because the weather would change soon, but it was hard enough to breathe, let alone give out lectures. So we left a trail of coats and blouses behind us. I figure there were a great many of our boys lying on the battlefield that night, the wounded and dying we had to leave behind, who wished they had something to keep them warm. God was fickle, and it got real cold that night. Hot and cold, hot and cold, whatever He wanted. It was as if He had turned His back on Franklin.

I thought we were almost there when we ran up against this long line of chopped-off Osage hedges, ripping and thick, which the Yankees had put out at the bottom of the hill leading up to their position. It was mighty clever of them. We were running, and then we were stopped in our tracks, just sitting there waiting to be shot. One of our officers, seeing what was happening, tried to run his horse through the hedge but got stuck. We stood there, listening to the sound of the air pulled apart by bullets, to the sounds of bullets striking wood, dirt, flesh. The horse got punctured everywhere and bled heavily. He kicked and screamed, showering blood and spittle on me. He finally threw off his rider and escaped. We were still watching that officer chop at the hedge with his saber when he got shot in the head. He was screaming at us to join him when he fell at my feet. I got his pistols.

We would have stood there all day if the Yankees hadn't started picking us off, one by one. It was obvious that we were going to have to make it through that hedge if we were going to save ourselves. There was no retreating now: it was too far to run, and we'd come too far to be shot facing away from the enemy.

And so we all started chopping at that hedge. It was a bloody mess. Men would chop and beat at the branches until they got shot, we'd drag them back, and someone else would take their place, over and over again, until we'd cut some holes big enough for a couple men to pass through. I wonder how many men would have walked off that battlefield instead of being buried under it if we'd just left it at that: bravo, job well done, let's go home. Because it was worse when we tried to go through those gaps in the hedge. We'd given the Yankees something to shoot at, a few places to concentrate their fire. Men would get to the other side of the hedge only to be sawn in half by the Yankee lead. After a while a few of the gaps we'd cut in the hedge were so filled with bodies that they were impassable again, as if the hedge had clotted itself shut.

It's odd to think about all this now and to realize that it all took place in the span of just a few hours. It doesn't seem possible that so much could happen in so short a time. It was a whole different world after the last shot echoed out over the field. I wonder sometimes about the person who fired that last shot, whoever he was. I wonder what it was like to be the man who finally said, *Well, that's enough.*

We didn't all die at the hedge. The thing about fighting is that if you throw enough bodies forward, eventually a few will break through almost anything. Those of us who ran through the hedge without getting shot got a little ways up the hill before we quit screaming and realized we hadn't been killed yet. You can get so that every step, every little obstacle on the battlefield, becomes so big that you can't see much past it, and when you do get past, it's sometimes hard to remember what the hell you were supposed to be doing. We dropped to our bellies and hunkered down in the grass, wondering what to do with so few of us still alive. I had those two pistols I'd taken off that dead officer, and I just stared and stared at them, noticing every scratch and powder stain. Everything was bright and crisp. The smallest things became clear. I watched an ant crawl over the dirt and get to his hole, waving his head around once before descending. I counted the veins on a blade of grass. I lost my other powers of observation. I heard nothing, smelled nothing, felt nothing. I had forgotten my truce with death, and I was afraid.

I was no longer paying attention to the fighting, so I didn't notice at first when the young assistant quartermaster on the general's staff came riding down the line on the enemy's side of the hedge, trying to rouse us for a charge. I looked up as his horse passed by. He was a tall and gangly man with a mop of dirty blond hair poking out from beneath his slouch hat. I remembered the horse's name—Guidance—because it was so odd. I remember thinking, *He's a fool; this is no place for a quartermaster. No one expects him to fight, and here he is risking his hide.* One of the sergeants jumped up, caught the bridle of the horse, and had words with him to that effect. *Go to the rear, sir, go to the rear!* I remember that clearly. But this young officer was too worked up already, waving his hat around and shouting that he would fight for his own town, by God. Slowly, man by man, the lot of us picked up and got on line. I think the last thing anyone ever said to him came out of that sergeant's mouth: *Don't start the charge too early, sir. You'll get 'em tired out.* I thought that was pretty good advice at the time. But after we stood up, the Yankees opened up on us again, and when men started to drop dead, we all began to waver, and some of the men leaped to their bellies again. I think that young officer saw what was happening and decided he didn't have time to hesitate. Whatever the reason, he turned that big gray toward the Yankee line, shouted something about his house and his family, and yanked his saber out of the scabbard. It was an impressive sight, and when he began to charge, we went with him.

He lost his hat early in the charge, and those blond locks of his were whipping back in the breeze as he got farther and farther ahead. Too far. In a few seconds he was all alone out there in front. We were huffing and puffing behind him as he got smaller and smaller, and when I noticed that the Yankees were shifting their fire away from the rest of us and toward something else, I knew he didn't have long.

When he went down, his horse was already dead. He went careening over the horse's head and into the air, and when he landed, he had been shot maybe half a dozen times. I know this because as we passed him by, he was screaming for help and shouting about how the bastards had shot him in his own yard. He was bleeding from his neck and his hip, and he'd gotten a mouth full of dirt when he landed. One odd thing, though. He didn't look like a lot of the wounded, who look at you with their innocent, pleading eyes as if you could explain everything in the world to them. This young man, he just looked angry. He also looked like he'd never needed to shave in his life. The last I saw of him, he was losing his voice but still shouting at us to keep moving. And we did.

Just as I got past him, our color-bearer went down with a bullet through the mouth. He fell upon the flag and became entangled in it up ahead of us. He looked like he'd been sleeping in the damn flag when his body came to rest.

I'll never be able to explain what happened next, not ever. It's still mysterious. That loudmouth who had insisted the band play him a tune while we were on the march, a man who had never stuck that thick neck out once, not as long as I'd known him—that man left his place right next to me and ran to take up the colors. He was named Warren, he had a dark beard, he came from Nashville, and he stole food sometimes. Up to that moment that's all I had cared to know about him.

I don't know what set him off, but he got those big legs of his moving, and before long he was bent over the color-bearer, straining his broad back and rolling the man over like a barrel. He took the colors in one hand and his rifle in the other, and he turned around as we approached. His face was red like a cabbage. He shouted, spraying spit: "What, you wanna live forever?" Then he turned and sprinted forward, and we got behind him like a pack of dogs. Nobody said a word.

Up and down the line, I could see dozens of groups like ours lurching their way toward the Yankee line. I imagined each group had witnessed its own tragedy and drama, hundreds and thousands of moments like the moment our colors lifted off the ground and went forward in those stiff, fat, outstretched arms. I looked to my right, down toward the pike, and saw a squad of Arkansans disappear in the smoke of a whizzing shell, leaving behind only a faintly pink mist as proof they had once been there. Off to the left, at the bottom of a particularly steep part of the Yankee line, I saw some Mississippians crouched against the earthen wall like shadows, each craning his neck toward the sky as if he might see over the battlement if he just looked hard enough. Periodically they would steel the courage to lift a man up on their shoulders to shoot at the enemy and he would be either killed or captured. Farther down the line another group huddled against the wall and lifted a white rag on the end of a bayonet.

I ran on, slowly catching up with our new color-bearer. I was shocked by how insubstantial the pistols felt in my hand. It didn't seem right that they could kill; they were like toys in my hand. Our new color-bearer began to stagger. The handkerchief around my neck began to itch, and I ripped it off. Warren resisted the urge to collapse and sprinted out ahead one last time. I thought then of that blond officer and his beautiful horse, their deaths so impressive and so unnecessary. The pike and field stretched upward and seemed to get longer as we ran. Men fell on each side of me and crumpled in heaps that were soon far behind us. They vanished, just like that. I wished I had once had a conversation with that young officer. I thought, *There is no good way to die.*

Our new color-bearer had sprinted to within twenty yards of the bulwarks when he stopped to get his breath. He turned to us and waved the flag back and forth, as if he had already taken the Yankee position and he wanted us to know about it. Warren's eyes were wide, and sweat dripped off the end of his nose, and he was screaming again about living forever. That's when he got a bullet in the back of his neck, and his small role in our tragedy played itself out.

There was no good way to die. But dying his way seemed easier than most, and that's the only way I can explain what I did next.

I made my way up to the colors and grabbed them up, yanking them out of his left hand, which was flung far out from his body. I saw how perfectly still he was, how his neck had quit flexing itself, how that strong back had grown smooth. I realized then that we are never still in life, that even when we think we are motionless, we are still vibrating a little. It was odd and confusing, yet reassuring, to see a man at perfect rest, and I went to join him.

I didn't need my pistols anymore, so I flung them to the ground. I didn't say anything; I'm not one for speeches. I just turned and walked toward the bulwarks expecting at any moment to be cut down. I wasn't happy. I was euphoric.

11

Carrie McGavock

I would always think I heard the footsteps of the men echoing through the house hours after they left. I stood out on the porch for a long time afterward, peering out at the countryside and trying to see what had disturbed them so much. I saw nothing but the slowly rising hills, the little creek running across the edge of my sight and off into the distance, the jittery killdeers flitting across dormant fields and guarding their nests. Whatever the men had seen lay only in the future, a premonition of what the landscape might make possible. I could not see such things.

I looked over at Mariah, who waited expectantly, her hands clasped in front of her.

"What will we do?" I said. "They cannot do this here, they must know that. We are not nurses."

I realized Mariah could not know whether I was referring to their plans to make the house a hospital or their plans to make war. Either way, there was no stopping it now. They would be back. I felt something clenching and cold pass through me like a ghost and sail out into the yard, where it shook the remaining leaves in the pecan trees. Mariah spoke up.

"We got to get ready. They coming whatever we say."

"They cannot come. They will not come. I will ask Colonel McGavock to speak with General Forrest. He will attend to it. He won't let this house be violated, he won't stand for it."

"Yes, ma'am."

But I knew they would come. If I had learned anything during my life here, it was that I could not keep things out. I had not been able to prevent death from waltzing in, and so how would I prevent this? I imagined what my house would look like when the wounded and their attendants had come here and gone. *How many? A dozen? Two dozen?* My stomach twisted when I thought of men in my home and their blood. Perhaps I could be of use to a few. Maybe the war would spare the rest.

She seemed to never quit moaning and crying. Sometimes she screamed for me. This was the way it was to the end. Her skin was so dry and red and flaky. It almost seemed to burn my hand. Every day I sat by her and applied cold wet linens to her forehead, and her body seemed to take up every bit of moisture without returning anything—no coolness, no relief.

A breeze blew across the porch, stirring up the air. It was almost noon, and the sun hung faded and fuzzy in the gray sky, a palimpsest of summer. I felt my forehead grow cold with sweat and my heart pulse in my throat. I resisted the urge to gasp for air.

"Mariah, begin the preparations, will you? I'll come in a moment."

"Yes. Yes, ma'am."

I walked into the house. It was cool in the shadowy corners and in the darkened hall. I wondered if anyone would miss me if I spent the day hidden away in the dark. I walked on.

Out the back and into the yard the warm breeze wrapped me up again. I wasn't thinking about where I was going. My feet carried me across the yard toward my garden, but my eyes were drawn off to my right, to a small stand of trees ringed by a black iron fence. The grass was still soft. The breeze kicked up again, and I felt I would suffocate. I wanted to strike out at it, to slap it away.

I stood in the garden and stared at the cemetery across the way.

I felt the grave markers marching toward me. I thought of it as another grove, a grove of trees and of limestone and of children beneath my feet, and it was for this reason that sometimes I could only bear to look at it by hiding in the garden and peeking through the foliage.

The garden had once been so lovely, so trimmed and neat, packed between the paths with obedient rudbeckia and peonies and roses and boxwoods and sunflowers and crape myrtles. I had loved it unequivocally and had taken pleasure in its boundaries and distinctions, the concentration of its colors and textures. It had been a rebuke to the very idea of uncertainty.

Now the garden looked nothing like it did that first day sixteen years before, when I was an eighteen-year-old riding up in my new husband's carriage. It had become ragged like everything else in my house, in Franklin, in Tennessee, and, as far as I knew, in the world. In the summer the rudbeckia took over much of the sunny side of the garden, and even in the night I could see their bright and insistent yellow blooms from my porch. Bleeding heart, cemetery vine, and ivy had taken over the rest. The peonies fought for light, and their occasional breakthrough was cause for mild celebration. I would not help them, but I took solace from their little successes.

So many years had passed since I had first gone to sleep at Carnton. The house had collapsed into itself. *Like me,* I thought without surprise.

I stood there like a shadow among the browns and beiges of my once precise Italianate garden, and I remembered the first time I had seen the house. It was not the same house anymore, although this would not have been obvious to the casual observer. Its bones were still there, but very little of the rest seemed familiar to me anymore. This redbrick neoclassical pile, with the Grecian portico on the front, and its massive, two-story Italianate galleries running across the entire back length, was empty: we had retreated back into the wing on the east side, which had once been the original frontier homestead. *We cannot run that house without all the slaves.* John had insisted that we send most of our slaves off to friends in Alabama before the Federals could requisition them and everything else they could get their hands on. *The house is much too big for Mariah to keep up,* John had said. I had known this to be only partly true. The rest of the truth, I knew, was that my husband wanted me to quit living among our dead children, if only for a while. This did not stop me from drifting through their rooms and listening for them.

I remembered the voices of my children and the sound of my own voice teaching them their lessons and reading them Bible stories, the sound of the piano, the sound of the tall case clock ticking in the hallway. *Nothing disappears.* I imagined that the sounds and smells of the children existed somewhere, borne away by the wind. That was a comforting thought. They also existed in my mind, as memories, but of late I had come to distrust those.

I could never leave those memories behind. They buzzed at me like gnats.

There was the central passage that ran the full length from front door to back, dividing the downstairs. There was the stairway that led to a similar hall upstairs. Heavy poplar doors led to two rooms on either side of both hallways. On the first floor the best parlor lay to the left of the entrance, my husband's office to the right. At the back of the house a door opened into the family parlor, where the portraits of our family had once hung. Across the hallway there was the dining room, the table now covered in linen. Upstairs, the only place I spent much time anymore, the doors to my children's bedrooms remained shut. Above the foyer there was an odd little room with no discernible purpose—an architectural accident, unintended space—and it was there that I spent my days sitting in a small haircloth rocker.

I was a medical puzzle. Like every other lady I'd known in Franklin, I'd been given my bottle of laudanum when the grief had overcome me, but unlike the other women, I had sunk deeper into my despair and—yes, I knew this—my eccentricity. This was not the usual outcome, according to Dr. Cliffe. In the little bottle the ladies of my former circle found the strength to sleep without dreaming as they sent their husbands off to war, or their children. They could move about and pretend to run their households, but in truth they spent their days moving through a sludgy torpor, never completely sure when a conversation had begun or when it should end.

But I had, in fact, never taken the laudanum. Every day I poured a little from the bottle into an empty perfume bottle which I kept hidden in a compartment of my dresser. Every month or so John dutifully went to get my next bottle, and every day I poured a little into my perfume bottle. *I won't prescribe more than this, because any more would kill her if accidentally taken all at once,* Dr. Cliffe told John when he thought I hadn't heard him.

In the years since I watched John Randal die when he was just three months old, the first of my children to leave me, I had collected the dozens and dozens of deadly doses, graduating to larger and larger perfume bottles as the months passed by. His eyes were so big, and he was so little, and when he looked up at me, his brows permanently wrinkled by pain and pleading, I saw the possibility of true innocence and the monstrous crime being committed against that very idea, against me, *against my son.* Sometimes the pain would ease, and he would smile, but only tears came when I tried to smile back and show him that I loved him, that he was the most wonderful thing. After a time he quit smiling. He was defenseless in this world, and so I loved him all the more and hated the world. Every day when I awoke I went to the wardrobe and pulled the bottle out. I'd feel its weight in my hand and ask myself if I would drink the bottle that day, and every day the answer was no. Then I'd put the bottle back in the secret compartment and slide the secret door shut. Some days I thought harder about the bottle than others, and once, I took the stopper out, but I had always put it away.

I knew it was there, though. I knew every day I could die, and this helped me. It was not the reminder of death that I desired. Everything around me was a reminder of death, every room, every length of wallpaper, every window. I needed no more reminders of that. What I wanted was to know what my dying children knew in their greatest moments, which were their moments of bravery and strength as they struggled to live. I had never seen my children so powerful as they were then, choking and shaking and whispering their apologies to me. Their *apologies.* They were at their best in the hours before death. I thought that if I could know it as they had known it, we would all share something that would not fade from my memory or disintegrate like the stones on their graves.

> *Dear Mother,*
>
> *I must amend my earlier letter to you regarding Martha. It has weighed heavily on me, and though I meant to pay her a proper tribute, I feel I must correct a few misrepresentations. Martha did not go to her Maker quietly. She was frightened and she cried out to me, and I could not help her though I wished to. I am not sure what she saw when the light dimmed in her eyes, but I will always remember the terror. I pray that she was welcomed into the arms of our Savior, and if anyone is welcomed thus it would be Martha, but I cannot be sure. I hope that I will never see such a thing again before I am myself taken away to my blessed rest. I tell you this now only because I do not want to mingle the memory of my Martha with certain untruths, how-ever kindly meant. Please forgive me.*
>
> *—Your Loving Daughter,*
> *Carrie*

I stood in my garden and let the cold creep up my legs. I had let the delicate roses die of thirst, and in their place had come the weeds and the other invasives—living things that looked like death to the undiscerning eye. The decline of the garden was a sad thing, people said, but I knew differently. Decline was natural. I was embarrassed to remember the times when I tended the plots, weeding and hoeing, beating back the inevitable. I was not saddened by my garden, nor by my house, nor by the little family cemetery and its fresh gravestones.

Death had been with me from the beginning, and now my house would be a hospital. I was not a morbid woman, but if death wanted to confront me, well, I would not turn my head. *Say what you have to say to me or leave me alone.* I did not look away. I *saw.* The garden, the cemetery, Martha's room—I had power. I had a power others did not. No, I would not have another child. No, I would not sow new seeds. I would not leave my house or change its decor. Nor would I sink into days of soft, drifting, opiated conversation with the ladies in town, fondling their laudanum. I did not have to run. I did not have to forget, I did not have to soothe myself, I did not have to ignore the most obvious fact of my life: that the things I loved had died and that I had failed them. *Let that wound stay open.* I understood that I could stand that pain and that I could even crave it sometimes. Dr. Cliffe advised John that I was spiraling down through the dark circles of melancholy, but it only felt like strength to me. Death could not make me afraid anymore.

If the price of that was seeming crazed and ignoring the doings of the living, it was a price I could pay. It was a price I was happy to pay, because it felt like vengeance. I took another look around my garden, and with a brief sweeping stroke I knocked down the brown stalks of two old sunflowers and watched them settle to the dark ground among the rotting leaves. Then I went inside.

12

LIEUTENANT NATHAN STILES, 104TH OHIO

I watched a little rebel boy, couldn't have been more than twelve years old, suffocate under the weight of the dead piled atop him. Suffocated. I had never considered the possibility. Only his head stuck through the pile, and I thought for a second that he was looking at me and trying to say something, only he didn't have the air to do it. He couldn't breathe, and God knows where he'd been shot. His jaws moved, and his eyes welled with tears. The last I saw of him he was closing his eyes just as another body landed on him, covering him completely. It was as if a wave had crashed over him and he'd been pulled out to sea.

We passed loaded rifles to the shooters at the battlements, and they passed their hot, smoking, and empty weapons to the back for reloading. The dead Confederates that filled our ditch were those who had made it to the top of our works, only to be instantly cut down. We had our own dead in that ditch, too, most all of them shot in the head after trying to take a peek at the onslaught. Most of our boys just raised their rifles over their heads, pointed out over the logs of the trench, and fired in the general direction of that god-awful screaming. There were so many dead in the trench we were forced to walk upon them, and I was afraid that soon they would fill our fighting position and force us out and that after that, they would fill every space around us and we would all suffocate like that grubby, breathless rebel boy.

If I had known what it meant to be defending a salient, I wouldn't have joked about the colonel's fancy language. We were surrounded on three sides, jutting out from the main line, and if the regiments on either side of us got a little too exuberant and shot at anything that moved in their front, they would start shooting into our position and we'd have to send someone over there to tell them to cut it the hell out. I lost two messengers that way.

We had robbed the cotton gin of much of its wood and steel—planks, joists, screw-press levers—in order to build our works, and in doing so we exposed the cotton bales in storage to the rebel volleys. Soon we were all covered in white puffs from the disintegrating bales, and much of the rest of it went floating out over the battlefield in front of us. In those rare moments when I risked a look over the top of our position, I watched how the cotton settled over the dead like a new snow. This is one of those things I can't forget about that day, one of those things that made me think I was living in another world. It was horrible and lovely and unexpected.

Why did they keep coming? By the second hour of fighting the killing had become so distasteful that when a rebel appeared on top of our entrenchment waving a flag or a rifle around, we'd yank him down and make him a prisoner rather than shoot him. That is, unless he seemed particularly dangerous. The dangerous men ended up in the trench.

The prisoners seemed relieved more than anything. At first they wouldn't be sure of what was happening, and then there'd be a brief moment of shame followed by the sunny, overwhelming realization that they were going to live. I saw one man begin to cry and another start slapping the backs of anyone within reach.

"Y'all fight like dogs, damn. Give them poor boys a break, ya

hear? You got food? That's one pretty rifle. Can I have it? Only
kidding, friend, only kidding. I ain't never seen a thing like that
field out there. You can't see it from here, too much smoke. You
tearing us up, though, sure enough. I'm just saying. You won't
believe it when you see it. Which way to the rear? I don't mean to
be pushy, but I've had enough of this."

And still they kept coming. They kept breaking against us, over
and over and over again, each time ebbing away and leaving
behind twisted and crumpled figures in the grass, rifles abandoned and glinting in the fading light, flags limp in the hands of
fallen color-bearers. Some of our boys began to pick out their tro-
phies, the things they would collect up later.

"That boy right there, see him? I'm going to take his pack. No,
right there, see? The one that had his jaw shot clear off? How can
you miss him, he's got his tongue lolling out right there on the
ground. Looks like he might have lost an eye, too. Can't quite tell.
There, now you see it? He's got a good-looking knife, too. I'll be
taking that also."

I put a stop to that talk, but I understood the urge. I wanted to
take something away from that place, too. I looked up above my
head and watched the cotton gin disintegrate bullet by bullet. I
wanted to leave the whole war behind me, and yet I was seeing
something on that battlefield that demanded commemoration. It
was unholy ground, but I wanted to thank God for showing it to me.
I would never again look at a man without wondering what crimes
he was capable of committing. That seemed important to know.

It was in the midst of that reverie when I realized that the
cracking sound I'd been hearing was not the sound of balls hitting
the gin house. I looked up once after being sprayed by splinters,
and realized the balls made a *thump-thump* sound against the wood
slats. The cracking sound came from the opposite direction, out
on the field. The dead and dying were packed so tightly that men
were charging right over them, shattering legs, arms, and ribs. It
was the sound of bones snapping.

I tried to keep them from shooting the color-bearer, but it was
beyond my power. If anything, the sight of those colors made the

men more vicious, each for their own private reasons, I assumed. And so the husky young man bellowing God knows what all, he fell just in front of our works as he waved the flag to rally the troops. He didn't see it coming and pitched forward toward his men with his arms out wide like he meant to embrace them. We had watched this unit struggle its way through the abatis while we shot them dead. We had watched the survivors be rallied to the charge by a fiery-eyed young officer, and we shot him dead, too. And his horse. We shot a lot of men dead, and still the others kept stumbling up the field. The big color-bearer took the colors from a fallen comrade halfway up, and then he came on like a huffing train engine, occasionally bellowing something that seemed to make the other men hesitate for a moment before going on. He wasn't a natural-born leader; that was obvious. Then he was dead.

I had lost my squeamishness. Killing was no longer distasteful. I was killing as many of them as I could by then, having seen enough of our boys get killed, almost all of them in the eye or the forehead as they peered through the slats in our position. Our trench was filled with dead from both sides, and I had to assign a couple men the task of hauling out as many corpses as they could, just to give us room to stand. No, I didn't have any problem killing Confederates by then. The initial shock of battle had passed. I was numb.

But there was something about shooting an unarmed man, even if he was carrying their blasted colors, that still seemed beyond the pale. The zealousness, the absolute faith in the cause, that prompted a man to take up a largely symbolic task at the risk of certain death: I had to respect it, as foolhardy as it seemed. Someone given over to such blind courage had made contact with a primeval thing, perhaps best forgotten but nonetheless extraordinary.

But I was too late to save that first color-bearer, and he went down. It was then that I noticed the other man.

From just twenty yards away I could see that he was going to pick up those colors. He was tall, and he had sad brown eyes, and he seemed to sigh when the colors wavered and fell. The most memorable thing about him, though, was that he quit running. He walked up to the colors, flung down his pistols, took the pole in his hands, and then turned and walked toward us like he was at the head of a parade. He was silent, just holding the colors high above his head. He was smiling, too, and I think it was that one fact about him that caused our boys to hesitate, and gave me the chance to intercede.

"Don't shoot the color-bearer!"

Weiss picked up his rifle as if he hadn't heard me, and I leaped at him and knocked the rifle out of the way. It was like I had woken Weiss from a bad dream, because he looked around and began to shake his head as if to clear something out of it. I shouted again.

"Shoot past him! Shoot past him! Let the color-bearer come."

For the most part the men did what I said, but a few shot at the colors, and it was a miracle that not a single shot hit that man, even an errant one. He strolled—and I can think of no better word to describe his gait—up to our line, climbed up on top, and planted that flag right in front of my face. He was still smiling, and he stuck his big nose in the air and laughed like hell. If there weren't other things to worry about, other men to shoot at, the men of my company would have goggled at him longer. But finally it was just him and me. He was looking around like he'd conquered a mountain, and he held his arms out from his sides the way a supplicant might. He was waiting for something.

I reached up and grabbed him by the belt and dragged him down into the ditch, where he looked up at me, his eyes buried in the leathery tan of his face. He then pulled his collar down and exposed his neck. He pointed to it, as if to say, *Get me right here, and be quick about it*. I kept my foot on his chest, staring at him, until the expression on his face changed. He became angry and struggled against my foot. He called me a coward. He spit at me, and I almost became angry enough to slit his throat, but there was something about him that stayed my hand. A man like that shouldn't die. He looked older, too old to throw his life away unthinkingly. Even as he struggled against me, his face relaxed and the furrows between his eyes smoothed out. He looked at me as if he knew me, and he smirked. I almost killed him then, too. But then he quit struggling and lay quietly.

"You are my prisoner," I said.

"I reckon so."

"Why do you want to die?"

"I don't want to die, Yank. I want you to do your duty."

"My duty?"

"If it's not your duty to kill me, then what the hell are we doing here?"

"It's not honorable now."

He laughed then, a wheezing laugh that reminded me I was probably squeezing the air out of him. I stepped off his chest, and he didn't move. He looked at me.

"When did they make that rule?" he said, still in the fever of battle. His mind wasn't quite right, talking gibberish. I'd saved his life, that's all I knew. I'd done something good for once, and he wasn't going to talk me out of it. I picked him up by his collar and dragged him back to the rear, where I handed him off to a guard.

"This man is a prisoner."

He looked back at me as he was led away, and laughed.

"Don't I know it."

13

CARRIE McGAVOCK

I stood looking down from the landing on the stairs. I watched Mariah striding about, carrying tables over here, the chairs over there. When Hattie and Winder tried to help, she slapped at their hands. *I whip you myself you drop that vase, youngun. Don't look at me like that, now. Get going, we got to clear it out.* I had not seen Mariah so happy in a long time. Or perhaps I hadn't noticed.

Hattie and Winder had finally retreated to the corner by the front door, where they took turns brushing each other's hair with Martha's brush. Hattie was wearing an old dress of Martha's, blue taffeta with white organdy collar. It was still too big for her, and it billowed out like a tent from where she kneeled behind Winder, his curls in her fingers. Chaos swelled and crested around them, but they took no notice.

"We getting ready, Missus Carrie. We clearing out some space and getting the nice things out the way. They be mens with muddy boots in here before long, and I figured you wouldn't want all them filthy things on the carpets. Let 'em stomp around on bare wood, I figure."

During those months and years I spent sitting in my Grecian rocker in my little room above the foyer, rocking and rocking, I had passing thoughts of the house's substructure, the walls behind the walls, the floors under the floors. I had wondered what it looked like. I had wondered if it had decomposed over the years and whether it could hold the weight of my household much longer. There were things that smelled like rot in the house, and walls that bowed out slightly. (This last fact I knew from time spent lying on the cool floor with my head against the wall, looking up.) I imagined that things lived beneath me and around me and that I would never see them. But I assumed that someday the house would come crashing down, and then perhaps I'd catch a glimpse of whatever it was that had been feeding off me for so long. It was thoughts like these that had reminded me that I oughtn't go to town and see people. I was no longer presentable.

Now the windows had been thrown open, and it felt as if the house itself was breathing deep while I stood on the landing taking quick, shallow gasps. The outside had blown in, sure enough, along with a few dead leaves and a mouse that one of the house cats was tossing about in the corner of the dining room. The house had peeled itself back and given way to the onslaught of folly and time. I felt euphoric, as I imagined I might feel if I were drowning and had finally abandoned myself, letting the water fill my lungs and cover my head. It was all out of my hands now.

"That's right, Mariah. Very good. But I'll take care of the children's things."

"Yes'm."

I descended the steps and glided across the hall to the front door, where I stood over my other two children.

"That's a pretty dress, Hattie darling."

Hattie was dark like me. She never seemed quite as aware as she should have been, even for a nine-year-old. She was ever stumbling over tree roots and laughing at stories a half-beat too late. I thought her merely a dreamy girl who would come to no great harm in her life, but on this day I could see peril looming for my little one—men crashing around knocking into things, screaming and crying, bleeding—and I vowed to keep my girl close.

"Yes, Mama. Mama? All of Martha's dresses are there in her room. Thrown up on the bed in a big pile, with everything all mixed up and going every which way. I told Mariah to be careful and not to wrinkle them, I did, Mama, but she weren't listening to me, which is quite rude, I do believe, but they aren't too wrinkled laying out right there, just as plain as you please, and this one is so pretty and I always liked it and . . ."

She paused to take a breath.

". . . can I have it, Mama?"

I stroked Hattie's dark hair and resisted the passing urge to cut it off and stick it in my pocket, which reminded me of something I would have to do later. *Later. For now I have this one, warm and delicate and awkward. I never knew her hair was so smooth.*

"You can have whatever you want now, little girl. But we must get to work."

Winder whirled around to look at me and yelped when Hattie forgot to let go of *his* hair.

"What work, Mama?"

Winder was seven and fancied himself a big boy, a man even, and cried each time his father refused to let him plow or shoot the crows that stole their seed. I looked down on my two children and wondered how I had missed noticing that they were getting bigger. It seemed ridiculous, but I was momentarily surprised by the idea that children grow. I had become too accustomed to looking at the portrait of my other children hanging on the wall opposite the foot of my bed, with their beatific smiles frozen for all time.

"There will be men coming, little one, and they will be hurt, but we're going to take care of them."

"Are they soldiers, Mama?"

Winder was also unclear why he couldn't be a soldier, a "caffryman." John had given up trying to explain and had given him a little cavalryman's hat at supper one day, which he promptly lost out in the yard, where it was torn to pieces by two stray dogs and devoured by our boar, Prince Edward.

"Yes, they will be soldiers. Now stand up—you, too, Hattie—and brush yourselves off. You're to help me pack."

* * *

I could see Mariah watching the scene out of the corner of her eye, but I'm sure she hadn't been able to hear what was said, even if she strained her ears mightily over the din of furniture scraping.

We had known each other since we were children, back in Louisiana, on my father's plantation. She had called me Miss Carrie, and Miss Carrie had briefly scandalized the household by calling her Miss Mariah. We had explored the lowlands together back home, when we could sneak away, braving the snakes and the leeches in search of ferns and tiny sleek tadpoles. But time had snuck between us, and now it was impossible to reconcile our previous history with life at Carnton, especially since I had begun to lose my children.

I'm certain Mariah was surprised to see the children stand up quietly and follow me into Martha's room. She would have expected the two of them to stay underfoot and cause trouble, which was their usual manner. But I had them marching behind me like two wee attendants, and I hoped Mariah was impressed. She wasn't the only one who could make people jump.

We hid away most everything in the main house. Casualties of war. Much later, when the house was finally empty of men, I imagined that the house—as I had known it—still existed somewhere, only disembodied, its pieces hauled off here and there, buried beneath a tree or hidden in a hayloft: the rolls of Brussels carpets, the books, the canopied beds. The only familiar thing was the wallpaper in the dining room, once gaudy with scenes of Egyptian ruins and Mayan palaces that had gone gray with mildew and dust. *Nothing disappears entirely,* I thought.

The house was transformed into something harder, barer, tougher. I presided over the boxing of my children's clothing and toys and stole some of Mariah's younger workers, the few remaining servants not yet sent off by John, to lug them up into the attic. Hattie and Winder were no help to anyone but me, and they amused me.

Trains and hoops and wooden horses went into the attic, balanced on the heads of young Negro men who had never played with such things except when they were broken and cast off, and who stole a few brief moments pushing the train around the attic when they thought no one was looking. Most of the furniture disappeared. We took the portraits off the walls, then the candlesticks from the tables, and then all my Parian figurines I had once so cherished.

We put these things away in places even I didn't know existed—cramped crawl spaces under loose floorboards, sideboards with hidden compartments, dark places behind corner cupboards. Mariah took the silver and the china, boxed them up, and had them buried near one of the cedars in the garden. The floors were swept and scrubbed, and old sheets were torn into long strips for bandages. Mariah searched the house and the old wing for buckets and basins for water, and she scrounged every bit of lye soap she could find, even the crumbs some of the slaves kept squirreled away under loose boards in the cabins, hidden for special occasions.

There was one place I felt I had to make safe before the onslaught, before things I could not imagine took over my home. I went to my desk and unlocked the slanted lid. It was filled with toys, worn-out dolls, a spelling book, a rattle. I opened one of the little drawers and removed two daguerreotypes and studied them. One showed Martha holding Mary Elizabeth's hand on Mary Elizabeth's sixth and last birthday. Mary Elizabeth's party dress looked a little stained and wrinkled, a casualty of playing with her cousins and friends during the party. The second picture showed a baby in his white dress sleeping—no, dead: John Randal. It was my only picture of him, he had died so young. I put the pictures back.

Martha didn't die at once. It was slow, so slow. She seemed to melt away. Every day she was a little smaller than the day before. After two weeks she rarely spoke, but her eyes were on me, and I thought I could tell what she was thinking by the way she held her eyelids. Perspiration was ever dripping into her eyes, and it stung so much that she often spent minutes at a time blinking uncontrollably. If I wanted to listen to her—I thought of it as listening—I had to sit there next to her and mop her brow. Sometimes I applied the wet tobacco leaves, but that never seemed to bring the fever down, and it stained her forehead a dark orange, which was unbearable to see. So I just sat there, tossing the linens on the floor as they became sodden and heavy.

Tucked into the back of the desk was my sewing basket. I lifted the woven straw lid, and on top of scissors and ribbons and needles and spools of thread lay a folded piece of lace. I took it out and placed it on my lap. I unfolded the top panel, revealing the three locks of hair, each tied with a thin black ribbon. For years I had kept the desk as a little shrine, occasionally taking up the locks and placing them against my cheeks. Now I just looked at them, lying there in a row on my lap. I stared, until I could distinguish every hair in every bundle. And then I wrapped them up, stuffed them in the pocket of my apron, and called for one of the servants to haul the desk away. With the sound of the wind whistling from the front door to the back door and the loud tearing of sheets and the general pandemonium, I didn't hear John ride up to the house until I saw his head (and Theopolis's behind him) bounce along the driveway. He was scowling, and that was another thing I hadn't remembered him doing before. Was that new? Had John scowled before?

I watched John slide off the horse. Theopolis strode off with purpose and vigor toward the kitchen porch on the other side of the house. He was the most unlikely Negro I had ever known, and I wondered idly what kind of man he would be if he were white.

John opened the front door and stared at his house turned inside out. He looked puzzled.

I walked up behind him.

"What is going on here?" he said.

"It's like a fire, come to purge us and burn away what's rotten."

John turned slowly. I could see it in his eyes. *She's still not right.*

"I think you must lie down."

"I am not tired."

But I was.

14

SERGEANT ZACHARIAH CASHWELL, 24TH ARKANSAS

I was lost. It was so easy to become lost. I was amazed at how quickly my life was transformed, from one moment on the brink of death to the next tied at the wrists and seated in the dirt against an old smokehouse. The thought *This ain't right* never crossed my mind. I became a prisoner and accepted all the duties of a prisoner just as easily as I'd picked up the damned colors and walked forward to the bulwarks. And it happened without thinking on it one bit. I suffered, and I accepted that suffering was my appointed job now. We had been routed, and the Union men who passed me by on their way to the rear—dragging their own wounded, wiping the smoke grime from their faces—gave me grief.

"Where are your friends, reb? Left them behind, huh? Saved your skin like a good little coward." A slight, balding private with an arm tied against his body with a length of cord, he walked right up to me and spit in my face. I would have broken him in two once, but now I just took it. Felt the spit run down my cheek and dry there.

This was my new life. My mind was packed up with thoughts falling all over themselves, thoughts I hadn't had in days. Thoughts about what would happen to me. In the minutes after that lieutenant put his pistol down and made me his captive, my mind went from thinking of nothing else but going forward, of nothing else but each footstep and each stretch of dirt in front of me and each bullet that tumbled past my head, to a fire of thoughts about my life and the new world I'd fallen into. It was too much to be thinking about and left me no energy to worry about spit in my face. I became a different person. Who would I become? Where would I go? Why was I spared, for what purpose? When would I get something to eat?

Occasionally I looked up from staring at my boots and their frayed laces to watch the things going on around me. There were five of us lined up against that smokehouse, and none of us spoke a word. I reckon we all had things to think about. I was seated against the corner, with a view of the road passing by to my right. To my left one of my fellow prisoners kept raising his bonded hands to his face to scratch at his head, and little flakes of his scalp fell onto his pant leg, where they sat until the wind picked up.

As the sun went down, I watched the Yankees begin to move their gear and their men down that road to the rear, and after a while a couple of big Union men came over.

"Get your asses up, rebs. We're moving."

They had their Springfields trained on us, and one was worrying a fat, unlit cigar in his mouth. We got to our feet and shuffled alongside them, out into the road. They were as confused as we were, I think, because they kept stopping us and starting us again, taking us down one way and then back another way.

"Why the hell are we taking them with us?" the taller one said. He had a scar on his neck that went from white to red every time he started talking. He sounded English to me. The other guard, just a little shorter but built like a brick, kept looking for a fire to light his cigar.

"Just do it, Campbell. What we got here, we got us the spoils of war." He laughed when he said that, a little laugh, like he didn't really believe what he was saying.

We were stopped under a big oak, waiting for the carts and caissons to pass after we were almost run over as the supply train made for a bridge in the distance. A limping soldier carrying nothing but a shovel slapped me on the back of the head as he passed. Then he stopped and began to rifle through my pockets.

"Get the hell away from that man, or I'll shoot you dead, Private."

It was the man with the cigar talking.

"But he's got some matches."

The man with the shovel pulled out my little round tin of matches, which I had been saving since Atlanta. He waved them in the air, in front of my nose.

"Put 'em back," the guard with the cigar said.

"Why the hell do you care?"

"I don't like you all of a sudden, that's why. Get movin'."

"Shit."

The man jammed the matches back into my pocket and elbowed me in the stomach in one slick move, and then he went and jumped up on the back of a cart and yelled out, "You aren't going to need matches where you're going, reb. It'll be hot enough without 'em."

"Go to hell," said the cigar man.

"Well, that's exactly what I mean."

As the cart pulled off, the stocky guard walked up to me. We were still standing there, and the cart train just seemed to get longer and longer, and I figured we'd be standing there quite some time.

"You got matches, reb?"

"Yes."

"Could I have one?"

I must have looked at him funny, because his scar got all purple and he frowned.

"I meant, give me a match."

He wasn't cut out for this, I knew that then. No sense of place or position. Probably a good man, but you never know. Could have been just stupid, not recognizing the power he had. Or not used to it yet. The funny thing was, I sympathized with him a little, even though I came to realize that I couldn't allow myself to stay under his control. Or any man's control. This, I reckon, was what all those piercing hard thoughts jabbing inside me had come to: I had to go. I was a prisoner. I was a reviled man, all right. That's who I had become. But I would not live like that forever. I would not allow it.

He reached into my pocket and pulled out the tin, took one out, struck it against the barrel of his rifle, and lit his cigar. I smelled that tobacco, and it smelled good. He looked at me and said, "I saw you run up that hill."

I didn't say anything.

"You ought to be dead."

I nodded.

"Maybe you could use a cigar."

And I nodded again.

His partner was getting hot and mad. "Don't fool with that son of a bitch. Let's just get the hell out of here."

I looked over at my fellow prisoners, and they all had their heads down, staring at the dirt. They'd remain prisoners for a long time to come, I thought.

"Shut up,"the man with the cigar said. And then he pulled out a tin case and popped it open to reveal some of the worst-looking cigars I had ever laid eyes on. He put one in my mouth and struck another match, lighting it. Then he took my matches, stuck them in his trousers, and walked off. I took a deep breath and let the smoke burn my throat and struggled mightily to keep from coughing and spitting the thing out. I hadn't smoked much before.

The two soldiers conferred, and then the taller one said, "Let's go, we're taking a shortcut."

They led us down an alley between two houses, through their yards, and through the fence of a stable that had been riddled with bullet holes. As if I had willed it to happen in just that way, they had decided to march us around the main line of traffic and head for the bridge by a back route. And that route brought us into the stable yard and past the stable with its manger of hay lying just inside the door.

And when I passed that manger, I hacked up a god-awful cough and let that cigar fly into the manger onto the dry hay before my keepers saw me. And when they turned back to me, I was busy mashing the ground with the toe of my boot, as if grinding the cigar into the mud.

"Got to take it easy with that tobacco," the shorter one said. "That's some powerful Tennessee bounty."

I nodded, and we walked off toward that bridge to God knew where.

There was a fire, of course. They were trying to sneak themselves out of town, all of them Union boys, and I set off the biggest damn signal fire you've ever seen, and it queered their plans a bit, I reckon. There was a lot of running around, and a captain grabbed our two captors for a firefighting detail, and while they struggled to explain that they had to keep an eye on us, I slipped off. Down through a little alley, down the bank, and into the waters of a little river. When I looked back, I saw the two men still arguing with the officer, and my fellow captives still standing there with their heads down, black against the firelight.

Stretched out before me in the dark lay everything, and I walked toward it.

15

LIEUTENANT NATHAN STILES, 104TH OHIO

I did not see that color-bearer again that day. That night, when the fighting had died down and all you could hear were the plaintive bleatings of the wounded strewn before us, I thought, *I saved one of them.* God knows what I consigned him to by not letting him be killed, but I hoped he would appreciate it someday.

We sat there for hours after the sun went down, listening to the occasional crack of one more gun in the hands of one more wayward and stubborn rebel soldier, but the battle was over. And as soon as the battle was over, the rhapsodizing began.

"Hood has crashed and broken upon our shoal," cried one of the bad poets in our company, and I was sure every man would file that little bit of doggerel away for future use in letters or in their memoirs or while sitting on one of a hundred porches scattered all over the Union. What garbage. Men from other units went out onto the battlefield to gather souvenirs, but I kept my men back under great pressure. What were they going to get off those sorry corpses? *Just another chance to get their hands bloody,* I thought. I wouldn't go along with that.

We got the word to pull out, but we had to sit there and wait our turn. We were going to sneak out again, just like the night before. While I sat there, cleaning my pistol, I thought about my precious Greek books back home in my parents' house. I wondered if I'd be able to pick up my studies again, whether there would be anyone left to run a college when I returned. I knew I would not be able to read those books again with the same mind. I had seen Spartans and Thebans and Atticans for myself now. The only glory to be had was the glory of surviving. Crashed and broken upon our shoal—well, that just meant we were living and they weren't. What man could take pride in the killing of another man? Not pride. Relief, yes, and damn them who would put a man in the position of even being relieved at the death of another. That's what made the sentiments of glory and honor, on that battlefield, such lies. If we were lucky, we might live to an age when our memory would fail us.

At one point, while awash in my dark ruminations, a fire started in town far to the rear. *There goes our stealthy retreat,* I thought. But it was quickly extinguished, no harm done. No harm done.

16

CARRIE MCGAVOCK

I returned to the garden. I stood in the diagonal plot formed by intersecting walkways, upon the dirt which, despite the brief hours of warmth, remained hard underfoot. I was listening to the new sounds echoing back to me while absentmindedly running my hands through the brown hollow stalks of the dormant liatris and coneflowers. Seeds sprang from their pods and attached themselves to the back of my long black wool skirt. I stood silently so I could listen clearly. The sound had stopped me and demanded my attention.

It was the sound of battle. What I took to be the report of rifles seemed, two miles distant, like the crackling of a new fire in a cold fireplace. I was surprised by how innocuous it sounded, and yet it was pervasive and never-ending. Once I heard the first shot, I could hear almost nothing else. I could also hear the occasional deep *shhthump-shtthump* of artillery shells, each of them gathering the air and transforming it into the deep percussion of something like a parade drum. I strained to hear other things—the twitter of finches and titmice, for instance, but either they had departed or

I had become deaf to them. There was no other sound. Not even a rattle from the last dry leaves clinging to the trees above my head. The sound of the artillery shells became louder and louder, and suddenly I realized that they were exploding on our land, in the remnants of our own grove. We, who had spent what seemed like a lifetime waiting for this war to pass, now found this war passing all too close to our world. Why would anyone turn their guns on our land? Surely there was no army at Carnton.

The two surgeons, each with a little group of attendants, had arrived just as the fighting began. They had taken down two of the interior doors, long, thick slabs of poplar painted in delicate faux mahogany, and transformed them into operating tables lying across hastily fabricated trestles. The first doctor to come through the door was a slight, frowning, bald man with a limp, who trailed dirt across the floor and smelled of ether and horse droppings. He was the one who demanded more bandages after seeing the pile of torn sheets Mariah had laid out in the foyer.

The second doctor moved slowly. He was heavy and old, and his cheeks glowed red in an otherwise pale face.

"Good Lord, Winston, there's never enough bandages. We'll run out sooner or later, always do. Calm *down*."

The old doctor said this as the little one shook his finger in Mariah's face, and I was grateful the old man had stepped in. I could see Mariah balling her fists and struggling to keep from frowning.

Their voices echoed against the bare floors and through the empty rooms, and the house seemed to be getting bigger and bigger, as if the walls were moving away and soon I would be lost within them, something small and forgettable. While the surgeons and their staff prepared the house, I had paced around the grounds with my children. John had walked with me for a time and tried to hold my hand, but I would not let it out of the front pocket of my apron, where it was buried. It had been years since we'd walked together without a destination, and I thought it best not to mention this fact. We passed between the garden and the house, through the rows of cedars lining the front walkway, down around the old wing, and past the slave quarters. As we passed the cistern, John looked in.

"They'll be needing more water, I expect."

"Yes."

"Theopolis and I can go to the well and start hauling it up. You can stay here."

"Of course."

John put his chin on top of my head and pulled me toward him. I stood stiffly in his arms, and John seemed embarrassed again. He let me go.

"I must get the water."

I continued to walk around the house grounds, listening to Mariah's shouts through the open windows. *Listen to the man, bring those chairs over here, get me the scissors*. I didn't know what to do with myself, so I walked. I didn't know what I was expected to do next. *Lord, give me the wisdom to know what you want from me and the strength to do it*. I offered that prayer each time I passed the front door of the house, at least a dozen times.

Then, finally, a husky boy stood at the end of the brick front walkway with his arms around another boy, who leaned hard against him. They couldn't have been older than fourteen. I walked over to the front of the house, and the two of us—the unhurt boy and I—stared at each other down the corridor of cedars. I would have waved them forward, but I could not bring my hands out of my apron pockets. I stood mute. The boy shouted across the bricks.

"Some men told me this here's a hospital."

I nodded my head.

The boy stayed where he was, shifting his friend's weight around to get a better grip. He shouted in the high-pitched singsong of a boy who knows he's in trouble.

"My friend got himself whumped on the head after a big explosion when we was just watching and not doing nothing wrong. Wham, just like that, and he flying through the air and the dirt was in my eyes, and he's sometimes awake and sometimes asleep, and I had to carry him some of the way, and, ma'am, I think he's hurt."

Not a child. Not another child. General Forrest had said soldiers, hadn't he? Soldiers were men. Not children.

I would have run. I thought to run. I saw before me another

child waiting to die in my arms, waiting for me to take him up and
nurse him so that he could be forsaken and abandoned by a distant God who had not once—*not once*—interceded in consideration
of what I couldn't endure. What did it say in Deuteronomy? *As thy
days, so shall thy strength be*. I had believed this! We had all believed
this! Every widow and mother, every one of the foggy-headed
wraiths wandering through their houses in town, every black-
shrouded figure casting her eyes upward while Negro men throw
dirt into the graves—we had all *believed!* And our reward had been
more than anyone could endure. I did not forget God's anointed
earthly intermediaries—the men. Carrying on their holy, hellish
war as if there were an unlimited supply of bodies and strength to
draw on, as if there weren't enough despair. What did God want
from me? I could witness no more. My heart had become flinty
and cold, concealing nothing. It was a rock, and He could have it.
But another child?

Get away, little boy, I thought. *You will die here. I am a killer: it's
what God has revealed to me, His great plan for me.*

I shuddered. I loved God. No, I didn't. I feared Him, I was in
awe of His strength, and I had always obeyed Him. Here was a
boy, now. Right in front of me, standing at the end of my walkway,
his friend crying little tears and staring at me for a sign. What was
unbearable was not the dying, but the idea that the dying was part
of His plan and that we had trusted Him to deliver us from evil. I
hoped the little boy in front of me would wait while I sorted it out,
looking for a way to help. The little plump boy, so steady for so
long, had begun to sink under the weight of his friend, and as his
knees buckled, he brought his cheek to the top of his friend's head
and pulled mightily under his arms to keep him upright. The
blood, when he pulled away, stained his wide, pale cheek.

As thy days, so shall thy strength be. *Thy* strength. *Thy* strength. My
strength. Mine. Not His, but *mine*. He was not responsible for this.
He was not responsible for Martha or for John Randal or for Mary
Elizabeth. *He was weak*. The sudden realization of this brought
spots before my eyes and made it hard to breathe. He was weak?
My children had not been taken, they had *just died*. Just died, no
special significance to it, no betrayal. He had not been there, there

had been no purpose to their deaths, no purpose to the intervening years of my mourning.

I passed from fear to love in that instant, while I stared down at the little boy and his dying friend. I no longer feared God, I loved Him. I loved that He did not even save His own Son. He had not taken His Son, He had *lost* Him *because* of the sin of this world.

I would not blame Him anymore, but neither would I ever again pray, *Thy will be done.* His will was never that His own Son die or that my children die any more than He had *willed* sin into this world. I would not pray to God that His will be done, as if He could make it so. *I* would make it so, as far as I understood it. He was not the author of children's deaths.

I would serve Him because I could. It was men who hurt that boy. Powerful men all around me. I heard them in the distance and smelled their fires.

Run.

Run.

Run.

I took my hands out of my front pocket and ran toward the boys down the walkway. The boy wiped at the tears on his cheeks and almost dropped his friend. He lifted him up again and started toward me.

And so it began.

I took the injured boy around the other shoulder, and between the two of us we got him up the front steps, through the portico, and into the house. As he passed under the portico, his head lolling back on his skinny neck, the wounded one awoke and saw the blue ceiling.

"The sky is damn beautiful, ain't it?"

His friend looked embarrassed and apologized to me as we sat him down in a chair.

"He's been talking funny like that all the way back here. He doesn't normally swear. Much."

He continued on, telling me all about how he'd lost his spyglass, which was a crying shame, and how he was named Ab and his friend was named Eli, and how the Confederates had flags and guns that could shoot a man at a hundred miles, and how they were spies but not really, and how he wished that rock hadn't been there.

I wasn't listening. I wanted to tell the boy to go inside, to bring out one of the surgeons or orderlies. I ran my fingers through the back of Eli's brown sticky hair, looking for the wound. I started when I found it—a three-inch gash at the base of his head, wet and warm. I looked at the back of his shirt and saw how it had been stained brown by the blood. My heart began to beat in my ears, but I kept focused by gently caressing the boy's head and face. He looked like a good boy.

I called out for help, and then again, until I heard Mariah and one of the doctors clatter down the steps behind me. Mariah grabbed Ab without a word and pulled him toward her and away from the wounded one. Ab didn't struggle. The short, sour doctor picked at his mustache and snorted.

"What's this?"

I told him the boy had been hit on the head and was cut. The doctor laid his delicate hand on top of the boy's head, shoved it forward, and roughly poked at the back of his head.

"He's just bumped his damned head, he's got a little cut. Where the hell did he come from? He needs to be out of the way right now. Wrap his head and send him out of here. Right now."

He spoke to me as someone who didn't know me, for whom my house was just a hospital, one of probably hundreds he'd haunted over the years. He knew nothing of me, not even my name. I could be anyone. He stood waiting for me to reply to him, twiddling his thin mustache and rolling his eyes, but I only nodded. He stomped back up the stairs and into his operating chamber. I looked after him briefly and then turned back to the boy.

Mariah, who had been conferring with Ab in the corner, sent the boy off to tell Eli's family about what had happened. Ab ran out the door and disappeared down the walkway.

The injured boy was unconscious again. I pulled his chair sideways and pushed it against the wall so that he wouldn't fall over. Without being asked, Mariah found a basin of water, a clean towel, and one long, narrow bandage.

I knelt down behind the boy and felt the hard wood on my knees. I took the towel, wetted it, and began to dab at the boy's wound. The pain and the cold woke him, and he groaned and cursed, but then he relaxed and let his hand rest in the palm of my free hand. I dabbed some more, lightly, and rinsed the towel out in the basin. Slowly the water turned a light shade of pink. I worked at the long, thin line of the cut, drawing out the dirt and exposing the healthy pink flesh. Soon I had forgotten that Mariah was standing there, watching me crouched on the floor like a washerwoman.

I remained kneeling behind the boy as the second wounded man arrived. And then the third and the fourth. I was there when the fiftieth man came in with his ragged pant leg dangling half-empty off the side of the stretcher and a belt tied around his thigh. They all brushed past me in a blur—the orderlies, the wounded, the dying, the members of the burial detail. They were only a tapestry of muted colors and muffled sounds so long as I dabbed at Eli's head. My knees went numb, and my house filled quickly. I continued to kneel and wash the wound of the little boy.

Men filled up the rooms on the first floor, and soon orderlies began hauling their burden up the stairs. In the parlor the men were lined up in rows, most unconscious, some groaning, but I didn't go to them. As I rubbed the last piece of dirt from Eli's head, I was deaf to the sound of the doctor's saw upstairs. I slowly wrapped his head with the bandage, three times, and the only thing I noticed was how precise Mariah had been while cutting up my old cotton sheets. I did not respond to the redheaded North Carolinian lying a few feet from me, holding his hands over the hole in his stomach. *Please, ma'am, if it ain't any trouble, I would very much like some water.*

". . . please, ma'am, please. I'm fine, please. That man, that man . . . he needs you."

The boy—Eli—had awoken a few minutes before, and *he* had not failed to notice the men passing by him. He did not know me, the woman with her arm around him. He just saw that man, the man who needed the water. He could see only the blood seeping between his tightly clenched fingers and soaking into the floor. I saw this in his face.

"That man."

"You're all right."

"That man."

"You didn't die. You're going to be fine."

"Please, ma'am, please. I'm fine, please. That man, that man . . . he needs you."

The man's eyes rolled up in his head, and his throat convulsed, and he screamed until he had no air left.

I nodded my head and ran my hand through my hair, loosening it. I had somehow, inside me, indeed heard the sound of men filling every corner. I had seen the unimaginable and understood what helping the Lord would really mean. But I had saved a child; a child had not died in my arms. The Lord had made good.

Calling to Mariah to follow me, I stood up, turned on my heel without a word to Eli. I stepped over the screaming man and mounted the stairs, climbing quickly. When I burst into the room containing the operating table, the little surgeon was smoking a cigarette and staring out the window while the older doctor cleaned the table of blood. I crossed the room so quickly the little man almost swallowed his burning tobacco when I came upon him.

"This is my house. Do you understand?"

"I never doubted it, ma'am."

"I mean to say, this is *my* house, and I won't be talked to like I don't have anything to say about what goes on here."

"Well, I'm afraid, ma'am, that we've requisitioned this house for a hospital, as you can see. You will be well compensated by the quartermaster, who will—"

I looked down at the operating table and put my hand over a small, sharp knife. I looked down at my hand intently while I spoke.

"I will cut your tongue out if you talk back to me again."

Behind me the old doctor laughed out loud, with wide and amused eyes. He made no effort to stop me.

"There is a young man downstairs screaming that his belly has been exploded, and then I come up here and you're enjoying a little break. I want to see him on this table right now."

The little surgeon backed away and leaned against the wall while trying to puff out his chest.

"We are in the process of triaging these men, ma'am, and we have everything under—"

I clenched my hand, taking the knife into my fist, which I left resting on the table.

"I swear."

The old doctor spoke.

"Winston, we ain't triaging a damn thing, and you know it. One dying boy is the same as another. That college has spoiled you. Let's go. I'll cut on that stomach if you won't."

I looked up and began to back out of the room, all the while staring at the little surgeon.

"I want to know if you're having any problems keeping this surgery operating. I want to know immediately."

The little surgeon wouldn't look at me, but he had begun to wash his hands. The old doctor spoke.

"Yes, ma'am. Thank you. Would you mind having that young man sent up here?"

I stopped in the doorway, crossed my arms, and nodded my head.

"And there will be many more."

"I expect so, ma'am."

Outside the room, I turned to Mariah and began breathing hard. Mariah put her arm around me for a moment, and then I shrugged her off. I told her to start tearing up more linen for bandages, and then I went back down the stairs.

Now hundreds of men lay about me, maybe thousands. Millions. I saw them clearly, the twisting limbs and the trembling chests, the rolling eyes in every head in every direction. I saw the letters peeking out of their pockets, waiting to be delivered to Lord knows where. And every one of them seemed to beg me for water. *Please, ma'am. Please.* This was the price of my redemption.

"I'm coming."

Outside, the orderlies began lining the wounded up in the yard. The red sky of dusk was disintegrating into black. There was no more room in the house. There would be no room for days.

17

NOVEMBER 30, 1864: TWILIGHT

It was said you could walk across the battlefield upon the bodies of the fallen and not once touch the ground. Others have described the dead as being stacked like cordwood or like sheaves of corn or like sacks of meal. By different accounts the ground ran with rivers of blood, or it was stained with blood, or it was blood. The wounded moaned, their teeth chattered, they screamed, they howled. Again, it all depended on who was talking. For many years afterward the survivors wrote beautiful letters and memoirs that always, always stumbled when they came to the task of describing the dead. On the morning after the battle, in a town of nearly 2,500 living, there were almost 9,200 casualties. There were no words to describe such a sight, and within a month the dead had either been buried on the battlefield in shallow graves or been hauled off to the new Union cemeteries in Nashville and Murfreesboro: in other words, they quickly disappeared out of sight.

There were thousands of dead men lying on the Confederate side of that battlefield and perhaps a thousand Union dead on the other side. To that add a few thousand horribly wounded men on both sides, and then there were a few hundred men that were missing—that were never again found. Then add to them the men who were so disfigured and broken that they were of no use to their armies anymore, who went home bearing the physical and mental scars of that battle for the rest of their days—lives often cut short because of what had happened at Franklin. The dimensions of the violence begin to emerge, its measurements a tidy table of dead and wounded. But it is impossible to see it all fully. It would drive a man mad to apprehend the whole tragedy, to know every effect and consequence, to know the names of every good man and woman, every genius and every saint, who was never born because their lineage petered out there on that rise at Franklin. It would be like looking into the face of the Gorgon, or for that matter, the face of God.

The thing to remember about the dead (stacked up like wood or like sheaves of corn, whichever you prefer) is that they're just flesh, and rapidly mortifying flesh at that. The mind reels, it refuses to look closer. The dead are objects, they are litter to be removed. And yet, if one did look closer, as a few rare and intrepid young men did, there was more to see: more than the flesh, the blood, the numbers. Such facts disappear from memory, but the memory of certain faces can be eloquent even in death if one looks closely enough.

"I saw scores of wounded men who had put their thumbs into their mouths and had chewed them into shreds to keep from crying," wrote a young Mississippian to his girl, "coward-like, as they lay exposed to the merciless fire. Franklin was the only battleground I ever saw where the faces of the majority of the dead expressed supreme fear and terror. Their eyes were wide open and fear staring. Their very attitude as they lay prone upon the ground, with extended, earth-clutching fingers, and with their faces partially buried in the soil, told the tale of mental agony they had endured before death released them."

The Confederate dead lay on one side of the entrenchments, the Union dead on the other, and, in the night, the living Union troops *quietly left town. They left town even as the Confederate commander planned his morning attack. A number of Confederates wandered the field looking futilely for their friends, taking in the full extent of the horror that lay at their feet. It was only then, later in the cold night, that they noticed the silence. It was not a total silence; there were still the moans and pleading of the dying in the air. But the aggressive sort of noise that had throttled their ears for near five hours—from the hour before twilight into the moonless night, the gunshots, the report of cannons—that noise had dissipated to nothing.*

The Confederate general heard of this, and he wept. The next day he marched toward Nashville to complete what he had begun. Within months the Confederacy would surrender.

Yet the Battle of Franklin was not over. Though the cannons and the wagons had rolled out of town, for some the fighting had just begun. Some fought for their lives in the cold rooms of makeshift hospitals. Others fought to remember what Franklin had been like before November 30, 1864. Still others fought to hang on to whatever vain hope or benighted purpose had brought the war into the town, on the theory that to abandon that hope and purpose would be to render the killing meaningless and the whole affair a cosmic joke. And some fought to quash everything that remained of such sentimental notions.

BOOK II

18

November 30, 1864: Night

In the center of town an old man named Baylor, gray-haired and dressed in black, watched a procession approach his porch: his son, delirious from the pain of his mortal wounds, carried upon a stretcher borne by his slaves.

"Take him into the quarantine room," he said when they tried to enter the main house. As his son passed him, he resisted the urge to touch the long locks of blond hair which swung freely over the edge of the stretcher. His son began to cry from the pain.

"Keep him quiet, for God's sake. Make him comfortable, but make him quiet."

He would not go to see his son, not until the boy was dead. The old man knew he would die, as surely as he knew he'd failed to raise the child with any sense. He didn't need to watch it happen, to feel the rebuke of his son's last breath. If only he'd had more time to teach him before the goddamn war began, he thought. Who had taught him to throw away life for a cause? Or for a girl? Did his son really believe he hadn't known of his little country whore or his trips to see her?

His son would always return to the Cause, that thing he wrote so glibly about in the Rebel, *disguising himself as Cotton Gin as if his father wouldn't recognize the words. The words he spat in his father's face. The Cause.*

There were no causes in the Baylor house, no such romantic notions. He held the world responsible for the boy's death, but especially the charismatic criminals who had led him into battle. They would pay. He heard a man calling for water from the battlefield, and he cursed the voice in the dark.

19

ZACHARIAH CASHWELL

It took a while to realize where I'd ended up after stepping away from those Union boys. There was a gap in time, I reckon, and I couldn't fill it right off. My senses came back slow, one at a time. At first I could only feel things outside my body, like the vibrations of whatever I was resting on. I could feel footsteps. *That's a floor,* I thought. *That's a wood floor.* And so I spent some time just paying attention to the way the floor moved under me, and how I could almost feel its grain against my shoulder blades. *Those are my shoulder blades.* I could feel the dull rumbling of boots against the floor, and sometimes I thought I could hear a set of lady's shoes walking quickly someplace. Her shoes were sharp and quick against the floor, that's how I could tell the difference. I hadn't heard a lady walk across a floor—hell, I hadn't *seen* one walk across a floor—since before I could remember.

Once you start in on your senses, they all come back eventually. Unless you got your eyes plucked out or your ears blown up. You only got two choices in this world—you're either asleep or awake, and you're never one or the other for long. After feeling the vibrations of people walking across the floor, I could soon hear them. And then I could hear voices, voices all around me, voices of men who seemed to be right there on the floor like me. I thought of my eyes, but I didn't open them. Didn't want to. I heard men groaning and crying and coughing and yelling and making the same jokes over and over again. The jokes was what made me finally understand where I was. They were the kind of jokes you tell when you're thinking about dying, and so I knew I was in a hospital someplace.

Why in God's name would I be in a hospital? I'd made it out clean, like a proper sneaky razorback. I'd burned that barn to the ground, and they never saw me go. I was a free man again. I heard the woman walking across the floorboards again. I might have chosen, as a free man, to spend some time in a place where women walked, but not if it meant lying still on the floor among the criers and the yellers and the jokers. They smelled bad. They smelled of sweat and shit and that ammonia smell people get when they's hungry for too many days in a row. My nose had come back. I opened my eyes and saw the stark white ceiling above me and saw men trembling and rocking all around me, and I thought, *So what's the matter with me?*

That's when the pain came, and I knew all my senses were back. There was fire in my right leg and in my hip and up my back, and the fire burned so goddamn hot that I had to grit my teeth to keep from screaming for a bucket of water, but that scream must have snuck out because I could feel some of the men looking at me for a moment before turning back to their own troubles. I gritted my teeth and felt the pain get all around me until I was just a little thing within it, and then I must have fell asleep again.

In my dreams I heard a voice: *So the man gets to the pearly gates and sees his own Negro up on that there cloud with a big ring of keys, and the Negro says, "Guess da top rail on da bottom now. But you a fine-lookin' buck, massa."* And I awoke again. The voices were everywhere around me, like the pain. I wanted someone to cut my spine out to relieve me of the hurt, but there was no relief. I listened to the other men to take my mind off things.

It was hard to see the men around me because it meant I had to move my head, and moving around only made things hurt worse. So I looked out the corner of my eye at the men in gray lying around me, each blending into the other so that the whole room seemed infested with gray, and it crossed my mind that a floor covered in rats would look a whole lot like what I was seeing. *I'm feverish*, I thought. After a time I could pick out individual men and put them together with their voices and listen to their pleas.

The two men on either side of me were dead, or else they didn't have much to say. On the other side of the man on the left I could see a young blond man trying to sit up, over and over again, each time too tired to hold himself for very long before sinking back down to the floor. Finally he gave up and just talked to the ceiling.

"Somebody help me get this letter out my pocket."

There wasn't no one answering him, and I'd have helped him myself if I could. I was balancing myself, up on a high wire like they got at those carnivals, and on every side was hot white fire. If I moved to help him, I'd fall off, and I couldn't do that.

"I got a letter for my mother. She don't know where I am, dammit. It's just right here. Please, somebody."

Another man spoke up across the room. He had an old and gravelly voice.

"Hold on, boy. Maybe that lady come back here in a minnit. You just hold on, now."

And that must have put the boy at ease, because I didn't hear a peep from him again, and I didn't see him move after that.

Finally a Negress came into the room, and I could see her down the end of my nose, standing in the doorway with her hands on her hips and shaking her head. She was yellow-skinned, like you saw sometimes around towns. She wasn't a country Negro, and she didn't act it, either. We must have been a hell of a sight to her, and she was about the cleanest thing I'd seen in months. Years. Maybe ever. She had a wooden bucket in one hand and a ladle in the other, and she moved around the room pouring out water into our open mouths, like we was baby birds. We just open our mouths wide, and in come the water. I blessed her in my head, even though I didn't think much of God then. I figured it wouldn't hurt.

The water made my pain go away for a little bit, and I sunk back almost to sleep again. I tried to remember what had happened to me. The Negress moved around the room, stepping in between our legs and occasionally stumbling over a boot here and there, and I could hear her cursing quietly under her breath. I wondered if she knew what had happened to me. I watched the dust roiling up off the men around me each time one of them coughed or spat or puked or laughed, and in the dust I finally seen what happened. The dust reminded me.

I'd made it away, and I was headed out from the fire and those guards. I didn't care where I went after that. Every place was a possibility. And I was running toward the creek, thinking I'd slip into it and hide against the bank until they moved off, and then make my way down the creek and away. But something slammed into my right side like a hammer, and I was knocked flat to the ground. I don't remember the pain right then. That came later. I just remember being knocked down, and rolling over, and looking back up the hill to the crest where the other prisoners were standing with their heads down, and a man with a rifle was silhouetted against the flames and the smoke of the fire. *What do you need me for?* I remembered thinking. *Why do you want me? Here is my body, take it if you want it so damned bad. But why?* There was no answer. And then I got to my feet and began to run again, but the first time I came down on my right leg I fell. The pain came then, and it was such a heavy pain I could barely keep my eyes open. It was worse than the first time I was shot. As long as I could keep my eyes open, though, I could move. I crawled and crawled, and when I got to the creek, I slipped into it and felt my head go under the water, and I screamed and sucked water and coughed, and felt my body borne away down the stream, and that's the last I saw of the war. Or, at least, that part of the war with the guns and the fire.

That's all I could remember. The Negress stepped lightly over me and looked down. I could see the freckles on her nose, and I noticed how she'd hitched her skirt up on one side so that she could move among us without getting dirty. I opened my mouth, and she poured the water in. I couldn't swallow all of a sudden, and the water streamed out the sides of my mouth and pooled on the floor beside me. I looked up and felt tears coming up in my eyes. I hadn't wanted to disappoint her, and I was making a mess. I looked after her as she walked out of the room, and I wondered if she'd ever come back. I slept then, and I don't think I woke up for a few minutes. I have a hard time remembering.

"Hey, friend."

I was woken up by a gray-haired fellow who was lying at my feet. Some of his hair was matted with blood at the back of his neck, but I couldn't tell whether it came from him or someone else or me. I reckoned I was bleeding, but I hadn't wanted to move around enough to check things out. Cranking his head back so I could hear him better, the man spoke again.

"This here's a prison, I reckon."

I thought about that. "Funny prison. No guards."

"Do you want to be here?"

"Well, no."

"Then it's a prison, ain't it? Whatever they want to call it."

The old man rolled over on his right side so he could look up at me better. I couldn't figure why he wanted to talk to me so bad, since there were men lying all around him. But he got over and looked at me, and I could see that he was a foreigner. Or from down Louisiana someplace. He had dark skin, and his nose was hooked over like a fish hawk's. He kept snuffling and hacking while he talked, like he had a cold, and every time he had a real bad coughing attack his bad eye scrunched down into his head and his whole face was cut through with dark lines and valleys of loose skin. I admired the stubble on his face, which was perfect white and reached up high on his cheekbones. He talked faster than I was used to, and I took him for a New Orleans man. We'd seen men like them running their flatboats down the river back in Arkansas, full of cotton and whiskey. Fast-talking men who'd speak in tongues when they didn't want you to understand what they were saying to each other. But this one wanted me to understand.

"I ain't staying here. No, sir. This ain't how I'm going out. Not like this. I got to get my ass up and walk it out of here, only I think my left leg ain't going to work, so I need me some help. This leg is all smashed up, and the Lord knows what's happened to this eye here. I keep trying to move it around, but I can't tell if it's there. I reckon I can pay you to help me out of here; I was a rich man once, you know, and you look like you'd take just about anything I could give you. Where you from?"

When I didn't answer, he went on.

"Well, shit, I don't really care where you from. I just need you to help me sit up, and maybe let me lean on you while we walk out of here and put the rest of these sorry cases behind us. I can't stand being around all these dead boys, even the ones who're still breathing. They're dead, sure enough, and I *ain't*."

The man yelled that last part as he yanked himself up to a sitting position and wobbled there. His little speech seemed not to sit well with the others. One man was standing in a corner over by the window, one of the only ones I could tell who could stand on his own. He was leaning on a piece of wood and kept pressing his hand to the wound in his stomach. He was tall. Maybe there hadn't been room for him to lie down, maybe he didn't fit among the rest of us, like a miscut piece of lumber. He was one of those fellows who looked a lot skinnier than they were, on account of being so long. You look close, you could see he had been a powerful man. His arms were thick. He had no beard, and this made him seem harder than the rest of us, like he had nothing to hide. Nothing to hide, or nothing he cared to hide.

"Oh, shut the hell up, old man. I'd wager a week's pay you got bullets in your back. You just don't want us to see 'em. You don't want that pretty little lady to come in here and roll you over like a damned baby and tend the holes in you. In fact, I'm going to write me a note right now and send it off to the newspaper, all about how I met a jawjacking Spaniard with holes in his back, and I wonder how they got there."

Voices came from all over the room.

"A week's pay? What week's pay? What pay? Who's getting pay?"

"Might not be a Spaniard. Could be a nigger, you know."

"Somebody go get that little lady. I wouldn't mind another look at her."

"She'd mind another look at you, that's a fact. You missing an ear and half your nose."

"I still got the important parts."

"Hell yeah. I got them, too."

The old man at my feet just smiled, like he'd heard such insults before. Me, I started to get hot just thinking about what I'd do if someone had insulted *me* like that. But you can't figure those boys from New Orleans. They think different. He ignored the biggun in the corner and kept talking to me.

"What do you say? Let's get out of here."

I sorely wanted to escape, just as bad as I'd wanted to escape from those Yank guards. But I couldn't move. I told him so, and he looked down at my leg and his eyes turned up and the wrinkles in his head smoothed out.

"I'm sorry."

"What?"

"You can't go anywheres. You're right."

"What are you saying?"

"That leg of yours is going to come off, if it doesn't fall off first. You can't feel it?"

"No."

"That ain't a good sign, either. They need to get you on the table right quick."

He began to yell. "Hey. *Hey! Help!*"

I didn't want to get up on any table. I tried to kick at him to stop him from yelling, but the pain made my breath stop, and I almost went to sleep again. I kept my eyes open, and I tried to get him to keep quiet, but I could only whisper.

"Please, no."

The man in the corner was watching all this, and he came stepping over the rows of men and stood above me and the old Spaniard. When I looked up, I could see a small drop of blood make its way down one of his big fingers where he kept them pressed against his gut, and fall to the floor.

"I think the man wants you to be quiet, El Conquistador."

"Look at his leg. *Dios mío!*"

"I see it. I don't care. He wants you to be quiet, and I'll make you quiet if that's how it's going to be."

"No need for that."

"I mean, you ain't in much better shape. You look pale like a real white man."

"And you talk like you had your brains shot out. So what?"

The big man stroked his chin, like he had hair there, and that's when I noticed that he wasn't clean shaven exactly. He had scars on his face where he must have been burned a long time ago, and where there were scars there was no beard. He looked like someone had taken an iron to his face, only they'd missed a few spots, and up underneath his chin I could see a sprout of red hair. I tried to catch his eye by staring at him. I wanted him to tell me what was wrong with me. He didn't see me, or chose not to see me, I reckon. He kept talking to the Spaniard.

"If you want out, let's go."

"With you?"

"Just play dead when I carry you out of here. No matter how bad you want to run your mouth, keep it shut. We can get you out of here if you're dead. They let the dead go free, and I'm going with you."

Then he took his hands away from the hole in his stomach, which got redder and redder. He reached down and picked the old man up and slung him over his shoulder like a bag of flour, and the old man screamed a little before choking it back.

"What did I say about keeping your mouth shut?"

The old man closed his eyes, and that squeezed a couple of tears out, which fell to the floor at my feet. I wondered how anyone would credit a crying corpse.

The big man walked toward the door and was almost through it when a white lady came into the room, pushing him back with the end of her finger. This must have been the lady with the sharp shoes.

She was dark-haired and pale, and she was dressed all in black. This was the lady they'd been making jokes about, about wanting her to return, about how their important parts would react to her arrival. I thought then that I could not be dying, because her arrival felt like a punch in my chest, which I reckoned to be a sign of life. I saw her and felt grateful and heated and afraid, all together.

I had no power to do anything; I was pinned to the floor by nervousness and pain. Her eyes sat wide apart on her face, and her bottom lip was thick and swollen like a doll's, and she might as well have been a picture on a wall in a castle a thousand miles away she was so beautiful. Right then I wished to God that He would show me no more of the world that I could never have or touch. *No more beauty for this old boy.* I felt the world receding from me every moment she stood in that room, glaring at that big piece of human kindling and the Spaniard playing possum on his shoulder. She reminded me of how much I had lost and how little I had and how far I'd gone down the road to the next life. I wanted her to leave the room only because I didn't want to have such thoughts and so that I could sink into sleep. I hated that she made me think these things, and at first I thought this meant I ought to hate *her,* rather than the man who had aimed his rifle at my leg.

"I don't think you-all should be moving around."

She talked with a hard voice, but like she was trying to convince herself she was hard. Her voice wobbled in places, but you had to listen close.

"This one's dead, ma'am. Just clearing him out. Making us a little room."

"He doesn't look that hurt to me."

"Bled out, I reckon. Got hit in the leg, lots of blood there, you know."

I watched her. From my angle, lying there on the floor, her head was framed between the carved door trim and the old wallpaper molding running around the ceiling, like she was a portrait. She looked past the big man and took us all in, the roiling and groaning floor of men dumb enough to let ourselves get shot up. *Dumb enough.* I hadn't thought of it that way before, but it was sure enough true. There was no sense in running into bullets, for whatever reason. Honorable maybe, but not smart. How many dumb things had been done for honor? I remembered watching two men gouge each other's eyes out back in Arkansas because one had insulted the other's fat wife. Blind but honorable they were. This was the wisdom of dying, I reckoned. Wisdom. Well, shit, that wasn't something anyone had ever accused me of having before. I took some pleasure in thinking I'd become wise, I don't mind saying now. A lot of pleasure. I sunk back and contemplated my new self and watched the lady out of the bottom of my eye. She said:

"Put him down. He doesn't look dead yet."

A voice piped up from across the room. "Ah no, he's dead, ma'am. Dead like a sack of potatoes."

Another voice, squeaky and giggly. "More like a bag of flour."

A chorus. All eyes on the lady and the soldier. Lots of chatter.

"Dead as doornail."

"Dead like a smoked mullet."

"Them Spaniards do like their mullets, I heard that."

"Dead like Stonewall."

"He ain't a thing like Stonewall."

"He dead, though."

"Dead like Lincoln."

"He ain't dead."

"Shhhh."

You could tell the big man carrying the Spaniard was getting angry at the gabbing. He looked around and glared at everybody. His game wasn't going as smooth as he'd wanted, and the yacking wasn't helping. He'd wanted to slide out smooth and slippery, no one noticing a thing. Now he was the center of the attraction, and the lady wasn't moving out of his way. He looked around and tried to look mean, but the skin on his face only let one side of his face get hard, and so he looked more like he was in pain than anything else, I reckoned. And maybe that was the truth anyway. He was still bleeding, I could see that.

"Ma'am, this one's dead, and I'm fixing to take him outside to the pile. I reckon you got a pile going out there, ain't you? This one needs to join it, or no telling what rot he'll bring in here. It ain't sanitary."

"He's crying, sir. I've seen dead people, but I've never seen one cry."

"Well, those are just the death tears. Like the death rattle. Rare, you only see it when a man dies a real painful death. But look, he ain't moving."

At that point I guess he figured he might as well take a gamble to make his story go, so he hopped up and down to demonstrate that his corpse wouldn't make a peep. I could have told him it wouldn't work; I could see the Spaniard's face, which was hidden from the lady on the other side of his rescuer's broad back. He was gritting his teeth and biting his lip and rolling his eyes up in his head like he was trying to make eye contact with God, and when he got bounced like that, it just wasn't anything but natural for him to scream like he'd been shot. It was a short, high scream that he choked off, but that was it. The game was up.

The big man wasn't giving in so easily, though, and he tried to get past the lady by faking one way and going the other, but she was quick on those lace-up boots of hers, and she kept in front of him, and I was waiting to see him knock her down, but he didn't. He hadn't lost that last shred of decency, I guess.

"Dammit, just let me out. He wants out, too. We just want to go."

The corpse spoke up between gasps for breath.

"Yes. Ma'am. Just. Want. To. Go."

I closed my eyes, figuring the show was over, that she'd call a guard or somebody to settle things with the two men and get them back down in their places where they belonged. I settled back into my daydreams about wisdom. It was our place to die here on the floor. That was our fate, for falling out on account of honor. I was feeling warm and proud of myself for seeing this, and it took me a few moments to realize that the lady hadn't sent for no one, that she was just standing there. I opened my eyes and saw her looking up at the big burned man, right into his ugly face, like she was studying it. She crossed her arms and rested on first this hip, then that hip, and she pooched out her lip some like she was concentrating hard. So beautiful she was.

"All right, go."

I don't think the big man understood what she was saying, because he dropped his head and turned back around and made like he was going to put down the Spaniard and go back to his corner.

"I said go. Get on. If you would like to go, with that hole in your stomach and that man with a leg that will never be right, then go. Go. You're a man, you can take care of yourself. You don't need any of us. Just get on."

She was looking up at him with an unusual look on her face. She wasn't frowning or smiling or looking worried or afraid. Her face was smooth, and her mouth was relaxed and straight. Her big wide eyes were pointed in his direction, but she didn't seem to see him anymore. It was as if she'd already forgot him.

The big man seemed a little confused by her words. At first he looked like he was going to protest that he should stay, after all. He put the Spaniard down, who accidentally stepped on an arm and got cursed out by the young boy to whom it belonged. I could see him trying to figure her out. Her expression was so cold I didn't blame him trying to get out from under it, to make it go away by giving in. But, finally, he wasn't *that* worried about it.

Once he'd seen she wasn't joking, he yanked the Spaniard back up on his shoulder and marched right on out of there.

She let him go. She looked around at all of us, and all of us looked right back at her.

"You can go, too. No one's keeping you here. Maybe you should go, go off and die in the woods somewhere. We only have but two doctors here and some bandages. We can't do much for you, really."

She seemed not to be talking to us, but to something beyond us, out the window. And yet what she said made the room quiet. Men quit groaning and bitching.

"Come on, get up, now. I'm not anyone's jailer. Let's go, get out."

Nobody moved. Nobody dared move. Every word she said about how little she could do for us, and how likely we were to die no matter where we were, and how easy it would be for us all to leave and find a more pleasant place to die—these were the words that kept us quiet and still. At least it kept *me* quiet and still. Any woman who could talk like that could save you, no matter what she said. To leave her would mean to leave one of the last people who cared to help you. You didn't dare do that.

Of course, moving wasn't an option for me. I wasn't going any-where, whether I wanted to or not.

Having received no takers on her offer of freedom, she turned around quickly; her skirts brushed the faces of the men nearest the door, and she stomped smartly out of the room.

20

CARRIE MCGAVOCK

The future lay out ahead of me as a daisy chain of days spent boiling water and tending wounds. One day after the other. There were so many men in so many different states of disrepair it didn't appear possible that there would ever be an empty space in the house.

Yet it was not long before I began to enjoy myself, although there was no joy in seeing men suffer. Their suffering visited me in dreams. I had very vivid dreams now that we were all—Mariah and the children and I—sleeping on hard pallets made up in the kitchen so that the soldiers could have the bedrooms. I wondered which I would remember when I was an old woman—the soldiers themselves or my dreams of them. I guessed it would be the dreams, which even in those first few days had come to insinuate themselves upon my waking hours, obscuring the line between what was real and what was not. This did not worry me as much as it could have, because Mariah admitted to me once as they were bedding down for the night that it was hard to see how the things around us were real, and that often she caught herself looking at a man and wondering if he was really there and how his wounds could be real. *It don't seem possible sometimes,* she whispered to me, over the sleeping forms of Hattie and Winder.

It was not the violence and the suffering that gave me my momentary feelings of joy. It was watching my linens be torn and cut into bandages. It was seeing some of my doors and moldings carried out the front door and smashed into kindling for fires. It was the stains upon the floors and the walls. It was realizing that I hadn't seen John for two days while he was busy hauling water for our patients and not noticed. A break had come, and I took pleasure in imagining the consequences of it. Children can't help but laugh when they're spun in circles and made dizzy, and I felt something akin.

One of the delights of my work with the men in the house was realizing that they liked me to boss them around and to dismiss the severity of their injuries. At first I had entered the rooms of the wounded and dying with fear and a desire to comfort, and so I would kneel next to the most gravely afflicted—a man shot in the stomach or one without a leg whose wound would not stop bleeding—and stroke their hands and tell them how sorry I was, and ask them whether there was anyone I could notify and whether they wanted me to pray with them. They all shook their heads and closed their eyes and did their best to ignore me, quietly. It took some time before I realized that there was nothing I could do for a dying man except ease his journey a little, and that wasn't accomplished by staring sadly into their faces and making it clear to them that, indeed, they would be dying soon.

When I realized that my gestures of comfort were only extinguishing hope, and therefore creating another agony, I began to bring the gravely injured men whiskey, which I poured down their throats with a smile. And when the other men in the room complained about not getting their dram, I'd stand up and declare that the whiskey was only for the handsomest among them and that the rest of them should count themselves lucky to get water. The other men would curse and laugh. The dying men with the taste of whiskey on their tongues knew the charade meant they would surely die, but I thought it possible I made them hopeful by swallowing my sadness. At least death was not something to fear, if a proper woman could treat it so cavalierly, and that was a form of hope. That's what I thought, at least.

None of those men ever saw me walk out of the house and down behind the slave cabins, where there was a tree I could sit against and cry. I was at the mercy of a host of passions in those first few days after the battle, and their buffeting was not unwelcome. I cried or laughed as I pleased. When Mariah called up the stairwell for more bandages, and if I felt pressed, I'd snap back that the bandages were coming in their own good time and that I didn't need Mariah telling me anything. And then, if I felt moved, I'd catch Mariah out by the cistern and stroke her hair and tell her how dearly sorry I was. If others would have been shocked by me making an apology to a woman like Mariah, well, they could just leave me be. I sometimes felt the old paralyzing darkness draw around me, but it was always tempered by the inescapable fact of the men lying around my house and in my yard, and the suspicion that they were harbingers of something I had not known before. How horrible, I thought occasionally, to think that these men were welcome and not a burden.

I was freer than I'd ever been. I felt obliged to the world, a world much larger than that contained between the four walls of Carnton, and although the burden seemed larger, I was similarly enlarged by the burden of shouldering it. I walked through my house and sat down in the chairs that were left, chairs I'd brought up from Louisiana when John had taken me here, and I looked at them as if they were new and saw details—scratches and stains and carving—I'd never seen before. Or noticed. That was the thing that was truly new: I noticed everything.

It was in that state of mind that I first saw Zachariah Cashwell laid up on the floor of my upstairs guest room, his right leg stiff and still while the other trembled and fidgeted. His face was rough and scratched and smudged with red mud. He had a wispy beard on the end of his chin that made me want to laugh. He was thirty years old, I later learned, and that seemed too old to be having difficulty with chin whiskers. His eyes, though, were the thing that drew my attention. They were watery and green, and they were the only eyes in the room that I couldn't feel on me when I walked in to confront the large, scarred man and his poor excuse for a corpse. I would have let one of the guards deal with the two men had it not been for the eyes of Zachariah Cashwell. He kept his chin in the air and stared up at the ceiling. Unlike most of the men, he looked ready to die. He looked as if he were welcoming it, urging it along. I wondered if I should go get the whiskey. I wanted his eyes on me. I didn't understand why, not then. But I stayed.

I made a scene and invited a giant man and his possum-playing friend—and anyone else so inclined—to leave, to crawl off and die elsewhere if they liked. I would not miss them, I said, all the while twiddling with my handkerchief in the front pocket of my apron and hoping the men would stay put. I watched Cashwell out of the corner of my eye and could see that my speech had produced the proper effect—he was watching me curiously and even moving around a little to get a better look. His right leg seemed attached to the ground and immobile, but he was able to adjust himself up on an elbow to get a better look. He grimaced as he did so, and I was flattered.

Silly girl. Silly, silly, silly. What did I care for the opinion of a stranger, all broken and arrived from a world I would never understand or care to see? I did not care. I cared less now that he had acknowledged me. I was vain, that was all. Vanity was a new passion perhaps. When I left the room, I decided to let Mariah tend those men from that moment forward. *No sense cultivating vanity*, I thought. Later I asked Mariah to get his name.

Every room and every foot of porch had been given over to the wounded. There was no logic to the arrangement; the little doctor had never realized his hope of triage. The first men to arrive took over the best rooms inside our house, whatever their wounds. As the first day wore on and new waves of the wounded—walking, riding, carried upon shoulders and in horse carts—crashed upon Carnton, they settled in ever-expanding rings that drifted out from the operating theater at the center, through the house, onto the porches, and into the yard. Every one of them would be a prisoner of the Union, property of the U.S. of A., but at first there was no one to claim the spoils. I guessed they would come sometime, when order returned to Franklin, but I had no earthly idea when that might be. But it was silly of me to think they'd wait for *order*. The first prison wagon appeared weeks later to take away the healthiest of our wounded.

When I needed fresh air, I'd find Mariah and we'd walk out into the side yard near the garden, gently stepping over prostrate strangers in various stages of dress. There we could survey the entire scene. I remembered my father reading me little bits of that book about the war for Helen of Troy, the one with the Greeks, and the long descriptions of the Greeks encamped around what I believed as a child to be a very large house made of stone. Around us the soldiers sparked fires and boiled water, and the ones who could walk paced back and forth and told stories and danced away from the sparks when they flared up in the wind. I imagined that this was what the Greeks' encampment looked like, although I decided the Greeks wore less clothing and weren't so pale when they stripped off their shirts. Was there an Achilles among them? That was hard to imagine. They looked so tired, so incapable of rage anymore. I wondered where Helen had gone off to and what kind of woman Helen must have been to have inspired this, this scene that spread out around her and into her garden. *No woman is that beautiful*, I remember thinking. *The men are fools.*

During one of these walks John rode up on his horse from Lord knows where.

"I have found another spring, so we should be able to have more water up here soon."

I walked to his horse and put my hand upon the harness gently, while Mariah walked back to the house.

"That's good, John."

"I also have news from the town, if you can call it that now."

"It wasn't much of a town to begin with."

John looked at me hard. He was losing patience with me every day, every hour. I didn't care.

"Whatever you want to call it, Carrie, it's not anything you'd recognize anymore."

"Then I must go see it, John. Perhaps it's been improved."

"I think not. I think you should stay here for a while."

"That shouldn't be hard; I have had a lot of practice."

John pulled up on the reins of his horse and turned its head so that it moved away from me, and I stood back. He looked pained and confused and angry, like a man who's just woken from a fall and isn't sure where he is.

"I have not kept you in this house. I've begged you to leave before now."

"And now I want to leave. For a couple hours, just to see things."

"It's not possible now. In a few weeks, perhaps things will have changed."

I looked over at one of the campfires, where a young man beat out the tiny flames in his trousers that flared from errant sparks. *I should go help*, I thought.

"Things will change, that's true. Thank you for finding the water."

"Send someone down to start running buckets when you have a moment, Carrie."

"I will."

"I have a man to see in town, as much as I dread going back there."

"Should I have Theopolis fetch your rifle?"

John shook his head.

"No need for that anymore."

John turned his bay all the way around and rode out around the house to the long driveway, picking his way carefully around the clusters of men camped out and burning what was left of the garden fence. If he cared about the destruction, he didn't seem to show it. An old man drunk on a bottle that was being passed around got to his feet as John went by, and flipped him a snappy salute before losing his balance and falling to the ground. John rode on.

I walked back into the house having decided to change my mind about something. I stepped around the men lounging on the back steps and went into the back hallway of the house, where the smell of men overpowered me. My nose had no experience with such a smell. It could not parse its elements. The smell was heavy and sour and musty, and I took it to be the smell of that world which had been kept at bay by my house and my husband these many years.

I gathered my skirts before me, climbed quietly up the stairs, and entered the guest bedroom again. I stood staring at the men, most of whom had sunk into sleep or into the final retreat of consciousness before death. But the man with the green eyes watched me, and I turned to him. Zachariah Cashwell.

"You're next, sir. What do I tell the doctor is the matter with you?"

He looked like I'd kicked him in the stomach. He squeezed his eyes shut and shook his head. His voice came out scratchy and metallic, as if he hadn't spoken in centuries.

"I don't think I should be next. I'm too far gone. I reckon there are other boys in here who got better chances. I been shot good in my right hip, I think, and I been bleeding for days, seems like. The fever's coming, I can feel it, and my leg is starting to smell bad. It's too late, I think. Just let me be. I should have been dead long before this anyhow."

This is the way a man is supposed to talk, I thought. I stepped out of the room into the hallway and summoned two orderlies, or guards, or whatever they were.

"Come get this man here."

When the orderlies lifted him up on a makeshift stretcher formed from their crossed arms, he screamed and cursed me. I slapped him, and he stopped and stared up at me, disbelieving. If the men in the room weren't aware of my presence before, they became aware of me quickly.

"Get this man to the table and keep him quiet."

The orderlies were two boys too meek to be soldiers. They nodded their heads and carried the man out of the room. One of them kept his hand clamped over the screaming man's mouth, and his curses reached me only as a low drone.

He'll thank me. He'll thank me, I thought.

I watched the doctors wrestle with the man until they had him fixed to the table. I stood in the doorway and watched as they calmed him with ether. His head lolled to the side, and his eyes fixed on me. Those eyes, intolerable and inescapable. The doctors debated over him. The short one, the bolder of the two, had proven to be a skilled surgeon even if he was an insufferable little rooster.

"This leg's got to come off, that's clear, but how high up?"

The older doctor was cautious. He seemed like a man who ought to be with his grandchildren. He never wanted to cut anything. He'd furrow his brow and scratch the back of his head and look at his patient with pleading in his face, as if the patient might solve the problem himself and take the guesswork out of it. He looked at Cashwell this way.

"Do you reckon it's gotten into that hip?"

"If it's in his hip, he's dead. Nothing we can do about that."

"So we just take the whole leg, all the way up?"

"Every bit of it, and see what happens."

Cashwell turned back to the doctors and spoke. "What makes you all think I'd prefer to be a cripple than to die?"

The little rotund doctor, already disinfecting the saw, looked at him, startled. "You don't get that choice, boy."

"I ain't a boy."

"Sir."

"You goin' to cut my leg, and you want me to call you sir? You want me to give you a kiss, too?"

The old surgeon intervened. "Quit talking. Let's go."

This was normally the point when I'd leave the room, when I would stick pieces of cotton in my ears and shut the doors to the sickrooms so those waiting their turns wouldn't hear so clearly. The growing pile of limbs underneath the surgery window told me what had happened. It was necessary. These men were to live. Life of any kind was superior to the alternative. This I had learned from watching my own children pass, this was what I believed the Lord intended. The Lord needed me—and the doctors and Mariah and the little orderly boys—to keep His children alive. He could do it Himself, but His intent was clear to me.

And yet I knew I had betrayed the green-eyed man, this

Zachariah Cashwell. He had been ready to die, he had wanted to die, and I had not let him. He was deluded, I was sure, and yet this would be no defense against his accusations if he cared to lodge them against me. He was the poor child of God who would have to hobble around the rest of his life on a stiff, splintery post fashioned to look a little like a leg. *I* decided this fate for him, on behalf of the Lord. I would have to take responsibility. Why I felt more responsibility for this one act, this one small betrayal, than any of the other decisions I made in those few days, I do not know. I had never seen a man like him.

So I stayed in that doorway, watching. I watched him sink deeper into the fuzzy warmth of the ether, but never so far that he didn't know what was going on or that I was there. I saw the doctors cut his pant leg up along the seam, and I saw the mottling on his skin, the red patches and the dark blue patches, and the black along the edge of his wound. I saw them tie off his leg at his hip with a strap, and then I watched them press their sharp, impossibly clean knife to the flesh above his wound, cutting deep. I watched the thin lines of their incisions bead with bright blood, much less than I expected. I saw the green eyes roll up into his head and heard the short gasps and quick grunts of a man holding pain down, like he was afraid it would rise up and absorb him. I saw the short doctor pull out the saw and slip it into the incision, where I assume it rested against the man's bone. I saw the older doctor look worried when he saw the man's white and sweaty face; he reached to the ether bottle and filled another rag with it and placed it over Zachariah's face, telling him softly to breathe deeply. He was whispering to his patient, as if there was something or someone in the room that he didn't want to disturb. I watched the green-eyed man roll his head to the side again, his eyes pointed in my direction, but so unfocused that he couldn't have possibly seen me or anything else. And yet those eyes never left my face. I found that I was gripping the door frame so tightly that my fingernails had dug into the wood. I held my hand to my face and saw that my fingernails had chipped and frayed, and then I was so horrified by the nonchalance of this gesture that I shoved my hands into the pockets of my apron and leaned against the door frame, resolving not to quit watching until it was finished.

It was over faster than I had imagined. The saw bit into the bone, and the bone yielded. There was hardly any sound, not like the sawing of wood. The leg was there, and then it wasn't, as if it had been released from the body and floated away. I was fixed on Zachariah's face, which was still awake but unmoving, and so I didn't pay much attention to what happened to the leg, although I knew it must have ended up in the pile below the window. He cried, and I shook my head and kept shaking it as if I could stop him. His tears were small, like beads of perspiration, but they were the worst thing I saw in that room that day. I walked away then and went looking for Hattie and Winder, whose tears dried easily. They had no reason to hate me.

Those days were the most important of my life. It is possible to know yourself—every kindness, every urge to violence, every petty resentment—in chaos. I discovered that my mind sharpened as my surroundings grew more uncertain and unfamiliar. I would choose one thing of the many competing for my attention, and I would hold on to it. I moved the wounded around the rooms, organizing them, freeing up space so that the men shivering out-side would have room. The men grabbed at me and handed me letters, and I took them. I didn't know what I would do with these letters, but I knew without hesitation that I had to take them. It was puzzling to me, how I would know that. How I would know what was right in a catastrophe. And yet I did.

After Cashwell I learned to stand by the surgeons as they did their work, when I wasn't needed elsewhere. I learned to hand them their tools and to fetch the ether when they needed it. I watched men do things to other men that should not have been allowed on the earth. Saws cutting through bone. I held the hands of the men losing their limbs until they would begin to grip me too hard, and then I would try to stomach the pain as long as I could, figuring it was the least I could do, but I had very little tolerance for it, and I always pulled away. My hand slipped easily out of their sweaty palms, and I wasn't sure they even noticed when I was gone.

I watched my children bring water to the men and play jacks with the ones who could sit up. Some told them stories they remembered from their own childhoods, thinking Hattie and Winder needed respite and comfort and that they could provide this with a tale or two. But memory is so fragile, and very few of them could remember the stories all the way through. Their tales of magical backwoodsmen and beautiful belles trailed off, were never completed. I wonder sometimes if this—and not the actual presence of these men mangled by war—was the thing that Hattie and Winder most remembered of those days. I look back on that time and wonder if it was then when they learned that the story never comes to an end, that it goes on and on, and that people eventually forget how it began and where it was supposed to end. I was more afraid of them acquiring this knowledge than anything else, and yet I could not shield them from it. My dead children had been shielded from it, but it was impossible to keep Hattie and Winder from that knowledge any longer. Not during those days.

The men moved in and out of the house. The living ones stumbled in, the dead ones were carried out. Soon a field of dead lay out in my garden and in the tall brown grass between the house and the small family cemetery. It was cold enough to lay them out like that, I was told, because they wouldn't smell so very bad. There were very few to bury them, and it wasn't clear where they were supposed to be buried. Once a day or so an officer would ride by the house and look around the grounds, see the field of dead, and ride off without saying a word. I took that to mean that they didn't care much about what was happening out here, so long as everyone stayed put. A few escaped, I know, and once I watched a man hobble across our cornfield and into the woods, leaning heavily on a homemade cane. Where would he go? I thought. Did he even know where he was? I suppose that was the thing that kept most of the walking wounded close to the house: they had no place else to go. Out there across the field was freedom, yes, but

also starvation and confusion and loneliness. Of these, I decided
the last was the worst. Loneliness, I learned from one of the soldiers in my charge, could be more frightening than almost anything. Loneliness was what we feared about death, he said, and to
embrace it in life seemed mad. I'd never thought of it that way.

21

FRANKLIN

Nearly every day John rode into town looking for food and clothing for the men at his house, and a little whiskey for himself. Brandy, too, if he could find it. He drank alone, out of sight of Carrie and Mariah, who were always bustling about and saving people and having men thank them oh so sincerely. *Thank you, ma'am, thank you kindly, Lord have mercy, thank you.* Carrie looked better than she had in years.

He watched her once from the other side of the slave cabins, where he leaned against a tree sucking from a bottle of old bourbon he'd found hidden in an abandoned hay cart. She was flushed, and her hair looked as thick as the day they'd married. She didn't look like the wasted and stooped ghost, bent and tucked, that he'd lived with since the first of their children died. She stood up straight, and hair escaped her comb and blew in the breeze, and men who had killed and were maimed looked up to her standing there on the back steps and saw their rescuer. *She brings salvation,* he thought, taking another sweet pull at the bottle. *Had I known this about her, I'd have invited the armies to fight it out here earlier. How was it that they waited until so late to decide Franklin was the best place to locate a bloody hell? I could have suggested it to them long ago, provided incentives. Taken another loan from the bank, paid off the generals. I could have built viewing stands and charged admission, and Carrie could have had a steady supply of the ravaged to ease off into the eternal beyond. Stupid McGavock, stupid McGavock.* He was not a drunk, not yet anyway. He just needed something to do. There was so little for him to do anymore. He drank just enough to help him ignore the smell of the house and grounds.

While John was overcome by the ugliness, it seemed to him that Carrie saw only beauty and sweetness. He watched her from his drinking tree and recalled the morning of the first day after the battle, when someone dragged the carcasses of four dead Confederate generals onto the back porch and laid them out like dolls on a shelf. He remembered thinking then, *These were our generals?* Almost every single one of them was ten years his junior. They looked like children even behind their fresh, strong beards. John and Theopolis had just arrived from hauling water to the cistern when they came upon the scene on the porch: some captains and lieutenants standing around the four bodies, their hats doffed. He himself was unmoved, although he understood the novelty of seeing four dead generals all at once, something like the feeling you might get seeing a thirty-pound catfish leap out of the Harpeth and fall dead before your feet. Not something you see every day.

But then Carrie came out of the house, and she stood by watching, and then she pushed through the young officers, bent primly and slowly over each of the dead generals, and laid one of her handkerchiefs upon each of their faces. *What's that supposed to mean?* he remembered thinking. The officers seemed to know, and when Carrie pushed back through them to return to her work in the house, they looked at her with awe. He thought, *I don't have any idea what that means! What is the significance of that? Who taught her to do that? Who is that woman?*

John had become used to being alone. It was his natural state, whether he was at home or riding alone on the pike to town. A great battle had been fought all around him, and he was no less alone than he would have been had he been standing on an ice floe in the ocean. He had never seen the ocean, but imagined that there was nothing more isolated than a chunk of ice in the middle of it, the ice being of water but still not part of it. *John McGavock: of the world, but not part of it.* This is what it felt like to be the husband of a woman who had no use for a husband. *I should have known better,* he thought. *She wasn't a normal child.*

He had known her as a child and then as an older girl orbiting her father when John came to visit their plantation in the winters, and then as a young woman—*briefly, so very briefly*—and then as his wife. What had he known of her before he married her? The one thing he'd known, and which was still true despite appearances, was that she was strong enough to live on the outskirts of the tiny town of Franklin, in Williamson County, Tennessee, which had been frontier when they were married. She wasn't as fragile as the other girls.

After watching her for a time McGavock mounted and rode the pike in silence, dipping out of sight of the house after a half mile or so. He had the vague notion to go to find Mr. Baylor, who controlled the bank, to plead for leniency on his debt. The carnage of the army had convinced him he had very little hope of ever recouping his contribution to the Confederates, which meant he would likely lose much of his land to the bank. Of course, Baylor would know this, too, and being a hard and unforgiving sort, would be unlikely to wipe the slate clean. But perhaps John could plead with him to put the slate aside for a while, to give him time. Time was his only remaining asset. He thought he ought to try, at least.

He was wary of what he would discover on arriving in town. It wasn't the mess of war that gave him pause. He reckoned the war was almost over. How much more could anyone take? The Unionists were already planning a convention in Nashville to set up a new government of loyalists and anti-Confederates, despite the fact that the Confederate army was still stumbling around in the vicinity. There were probably some who took joy at the slaughter visited upon Franklin, since it made their plans all the more timely. How any Southerner—for they were Southerners, these Unionists—could take joy in the death of another Southerner was beyond

McGavock. But then, he thought, they probably didn't even think of themselves as Southerners. At least that wouldn't be the first word that sprang to their minds. *Businessmen, politicians, victors.* Those were the words. Somewhere down the line they'd get around to *Southerner*, but it probably wasn't something they talked about a lot in their circles, not at the moment. That would be a word with flaws in it, connotations they'd just as soon leave behind.

Carnton was not the only hospital in or around the town. Now, with supplies dwindling—they hadn't much ether left, and the little surgeon broke his saw on a thighbone only that morning—John had volunteered to canvass the other makeshift hospitals all over Franklin to scavenge what he could.

He stopped the horse to drink in a creek running across and under the pike, but then thought better of it. *No telling what's in that water now*. He rode on.

Franklin had been transformed into a grotesque thing, as if the skies had opened and God had reached down and twisted and broken and snapped His creation—buildings, trees, people—just to see what would happen. Men sang, cried, and fought with each other as they dragged the dead here and there: to that waiting cart, to this gaping hole in the ground. As he was about to enter town, he stopped to watch one group of men pass around a bottle, not forgetting to give the corpse they were supposed to be burying a taste. A young soldier with a red cowlick and unfocused eyes giggled each time the liquor dribbled down the dead man's chin.

"Got to hold your liquor better than that, my friend."

"Aw, quit wasting it on him."

The redheaded man drew himself up to his full, unimpressive height against whoever it was who had spoken. John couldn't tell which one of them it was; they were all red with mud and looked alike to him. Almost exactly alike.

"He's got need of it now, if he ever did."

"He didn't even drink when he was alive. What are you talking about? Look at that Bible in his pocket. Those boys don't drink."

The redheaded man considered it and took a swig of the bottle.

"That's what I mean. Look at all he missed for that book. He's got one last chance to wet his lips before the dirt gets him, and I aim to help him."

"Aw shit. Just dig, boy."

Little boys ran through the streets playing with rifles they'd confiscated. The guns were almost as heavy as the boys themselves. They lurched under the weight of the weapons and pointed them at soldiers and at horses and at each other. He did not recognize these children, even though they must have been locals. They did not look right. They wore hats removed from the corpses and were possessed of enraptured, frenzied expressions, as if they had been granted the greatest toys imaginable and the only price of them had been a glimpse of things beyond their ability to describe. These were the crazed grins of beings who had agreed to a terrible price and were getting their money's worth while they could.

What will happen to our children? John thought.

22

ZACHARIAH CASHWELL

I don't really know how long I was asleep. Days, a year maybe. Hard to tell. Made me wonder whether putting names to time made much of a difference anyway. What did it measure? Not how much life passes. Hell no. Your whole life can pass and be changed in a second or in a century. Don't matter.

I dreamed dreams that were weird and colorful and comforting and scary and perverse, but the details ain't really important enough to tell about. I reckon they weren't any better or worse than anyone else's dreams. The flashes, the lights, the things you think are there but aren't—none of it makes a lick of difference. I ain't one to talk about dreams anyway. But there *was* something important about the dreams, and that was the fact that I could remember them all when I woke up. I remembered the details, every color and every word. I knew that I had dreamed for days and that the dreaming had not stopped, that I had thought things I had rarely thought before. I had *dreamed* before, but I'd usually lose the foggy impressions of those dreams after a few minutes awake, after I'd had time to splash water on my face.

But this time it was as if I'd lived another life, like I'd been gone somewhere for God knows how long. In this place were things I'd seen before but had forgot. I was a child in those days. I was close to being the child I'd once been, when my brain was full of fancy notions and impossible feats. When I awoke, I was as alone as a child, too.

I knew what had happened to me, how that damn woman had reached into the room and plucked me out and sent me off to see the surgeon and his saw. I could remember that, and I could remember staring her down as the surgeon drew the blade across my leg. Folks can't stand that, to see the evidence of their badness, and I made sure it was right there in the room, plain as could be.

When I awoke, I knew that my leg was gone, but I couldn't *feel* it gone. So I didn't look down for a few hours. They'd given me a hell of a lot of medicine to take the edge off, and I thought it was possible that I had been asleep and someone had changed their mind, and so I didn't make no big effort to get the fact straight. I even felt that I could wiggle my toes, and that gave me a powerful urge to look down at my leg, but I'd heard of men and their ghost limbs, and I wasn't going to be tricked like that, not right away anyway. I kept thinking the leg was there, resisting the urge to find out it wasn't, until a colored servant came into the room I was in and flipped me over like I was no heavier than a child. *I have lost my leg. I am smaller. I am less human. I am lighter upon the earth. I am of less significance.*

"Get your nigger hands off me."

Her hands, the hands of this beautiful Negro woman with the freckles and the hard look, those hands made it clear I wasn't a whole man. In her hands I could feel a lifetime of hobbling around like an old man, whittling peg legs in my spare time, trying to ignore google-eyed children. I would never be able to escape, I would never run again. I felt that I had been chained and bound and made to live at the end of a rope like a dog pegged to the earth. I was *contained*, to use the word the officers like to throw around. *Contain the enemy, that's the plan.* The bed, the room, the bandages on my right leg, none of that was in my plan. There had been no plan, just fire and shrapnel and running forward. I wondered how I would earn a living.

"There's no need to talk to her like that."

I knew that voice, but at first I could not tell where it was coming from. It was the woman, the bossy one, the thief who stole my leg.

"She's just trying to get you clean again."

The voice came from above and behind me to my left, and I tried to flip over to tell her what the hell I thought of her and her Negress, but I couldn't push off to roll over to my left. No leg to push with. I flopped like a fish in the summer shallows and snorted out my nose.

"Don't remember being clean, and I don't believe I want you this close to me. Liable to take an eye from me, or my liver. You want some other part of me? Here, take my head. This here is Zachariah Cashwell's head, and you can have it."

Finally I pushed off with my right arm and rolled onto my left side. The Negress had joined the white woman on that side of the bed, and they both stood there with their arms folded over their chests like they were sizing up livestock.

"I don't believe I will be the one to clean you. It wouldn't be proper, though Lord knows what's proper these days. I don't suppose it's proper for a woman to be alone in a house with hundreds of men, but there isn't any helping that, is there?"

She spoke direct to me without fear, like she'd spoken to those men back in the room where we were all laid out. She had spoken to us like little boys who weren't aware of something she knew all about and was tired of having to explain. I wasn't used to being spoken to by a woman that way. I wasn't used to being spoken to by a woman, truth be told, but I knew this was one woman who was taking some liberties, who knew she was in control for once.

"Who are you?"

Carrie McGavock, she said, and this was her house and her bed. *You are lying in my bed, so I believe it would be best if you watched yourself and treated Mariah with a little respect.* She said this, and her eyes seemed to get bigger and a little darker all at once, like a cat that's been startled by what it sees. *This is all mine,* she said, and I don't mind saying that those words scared me a little.

The Negress shook her head slowly, from side to side. I was scared of her, too. I was scared of every damned thing at that moment. My leg hurt like hell, sometimes like it had been ripped off by giant men and sewn up with baling wire, and sometimes like a band of swamp elves were gathered around my stump and poking flaming cypress branches into the wound. I hadn't thought of swamp elves since I was a child. I was asleep again.

I dreamed lightly and moved in and out of wakefulness. I dreamed of the McGavock woman, who led me by the hand through a grove of trees, each of them perfectly aligned and identical, row upon row of trees with deeply furrowed bark that scratched my hand as I tried to grab them, to keep her from taking me farther in. But I was dragged along by something, and the trees would not help me. She was saying something I couldn't understand. She turned to me with black eyes and said something so nice it sounded like bells, and after a while I come to think that she was telling me the names of the trees. Not their kind—they were all the same kind, whatever they were—but their *names.* She'd named them and knew where each stood. I tried to say, *You're crazy,* but somehow it came out as a speech to a squad of faceless men, and I was telling them that there was no hope at all and that there had never been any and that we might as well enjoy it while we can, and how bad could a bullet feel anyway? And they nodded their faceless heads and jumped to their feet and went tear-assing through the grove until all I could see was the glint of their rifle barrels in the distant dark. The woman stood beside me, and her face changed and her eyes lightened, and I could see a glimpse of my mother in those eyes, before she left me with my aunt. *I'm going West, and I'll send for you right soon, son.* The words twisted my guts like they always did. The McGavock woman's face changed again, and she was herself once more. When the trees began to sway and topple in the wind, crashing about us, we went striding out like gods, pushing the big trunks aside as if they were old weeds.

I awoke again and thought, *Is she Death?* How could Death be so pretty?

The room was empty, and I could barely hear the shouts and cries of the men in the surgeons' room. I reckoned I was in some other, distant part of the house. Why had I been put there, in the big bed with the soft ticking and the clean sheets? I saw the sky through the window and was surprised that it wasn't gray, like a proper winter sky. It was bruised and yellow like it had been punched, like a sky looks when a storm's coming up the river and dumping buckets of rain every which way. It was low and pressed in on me, even through that little window, and I thought I could feel it lying heavy on my chest. Occasionally I'd see soldiers walk by the window, and occasionally one would slip and fall like he'd been tripped up or pushed from above.

I decided against ever getting up again, but the Negress came back and she had other plans.

"Sergeant Cashwell, it's time for you to be gettin' up."

"No, I think I'll be stayin' here awhile. It's right comfortable, and it's the least you-all can do for me, having hacked me up like a hog. I ain't been in such a bed before, and I'm just startin' to get used to it."

The Negress ran her hand along an old chest of drawers that sat along one side of the room, and studied the white dust that attached itself to the edge of her hand. She looked over at me like she was fixin' to bring the edge of that hand down across the bridge of my nose, and I wasn't sure I could stop her. I was weak, which was also a new experience for me.

"What we done . . . what Miss Carrie and those doctors has done . . . is the *most* that can be done for you. But I ain't been sent here to argue with you. I been sent to give you these."

She reached outside the door and pulled in a pair of rough-cut crutches. The tops of them had been wrapped with cloth and twine, but they still looked pretty hard.

"What you goin' to do with those?" I asked.

"Give them to you, Miss Carrie says."

"I appreciate that, but I don't think I'll be needing them. Give 'em to one of those boys who keep stumbling around out there, outside that window. I plan to stay right here. Comfortable and safe, that's my new plan."

She laughed. "Ain't safe here."

"Is that right?"

"Ain't safe nowhere around here. You a prisoner, you know."

"This is prison? Hate to see freedom, then. Couldn't take it. Too much pleasure in it, I reckon."

"You laugh all you want, but you'll be wantin' them crutches right soon when they come to take you all away."

"Who's they?"

"Who do you think?"

"The Yankees?"

"The very same."

"The men in blue?"

"Them, too."

"Unionists, then."

"I reckon I heard that word, yes."

"Republicans."

"Hard to tell who's a Republican these days."

"I guess that's the truth."

"Don't doubt me, Sergeant Cashwell. I know a little more than your average nigger."

"I didn't doubt it."

"Yes, you did."

I liked her. She was like me, only she was a Negro and a beautiful woman. She was tough and smart-mouthed, and I liked it. There were a lot of men who would have smacked her down for talking like that, but I had never been bothered by such talk. I never did care much one way or another about a Negro and never gave much thought to what was proper coming out of their mouths. I was never obsessed by 'em like a lot of other white folks. I didn't get scared by the thought of a Negro uprising, which made me a little unusual where I come from. I just reckoned I could always take care of myself and fade into the swamp. Disappear. Now I had a Negro handing me a pair of crutches so I could try to take care of myself before the Yankees came for me. I wasn't at all as confident about things. The swamp could drown me now.

"All right, I'll take 'em."

"Miss Carrie wants to see you on the back porch."

"Anything else she want? She want me to dance for her?"

"That be it for now."

That wouldn't be it, though. That Negress knew a lot more, she just wasn't going to let on. I liked her less for that, but not until later.

I rolled over onto my right side because I could get some push from my good left leg. *Still strong, yes, sir, like an oak.* I took the opportunity to check out my pecker, too, and everything seemed to be working proper once I pulled my trousers down a bit. *Like an oak.* That made me laugh. Next to the empty air where my leg had once been, my pecker was as solid and impressive as it had ever been, which had never been much, to tell the truth. That had never mattered to me much. Now it did. Now it mattered, and I suddenly couldn't imagine the woman who would want to see me now. *The Lord giveth, and the Lord taketh away. The Lord likes His jokes.*

I got so I could sit up on the side of the bed, and I pulled the crutches over the bed and set them standing on either side of me so I could lift myself up to stand. My arms trembled as I tried to yank myself up, and the crutches got so wobbly that one scooted out from under me and clattered to the floor. I fell back on my ass and lost the other crutch. I lay there for a few minutes looking up at the ceiling and admiring the wallpaper moldings and the almost perfect plaster ceiling, with only a few mold marks here and there. I counted them. Seven. I wondered how mold chose where to appear and blossom. Was it random, or was there some sort of plan for it? Don't matter. The mold looked like it was meant to be there to make the room seem real and worldly, where things were never quite as clean and smooth and perfect as you thought they ought to be.

I rolled over on my stomach and felt the wool blanket scratching my belly. I hoped they hadn't used one of the army blankets, or else they'd have fleas and mites everywhere in the house in no time, but I looked at it and it was too finely woven and too colorful to be one of ours. I pulled myself over to the side of the bed and reached out to try to snag the crutches. I got far out over the edge until I could feel myself wobbling and about to fall.

Got to remember I ain't got so much ballast anymore. It was just enough to snatch up the crutches and get them situated again. This time I set myself up on the side of the bed and rocked myself into a standing position, and this seemed to work pretty good. The crutches were hard on my pits, though.

Once you get the swinging action going, you can move steady on crutches. My leg hurt awful, but they give me dope for the pain, and I made good use of it. I stumbled a few times right off, and I took a couple of practice laps around the bed to get the hang of it. But finally I went out the door of the bedroom and into the sunlit hallway, keeping my eyes on the floor ahead of me in case of divots in the wood or other things that could trip a man up. The floor was joined tight, though, and I admired it. Clean, too.

I saw a small door up ahead that looked like it led out onto a porch, and I reckoned that was where the McGavock woman was at. The door was solid poplar and fit perfectly in its door frame, and I had a time trying to get it pushed open. *Someone around here knows how to cut a piece of wood,* I thought. But I finally got the door open, and I stepped out into perversity. That's the only word I got for it.

I'd seen my share of battles, and after the battles, to be sure; so perhaps it was the sudden chaos of this, after all the quiet and solitude of the room. Now I thought it was like being at the carnival that came through our town back in Arkansas, only the things that were promised on the sides of the wagons—great terrifying freaks that oughtn't to ever have lived—were real. The knowledge I had had as a kid, that the terrors were illusions, was not there for me now. I tried to think *fake, fake, fake,* but it was impossible to keep up with what I saw.

The carts were loaded with dead men, and the smoke that blew everywhere and kept me coughing only partially obscured the stink. Men limped and crawled across the ground below me, calling for water or friends or their mamas. I saw one man over by a fire dancing a jig and whipping his empty shirtsleeve around like he was some kind of scarf dancer. The men around him were laughing, as if there was nothing special going on. They all looked partially human. You could stitch 'em all up together and make something perfect. All parts of a whole, like me.

"Good morning, Mr. Cashwell."

I saw Mrs. McGavock boiling bloody bandages in a pot off one end of the porch. I couldn't speak.

"Things look bad out here, but I'm sure you've seen worse."

But I'd never seen worse.

The worm is among us, the preacher said, before he took my mother away. The worm is among us, heed the signs. He breaks the hearts of men, snaps their bones, tears asunder the bond between man and woman, turns child upon child, rains injustice upon the fields until they have blackened and wilted from the poison. And the worm will leave the broken and the poisoned in his slimy trail, as the serpent left wormwood behind in its escape from paradise. The worm is here, oh yes.

My head hurt, but soon I was used to it and the sight of the men in front of me. A young white woman I'd seen once or twice moved among the men, bringing water and what looked like boiled potatoes in pots. The McGavock woman called out to her, directing her here and there, from this group to that group. After a while Mrs. McGavock sat on the back steps to watch, and I stood over her, trying to get used to balancing on my new crutches.

"Becky, mind you don't give out the water all at once. Move around. There are some fellows over there who look thirstier than those."

Mrs. McGavock turned toward me without looking up and began to talk.

"That girl's brother, a little boy, almost had his head shot off."

"Was he in the fight?"

"No, of course not."

"Bad luck, then."

"I don't believe in luck anymore, Mr. Cashwell."

The girl looked like she'd worked hard her whole life, and yet she was soft around her mouth and her chin, the places where you look for signs of kindness. She was hauling those buckets around like a man, two at a time. She looked up at Mrs. McGavock, nodded her head, and smiled.

"She's in love."

"With one of them?"

"Of course not. With one of the boys who ought to be here but isn't. Lord knows where he is."

"Who is he?"

"I don't know."

"She didn't tell you?"

"She didn't tell me anything. I can just see it on her. The things she's hoping for are right there on her face."

I didn't know what the hell she was talking about. Mrs. McGavock talked like she was talking to someone else, even if her mouth was pointed at you. She acted like she'd seen everything, and that made me a little angry. How could a woman who had spent her life wrapped up in shawls and waited on by nigras know a damn thing about anything? *I'd* seen things. I'd *done* things. Once. Once upon a time.

I reckon the old boy didn't think we could see him, crouched down behind the pecan tree in the yard, one of hundreds of men lying about. He was off by himself a little, and I wouldn't have noticed him except that when Becky came walking by the tree, swinging the buckets and calling out to the men—*Water? Water? Got potatoes, too!*—he grabbed her, and the buckets fell to the ground and clattered down the slight slope until they came to a rest next to the fence.

There wasn't a man who got up to help her, and I can't really blame them. Who could pay attention to anything but their own new circumstances, their own odds of life? Mrs. McGavock didn't see it, either, having turned her attention to the laundry again, her head taken up in a cloud of white steam over the black kettle.

I shouted, but it had been days since I'd last used my voice like that, and all I got was a coughful of spit. I hacked out another shout, but it was indistinguishable from the sounds the men were making on the lawn, and no one seemed to hear me. I thought to go for her myself, but I looked out and couldn't see how I'd get myself around all those bodies on my new crutches. Such a beautiful, hard girl, though. She reminded me of the girls I'd grown up around, the ones who'd had to work like the boys, who wouldn't take no shit. I wondered if she could take care of herself. I decided I couldn't wait.

I threw the crutch on my good side away and realized I could move pretty quick if I hopped most of the way and just used the crutch to prop myself up when I had to stop or turn. I leaped across the field. I could see the faces of men, their gray uniforms, their white bandages, the ground they lay on, all passing below me when I looked down. I could feel them sit up to watch.

At the tree the old-timer hadn't gotten very far. During the battle he must have been shot in the head, grazed probably, but you can lose a whole lot of blood that way. He was weak. His beard was mostly gray with black speckles, and it grew high on his cheeks but not high enough to cover the divots and marks in his skin. He was an ugly man with a full head of stringy hair and his pecker in his hand. He was bigger than me, but I figured I was meaner.

The girl had kicked him a few times, but he'd still managed to get her on her back, wedged into the space between two of the tree's roots. She spit and clawed at him, and I picked up my crutch, balanced on my left foot, and took a swing at the geezer. I didn't get him good, but it was enough to knock him back and start his head bleeding again. The girl just lay there, panting, covering herself, looking at me. The old soldier sputtered and cursed.

"Who the hell are you? Get out of here, gimp. This don't concern you."

"Just leave her alone, old man. Ain't need to go any farther than this."

"I'll say how far it goes."

A woman spoke from behind me.

"I believe Mr. Cashwell will tell you how far it goes."

The lady of the house never missed anything, I would learn this later. But damned if it wasn't a little frightening to have her come up on me like that, like a ghost. I began to turn to see her, but I saw the old guy coming at me right then, and so I turned back and whapped him again, this time in the gut, and he had to sit down for a second.

I meant to wallop him a couple of times and get my one-legged self out of harm's way before he got a chance to do me much real damage. I couldn't be in a fight, not no more. Even the old man was my superior now. I'd ambushed him, but that couldn't last.

Surprise never lasted. There was a crow in the tree sitting on a branch above the girl, and it moved back and forth looking at us, stretching its neck and opening its beak like it was going to say something but never succeeding.

The old man rocked on his haunches and hauled himself up. I turned to look at Mrs. McGavock again. The crotchety old pervert came at me again, and this time I got him on his jaw, right under his ear, and that knocked him out but good. He stumbled around for a second and then fell to his knees and rolled over like a baby.

The girl, in the meanwhile, had got up. She walked over to the man, his mouth lolling open, and stood over him.

"No, Becky."

Becky looked over at Mrs. McGavock with hate in her eyes at first, until she realized who was talking, and then her face softened and the lines between her eyes disappeared. She turned and walked toward the buckets. She began to dust off the potatoes.

I stared at Mrs. McGavock. She said, "I just wanted to see what you would do. You don't have a leg, you know."

23

Carrie McGavock

Becky came to us the night I discovered Ab and Eli at the end of our walk. There were flurries of snow throughout that evening, but she looked as if she had been through a deluge. Her lovely brown hair, which she kept long and unhindered, traced lines across her cheeks and forehead, and not once did I see her bother to put a hair back in its place while she stood there on our front porch shouting at Mariah about her brother. My, she could have been a handsome girl. But someone had chosen to make her a farm implement; that was clear. Her hands were rough and brown and scabbed like a man's.

The newspapers were always on about how the best men of our country—and by that, they meant this new country of ours, these Confederate States of America—went off to fight and were lost forever. But what of the best of our women? How many lovely young women were sacrificed behind the plow in those years? Oh, I'm not saying that a woman oughtn't guide a plow, although I shudder at the thought of my own incompetence at the reins. It's not the plowing, you see; it's the elimination of everything *but* plowing, the possibility that you could be anything *but* someone who walked behind a mule and gathered in the snap beans. A man could transform himself, and although these last few years that transformation had been completed by war and sometimes death, it is impossible to say how much bigger life must have seemed just knowing that it could be changed. A girl like Becky could not change anything for herself, and she had been called upon to take up the work and life of a man. Her charms had leached away, leaving something bone-hard in its place. Sometimes when I looked at her, the gulf between us made me dizzy. We could not move lightly between our worlds as a man might move easily between church and saloon, battle and sport. I was soft where she was hard, and when I caught her sitting off by herself and stemming tears, I knew that there were things I had mastered that she had not. We were halves of a whole, and the fathers and mothers and families and houses and histories that had sundered us were insurmountable. I wanted to love her, but I did not find a way. I pitied her, as she must have pitied me from time to time.

I pitied Becky for reasons other than her station in life. What was station anymore? I could feel my own station slipping away, and good riddance. I wore plain clothes and quit bothering to powder my neck. I swore occasionally in front of the men and committed to memory the new curses I heard the men sputtering. I thought of the curses as passwords, the lingua franca of my new life, one I could not yet envision but which I knew would be coarser and not possessed of the layers of fine scrim that had kept me in gauzy ignorance of the clang and stink and sharpness of things outside Carnton.

I pitied Becky because she was in love. There were many signs of her condition: the systematic way she attended to all the men under our care, pausing to overhear their conversations; her questions about other hospitals and whether there were any Tennessee boys in any of them; her particular interest in the opinions and recollections of any Tennessean she happened across; the vehemence and violence with which she repelled the attentions of the men. When she stood over the man behind the pecan tree, I saw the cold hate of a woman who has lost something and was outraged by the idea that someone would think to take even more from her.

She was just a girl. I was reminded of this when she sat by her brother, Eli, during slow moments, and I could see the family resemblance and their youth. They leaned into each other comfortably, a position obviously familiar to both of them. She stroked his head and ran her hands across the scab in his scalp. He picked at the folds of her skirt and gathered a few in his fist. She tickled him, and he tickled her back. She laughed and called him a little piglet. He stuck his tongue out at her and tried to yank at the long hair that spilled down her back. She slapped him on his knee, hard, and he pouted a little before getting up and dancing a little jig in front of her, teasing her about something, staying out of her reach. He was confused by her reaction, which was not to come after him and give his ear a yank, but to turn inward and shrivel a little before slowly getting to her feet and moving quietly into the house. Eli watched her go and then walked slowly among the men in the yard without listening to them or acknowledging their appeals.

Eli had become a little master of the place and had found an acolyte in Winder. My son tagged along after the older boy as Eli carried water and food and contraband among the men. He was resourceful and kind: he took no money for the little bottles of whiskey and the sweets he brought to his favorites among the patients. He just passed their money along to his supplier. I'd seen him huddled with the quartermaster clerk who ran errands to town, the older man laughing but still pocketing the scrip that Eli held out in his little hand. Once I would have forbidden Winder from fraternizing with such a boy, but now I hadn't the heart or the inclination. Winder was in love with the older boy in the way little boys fall in love with train conductors and frontier fighters and famous generals. Eli was Winder's new obsession, the reflection of himself in a darker and deeper pool, one containing greater possibilities. That Eli could make himself not just tolerated but useful and even desired by the great men strewn around them—this achievement impressed Winder, who started walking bowlegged like Eli and never stopped for the rest of his life.

I had my own obsession, my own little project. The man Cashwell was as foreign to me as Eli was to Winder. I can't explain why I needed him around. He held no attraction for me, and I sometimes doubted if any man could. In the beginning I believe I was shocked to find a person, in this case a man and a soldier, who wanted to die. Once I had thought that I wanted to die, but I could see from watching Cashwell that I was only a pretender, a histrionic fool. Cashwell took no pleasure from the thought of dying, not that I could see, and that's what made our difference clear to me. There had been a perverse pleasure to be taken from contemplating the big vial of laudanum I'd kept hidden from the world, and it was that contemplation that had sustained me and, if I'm not wrong, that had kept me alive. If what I could become, my potential for transformation, was as severely limited as Becky's, at least I knew I could be transformed by death. The possibility of an option in a world empty of options had been liberating. But Cashwell, he *wanted* no more options. At times I'd come to his bedside and he'd ignore me for a while, but then we'd talk a little. He never said it, but I thought I detected the weariness of a man, a person, who had seen *all* the options of life. Of late these options had been brutal and unfair and ungodly. It thrilled me to stand next to a person who possessed a record of experiences entirely unimaginable to me. If he felt the pressure and weight of being alive, I felt its mysteries when I was with him. It was a relief to know there were still mysteries.

A day or so after Cashwell's debut as the knight-errant of that macabre little scene under our pecan tree, played out under the unseeing eye of the surgeons sawing away upstairs with our brandy still on their breath from the night before, he and I came to an understanding. I didn't know where John was, and I didn't care.

Late one afternoon I went into Cashwell's room—I thought of it as *his* room now—and fussed with some of the things lying about on the dresser. There was a hand mirror there, my old hand mirror, and I looked into it and saw a face that seemed younger than I imagined possible. I would have wagered that years had passed since the first of the mangled had been brought to our door and that I had become a gnarled hag left to sift the bones. That was not the case. I even looked, how would I put it, *vehement,* for once in my life. Assured. I smiled at myself, and it didn't feel at all unnatural. I felt heavy. Not fat, but just less airy. I could feel the floor through my shoes and the pull of gravity through my knees.

I straightened the dresser: moving the mirror to one corner, a tin of matches to another, a stocky little candle in its holder to another corner, and Cashwell's belt—rolled up tightly like a snail's shell or a snake—to the very middle. I thought he was sleeping, but he must have been watching me.

"What you doing, Mrs. McGavock?"

He startled me, and I jumped a little before recovering and turning to see him there in the bed. *No flinching.* I tried to look at him coldly.

"I'm straightening things. This is still a house, a fine house, and no matter how long you and your friends lie around here, it will remain a fine house."

His face was still pale, but it was gathering a little color day by day. He sat up in the bed with his hands on either side of him, pulling the sheet tight across his waist. The sheet sagged in the emptiness where his right leg had been.

"No one said it ain't a fine house."

"Thank you."

"I didn't say it *was,* either. No offense, but I ain't going to exactly have pretty memories of this place. That might affect my judgment."

He looked at me straight on, like he was waiting to see something in my face, some reaction. A test. I struggled to hide myself behind feigned weariness. Weariness was a skill much practiced among the women of my acquaintance.

"Perhaps I could have the surgeon cut your other leg off, and then you would be symmetrical. Symmetry is beauty, correct?"

"Perhaps you could have let me alone down in that room. That place was pretty, with a nice blue ceiling that looked like the kind of sky I used to like to fish under. I could have died thinking of fishing, and that—"

"I am bored by that sort of nonsense. You bore me. Here I

thought you might be an interesting man, and you're as imaginative as a stick of kindling. *The ceiling looked like the sky.* How touching and perceptive of you. *I want to die.* How tiresome. You're a terrible conversationalist."

"Forgive me, ma'am, but I ain't really up for a lot of talking, or conversationing, or whatever it is you come to my room for."

"My room."

"You're welcome to it. Put me on the next wagon out of here, I'm ready to go."

I did not want him to leave on a wagon. *Not yet.*

"Get me the hell out of here. You've chopped me into a freak, and I reckon it's about time I got on with living my freak life. I didn't much care for you letting that girl get roughed up like that, and I don't want to be no part of whatever experiment you got cooking up in here. I ain't yours to talk to. Who the hell are you, lady? You've got some kind of sickness on you, I can tell. I seen it. You twisted up somehow, something ain't right. You're *watching* all the time, watching me, watching the men laid out all around you, watching that girl. What the hell do *you* do, besides decide who lives and who dies?"

I could not look at him, and he went on:

"I guess you're God, or God's messenger or prophet. You like Elisha, doling out miracles and leprosy as you see fit. You didn't think I knew the Bible, did you? I'm just an uneducated man from Arkansas who can be of some kind of use to you, which remains to be seen. But I know the Bible, I can read. Even if I couldn't read, I'd know the Bible. Mama was always spitting it at me before the preacher came. Yeah, a preacher ran off with my mother, ain't that something? Bet you never thought such a thing could happen. Nah, bet you *did*."

I knew he was raving, and I went toward him, as if to calm him down, but he continued as if he'd forgotten I was there.

"Bet you think that's how it happens all the time outside this place, that all the dumb and ignorant trash in the world fall over at the sight of a person with learning and clean clothes and proper talk. But that ain't exactly so. My mother knew what she was doing. She'd given me the name of Zachariah. She was the woman in the basket, you know that story? It's in Zachariah. They bring this woman in a big basket with a lead lid on it, only Zachariah doesn't know what the hell is in it, and the angels reveal a woman in it, and Zachariah says that ain't right, but he puts the lid right back down on her. And the angels agree, and they say it ain't right exactly, and so that's why they're taking her off to Babylon, and off she goes. Off to Babylon. See, I understand that prophecy better than my mother, who's now off someplace with a preacher. Or she's whoring or whatnot. She felt sorry for the woman in the basket, and she thought she *was* the woman in the basket, poor and boxed in by her family and that shack and her stupid son. But the woman was a sinner, and Babylon was the resting place of sin. This is what I learned when I started reading. I was Zachariah, who closed the lid, and my mother found a way to be lifted up and carried off to her rightful place. I ain't ever heard from her again, and I don't care to."

And then he turned his green eyes at me again.

"I have had my fill of women who think too much, so if you think I'm anything but a man who's going to have a rough time walking around and defending himself from here on in, you wrong. You dead wrong. You don't know God, you don't know shit. God will stick you in a basket if He wants to, and there ain't have to be a reason for it. There is no reason I am sitting here, in this nice and clean bed, talking to you. It just happened that way, and it don't mean nothing. You should have saved that girl yourself, you should have screamed, you should have let her shoot that old coot in the eye. That's the way it ought to be done. I don't need to be educated by you. I don't need to entertain you. I don't need to be convinced that I'm still a whole man, because I know what it means to be a cripple, lady. I been out there, I know what happens. I'll get me a box and a cane and a little sign, and I'll eat off people's back porches when they get it in their mind to take pity on me. I don't want your pity. Not your kind of pity. Not from someone like you."

"I don't have any pity for you, Mr. Cashwell. I don't have any to give to you."

"If not to me, I'd sure as hell not want to meet the man you did pity. Must be a real sorry bastard."

I wanted to tell him that it wasn't so, that I wasn't doing anything but attending to the wounded, that this hadn't been my choice but something, in a long line of somethings, that had been thrust upon me without my permission. But then who would have been angling for pity? Things are thrust upon you; that's just the way it is. But I also wanted to tell him that they were not all an undifferentiated mass of men to me, not something to be experimented upon. He thought I couldn't see them individually, but it was the man lying before me, this apparently insane man befuddled by Old Testament prophecies and the perfidy of his mother, who could not see them individually. He was the one who had spent the last years walking in step with them, wearing the same clothes and eating the same food, watching one man fall and another step into his place, like a colony of termites driven by God knows what to move ever forward together, stopping at nothing, sacrificing the weak. *He* saw them that way, and why not?

But I could see them as men and boys, hundreds of men living with me, individuals, each with a story and a different face and a different future.

My children could see the differences that Cashwell couldn't see. Hattie, who had become Mariah's own assistant in charge of tearing up sheets for bandages and checking the cistern's water level, told me many stories of the men. She kept a count on her little black lesson slate of the number of men with blond, black, brown, and red hair and then went back and counted up the bald and silver-headed ones.

Yesterday morning—had it only been yesterday?—she came to me in the kitchen, the only place Mariah and I and John (when he wasn't off on some other errand or drinking) could gather in peace, and she would tell us about the men who had talked to her that day or the ones she had spied on.

She told me about the boy crying in the upstairs guest room, the one who had been shoved into a corner by the bigger men and who faced the wall all day. He was a boy who had been shot in the arm, and the surgeons had removed the bullet and patched the wound, but he'd gotten the fever anyway and spent his days becoming paler and glazed in sweat. He was dying from the infection, and I could not tell Hattie this. But I think she knew it anyway. She told me that she had brought water to the room with Mariah and that she had heard the boy weeping. She stepped over the other men who had become so used to her flitting about that they didn't even bother to watch her anymore, and she went over to the boy. *I'm so cold,* he said, over and over again. *I'm so cold, I'm so cold, I'm so cold.* So Hattie, who is nothing if not a practical and sensible girl, went down to her own bed and pulled off the blanket that her grandmother had made for her of lace and white cotton and satin, and brought it to the boy. The boy looked at her and smiled, but pushed it back.

"And so, Mama, I said, 'Why don't you want my blanket?' And he said, 'My mama gave me a blanket she made for me with my name on it, and I brought it to the war, but some people took it from me when it started to get cold a month or so ago, and I ain't seen it since.' He didn't want to take a blanket from anyone, not even me, Mama, and it's a nice blanket and I was nice as I could be. He said it would be like stealing. I don't know about that, Mama, but he wouldn't take my blanket. He was shivering like he was real cold, and crying, and he said, 'I want my mama's blanket. I want the blanket she gave me.'"

Hattie began to cry, and I could see that she wasn't sure why. I was sorry and angry that she had already learned to cry like that, to cry about cruelty. From the sound of her story I didn't think the boy would live much longer before giving up, so I excused myself. John didn't even seem to notice I was getting up, but Mariah did. Mariah shook her head. I didn't care.

With a candle in one hand, a piece of paper and a pen in the other, I went upstairs to the boy. I could hear him as soon as I walked into the room. He was no longer saying *cold.* He was saying *no. No, no, no,* over and over again, barely a whisper above the rattle of the leafless poplars outside the window and the wind as it swept down the porch outside. I stood over him. He was a dark little ragamuffin, but I supposed he'd been shrunk by the war and by his wound. His hair was brown, and his face was streaked with the mud of sweat and smoke and dirt. He had his eyes closed, but his mouth moved. I kneeled beside him and shook his shoulder, and he started awake and looked hard into my eyes to make sure I wasn't someone else, someone better, before resting again.

"Can't I get you a blanket?"

"No blanket. Had a blanket. No more blankets."

"We have plenty of blankets."

"I'm going, I don't need any blanket."

"You're cold."

"I just wish I had my mama's blanket."

"Your mother made a blanket for you. That was nice of her."

He looked at me without any expression on his face, like he was still waiting for me to say something sensible. I didn't know what else to say. He spoke first.

"You ain't supposed to go like this. They never said this would happen, they never talked about any of this. We just signed up, give me a gun and a hat and let me get 'em, yes, sir. My mama is in North Carolina. Far away. You ain't supposed to talk about your mama if you a man, but shit. I'm sorry to swear, ma'am. You supposed to be around people who love you when you go, not all these farting and cussing sons of bitches. I don't love a person in this room or in this state or in this army. I love one person, and she could keep me alive, I know she could. And now I'm going to pass—no, I know it, don't shake your head, ma'am, it's nice but you don't have to do that— and she ain't ever going to know where I am. I'll just be gone. And she'll be gone from me. I won't be able to think of her no more, and she won't know where I am. I been thinking of her every day, and now that's going to end. I don't want to do this without her. She'd know what I'm supposed to do now. I don't know what to do, and I'm so afraid I'm going to do this wrong. I've been trying to pray, but I don't know much prayers—she was the one who always did the praying. What do I ask for now? I don't know. I don't know. I miss her. I miss her, ma'am. I do. I'm going to hell. She gave me a blanket, you know. I don't got it anymore. It was stole from me, and I couldn't get it back. I tried. Please tell her I tried. I didn't mean to lose it. Please tell her that. Can't you?"

I'd never made Winder a blanket, and I'd never prayed over him. I had only prayed over my dying children. I held the boy's hand.

"I've got a piece of paper here. Would you like me to write to your mother?"

"Yes, ma'am."

"What would you like to say?"

"I don't know. Just what I said, I reckon. Or maybe not that much. Maybe you can write her and just tell her that I was here and where she can find me when I go. I just don't want to be lost."

"Would you like to write it?"

"I can't write. And my mama can't read, so just address it to Pittsboro, North Carolina. Somebody will read it to her."

"What's your name?"

"Marcus. Marcus Sanders of Pittsboro, North Carolina. My mama's name is Mattie, but folks only call her Mat, so you better call her that."

"I will."

"You have a nice house."

I stayed with the boy through most of that night until he passed. I thought I could feel the blood stop moving in his wrist, which I held and stroked for hours.

Marcus Sanders was one of hundreds who died at my house in those days, and most of them left me with memories. They were not all the same men, they were not just bodies. Sometimes my memories weren't as detailed as those I had of Marcus. Sometimes they were just snatches of things: songs I heard a man singing in a weird, high-pitched tongue, songs that drew a little crowd and made some of the men stomp up and down on their boots like they were trying to rattle the trees at their roots; the time one of the men, who claimed to be college-educated, held forth and lectured to a room full of unconscious men on the betrayal of Achilles; the time I watched for hours as a young man from Georgia named Stace carved a leering, bucktoothed face in one of the spindles lining our back porch.

They all died, and I remember them all.

24

ZACHARIAH CASHWELL

There came a time when I didn't worry so awful much about getting my leg cut off. I remember that this happened on the fifth day of my stay at the McGavocks' house. I was sitting up looking for something to whittle and for something to whittle with when I saw two heads go bobbing past the window on the other side of the room. Up and down, up and down. I could see the man trailing behind yell at the man in front every once in a while, and they'd both stop, and the man in the back would shrug and make like he was heaving something up, and then they'd go on. They did this most of the morning. Finally, after not finding anything to whittle with, and after I'd got tired of trying to think about the things I would whittle if I could, I got out of the bed and hopped to the window. I could lean my arms on the sill, and that held me up pretty good. I looked out, and there were fewer men in the yard than I remembered from a couple days before. Just a few groups of men here and there. I looked for the men with the heads, and after a while I saw them come by again. They were carrying bodies, some of them wrapped up in stained white sheets, and others just as they were when they died. I saw that they were moving the pile from one end of the yard to the other, from down by the Negro cabins over to where there looked like there was a garden. Just moving them, that was it. The piles looked the same on either end of the yard, only one was getting bigger while the other got smaller. The dead men were stiff, but they still flexed a little. Sometimes they'd bend right in half if the two men bunched up too quick as they were walking, and then they'd have to put them down and step on the legs until they went back flat again, kind of like how you'd stomp saplings into something you could carry while clearing brush. I watched them for an hour, I think, one pile to the other, and every one of the dead faces was gray.

When Mrs. McGavock wasn't in my room harassing me, I had some time to think and to listen to the things going on around me. Every day the house got quieter, like it was going to sleep. I didn't hear screams much anymore, and the moans, even though I'd got used to them, were not so constant. I suppose it was just the natural course of things, that after a few days all the fuss over whether we were going to live or die was settled, and those who died went quiet, and those who were going to live shut their mouths and got on with it. I reckoned that a goodly number of men snuck out of there and headed home. I thought about doing it myself, but every time I thought to get up and go, I come up with a little reason not to do it right then. *I'll do it right after they bring me some supper.* But I was always hungry, so I never left. Seems like an excuse, but I didn't barely know where the hell I was, and food ain't always easy to come by when you're lost. You got to think about those things.

After I watched the men carry the bodies, I thought to start counting my blessings. I was still enough of a Christian to do that, and so I did it. I wasn't going to thank anybody for taking my leg, but I quit cursing about it. I thought I could probably get on without it. I even thought that maybe I wouldn't ever have to get out of that bed if I played things right, and let Mrs. McGavock have her words with me when it suited her. I would have done that if I'd gotten the chance.

As soon as I quit crying about the leg, though, I started taking

stock of the *other* things I was missing. And the one that made me
the angriest was that I knew, lying in that bed, that I was not any
longer the man who had picked up that flag and run into the
Yankee works. I was not the sergeant who knew every damn
thing about fighting. I was not that man. I was a man who would
not ever again think to pick up a flag like that. It was not that I
had become afraid. I was not and I had never been a coward. No.
The thing was, I cared about living now, and taking care of my
own business and nobody else's. I had been ready to die, and that
had made me strong and fearsome and in control. But now I
wasn't ready to die, and I didn't see as how I would ever be ready
to die again. I'd been ready to die even as the surgeons sawed my
leg off, and I'd been ready to die in the days after, when the pain
seemed like it was demanding that I die. But now, like I said, the
fuss was over, and I was going to live. I didn't know how to live,
exactly, but I knew I had to figure that out now. I had become
like any other man, like I had once been before. Before the war,
before the fighting, before the charge. Living did not seem like
a gift. It was a heavy weight, but it was all I had anymore, and it
didn't matter how low I sunk as long as I stayed alive. This is
what I thought, and it made me angry and sick. There was
nothing worth dying for anymore, and that made everything
around me seem smaller, including myself. The whole world was
cheap and mean, and I was going to be cheap and mean along
with it just so long as it meant staying alive. It made me
common. I was common again.

There was some good things about being common, I'll admit
that, about *having feet of clay*, as my old aunt used to say. She'd say
it when I got into trouble. I liked the way it sounded—*feet of clay*.
Or foot of clay, if you get my meaning.

One of the things about being common was you could get up a
game of cards for money and not think twice about it no more.
Gambling was a sin, but since sin seemed like it was going to be a
natural part of things from then on out, I figured I might as well
get started right away. There were still enough of the boys around
the house to go out on the porch and wager over a few hands, and
so I took to clomping around the house on my new crutch looking

for men who were awake and could move around a little. There was a fellow named Jerrod Smalls—missing an eye—who had a deck of cards he'd carried up with him from Montgomery. Smalls was young, maybe twenty or so, but he fancied himself some sort of master of the game since he was from the city, and so I could count on him for a game or two. He was not as good as he thought, and he couldn't count very well anymore due to being hit slap upside his head with the butt end of a Yankee rifle, and so he never seemed to know when he was losing, and I didn't always bother to tell him.

On days when I wanted to play cards I'd go find Jerrod first. He was usually up in one of the rooms overlooking the front drive, staring out the window at something I never could figure out. His hair was long and jet black, and he'd let it hang over his face so he looked crazy and people would leave him alone. *Just want to do what I want to do from here on*, he said. He didn't look like he'd ever shaved, and his one good eye was big and dark like a heifer's. He was thin and bony like the rest of us, but he still looked soft. I'd come into the room and call him Lefty, because that was the eye he was missing, and he'd just call me a gimp, and we'd walk out of the room looking for others. He'd start shuffling his cards in his hand. He was good at it, and so the cards made a loud sound like someone was ripping a tent, over and over again. The men who weren't dying recognized the sound, and the ones who could talk would call out, and soon we'd have us a game.

We played for scrip, which had never been worth much and I reckoned would be worthless soon enough, and so maybe we weren't gambling technically. But I felt it in my heart and my gut, wanting to have all that worthless paper in my pile. I didn't care what it was, I wanted it, I wanted all of it, and so I reckon I was gambling in spirit if not exactly in fact.

We played all kinds of games. Faro, euchre, poker, boo ray, even chuck-a-luck once when we found some dice in the pocket of a dead man, but Jerrod got so mad at the dice that he threw them into the tall grass off the porch, and we never did find them again.

We were playing outside in front of the house one morning when I watched Mrs. McGavock pack her children into a fancy covered carriage and stand at the end of the walkway crying and waving them good-bye.

"You see that?" I said to Jerrod.

"Yep. You just lost that trick, my friend."

"No, I mean over there."

He turned around to look with his good eye.

"Mrs. McGavock? Uh-huh."

"She just sent her children off. Don't look like she wanted to."

"Should have sent them off a lot earlier than this, you ask me. Ain't no place for a child."

Jerrod looked over at me quick, so none of the other boys throwing down cards would see him. He looked sad and was looking at me to see if I looked sad, too, I guess. I don't know what I looked like, but he was satisfied enough to turn his eye back to the cards.

It *was* no place for a child. Jerrod and I had seen that real clear. Mrs. McGavock's children, the little boy and the older girl, had been flitting around for days. They were always there, filling mouths with water or, in the case of the boy and his older friend, Eli, running a little trade in whiskey and clothing. I did not understand why Mrs. McGavock let them be around us so much. We were a horrible-looking lot, and what business did children have seeing us like this? I couldn't imagine what kind of cockeyed vision of the world they would have after tending to us, the crippled and the condemned. But that was her business; if she wanted to raise ghouls, then let her.

But that girl of hers, Hattie she was called, was the prettiest thing, and some of the men noticed. A lot of soldier talk is just talk, and so there ain't no sense in taking serious everything you hear. But sometimes you can hear something different in a man's voice, something calm and harder than the regular bullshit, that makes you know that what the man is saying ain't the usual bullshit. Could be he's telling the truth.

Jerrod and I started hearing that kind of talk around the card game a couple days before I watched the McGavock children go riding off, with their mother standing in the road behind, waving. We started hearing talk about that girl, Hattie. She was too pretty and too young and too trusting to be around men like us. I decided to tell Mrs. McGavock, and so I did. I told her that the thing that had almost happened to that girl Becky, at the hands of that broke-down old goat, might also happen to Hattie if she weren't careful. Mrs. McGavock had her apron crumpled in her hand while she listened to me, and her eyes got darker and darker. I couldn't tell if she was scared or angry. But then she told me to mind my own business and that if she ever wanted tips on child raising, she would be sure to come to me, but at the moment she was doing right fine, thank you very much. I figured she was angry at me for pointing out the danger to her own child, who was not just some country girl from down the road with a pistol in her pocket.

Then I went and found that boy Eli. He reminded me of myself, or what I might have been as a boy if I'd had a sister to love and love me back. He was a scrapper, I could tell it on him, and I could see he didn't let nothing get by him. He was taking orders for liquor from some of the men when I grabbed him by the arm and took him around to the back porch.

"What you think you're doing, Eli?"

"Nothing."

"You mighty busy for doing nothing."

"Reckon so."

Tough kid. I didn't scare him. I didn't want to scare him. I had the awful strange feeling that I wanted the little kid to *like* me and that I wanted him to do right and not get him or his friends in bad trouble. I wanted to protect him, even if I was myself a gimp who could barely protect himself no more.

"You friends with Hattie?"

"She's my friend's sister. I know her all right."

"You know what happened to your sister, right?"

"I know you walloped the hell out of a man over her. Thank you, sir."

He shrugged his shoulders and turned to go, like all I'd wanted was to be thanked. I hadn't even been thinking about being thanked.

"That same thing could happen to Hattie and your sister again if you and your friends and your sister don't get the hell out of this place."

Smart kid. He knew what I meant right off. He knew these men almost as well as I did now. Like I said, he didn't miss nothing.

"We got work to do."

"Not here. Not no more. You get them and your sister safe, hear?"

He was holding some crumpled Confederate scrip, and he looked down on it, and maybe for the first time he was seeing it weren't worth much.

"What do I do?"

He looked at me with real fear, for the first time, in his face, and I knew I could make that fear go away, at least for a minute.

"You go to Mrs. McGavock, and you tell her you been hearin' the men talking about Hattie and Becky. Just say that. She don't want to believe me, but she'll believe you."

"Why?"

"Because she will. Now, git."

He tossed the scrip back at the men he'd taken it from for liquor, and on his way back into the house he turned and waved and said something I couldn't quite hear. Sounded like *See you*, but I couldn't tell. I remember thinking, though, that maybe I weren't useless, after all. I also remember thinking that he sure did remind me of myself.

Just as the McGavock children were rolling out of sight at the end of the driveway, I spotted those two other castaways, that girl Becky and her brother, Eli, walking down the drive away from the house. The dust kicked up by the carriage must have hid them. They walked purposeful without looking back, and I reckoned I would never see them again. Or, maybe more true, I'd be seeing folks like them again and again and again. They were people like me, who ain't got shit, and I believed there'd be a whole lot more of us after the war had sorted itself out. I hoped they'd be all right, that they'd stay away from men like me. I was shocked that I felt that way, seeing as how I had barely known them. But those days at the McGavocks' had felt like forever, and every little thing like the only thing in the world.

At least Mrs. McGavock must have taken me serious about the threat, sending those two away also. No matter what she said.

Later, after Jerrod and I broke up the card game and headed back into the house, I said something to Mrs. McGavock about watching her ship off her children. I said I reckoned it was the right thing to do, and she turned to me slowly like she was having to take things real slow on account of she was talking to an idiot.

"I believe it is the right thing to do, but not for the reasons you're thinking, Mr. Cashwell."

"And what other reason would there be?"

She ignored me and traced with her finger the fancy pattern of the hallway's wallpaper. She had a soft look on her face, like she was thinking of something that had happened long ago.

"I do believe you and I shall have a conversation this evening. I shall bring you supper."

"Thank you, ma'am."

She squinted her eyes at me, and her face lined with sharp and dark wrinkles.

"How do you think they're managing in Nashville?"

That was the first clue that I wasn't going to be staying at the McGavock house forever. It's easy to think that your circumstances won't change once you've given up on changing them. But they get changed for you, sure enough.

I had mostly forgotten about the rest of the army. I reckoned I was shut of them, that they'd gone off to somewhere and *that* somewhere would never include me ever again. Nashville was it? *All right*, I thought, *so what?* I didn't mind the boys around the house. They were comforting, ugly and no count as they were. I just didn't have no need of the *regular* army, if you understand me. But it occurred to me when I was back in my room again, waiting out the couple of hours until suppertime, that if they were fighting in Nashville and things didn't go well—and they were sure not to go well after the beating we'd took—those boys would be coming right back on down the road to Franklin with the Union on their heels, and I was right in the path. *Well, shit,* I thought.

I hobbled over to the window, where I could see a group of men who had strung a rope from a branch high up in a large poplar and were taking turns seeing how high they could swing and how far they could jump after letting go of the rope. They swung back and forth like boys, looking up at the empty branches and the dusty blue sky, shouting nonsense and then jumping over what looked like a big pile of old coats. They *were* boys, I guess. Some of them. And then I watched Jerrod get on the rope and try to hold on, and he was doing pretty good until the rope got to swinging good and fast. I could see he was having a hard time holding on and that the happy look on his face had turned and become fear. He let go of the rope at the top of its swing, and that was a bad misjudgment. Maybe it was because he couldn't see so good with his one eye. He dropped straight down rather than gliding off and away, and he fell right into the pile of coats. He was screaming and thrashing and trying to high-step it out of there, and that's when I saw it wasn't a pile of coats, but a pile of coat *arms* and pant *legs,* with the arms and legs still in them. The other boys were shouting and whooping and pointing at Jerrod, who shouted curses at them and kicked the limbs out of his way. They were all so innocent, a pile of arms and legs was nothing to them. Didn't symbolize anything, didn't make them think about nothing. Just was what it was—a funny thing to see a man wallowing around in, dead and frozen things that didn't mean anything in particular. I thanked God that we had men like that, or boys like that, or elsewise we would have had our asses whupped by the Yankees years before. I had lost my own ability to jump over such a pile without thinking about it, and I envied them.

My mother would sometimes trace some symbols in the air when she was nervous and wanted protection: an *A* and something that looked like a horseshoe. She said it was the name of God. The window was fogging up with my breath as I looked out at those dumb cripples and heroes, and I traced my finger through the fog and drew my mother's symbols. I got tired then and went to bed.

* * *

Mrs. McGavock didn't bother to knock on the door. She came in with Mariah, and they bustled around with dishes and trays as if I was still an invalid who couldn't get out of bed but had to take it on his back, and not a man who got up every day to gamble and jaw with the others. Mariah looked at me straight, as if she was daring me to say anything about it. She knew good and well I shouldn't be having the mistress of the house waiting on me like that. *Ought to be getting his sorry ass out of bed and off to wherever he's supposed to get off to.* I could see what she was thinking, plain as anything. She was right, too, and I liked her the more for it.

When the food was all set out and ready to eat—we were having potatoes and some fried-up ham from the smokehouse, looked like—Mrs. McGavock sent Mariah off and bent her head to pray.

"Come, Lord Jesus, our guest to be, and bless these gifts bestowed by thee. Amen."

I said it with her. As soon as she said, "Come, Lord Jesus," I recognized the blessing and knew its words. I couldn't remember exactly where I'd heard it before.

"The Moravian blessing," she said. "You know it?"

I didn't know what a Moravian was, but somehow I knew their blessing. Didn't really know if there was such a place called Moravia.

"Yes. I know it."

"You're a religious man."

"No, I ain't. I just remember things in my head, and I ain't opposed to blessing food. Doesn't really matter where it's from, does it? It's something to be happy you got, that's what I know."

"You're a regular theologian."

"May I eat, ma'am?"

We ate without talking. I sat up in the bed, balanced the tray in my lap, and bore down hard with the knife on that ham. It had been kept up in the smokehouse a long time, was my guess. I didn't have cause to complain, though.

Mrs. McGavock was a hardy eater. It surprised me. She was so fine and pale and weak-looking I couldn't quite picture her bolting back salt ham like she did. She acted hungry, though. She balanced a plate on her knees, which she had drawn together with her feet perfectly aligned below. She had an apron on, and under-neath that she wore one of the black dresses she always was drifting about in, and for the first time I noticed that the black was faded and the seams had been mended a time or two. Between bites she'd sneak a glance up at me and then quickly turn her attention back to her plate and stab a little potato.

"Why are you here?" I said.

"What do you mean? This is my house."

"You may be thinking I'm stupid, but I really ain't, and so I've noticed that I'm being primped and pampered like I was kin to you and you reckoned to inherit a lot of money from me. Is that how you-all got your money, by the way? Is this family money? Because I've looked around this farm, and I have to say it's a sorry operation, and I can't figure you're making much money your-selves. So seeing as how I don't know you except that you decided I needed my leg sawed off, I've got to say it's a little mystery to me why I'm getting the special treatment while the rest of the boys got to sleep on the floor. But I'll say this. You've done enough for me, even if right this moment men outside are using my leg like it was a goddamn toy. You've done enough for me that you don't have to worry. Just tell me what you want from me, and I'll give it to you. I got to settle accounts here shortly anyway, seeing as how it's likely I ain't going to be staying much longer. I got to get my affairs in order and get on with it. So tell me what you want."

My potatoes had gotten a little colder, and so I shoveled a few into my mouth. She'd put her fork down and her plate aside, and sat there looking at me with her hands in a ball on her knees, her mouth drawn in a straight line I couldn't read. I was an ungrateful jackass, I knew that. I meant to be an ungrateful jackass, and that was the truth. I didn't want to owe no one nothing and I wanted to be free, and the best way to do that was to settle your accounts and burn your bridges so there was no going back. And, anyway, I couldn't understand her, and I couldn't understand why she was so concerned with me, with what I did, with how I was treated. I had thought it was guilt at first when she put me up in this room and made things more comfortable for me. But I soon realized it wasn't that, because she had not a fleck, not a spark, of pity in her eyes. She did not feel guilty; she would not have felt guilty if they had cut off all of my arms and legs and I had been able to do nothing but roll around and curse her. There was no guilt about her; she didn't cringe and talk soft to me like a guilty person would. On the other hand, I sometimes caught her staring at me when I was playing cards or when I was trying to hobble around the yard for some fresh air or when she passed by my room late at night. I didn't like being looked at when I didn't know what was being seen.

"You are my key. You will explain the things to me that I have not been able to understand. You can do this, Mr. Cashwell, because I saved you. I have known only the opposite in my life. The opposite of saving. The things dearest to me have been taken because I could not do what I did for you. And so I'm wondering, *Should he be dear to me? Was he meant to be dear to me?* And frankly, Mr. Cashwell, I've had a hard time coming around to the belief that you could *ever* be dear to me. I want you to explain to me why I wanted you to live and why I was able to make you live. Because I don't understand, not really, and the answer is very important to me."

She was out of breath, and I was out of breath just trying to keep from interrupting. I didn't have one clue about what she was talking about. She spoke in pieces of thoughts that I was supposed to understand, but I couldn't put them together. I was just a soldier, just a shot-up soldier, and I didn't want no more responsibility than that.

She stared straight down on me and seemed very tall in her chair.

"I don't have any answers to any of that, ma'am."

"You do, you just don't know what they are."

She relaxed in her chair, unclenching her muscles and folding in on herself. She smiled at me and scratched at the back of her neck, where her hair was starting to tumble down. I waited for her to speak again, because I was lost.

"You don't know what I'm talking about, I see that. That's all right. I'll know the answer when you tell me, even if you don't."

I kept my mouth shut, swallowed the last of my potatoes, put the tray aside, and crossed my arms over my chest. I waited.

"I suppose I'll have to ask you the questions."

"I reckon so, but I want to ask you some questions, too, if you don't mind, Mrs. McGavock."

"I want you to call me Carrie."

"Will you answer a question for me first?"

"All right, then, yes."

"Don't take offense at this, but I want to know what the hell happened to you to make you so goddamned odd."

I knew there was no way she wouldn't take offense at that, but it was the only question I could think of to ask, and it was the first one that came into my head, and after the words came out of my mouth I realized it was a question that had been banging around in my head for quite some time, probably since the first moment I'd seen her. I didn't know women like her. Didn't know many women, to be truthful, but the ones I *did* know weren't people like her. They weren't rich and well-born, and if they had their secrets and wounds, they came by them honest, in ways you could see real plain. *Her husband ran out on her. She don't have much food. Her daddy lay with her, they say. Her daughter died.* Things you can point to easy enough, that's what I'm saying. Now, I knew that Carrie had lost some children. I'd seen the big painting she had up in one of the rooms, three little faces in the clouds like angels, looking down on the world as if they were still alive and watching all of us. I guessed that was her story, but it still didn't all come together for me. It was the painting itself that made me suspicious, I guess. What kind of person wants to have a painting like that hanging around? The women I'd known did everything they could to get on from the past, to burn the past behind them. This woman didn't do that, and I wondered if it was just because I didn't know enough women.

"I'm odd, then."

"A little. A lot, actually. I don't mean to offend you."

"I'm not offended."

She closed her eyes, and her smile drew farther across her face, like she had just thought of something to look forward to. She sat like that for a few minutes. Without opening her eyes, she started talking again.

"What do you mean by odd?"

"I mean, this whole thing right here in the house."

"The hospital, you mean? I had no choice in that."

"But you like it, I can tell. You like what's happening here, as if you had wished it."

"Maybe I did."

"And that's odd, ma'am."

"Perhaps. What else?"

"What else?"

"What else makes me odd? That can't be all of it; you surely must have encountered the morbid in your time. Or have you been a sheltered man?"

"I don't know what you mean by morbid. But if you mean floating around this house like you were Death's angel herself, always watching and watching and watching, and letting your children see the worst there is to see in this life like it was no more unusual than the circus, and talking about answers I might have, when I've never had any answers for anyone except when it was time to charge ahead and get shot at, and—"

"That's what I mean. Tell me about that."

"About what?"

"You're not dumb, Mr. Cashwell, you know what I'm talking about."

"I'm afraid I don't."

"About *charging*. About killing. About fighting. I want to know that."

"I'm done with that."

"I don't think so. Not you. No. You're not finished, I can see it. You'll kill again."

"I'm done with soldiering."

"I'm not talking about soldiering. Do you know Mariah?"

"The Negro woman who was just in here?"

"Yes. She's got a prophecy about you."

"She don't look like a prophet."

"Would you like to know what she saw in her dream?"

"No."

"Well, then."

The sun was setting just then, and that low orange light seemed to light up every individual piece of dust on the windowsill. I'd never noticed the dust before, and I stared at it like it was something important, like there was something there. It didn't do anything. The back of my head hurt. Not like I'd been hit in the head, but like there was something wrong up in there. It tingled, like my arm did when it fell asleep and the blood had just begun to rush back to it. That part of my head felt empty except for the tingling, and I felt as scattered as the dust on the windowsill. I had no ground to stand on, no place from which to say, *This is who I am, this is what I am, this is where I'm from.* I could be one of any number of men. I *had* been any number of men in my life. The man who had rushed the barricade and who had killed other men was as dead as the boy who watched his mother ride off with the black-coated preacher. What could I say about him, the soldier and killer, except that he had lived? What could I tell someone like Carrie McGavock? I knew what she was asking, and the truth was that I had never thought much about what it felt like to kill other men. Killing was just another part of not being killed, at least the way I had experienced it, the unavoidable other side of the coin, and it had been my own willingness to be killed that had made it possible to kill. That's what I told myself, every day after every bad night of sleeping on the cold ground, hugging my rifle. It was a puzzle, though, and how could I explain that to this woman who had probably never been threatened in her life? I knew that death had been in this house, but it had snuck up on her unannounced, and to me that was some kind of mercy. She didn't have nothing to do with it, and I wasn't one of those folks who thought sickness and death was some sort of punishment for crimes against God, for sin. Sickness and death was like termites in the forest. Just something to take care of the dead wood and nothing special at all.

"Ask your questions. I reckon your husband wouldn't like it if he knew you were spending so much time with another man, even a man like me, so we ought to hurry up and get this over with."

"My husband is off on his own errands these days. He has no interest in you."

"He's a wise man, then."

"I suppose."

She said this like she didn't really know what I meant and was just humoring me. I took offense. My head hurt, and I was rapidly losing control of my tongue. I wanted to hurt her, to make it plain that I didn't take shit off rich ladies with too much time on their hands. The question came to me quick.

"Do you love him?"

I should never have asked that question, because that question seemed to break something open in her, and I became just something she talked at for the next couple of hours. Her talk had been in pieces before, and it continued to be, but as time went on, I began to recognize the pattern and put some things together. If I had wanted to insult this woman and push her off and get her to leave me alone, I failed. Instead, I fell in love with her, and as a result she never left me alone again.

She quit looking at me when she talked. She looked at the ceiling, down at her hands in her lap, and farther down at the cracks between the floorboards. But no matter where she was looking, she was talking. I could not quit looking at her and listening, even when it became plain to me that she was talking to herself, to the walls, to the ceiling, to the hard cold ground outside, which was just possible to see in little splashes of light that fell out of the window.

She told me she had been a little girl in love with her papa and that her papa had been the master of a sugarcane plantation somewhere down in Louisiana. She said it was in a place called Terrebonne, which sounded like *terrible* to me, but I never been good with languages and such. The way she talked about it didn't make it sound terrible. Sounded nice, although not in a way that I knew anything about, something like how a drawing of the western mountains looks nice and pretty, but you don't really know whether they're nice or not because you ain't ever been there or to anywhere like it.

She told me about her papa's wrought-iron porch rail and the gargoyles and cherubs that were molded into it, all connected by twisting iron wisteria and magnolia leaves. She said she thought she could see the whole world from the stoop of that porch, which appeared to be at the center of a conquered land, sugarcane in every direction and all things brought to heel and civilized under her father's command and then made to yield up riches. That was what she knew of the world, that it *worked*, that it made sense, that it could be brought under control. Everything fit just right in her home down there in Terrebonne, she said. She said that the order seemed to work its way out from their house and into the fields and marshes beyond. She said it was all so flat, like the Lord Himself had come along and leveled the imperfections so that they would know that their place was the center of His creation. *For example,* she said, *as a child I often wondered if other people had fig trees like ours in their yard, and it would not have surprised me at all to find out that our fig trees were the only ones in the world. It would not have surprised me to hear that the white herons that stood out like white candles against the green sward of the marsh were the only such herons in the world. That our wet, vine-twisted bayous marked the edge of everything and were the source of all that was good.*

Mariah, the Negro with the prophecy I didn't want to hear, had been her childhood companion. Her only friend, she said. I said that must have been lonely, having only a nigger for a friend, and she looked at me like I hadn't understood a word she'd said, and continued talking. She wasn't sure if Mariah was older or younger than she was, but it had always seemed that Mariah saw things before Carrie ever thought to look. She said that a lot of the Negroes on the plantation said this was because Mariah's mother had the second sight, which she had inherited from her own mother and passed down to her daughter. *Witches, they would call them, and that wasn't an insult exactly,* she said. *I remember Mariah's mother gathering roots, and, if she was walking up the way with the roots wrapped up before her in her apron, the other Negroes would move to the side and make room. She was respected and feared, which I thought were words for the same thing.*

It was the birth of Mariah's baby that changed things, she said. Mariah wasn't married, which wasn't surprising by itself, but they were only children. Mariah and Carrie had always been children, and even if they *were* sixteen or seventeen, the pregnancy and motherhood of Mariah came as a nasty shock to Carrie. The boy baby was named Theopolis, she said, and he came out every bit as pale as Mariah, maybe even paler. Carrie could not look at the baby. That baby was evidence of secrets between the two of them, and she couldn't stand that. *Why hadn't she told me?* I thought she was getting awfully worked up about a relationship with someone who wasn't even white, one of her people, but I had begun to notice that she didn't recognize that distinction, at least when it came to talking about Mariah. Nobody knew who the father was, at least the white folks didn't. Mariah wouldn't tell her. *Just some boy from someplace else, she said to me. I asked her why she hadn't told me about him, and she said it was because she didn't want me to think less of her. She said she wasn't afraid of being pregnant, it was just that she was afraid of me knowing the particulars. I said, "I know the particulars, I'm not as ignorant as you think I am." But in fact I was as ignorant as she thought I was, and I knew the particulars neither of the physical act nor of Mariah's own private performance of it. I could imagine it, though. I felt quite alone of a sudden.*

The world seemed at once more expansive and more pressing on her. *Oppressive*, she said. Where she had thought she'd seen order emanating in an orbit around her house and her family, she saw threat. It was as if every tree, curved so beautifully this way and that, had turned on her and that what she had taken for beauty—beauty created for her enjoyment, pure beauty—was the work of something beyond her control and understanding and was neither beautiful nor ugly, but just itself. *Without meaning. It was the disregard, my own insignificance, the idea that I was being laughed at behind my back or just ignored. And all because of one baby.*

The two girls grew apart a little, although Carrie eventually grew out of her bad feelings about the little baby and helped Mariah take care of him once in a while. Carrie began to wear black, though. I suddenly realized she had probably been wearing black for going on twenty years. *Young girls do not wear black, my mother said. But I ignored her and went about wearing black to show that I understood that none of us knew anything and that what was proper was arbitrary and meaningless. Then I just never stopped wearing it. I got used to it, like we always become accustomed to things. I thought I looked good, I thought the boys I saw every once in a while thought I might be pretty in my black. I learned we can become accustomed to anything, which is why things can seem to us like they're in their proper place when they really aren't. We just don't pay attention after a while.*

She moved her chair into the circle of light thrown off by the solar lamp on the table next to my bed. The chair squeaked and it rocked, and she took to moving it back and forth so that there was noise to fill the emptiness in the air while she thought about what to say next. I was uncomfortable having her so close, because I was uncertain how I might react. I was prone to sudden urges most of my life. When I was running around in the army, I would have the almost irresistible urge to kick someone for no reason or to start cursing at the colonel or to cry. Picking up the colors in the rain of Yankee bullets had been one of those urges that had gotten away from me. The most scary times were when I got the urge to put my arm around one of the smaller boys trying to hoist his rifle onto his shoulder, tell him that I loved him, and give him a kiss on the top of his head. The idea would shoot through my head and be out just before I'd ever have time to act on it. The idea was dangerous, and it frightened me how close I could come to doing something like that, or that I had even thunk it. I was never no "Nancy," for I didn't fancy men, I knew that. But those weird thoughts, urging me to act, would pop up, and they would be powerful. I fought them and they'd disappear. I'd wonder what would happen. If I got the urge to kiss this woman talking next to me, I didn't know if I could resist it.

"What's this got to do with your husband?"

"I'm getting to that. It's not a simple question, Sergeant Cash-well."

"Call me Zachariah."

"I can't just answer that question with a simple yes or no. It's scandalously presumptuous of you to ask the question anyway, so I think you should be quiet while I choose to answer it my own way, if I choose to answer it at all. Are you comfortable? Do you need anything?"

"I don't need anything."

"That's good, Zach."

"Zachariah."

She ignored me and went back to rocking on the chair that squeaked, in and out of the yellow light of the lamp. The shadows on her face got deeper and blacker, and she seemed to gradually disappear as the light from the sky faded. The black shadows on her face matched her dress, I noticed.

She went on about Mariah. She told me how she, Carrie, went about trying to learn to flirt with the boys from the parish and about the endless procession of cousins who came to her father's house for one reason or another. She was not good at it, she said. But she was by God going to get her a sweetheart to teach her the things Mariah already knew, if Mariah was going to keep such things a secret from her. But she was clumsy, and she was shocked to hear that boys didn't like to talk about the books on her daddy's shelf, most of which she'd read part through. She liked to talk about Milton, she said. I didn't know who that was, but she said he wrote about heaven and hell, so I nodded my head because I knew about those things. She'd try to talk to the boys about paradise, and they'd interrupt to talk about sugar prices or the weather or how the neighbor's bull had jumped the pen again or about the blue crawfish they'd pulled out of the swamp. She had nothing to say to them, these boys named Boudreaux, Landrieaux, Pontellier. She loved their skin, though, even their sunburned noses. *I had one thing I could give them, and I knew that they knew this, that they were thinking about it.* Carrie's mother was wise to that, though. She could see what her daughter was fixing to do with those Cajun boys, and she weren't having it. *Mama thought it was bad enough to live in a swamp without getting friendly with the swamp creatures.* And so she run off the boys and began to invite real suitors, and this was worse to Carrie because they were all so old and she didn't like the way they looked at her, like they were shopping.

This was the case until her cousin John arrived on business from Nashville. *They* said *business anyway.* He had been to the plantation on business many times before and was said to have a way with the Negroes and didn't mind spending a lot of time around them, teaching them new farming techniques and assessing their worth for Carrie's father. He was handsome, and when he talked to her, he didn't change the subject when she was talking. *Maybe he wasn't listening, I don't know. But he let me talk about God and poetry and death, and the way things weren't what they seemed, and he never corrected me. I was very appreciative of this. I remembered him from previous visits, of course. He was hard to miss. He was an interesting man.*

"So that was love."

"You're impertinent."

"Just trying to get to the answer."

"You wouldn't want to know what I think love is."

"And why would that be, Mrs. McGavock?"

She looked at me, and I could hear the chair squeaking and filling the entire room with its little noises. I could smell corn bread being burned in the kitchen, and for a moment I could barely keep myself from jumping out of the bed as best I could and going to save it. Keep it from going all black and wasted. Carrie's hair had fallen around her face. I hadn't noticed when it happened. It covered half her face, like a thin screen, and sometimes an eye would shine through, or a lip or a cheek or a tooth. Mostly her eye is what I noticed, though. She spoke from behind that veil.

"Why do you stay in this room?"

I was surprised by this question. She was poking at me. Why did I stay in the room?

"I didn't realize I had a choice. You put me here once you'd taken my leg and thrown it out on the trash heap. I reckoned you felt bad."

"Taking your leg saved your life. Anyway, it was going to be cut off sooner or later, and not by me, and so I believe you should leave off that argument once and for all. It's tiresome and childish. And I don't believe you've come up with the right answer anyway."

"Why do I stay here? Why wouldn't I?"

"I can think of many reasons. You've taken a special privilege over every other man in this house, and you don't appear to me as someone who routinely takes privileges. I'd call you a humble man. Am I wrong?"

"I think you've got the thing pegged all wrong. I may be humble, but no soldier is going to turn down his own bed and special dining privileges, not any soldier I know. Luck went my way, and I got the bed, and I been hunkering down here ever since."

"Even if it's meant hearing men talk about you like you thought you were special?"

"I ain't heard that."

"If I've heard that, surely you have."

The truth was, I had heard it, but every man I heard say something about it knew I could still whup his ass, and he shut up quick. She was right, though. This was a privilege I should have shared, and I hadn't. They had cause to hold that against me. I had never taken privileges. I had always eaten last in the field when we got chow, and I always filled my canteens last, and I always took watch in the middle of the night. That had been my duty as a sergeant as I saw it, and so I'd done it. Now it was different.

"Why are you here?" she asked.

"I don't know."

"Why do you let me, a woman and a stranger, talk to you like this?"

"I don't know."

"Why do you talk back? Why do you listen?"

I knew, I knew. I knew the answer to that. I was there because of her, because I had not ever been so close to a woman who seemed also possessed of that black thread that wound down through time and the fabric of my life, fraying here and there but never leaving me, always growing longer and stronger, pulling me toward God only knows what, nothing good. It surprised me that a woman of means, with such fine things and a family and a beautiful face like polished china, that she would also have been bound by this thread, which could spin and weave around a person until there was nothing left to see of this person, only the black cocoon. I could pull that thread, tie it onto my own, and I knew that I could be at some peace with myself if I did exactly that, spinning her away from the tangles of time.

Time, twisting on and on, always taking away and never bringing anything back, could kill people years before they extricated themselves from their bodies and flew off to God. I had heard her float through the hallways of the house, whispering the names of her children as she blew out the lamps. *John Randal, Mary Elizabeth, Martha.* It sounded like prayer, like some sort of invocation. I'd been in a Catholic church once, down on toward Natchez, and I'd heard the same sound when the priests approached the altar, muttering the sounds that would bring Christ back to them. I didn't much care for that sort of thing, and I had no faith that a priest could work such magic, but I found myself praying that someday, maybe, Carrie McGavock would perform that miracle, that time would get all wrapped up on itself and confused, and that those children would walk the hallways with their mother again. There was beauty in that woman. Not in her pain, but in the part of her obscured by the pain and the black crinkly dress and the black thread of time. I saw a young and beautiful woman, a woman who could lift burdens and redeem men. I wanted to be redeemed, I wanted to be absolved. And I wanted that woman, the angel who walked in the cemetery among her dead children and kissed their gravestones when she thought no one was looking, to be the one doing the redeeming. I had no name for that, no word. Just a feeling.

I answered her question.

"I don't know."

"No, you don't. So perhaps you might consider being polite and listening to me try to answer your question, rather than interrupting me?"

She smiled sweetly, but behind the sweetness I could see her thinking that she had won.

"John McGavock was a kind man. That was all the reason I needed."

"That's it? That's all a man had to be?"

"Yes. Now that I'm trying to remember, I believe that was it. But I hardly think of such things anymore."

25

CARRIE McGAVOCK

That night I told Zachariah everything, everything I could remember. I had never talked to anyone like that. He was captive, and he irritated me in a way that made me want to talk to him even more, to make him see, to make him understand me. I thought I could talk to him like this because he would go away eventually and take with him what I'd said. But that wasn't it entirely. He was so strange, and he was unafraid of me. He was a sinful, flawed man, and those sins lay upon his heroics as accents of color on a plain quilt. He was not like the rest of the men in gray. His sins were what emboldened me, because I knew I could not be judged by him. His sins drew me in.

He lay there like a fidgeting child while I talked, constantly brushing the hair from his eyes and running his fingers through it while trying to look at anything but me. His eyes drifted to the ceiling and then out the window and then to the dresser. He smelled tart and sour, like old vinegar. It was the smell of the Negroes who worked on my father's plantation. He reminded me of them, only he talked back to me. He *challenged* me. Who had ever taken the time to challenge me, to argue with me? This man, who I had presumed was illiterate, paid attention. If as a girl I had loved John because he was a mystery and didn't interrupt me, I became obsessed with the one-legged man in the bed because he was a mystery and he *did* interrupt. I had grown old, and I knew the pain of being left alone with my thoughts. The silence John had given me was no gift, as well intentioned as he was.

I had finished telling Zachariah about my decision to marry John when he abruptly swung himself to the other side of his bed, grabbed the crutches that leaned against the headboard on that side, and drew himself up to his full, now diminished height. I thought he was just fidgeting still, but when I looked at him, he was looking at me sadly.

"I don't want to hear any more. I'm going for a walk."

"I'll come with you."

"I wish you wouldn't."

"Do you know where you're going? In the dark?"

"I'll find my way."

He hobbled over to the far corner where his clothes were piled and awkwardly pulled an old coat over his shoulders. He didn't look back at me when he passed out the door and turned down the passage. I sat for a moment, deciding whether to follow him. I laughed a little. Of course, I'd follow him.

The moon was hidden behind the clouds, but it was bright enough to cast a weak gray light onto the grounds. I watched him turn a slow circle in the yard, always looking outward. I suppose he had been drifting in and out of sleep that day, because he seemed confused by the absence of men. There were no men in the yard anymore. They had all disappeared in the previous day or so, as if they'd sensed something they could not tolerate. Some had even volunteered for the prison wagon. They had escaped this place, one way or another.

He looked over to where we had piled the dead and the leavings of the surgeons, and they were gone, too. He was alone except for me. My hands looked odd in the light, hard to distinguish from the ground or anything around me. I felt my own self falling into the depth of an empty night. I felt light-headed, as if the boundaries that described my body and my head—the neat lines between here and there—were dissipating to gray, losing their definition and precision, and that I was becoming indistinguishable from the air and the colorless clouds of breath rising from each of us. If I looked at Zachariah just right, he seemed a ghost, too.

"Where the hell is everybody?"

"They're gone. Not everyone, but almost everyone."

"I've been left behind, then."

I walked over to him, where he stood between the house and the old cemetery. His eyes were narrowed, and he frightened me.

"Left behind is a matter of interpretation, I guess. It depends on knowing where you had wanted to go and where you are, and the difference between the two. Where had you wanted to go?"

He was frantic, and he began hobbling quickly toward the corner of the house by the garden, to see if the side yard was empty, too.

"Shut the hell up. Just shut the *hell* up. You talk too damned much. That little bastard Jerrod left me, too."

I shut up and followed behind him slowly. When I caught up to him, he was leaning against the side of the house and breathing heavily, looking out at the empty side yard and the empty drive. Flecks of paint fell onto his shoulders as he rocked against the side of the house, scraping his back against it like he was trying to push it down. *We must get the house painted*, I thought, and immediately realized that I wasn't all there, like I was floating above events. There was no sound except for the crunch of the ground beneath my shoes, and the hiss of air as he breathed through his teeth.

"The bastards left me. Almighty. How the hell am I going to get out of here?"

His voice broke a little, but he coughed and covered it up. The coughing became a hacking, and he had to bend over for a moment before straightening up and holding his hand to his head.

"My head hurts. Dammit."

"Come inside."

"I'm fine right here. You'll tell me where the hell everyone went, and then you will send me on that way, too."

"You're in no condition to go anywhere."

He moved quicker than I imagined possible for someone on crutches. His hand shot out and took hold of my hair, and he yanked my head back. My throat was cold and indecently exposed, I remember thinking, before the pain hit me and I gasped. He wound the hair tighter in his hand, and he pulled my face right to his, as if it were weightless and not attached to my body. His breath smelled like rotting hay.

"I'll kill you. Don't want to, but I'll kill you. I've killed many less deserving than you. I don't love you enough not to kill you. Did you think I did? You're a strange woman, and you don't know a thing about me and you don't care. I ain't your toy, your pet. You will save me, do you hear me? You will make sure I am not left behind, or I will kill you and your husband and your niggers, and then I will steal what I need and I will make my own way. Do you understand me? *Where the hell is Jerrod? What did you do with him?*"

When he slipped, he fell quickly and hard. His good leg went out from under him as he pulled back on my hair. He had forgotten his limitations. I could feel the tears streaming down my cheeks and the burn at the back of my head, and then I was released and he was lying on the ground.

He'd said he loved me.

I picked up one of his crutches and swung it as hard as I could at his head, and I felt it strike him square in the face. He screamed. Some blood flowed dark down his mouth to his chin. I swung it again and hit his stomach. He'd said he loved me. I swung it again and again like I'd seen men do when they were chopping wood, and again and again he yelled. I would be doing the killing now. I would not let him leave. I couldn't stop. He was vulnerable to me. *He loved me.*

I aimed at his head over and over and over, and his shouts became whispers and then silence. I would never stop. He would stay here.

There was pleasure, intense pleasure. I thought I could see every blade of grass in the dark and every frayed thread in his coat and every single drop of blood. I could see it all, so clearly, more clearly than anything I'd ever seen in my life. His arms flopped out from his sides, like a scarecrow.

Not since I was a child had I thought I could order the world to my liking, in the way I imagined it should be. It was the ordering that was important, not the beating of Cashwell. The killing and the beating and the violence were allowable because they were mine to dole out, they came from me. I was their bearer, no one else. He would not leave, not ever. I began to cry from joy, or from relief.

The hands that grabbed my shoulders and lifted me up were strong and black and callused. I thought they were God's.

"Miss Carrie! Miss Carrie! No, Miss Carrie. You ain't to do this, not this. No, ma'am. No, ma'am."

It was Theopolis, and when he spun me around and I looked up at him, he was as frightened and determined as I'd ever seen a man. I sobbed up at him, hard, like I was hacking something awful up. I looked into his face and hated him, too. He was the child who had complicated everything by his birth. His face was almost as white as mine, and I hated him even more for that. How dare he not be black as night? What right did he have to glow in the faltering moonlight, to hold me, to keep me from doing *anything*? I would have him whipped—yes, I would. I beat his chest, and he gripped me tighter. He had smiled at me once that night he was born, and I had known he was innocent. He was innocent, and so he was more monstrous for the havoc he caused. I cursed him and cried and leaned against him.

"Who is that, Miss Carrie? Who is this? What he done?"

I knew I couldn't tell him. This was an impossible situation. The Negro son of Mariah had his hands on me, and a Confederate soldier lay at our feet, possibly dead. *Someone's going to die for this,* I thought. Whatever had driven me to violence flowed out of me. I saw things clear again. I looked up at Theopolis again. *What a beautiful face, what a beautiful man,* I thought. He must not suffer. I looked down at Zachariah. *What a beautiful face, what a beautiful man.*

"Did he hurt you, Miss Carrie?"

"No."

"Then why you beat him like that?"

"I don't know."

I knew what to do then, right then. My mind was so clear I heard the beetles crawling through the dead leaves at my feet; I felt every tremor in Theopolis's hand, every contraction of muscle and sinew. I knew exactly what I would do and how I would handle this. No one would be hurt. Everything that had happened here would be analyzed and categorized according to my wishes, and all I had to do was remain silent.

Theopolis looked down at me and drew his lips tight, as if he thought he understood. *They'll believe I'm crazy, they've always believed I'm crazy. That will save us all.*

"You ain't all right, are you, Miss Carrie?"

I just smiled and smiled. I began planning Zachariah's funeral. We would bury him in the north corner of the cemetery, away from all the McGavocks. There would be no headstone, and after a time only I would remember where he was.

I cried. Who was the monster now? I told Theopolis to go away, that I would stay with the body until daylight, when we could see properly and could move it. He said I must not do any such thing, that I had to come into the house, that he could carry the dead man anywhere in the blackest night. I told him to bring me a blanket and leave me be. I told him I wanted to watch the sun rise. He shook his head and fetched a blanket, and I sat down next to Zachariah, who breathed shallowly next to me as I leaned against the house and waited for the day to begin.

26

FRANKLIN

John walked his horse through the town. The street was torn up, and the trees and houses on either side of the road were pocked with bullet holes or shredded by artillery fire. Articles of clothing lay in the road next to the sidewalks—shoes, hats, shirts—as if their owners had been snatched and lifted up out of their corporeal misery and made to disappear, leaving behind the things they'd no longer need.

Carrie had sent the children off, and since then she had not once noticed his coming or going. For all she knew, he'd been gone for a week. He had time. He had been coming to town for supplies he rarely found, and now he was in search of mercy from a man who would not possess it. Another wasted trip perhaps, but so what? He had time.

It was a few minutes before he noticed that the dead were gone. Elsewhere he had become accustomed to the sight of men lugging off the bodies, but here in its center the town seemed emptied of everyone, the living and the dead. He was looking down the road, straight down the center, and knew he was looking into the heart of the whole mess, the place where the violations of human decency had been the most common, and it was almost deserted. Denuded, like a field after a grass fire. The houses were still there, bearing their wounds, but there was no life about them. No one walking around. *Maybe they're still hiding in their basements, waiting. Waiting for what? For something to end? What would that be? How long had it been since everything happened? A day? Three days? I've lost track of the time.* He began to wander, his purpose forgotten.

His path took him generally in the direction of the poor side of town, called Blood Bucket by the locals because of their belief that much blood was spilled there every weekend after its inhabitants had drunk their fill. It had long been a white enclave for failed farmers, gamblers, and drifters. A few years before, though, free Negroes had begun settling there, and because their freedom was always an open question, they kept to themselves and stuck close to their homes. If there had to be free Negroes, the thinking went among the town's leaders and its hotheads, it was best that they kept quiet and bottled up by themselves. No sense bringing them into contact with the other Negroes, *their* Negroes. No telling what kind of havoc might be caused by open communication.

John knew that most of his neighbors were still flummoxed by the notion of a free Negro, but it didn't shock John much. There had always been free Negroes, freed for one reason or another, usually the magnanimity that occasionally came over old masters facing death, especially if they had no heirs. John himself had known a number of freed Negroes in New Orleans quite well, during that time in his life when he traveled to Louisiana on business, before he married Carrie. Some of them were as white as he was and twice as cultured. This had surprised him, and he had been forever on his guard against seeming less than refined in their presence, for fear of embarrassing himself in front of a Negro, however white their skin. The thing that had shocked John the most was that they were proud of being Negroes.

In Blood Bucket the houses were short and leaned this way and that. Porches sloped, and the piers they were built upon seemed to sag in toward each other, like drunks trying to catch their balance. Every manner of odd amendment had been made to the houses when it suited their occupants. A window tacked on here, an extra room there, maybe a fireplace. The houses may have once had a design, but they had grown and expanded like natural things, like things that bent and twisted toward the light.

There was a dry goods store in Blood Bucket. It was too much to call it a store, really. It was a house owned by an old black man who occasionally got his hands on some things—shoes one week, rolls of homespun the next, liquor every week—and didn't mind selling them. John strolled over to see the man. He had all the time in the world, and he didn't mind using it.

Joe was the man's name, just Joe as far as John knew. Little Negro children stared out from between the weatherworn balusters of their front porches, while their mothers went about boiling clothes and hanging the laundry on lines. He noticed the women didn't wear shoes and that their toes curled under themselves, conserving heat against the cold ground. They called to their children, but their children did not listen. Or they couldn't hear while the wind whistled down the alleys and through the eaves of their porches. They watched John walk by, their eyes glistening and crusted at the edges. Their mothers hung laundry and cursed the wind. They were the lucky Negroes, they were free. *They still look like slaves*, John thought. He could imagine ten thousand slaves hanging laundry on ten thousand lines at that very moment. Barefoot. The difference, John noted, was that their children watched him walk down the middle of their street. They paid him close attention, as if he and his horse, walking slowly and warily behind him, were circus animals on parade. But they didn't run away. Or, rather, they did not turn their backs on him. Maybe that was it, John thought. *They're keeping watch.*

Old Joe was watching him, too. John had been selling bits and pieces of Carnton to Joe for two years. Joe knew people who knew people who would buy such things as ceramic cigar stands and silver pens. These were the little things John could sneak out of the house without Carrie noticing. John wondered how much of Joe's apparent prosperity had been bought with McGavock heirlooms. He scuffed across the dirt yard and shrugged his shoulders. It didn't matter.

Joe just rocked back and forth on the back legs of the chair he had set out in the front yard of neatly raked hard-packed ground. John watched him stop rocking, balance on the back legs that had dug deep holes in the ground, and then slowly allow the earth to draw him back down until he was firmly planted again. Joe had decent clothes, clean dungarees without a patch anywhere, a boiled cotton shirt, and a coat made out of an almost new blanket, altered to fit his long arms and narrow shoulders. He let his head stay bare, and John wondered if that was not for poverty's sake, but because he had a fine, lustrous head of gray hair that looked like a collection of silver curlings. A manly head of hair.

John had never avoided Blood Bucket, as so many others in town did. After he'd sent his own slaves off, he'd found it necessary to come in and hire day labor occasionally, when he and Theopolis couldn't handle a job themselves. He never brought Theopolis with him. Sometimes he'd drive in with Mariah, who knew women who would sell her sundries for much less than the white traders. He didn't mind bringing Mariah because he knew her, and knew she loved Carrie, and knew that she would never get her head turned by the illusory promises of freedom. Mariah was smarter than that, he knew, but Theopolis was still too young.

He also knew that Mariah occasionally came into Blood Bucket on her own to visit an old root doctor. This was a side of her he chose not to know anything about. He just barely tolerated it.

"What say, Colonel John?"

"Just taking a walk, Joe. Making my rounds."

John didn't exactly know why he'd come to talk to Joe, and he had only a vague idea of what he wanted to ask him. He didn't have the words to put it just right.

"You seen anything, Joe?"

"Now, Colonel John, I got eyes. I see a whole lot. A whole lot. That ain't a question I can take good aim at. I *heard* things, too, yes, I have."

"What have you heard?"

"I'm not sure I know."

"Don't play with me. You know better than that."

"I'm not sure I do, Colonel John."

"Do what?"

"Know better than that."

The sun streaked through the clouds, and the light fell upon Joe's face. Shadows hid part of him, but his eyes gave off a shine. He smiled and chuckled and looked past John toward the end of the street. John imagined he was standing at the center of the earth and that lines of disruption radiated out from where he stood, from where the old man sat on his chair, like the lines of violence that emanated from the center of an artillery crater, thick gashes in the ground that tapered many yards away into a filigree of delicate lines traced by pebbles momentarily blown about and then left to rest again, forever. It was vertiginous, the feeling that came over him. For a moment he wanted nothing more than to sit on the old man's lap and have him whisper secrets into his ear, to tell him the things he needed to know, the things he might tell his grandchildren. He laughed out loud, and Joe narrowed his eyes at him. *Absurd, absurd! What could a Negro tell me? Children, all of them. What would a Negro be wise about that could ever concern me?* He had heard of people, white people, who claimed special wisdom for the Negro on account of their experience and closer proximity to man's natural, primitive state. John knew better. John knew they were no more primitive than he was, nor were they any more wise. Had they not fallen from paradise along with everyone else? They had. Along with their knowledge of the world came the same complication, and with the same complication came the scheming and the struggle and the betrayals and the inexorable slide into sin and disappointment. *When did I start thinking like a theologian?* He was fascinated by the man sitting before him, who chewed on the inside of his cheek and rocked in his chair.

"I seen your nigra girl go down the road just a little while ago. Gone to see Miss Eloisa for some knowledge, I do believe."

John was slowly emerging from his fog.

"Who?"

"That nigra girl. Mariah."

It had begun to snow. The flakes were hard, or seemed hard on John's bare neck. Joe looked up and let a few flakes strike him in the face before lifting himself up from his chair and dragging it back to his porch, which was protected by eaves. The legs of the chair left black tracks in the snow that already lay on the ground. John's horse stamped and shook his head. John watched snowflakes disappear into Joe's head—first they were sitting there upon the wiry gray, and then they were gone. John reached up and felt the wet upon his own head. Snowflakes were rare enough in Franklin to give pause, but not rare enough to bring joy. The flakes seemed to hurl themselves to the ground, white streaks shot directly to their appointed places and then, arriving softly, freezing the earth below them. Flake by flake, Franklin was freezing in place. *Good*, John thought. *Freeze it over. Freeze everything over. Stop this thing from growing.*

"Why don't you come out of the wet, Colonel John? Come on up here, it's warmer. Got the stove going inside, and I can feel it out here."

"Guess I will."

John tied his horse to Joe's fence, climbed the two wood steps, concave like saddles, and sat down on an old stool next to the door. Joe was right—the heat escaped under the door and through the chinks between the siding.

"You got whiskey, Joe?"

"Always got whiskey."

Joe went inside and a moment later came out with an old brown jar made of glass, the kind a doctor might have had on his shelf. Joe saw John eyeing the jar.

"You ain't the only one who sells his things to me."

Joe poured a jigger's worth into a tin cup and handed it to John. John sniffed. Flavored moonshine that smelled like rotted peaches. It smelled good. *Liquor changes everything, even the meaning of smells.* John threw it down like a practiced drinker.

"You said Mariah was down here? Where?"

"She gone down to see Miss Eloisa and her roots. Roots and powders and such."

"Eloisa puts on curses?"

"I wouldn't cross her, but don't know nothing about curses, though."

"No, you wouldn't. But you'd go see her, wouldn't you? You'd go see her if you hated someone enough, or wanted something badly enough, right?"

"I've been to see Miss Eloisa, yes, sir."

John found himself rubbing the beams of the porch, admiring the rough craftsmanship that had created a house whose lineaments could not be named, whose shape could not be found in any book of architecture, but which was solid nevertheless. He knocked his knuckles against the tan weathered wood of the doorway and listened for the note. *Cedar posts, that sound is unmistakable.* He wished he could knock on the heads of people and suss out their characters by the ringing in his ears. He wondered what Mariah was doing. Thoughts of Baylor and his debt had left him entirely, piddling things next to the fears that were beginning to rise up in his head. He felt nervous and prickly and couldn't immediately explain why.

Joe was staring down the road, toward the north end of town where the road met the pike and went on to Nashville. A figure appeared in the slackening snow shower. Shoeless and thin, thin like the ghost of one of the Confederate dead. He'd seen the body a thousand times before, only he'd seen it still and quiet, lying next to one of the holes that the gravediggers were still—*I can still hear them, the picks and the shovels!*—carving out of the frozen ground. This figure was not dead. It carried only a rifle. John stared with Joe, rapt. The man—it was obviously a man—came along a little farther before stopping at one of the houses across the street. He had an old blanket around his shoulders sewn with a boot lace into a cape, and he'd wrapped his head in a torn piece of shirt cloth as if he were a Mohammedan. He held his right hand high up on the porch rail and let his head sag down past his chest to his knees, retching. Nothing came out, which seemed to make him furious. He took his rifle and swung it like a club at the front door of the little shack, shouting for food.

"Give me your goddamn food, nigger. I see you in there with all your little bastards. I . . . can . . . see . . . you! Feed me, for God's sake. Just a biscuit. I'll protect you, I swear."

He had only enough strength to strike the door three times before sinking to the floor and letting the rifle clatter down onto the porch. He didn't move when it slipped down the steps and planted itself muzzle-first into the dirt. He didn't seem to notice.

The man had come from Nashville, John realized. He had heard they had gone on to Nashville after the Yankees, he just never thought they'd come back. The man was so thin it was easy for John to see that his chest was sunken, even through the mismatched layers of the man's clothing. His head drooped upon his chest, and the hinge of his jaw, outlined in shadow, was plainly visible from across the street. Here was what was left of the Southern ideal, the Southern man: starvation, filth, confusion, exhaustion. The man rasped and spit over the rail of the porch. He was hungry and cold and weak. He was human. His appearance undermined any notion of a special Southern exception, a separate branch of humankind. He was as broke-down and anonymous as any man would have been, Southern or not, had he fled barefoot from Nashville to save his life. He was the end and the beginning. The rest of the army would be coming, too.

The man across the street had fallen asleep. The soles of his feet were black and scabbed over. A hand parted the sheets that passed for window curtains, and John could see a pair of night-black eyes staring down at the soldier, whose age was impossible to tell. John thought of Mariah. He was quickly overcome by desperation.

"Joe, where did you say Eloisa lives?"

Joe was busy gathering his things—various bottles and jars, his chairs, a bag of old rice—and tossing them inside his house. He pulled closed the shutters he'd made out of scrap boards and was entirely uninterested in what the white man on his porch had to say. He'd figured out what was happening just as quickly as John.

"What, Colonel John?"

"Eloisa's. Where is it?"

"Down farther the way you was coming, turn left at the white chapel, look for the tin house on the right with all them whirligigs in the front yard."

"All right."

"You looking for that nigra of yours?"

"Mariah."

"You best hurry on. And I'd take that horse with you quick, or it be et up soon enough."

The whirligigs were preposterous. John marveled at how much junk and energy had gone into making them. Blades made of old rusted tin sheeting caught the wind and spun long wooden rods, hand-carved, which in turn moved the diminutive wooden figures at the other end in all manner of ways. There was the wooden man ceaselessly bending over with his bucket to scoop water, there was the preacher pounding his pulpit with the same fist, over and over and over again, and there were the two little men facing each other with shovels, each digging while the other tossed the imaginary dirt over his shoulder. There was a witch at her cauldron and a dog snapping at a runaway's heels. Each whirligig faced into the wind, and at least a hundred of varying sizes—some small enough to fit in John's palm, others bearing figures the size of midgets—cluttered the yard. There was no escaping the wind at Miss Eloisa's house, John reckoned. Even if you had wanted to.

The house itself was like every other in Blood Bucket—improvised, improbable. It was tin, every square inch of it. Although John knew there must be wood beneath, the tin facade looked entirely unnatural, like something coughed out whole from one of those big, black-smoke factories he'd read about in *Harper's Weekly*. It would not have surprised him if the house itself was attached to a spindle and spun around if the wind was strong enough. It did not seem the sort of place a person would live in; it was the sort of place one might store things.

John walked up to the door, which was also covered in tin but punched with small holes in the shape of a giant rooster. He knocked and heard only a murmur behind the door. He waited and knocked again. He thought he heard moaning.

He opened the door, and rows of jars winked at him from every wall. The beams that held the roof on were exposed, black from soot, and ran the length of the small room. There was a table in the slap dead center of the room, and a figure sat at each end of it. In all four corners of the room John saw piles of wild things, the reaching and weaving tendrils of roots taken whole out of the ground, redolent of damp Tennessee soil ground out by the slip of glaciers, the beating of the wind, the trodding of feet. Other roots hung from the ceiling joists. Under the room's only window, on the left, stood a small table bearing a pile of chicken feathers upon it, neatly gathered. The next thing John noticed was the flash of two sets of eyes, black and white all at once, as they took him in.

"Hello, Mariah."

He expected Mariah to be shocked, and maybe a little afraid of him discovering her, but neither emotion passed across her face. Nothing passed across her face. Both Mariah and Miss Eloisa looked at him, and he could see he was being assessed, not as a threat, but simply as a fact, as if he were one of the posts that supported the roof, so familiar that they were practically invisible. Miss Eloisa turned back to the mortar and pestle she had been using. The muscles in her forearm were stringy and long, and they flexed as she crushed and scraped a green root into powder. John tried again.

"Mariah, we'd best be getting on now. There are soldiers coming, and I think we'd all be safer back at the house."

Mariah stood, and Eloisa watched her, amused.

"Safe from what, Mr. McGavock?" Eloisa asked.

He was now conscious of her standing there, looking him in the eye like he was her peer.

"Gather your things and let's go."

"I expect you'd best not be going anywhere, mister." Miss Eloisa's voice sounded distant and thin, like the whispering that tall trees make when their tops rub against each other in the wind. It was a voice so tremulous it was ever in danger of cutting out altogether, and every word floated out after great effort. She was still grinding at her root, but now she had half stood and was leaning down on it as if to push it through the table and back into the earth. She talked without looking away from her work. John spoke up again.

"And why would that be?"

"They already here."

"I only saw one."

"They already here. You ain't a-making it out of town, not now. At least your horse ain't, and maybe not Mariah, neither."

"There's nobody in town."

"I seen them."

"I don't believe in your sight."

"That don't mean nothing. And if you don't believe me, ask your *nigger* what *she* seen."

Mariah was looking up toward the rafters, where cascading clumps of roots and leaves and herbs hung tied together. Her face had gone smooth, expressionless. The permanent wrinkles of a woman accustomed to squinting in the sun had disappeared.

"Mariah?"

"Mr. John, I think we better stay here for a time. It's safe here. They won't mess with this place."

John was beginning to feel that he was the last man in Tennessee and that all its women had decided they could get on without him. He was becoming angry. He wished Eloisa would quit with the powder and look at him.

"There is only one, and he was as unthreatening as a clod of mud. Practically dead, and he might be dead right now by the look of him. There might be others, but I didn't see them, and I think we've got time to go."

"You didn't see them."

"No."

"Look out the window, Mr. John."

John looked over to the window where the feathers rested upon the little table, catching the dim, filtered light. He walked over and felt the things dangling from the rafters sway at the vibrations of his feet upon the boards. The tin exoskeleton of the house creaked and clanked as the house shifted under his weight. He leaned on the window jamb and peered out. He had to blink his eyes. He blinked and took refuge in the dark and then opened his eyes again to a scene he could not credit.

He was not confused by the fact that the entire Confederate army was now streaming back through Franklin. This he had expected. It seemed natural. No, it was what the army had become. Or, rather, what the men had become.

In his youth his tutor had taught him Latin, and he had read medieval poems and accounts of armies of the dead arrayed against the chivalrous forces of good, skeleton men with terrible sunken eyes and permanent grins wielding sharp spears. His tutor had been fired for bringing those books into the house. They were not the Bible, nor were they the work of the Athenians or the Romans, nor were they the work of the pious Dark Age papists like Bernard of Clairvaux. They were godless ghost stories, his father had said, and blasphemous. His father had said, *In life we are imperfect but reasonable approximations of the character of our souls. In death we become a crystal of ourselves, a perfectly condensed figure of our souls, of our character. We are not then rounded up and sent off to battle like a raggedy bunch of conscripts. Skeleton armies indeed. Our souls have no business with the earth. The state of our soul is all, it's everything, it is eternal. Sow muddleheaded credulity in your soul now, and you will become a muddlehead evermore, a confused and misguided boy forever.* His father had allowed him to keep the Dante his tutor had given him, and he burned the rest.

But the men were nothing if not a collection of the skeletal and the empty-eyed, moving along as if under the command of someone unseen. They walked and hobbled down the street in front of the house and down every street John could see from the window, all headed generally south. They were an army, and yet not one of them seemed connected to the other by anything other than a common desire to move ahead. They scarcely spoke to each other, although occasionally one could be seen carrying another. There were no officers, no horses, no carts. Many had lost their rifles. Three men passed closely by the window without looking into it. The first had wrapped a bandage around his head, and John could see the impression of his ear perfectly represented in blood, as if someone had drawn it upon the white cloth. The second man was short, and moved with the help of a stick upon what appeared to be a smashed and useless foot. He sucked at his thick blond mustache, the only spot of color upon him, as it curled over his front lip. When he accidentally stepped upon his bad foot, he'd suck so hard at his mustache that the flesh of his face slipped down and his eyes deformed into permanent sadness. The third man, white as an albino, did not seem hurt at all. He walked slowly but without effort. His eyes roamed from side to side, and occasionally he'd stop to assess those around him. No one paid attention to him. He wore blue pants and a gray blouse and riding boots. He had no coat. John watched him overtake the short man with the bad foot, walking alongside for a while, before reaching over and lifting the man by his coat collar and removing it. He put it on, and his arms shot through the end of the sleeves by three inches. The little man never protested and began to shiver. The two men walked off together, and the taller one put his arm around the shorter one for a time before withdrawing it. They never spoke a word. As John watched, the short man fell farther and farther behind until he was alone, and then he disappeared over a rise in the road.

John turned to Eloisa.

"How did you know this?"

"I listen, Mr. John. It's no big thing. I pay attention. Don't need no roots to hear an army." She laughed at him.

"Can we stay here?"

"Oh yes, Mr. John. That was what I was hoping for."

"Just a little while."

"A little while, sure enough."

John walked over to Mariah and tried to say something to comfort her, but she needed no comforting. She had sat back down at the table and yawned. A piece of dried thistle floated down from the rafters and lit upon her shoulder. She looked at it and let it stay. John slid his back down the smooth paneling boards and rested on the floor, drawing his black coat around him and thinking that he would probably never see his horse again.

27

CARRIE McGAVOCK

I stayed with Zachariah long past sunrise. John had gone to town for one of his Temperance rallies, or in search of drink. If either one of us saw the irony in this, and silently we both did, neither one of us ever spoke of it. Mariah had gone to town earlier the day before and not returned. In the past I would have feared for her safety, but we no longer had the luxury to live in our past, so it was left to Theopolis to tend to me, to worry over me, to make me see reason.

I huddled against the side of the house and stroked Zachariah's head and his thick hair made thicker by ages of sweat. I had stroked the heads of Winder and Hattie this way when they were hurt, and this thought made me wish I'd never sent them away. Lord, I pined for them all, the living and the dead, whom I had brought into the world. Who was comforting them now? They were my children, my loves, and yet they were gone, and instead, I had in my arms a soldier upon whom I had beaten the fact of my loneliness. All was twisted and wrong.

I knew he was alive, but didn't tell Theopolis. He was breathing lightly, and so I piled another blanket on his chest to conceal its rise and fall. So long as he was dead he was mine alone, mine to reckon with and mine to make peace with. If it were commonly known that he was alive, I would not have been able to stop the others from spiriting him off and reviving him. I dreaded his awakening; in his sleep he could not accuse me.

Theopolis, unsuccessful in his various attempts to haul us both into the house, built a fire at my feet. I was watching the embers fade to white around midday when I saw the first of the soldiers rear up upon the rise at the edge of our property and stumble on toward us. The first was followed by two more, and eight more after that, and fairly soon I watched what remained of our army meander back down the pike and over our fields, never looking up and never stopping. I shivered and silently prayed that they would make it home.

"They came back. I knew they'd come back."

Zachariah was awake. I was mesmerized by the army in retreat and did not at first think the sound of his voice anything extraordinary.

"Funny thing, though. I got no interest in going with them now. If I did, you beat that out of me anyway. I'm hungry."

The sun was almost halfway through its arc across the sky when it disappeared and the snow began to fall. It fell slowly, and drifted this way and that like a soft curtain. The flakes disappeared on contact, sucked up into the fire and into the dark black dirt around it, until it had fallen long enough that it overcame resistance and turned the earth white.

Zachariah rose to his feet and fell.

"My head is spinning. I'm freezing."

"I'll get Theopolis."

"You know the Yankees won't be far behind. Those boys are running, and they don't run for nothing. Look at them. They're going as fast as they can. Maybe they can hear me. *Run, boys, run!*"

I got to my feet and began pounding on the side of the house and calling for Theopolis. The house seemed to angle out over me, as if it were watching, or as if it were about to fall upon us both.

"They'll come for me, you know."

I could only hear the shuffle of feet along the snow-dusted pike. It was loud, deafening. The men passing by the house looked at us but didn't say a word, just walked on and into the woods. The blood had frozen black upon their faces. I looked down at Zachariah, who was holding his head in one hand and trying to blow on the cold fire.

"Who will come for you? No one seems to be stopping."

"The Union troops. They've got me. They love a prisoner. They'll be here soon, I'm sure. To take me away. I'll go, too. I'll go."

I pounded harder and harder on the house until I'd cut the palm of my hand on a brick edge. Theopolis stuck his head around the corner of the porch and then vaulted the balustrade.

28

FRANKLIN

John hadn't moved. He had shut his eyes, leaning back against the paneling of Miss Eloisa's wall. He sat for five minutes, and then ten, and then thirty. He listened to the boots upon the road and tried to count the men by the distinction of their gaits. After a while he opened his eyes and looked over at Mariah, but she had put her head down facing away from him, toward the fire. He could hear her soft, unconscious breaths as she slept away the ebbing of the Confederate army. Eloisa ground and ground at her root.

He felt light, like he would float up to the rafters and bump up against the slats of the roof if he didn't hold on to something tight. He had trouble breathing and for the first time noticed the odd smoke coming from a pot in the fire. It was bluish, and as it gathered around the room, it was barely visible.

New Orleans was a sunken, decrepit, and beautiful place entirely run over by graspers and con men, and it was a matter of pride for me that I was not taken in by schemes. But it made me distrustful and hard, an uncomfortable way of living. On every business trip I always rode down into the southern parishes to my cousin's plantation in Terrebonne Parish, where I could rest. I am not a distrustful and hard man, I am not a grasper or a schemer or a thief. And so I enjoyed the hospitality of my uncle, who was none of those things, either, and who reminded me that I was to become a man of property and position and honor. There was a plantation waiting for me back in Tennessee.

Before one of those visits, I'd had a particularly hard time with a Creole trader who said he thought very little of our cotton. I learned that the Creole was taking our cotton and selling it at a premium as a special strain of Alabama lowland cotton, specially picked by slaves bred to possess particularly long fingers for stripping cotton without fraying its fibers. It was absurd, and a lie, and a con he had run on me. I was angry, and I went back to the Fauborg St. Mary to sit in my room and collect my thoughts. Then I returned to the St. Louis, where I found the trader again.

I challenged him. He fiddled with the button on his high collar, which sat below a thin, freckled face and eyes like a vole's. He laughed in my face and stomped his high-heel boots and said, "I'll kill you in your sleep before you see me out at the dueling tree, Americain." His fellows guffawed and slapped each other's backs.

I walked out and was afraid, afraid for my life. I had never before been afraid for my life, nor had I ever felt such hatred for that trader's kind. He's a Negro, he's a Negro, *I said to myself over and over as I walked to my hotel and cleared out, resigning myself to having been bested in the deal.* He's a Negro. He's low, he has no honor, even if his suits are made for him personally and his women summer in France. He's just a nigger. *The more I said this to myself, the happier I became. It was* my *fault for doing business with a son of Ham, not his. What could I have expected?*

It got so that I could chuckle at myself for my folly because I had not been bested by an equal, I'd been betrayed by a lower man, and that's what lower men do. Nothing more to expect.

I will say that this changed my view, temporarily, of the Negro. Or more to the point, it changed the way I was inclined to treat the Negro. And this meant that when I arrived at my cousin's two days later, when I walked up the steps of the house where my future wife lived, I was newly receptive to the invitation of a group of my cousins—there were always cousins of various degrees of descent hanging around the place— who enjoyed making nocturnal visits to the cabins. I suppose I'd always known what they were doing, but this time I was curious to see for myself. I was not appalled, as I'd once been, by the very idea.

It had never crossed my conscious mind to ask who the young Negress was. It had never occurred to me that she was anyone. She was a feeling, a smell, an event. It was not fair to think that such a memory had a name, a history. My memory with no name had never said a word, only gripping the rough edges of her hand-hewn bedposts with her black hands, knuckles turning gray. She never opened her eyes, and so I closed mine. She did not struggle, but she did not acquiesce, either. Her body did not receive me, did not ease backward with my motion as if catching me, but remained still and hard and impenetrable in every way but the crucial one. I felt shame. I felt shame while I was in her cabin. It was the shame that made me move harder and faster, that made her sweat smell so rancid and so wonderful. It was the shame that spurred me on, that gave me pleasure. I was degraded and I was degrading, all at once. Nothing lower than that, I reckoned. I did not last long, and I stumbled out.

Mariah's voice jolted him.

"They breaking your things, Miss Eloisa."

John opened his eyes and saw Mariah sitting up in her chair, looking out the window; he followed her gaze. Some of the soldiers stopped to watch the whirligigs, as flummoxed by the sight as John himself had been. Their faces softened, and they seemed like children for a moment. John thought he saw their eyes turning and turning in small circles a moment behind the motion of the whirligigs. One by one, with smiles on their faces, men walked into the yard and yanked the whirligigs off their posts or out of the ground and either carried them away or cast them down at their feet. The tin crumpled, and the figures bent under their boots. John, watching, thought of the word *wanton* and knew what it meant. There was no reason for the destruction except that it could be done and that it bestowed upon the men some sort of joy that John could almost understand. If he had gained nothing else from the long day, he had gained an understanding of the paradox he watched acted out in the root doctor's front yard. *In the random, order.* Many instances of order, a form of order for every man who stepped foot in the yard, an order known only to the man himself and therefore inscrutable. John had developed a new idea of order, and he knew there was no turning back from it. John could understand the trampling of the whirligigs in a way he wouldn't have the day before. The whirligigs, endlessly repeating the same motion again and again, could not escape the chaos. *Would* not escape the chaos if those soldiers had anything to say about it, by God.

Miss Eloisa slowly stroked her cheek with one long finger and watched the events in her front yard unfold without flinching or even frowning. Her face was immobile and knowing.

"They break anyway, Mariah. They break someday, why not today?"

She looked into the mortar where she'd been grinding the root, sniffed at it, and seemed satisfied. She pulled a rag out of her pocket and poured all but a little into it, then folded it up and handed it to Mariah. She took the rest and put it in her palm, and while looking straight into John's eyes, she blew the powder at him. John tried to watch it flutter to the ground, but it seemed to disappear. He became angry and got quickly to his feet.

"What was that?"

"Can't say."

"Damn you! What was that?"

"You don't believe in me, in these roots. What you care?"

John conceded the point silently while frowning down at the little black woman in her head scarf. He knew he shouldn't care, and yet he was afraid.

"I believe in you. Now tell me what it is."

Mariah quietly slipped her little parcel into a pocket among her skirts.

"I can't. It won't work then."

"It won't work how?"

Mariah rose to her feet and seemed to John to be decades younger. It was the light, he thought. She reached back into her pocket, pulled a pinch of the powder out, and let it drift down upon her head. Eloisa laughed and clapped her hands.

"You will never find out, Mr. John. Just a mystery . . ."

Her voice trailed off. She let her face relax until it was without expression, and then she turned her back and walked to the other side of the room, where she stood with her back to them and ran her hands through the chicken feathers. John had the odd feeling that time had resumed again and that he no longer existed in that room. He had been fearful of the two Negro women, even *deferent* to them. He no longer felt that way. His old sense of control returned. His sense of place. If the world had changed, he had changed with it. He would have to be sharp from now on, not only aware of trouble but prepared for it. This understanding gave him power, he thought, in an unpredictable and merciless place. It would take strength to be merciful now. He looked at Mariah.

"Let's go."

"Yes, sir."

They walked out into the yard and stepped around the whirligigs and mounted Josiah. Miracle of miracles, he had not been stolen.

Mariah held on to John around his waist, and John rode quickly the way he'd come, against the progress of the retreating army, which flowed in fits and starts toward God knows where. He sensed that they were in danger, but none of the soldiers even bothered to look up at them. Nevertheless, he desperately wanted to be home, to be at Carnton. Mariah hugged him tight, and he felt stronger for it. As they passed the houses on the edge of town, he looked around him and caught sight of Mrs. Baylor standing on her back porch in full black. She was wringing her hands and looking around, pleading.

Mariah had been following his gaze and answered his question before he had formed it.

"She in mourning. Her son."

"Which son?"

"The young one, Mr. Will. The one off at the war. He died close by."

"How do you know this?"

"I heard it."

"Will Baylor is dead?"

"Yes."

If he hadn't turned his head to look back at Mrs. Baylor, he might never have seen it through the window. Just a flash, a momentary glimpse of something he couldn't quite place. It was gray and it was bare. It was a quick motion, violent. A bare arm slapping at the air before disappearing into the dark. A door slammed closed. A shout and, perhaps, a half-choked laugh.

"Mr. McGavock?"

He hadn't remembered guiding the horse to the back of the Baylor house, but there they were. He stopped and stared hard at the old smokehouse back of the Baylors' place. *Why have I come back here?* he thought. He had forgotten he had business with Baylor, and now he had no desire to meet the man. It wasn't Baylor who fixed his attention, but the smokehouse all gray and pockmarked. He knew what was happening in there. He knew it instinctively; he could have predicted it. *This has been a very bad day.*

He stopped the horse and dismounted.

"Mr. McGavock, where you goin'? What we doin'?"

"You stay here with the horse."

On the back porch of the Baylor place, Mrs. Baylor stood silently, and he could see that she was not wringing her hands in anguish, as he'd thought, but in anger. She was staring at the smokehouse, too. He walked toward it, past the woman on the porch.

"Oh, thank God, Mr. McGavock. There's a man in there, and I think he's hurting someone. I didn't know what to do. I'm alone. Please do something."

John looked up at Mrs. Baylor, a woman thin and sharp as a finch, enfolded in layer upon layer of black dresses and frocks and long coats. She wore a hood, and her tiny white face looked as if it were receding into a dark cave, dragged backward slowly. For once she seemed honestly concerned about what was happening in her smokehouse, and John found himself warming to her.

"I will. You tell Mr. Baylor I want to see him, though."

He looked around on the ground and found a solid piece of

poplar board, split at one end so he could hold it like it had a handle. He swung it a couple times and hefted it over his shoulder. Mariah nodded as if she understood. She frowned at him, the frown of a mother scolding a little child for playing with snakes. But she did not seem worried. She did not look worried at all, only annoyed. He wondered why, but there was no time for that.

He turned and ran toward the smokehouse with the board held ready before him. Mrs. Baylor called after him.

"I don't want that sort of thing happening on my property. If anything happens to her, they'll think we're running a brothel here."

Should have known, he thought. *Merciless Baylors.*

She was dead by the time he broke through the door.

The man, one of the soldiers, was hitching up his britches and turned, startled. He had a heavy metal hook in his hand, one of the many that hung from the rafters of the smokehouse and which were used to suspend the meat for smoking. He was still just a boy, a skinny, emaciated boy whose hair was falling out in clumps, and who looked at John as if he had never seen anyone so disgusting and unworthy of his attention. The prostitute lay in one of the hollowed-out hickory logs that ran the length of the room, her legs and lower body stripped bare and hanging off the sides of the log. Her head was cocked to one side and resting against the wood, and John couldn't immediately see what was wrong with her—besides the fact that this man, *this boy*, had forced himself on her. John became strangely agitated by the darkness and the low ceilings and the lingering smell of ham. The ugliness of it was almost unbearable, although it was exactly like every other smokehouse he'd ever seen. *Who invented the wall and the ceiling, I'd like to know. Who started hemming things in? Only the ugly, dark, and dank comes of it.* He wished he were standing in the smokehouse a month before, when there would have been nothing to notice except the smell of food. He liked a smoked side of pork as much as any man. These thoughts flashed through his head in an instant without being consciously summoned. They separated him from the matter at hand, allowed him to float over it. He saw the blood streaming down the sides of the log just as the boy spoke.

"There's others coming. I might could have taken better care of her for them, but they'll be here soon anyway. I sent them word. So you be better just getting on."

John looked down at the girl, who wouldn't have been any older than Martha had Martha lived. *Where did she come from? Whose daughter is she? Who cast her out? Had they carried her with them? Did she know she would die?*

Strength in a twisted and random world. John swung the board so hard he almost lost hold of it. The sound of it hitting the boy's skull was very strange, he remembered later. There was a sharp noise and a moment of resistance followed by a soft, wet sound. He crushed the boy's skull. The force of the blow threw the boy ten feet, and he died somewhere along the way. His body hit the wall without any fight, limp and useless. He landed in a crouch resting on his head, as if he were about to begin a somersault.

He saw a tableau, not a woman. He reckoned there was a message in the tableau, a moral lesson, but he didn't bother to take it in. He pulled her underthings back up around her waist and straightened her dress. *This is the way of things now,* he thought. He left her there, where she looked at least a little peaceful. He knew he had just killed, and he detected a wistful sadness floating inside him, but no regret about it. *This is the way of things now,* he repeated again to himself. Why had the boy killed her? *He* hadn't killed the girl he'd been with so many years before, so why did this particular girl have to die? *I am responsible for this, for all of it. This is my penance.*

Outside, Mariah had disappeared, and the dead boy's friends had finally arrived. Mrs. Baylor fended off the others, three of them, with the handle of a broom. They laughed and grabbed at her skirts from the ground below the porch. She shouted her protest.

"Not me, you fools. In there, in there!"

She pointed at the smokehouse just as John emerged from it. That stopped the men cold, but only for a moment. Each of the three turned toward him, following the line of Mrs. Baylor's broomstick. Their faces were blackened by dark beards in the hollows under their cheekbones, and they looked at him with the same weary loathing he had seen in the eyes of the boy. The tallest of them wore a coat with rank that had either fallen or been ripped from his shoulder, leaving the shadow of a sergeant's stripes. His hair hung down in his face.

"What you got there?"

John didn't know what to say. How to explain? Where to start?

"You got our whore. Where's Jimmy?"

John didn't say anything.

"*Jimmy!*"

The man called out and heard nothing. He looked at John and saw the blood running over his forearm and smeared against his chest. It was the girl's blood, not Jimmy's, but the man was confused and agitated and quick to judge.

"What did you do to Jimmy?"

They had rifles. They had knives. John had nothing, he was alone in the world. The soldier shouted at the other two.

"Get in there and find Jimmy."

John would have picked a different circumstance for his death. The thing that most bothered him about it was not that he'd be killed in the presence of a whore, but that Mrs. Baylor was watching him and that he could see her. He wished she would go inside, but she was leaning against the porch railing trying to catch her breath and watching what would happen to John. John didn't want her to be part of his final memory.

Later Mariah would tell him that she had seen the men coming and knew they were too tired to chase her, so she lit out like she was fleeing, only to circle the horse back to hide on the other side of the smokehouse, where she had heard him kill the boy. It was from there that she and the horse shot around the corner, knocking the other two men to the ground just as they came running out of the smokehouse. She pulled alongside John.

"Come on."

John was so mesmerized by the thought of his own death he didn't move at first. He looked up at Mariah and wondered, *When did she learn to ride?*

"We got to go, Mr. McGavock. Right now."

The tall man, the leader, was getting his rifle ready to fire. The other two were screaming.

"Jimmy dead. Done killed him. Killed him dead!"

Mariah leaned down and pulled John toward the horse. John understood and was about to mount when Mariah dug her heels in and turned the horse's head toward the tall man. He was raising his rifle as they leaped upon him, knocking him to the ground and sending his rifle pinwheeling through the air. Mariah turned the horse back around and came alongside John again.

"Last chance, Mistah John."

John leaped up behind Mariah, and the horse shuddered at the weight. Mariah spurred him and leaned over so she could talk into his ear. He began to trot away, around the side of the Baylor house and out into the street again. As they passed Mrs. Baylor, she called out to them.

"I will tell Mr. Baylor you called."

They stopped only to switch places. The farther they went, the more the horse became confident in its strength, and as they passed through the woods that would lead them back to Carnton and away from the roads, he began to run. John only looked back once, when they crested the last hill. He thought he saw the glint of rifles and the movement of a blue mob, but he couldn't be sure. He sensed that the town had not died, that it had just been holding its breath.

29

CARRIE McGAVOCK

I had not been down to the servants' cabin in a very long time. *The slaves' cabin,* Zachariah said, hanging with an arm around the broad shoulders of Theopolis. *Into the slaves' cabin I go, I go, ho ho, ho ho.* He sounded drunk, although I knew that wasn't possible. *I could be a good slave, you know. Got a strong back. Maybe I'll just stay.* The cabin was a two-story box with a shake roof. On the front was a tall staircase that led straight up to the second floor's two cabins, and around back was a smaller set of doors opening onto the first-floor quarters. It was a very strange building.

We walked along the side of the building to the back, and Theopolis carried Zachariah into the door on the right. The servants hadn't lived in there for a while, and it had become a storage hopper for corncobs and other grain to be fed to the hogs. The cabin was on the side of a hill, and inside, under the floorboards, was a tunnel that led to a small underground room. This room is where we had hidden some of our most precious belongings: a coin-silver tea service and most of the family coin-silver flatware, long-ago wedding gifts from happier times, John's silver cigar holder, and such other things he had felt it necessary to hide. I had never been in the chamber, but I understood that it was not at all uncomfortable. This is where I sent Zachariah.

"Down into the hole. I ain't going. I ain't a rat."

"There's no time. You said yourself that they'd be coming soon."

"I *want* them to take me, Carrie."

He had never called me by my first name. I looked at Theopolis, but he pretended not to listen and fiddled with a couple of cobs.

"You'll be a prisoner."

"I'm sorry, reckon you're right. It's far better to live in a hole in the ground."

"You won't be living there."

"I won't be living."

"Don't say that."

"Why should I be your prisoner instead?"

"You're not my prisoner."

"What would you call it, then? Carrie?"

He used my first name again.

"I'll sit with you."

"In there?"

Now Theopolis was listening hard and seemed about to speak. I turned to him and looked him in the eyes and saw that he was frightened for me and that he would also do as he was told. He straightened his coat and clasped his arms behind his waist and waited for me to speak. He was an impressive man, and I pitied him.

"I will be sitting with Mr. Cashwell for a while, until he has become accustomed and while he is still recuperating from his . . ."

What did I call it? *The attack? My attack?* Theopolis knew how to keep up appearances.

"His injuries, yes, ma'am."

"His injuries, yes."

Theopolis pried the boards up and went first, carrying a small oil lamp ahead of him and dragging Zachariah behind him by the collar of his shirt. I followed behind in the narrow tunnel, my nose just inches from the worn, almost paper-thin sole of Zachariah's boot. I found it difficult to crawl in my skirts, and so I stopped to hike them up and proceeded again upon my bare knees. I felt many things, but mostly I felt like a girl again, exploring the outer reaches of my home place, the dark corners of forgotten outbuildings, and crawling through the tiny gaps in the dense vines that formed walls in the undergrowth of the swampy areas. I felt the dirt on my hands and under my fingernails, and I realized I'd forgotten that dirt could smell so clean. It was us, me, who was foul and dirty.

When I arrived in the chamber, Theopolis had already hung the lantern from a post driven in one wall, and was blowing into two iron pipes that had been driven into the ceiling.

"The tubes, they clear. They go up into the room right up there. You-all be all right here, there be some good air coming through. Not long, though. Can't stay real long, Miss Carrie."

Theopolis was obviously disturbed by this situation, and I imagined he was also frustrated that he could do nothing about it. I wondered where the air tubes had come from and why they were there. Zachariah sat on the dirt floor with his back against the sloping wall and one knee gathered to his chest, saying nothing. He rested his head on his knee and closed his eyes, as if he were nauseous. If Theopolis had decided to drag me out of there, which I could see he was contemplating, I would have made sure he was punished. I'd never ordered a Negro to be punished in my life, but I would have had Theopolis punished. I think he knew that. If his mother had been there, it would have been a different situation. Mariah might have shamed me into leaving. I think he knew that, too.

"Well?"

Zachariah spoke. He was quiet, his voice had no violence in it, no sharpness. I hardly recognized it.

Theopolis ignored him. "I'm going, Miss Carrie. You holler you need anything. If the army men come, I'll have to go put them boards back, and you'll have to stay here until I come and let you out. You might have to stay in here a good long while if you wait too long."

"I understand, Theopolis. Thank you."

"Yes, ma'am."

Theopolis lowered his head and shoulders into the tunnel and quickly disappeared. After a while I could hear his feet stomping around up above and then nothing.

I turned around to look for the Grecian rocker that President Jackson had given John so many years ago, but I couldn't find it. The truth was, there wasn't much in the chamber, none of the stacks and stacks of McGavock treasures I'd seen hauled out of the house. I saw no silver, no furniture, no paintings.

"What are you looking for?"

"Our things. The things that were supposed to be here."

"Oh."

He went silent again, but this time he kept his eyes trained on me. They followed me around the little chamber while I tried to find a place to sit down, as far from him as I possibly could sit without tumbling back into the tunnel. His gaze made me uncomfortable. I had beaten him to death, and then he'd come back to life, and the whole experience had made me closer to him and therefore more uncomfortable sitting in a crowded rat hole with him. I did not know where to begin. I pulled my skirts all the way down, as far as they could go, and sat with my legs folded beneath me. He kept looking at me, and I would have sworn that he never blinked. He was waiting for something, I suppose. His eyes had little white spots on them where they reflected the lamplight.

As I watched him, it occurred to me for the first time that I had never really understood how he'd been wounded. I'd heard the story, or overheard it rather, from some of the other men lying about the house in various stages of recuperation or disintegration. I had thought about it before, but there was something about his manner, his silence, his softness, that brought my mind back to it. I'd heard of the charge, and Zachariah grasping the flag and running toward the Yankees. I'd seen all this in my mind, and they were familiar images. Ancient. I had seen them when my father read to me those stories about the Greeks at Troy. He thought it a great romance, but all I had remembered were the lances and the charges and the great, self-conscious gestures of violence and wounded honor. It was the same scene, and I imagined it was always the same scene in every war, at least for those of us who did not fight them. They were familiar images, and because of their familiarity, they could be faced and accepted and sung into history. What would poetry be about otherwise? But there was something about that man sitting across from me deep in a hole in the earth. He was not an Achilles or a Hector. None of them were, not even those young men they called General who had lain upon my porch, dead and uncovered. If that was true, then there surely was more to Zachariah's story than the charge and the flag and his triumphant stand upon the Yankee ditch. Whatever it was, I began to think it would explain why I wanted to protect him and keep him close to me.

"Why did you pick up that flag?"

Zachariah seemed lost. He was smiling, which was not at all appropriate. It was a child's smile, the smile of someone who's happy but doesn't know enough to say why. The smile of the ignorant. He picked at a scab on the side of his face, the remnants of a poor shave job. He raised his head off his knee and leaned it back against the wall, looking up. He talked to the ceiling, and while he did so, I watched his coat fall open and felt the urge to reach out and feel for his ribs.

"You mean, why did I pick up the colors? Because they'd fallen."

"But why you?"

"I don't really know."

"All right. But how did you carry it with your rifle? Did you carry one in either hand?"

"No. I carried it in both hands."

"Where was your rifle?"

"Why are you asking these questions?"

I didn't quite know. But Zachariah's life—the fact that he was living—was a mystery that could be solved, and in solving it, I might find an explanation for my own actions and my desire for him. The lamp flickered, and Zachariah momentarily faded into the darkness and grew into a monstrous shadow. I paused until he was small again. My legs tingled and grew numb, but I didn't dare move. I acted as if I had trapped an animal, and guarded against sudden movements.

"I'm just curious."

"I'd lost my rifle."

"And so you had no weapon."

"No, I had some pistols."

"So you carried a pistol in one hand and the flag in the other."

"The colors. The colors. And no, I didn't carry a pistol in any hand."

"But you were armed?"

"No, I wasn't. I tossed the pistols when I picked up the colors."

"Why?"

We were silent a long time after that, as Zachariah began to understand my questions and where I was going. I wasn't sure exactly where this would end, but I knew the direction to go.

I had Zachariah's full attention now. He looked me square in the face. His forearms flexed and expanded across his one shin, which he had drawn up close to his chest. He looked much stronger than I'd thought he was, and I experienced a momentary shiver of fear, remembering our scuffle in the dark and realizing how easily I might have been hurt by him if he'd not been crippled. Maybe he was still more powerful than I knew, leg or no leg. Now his face was undecipherable in the wavering of the lamplight, but his voice was soft. I didn't feel threatened *now*. Something had happened. His body was still—not from tension, but from perfect pliability and torpor. The little room was warm and dry, which surprised me. It was not how I had imagined the earth to be. There was one wet spot in the dirt ceiling, and every few minutes a small drop of water would collect and cling to the ceiling before dropping to the floor, where it was immediately swallowed by the dirt. I supposed the little water drop would continue its journey through the dirt and rock until it reached the center of hell or out to China.

"I dropped the pistols because I didn't need 'em. Couldn't use 'em."

"You could have used one, or was the . . . were the *colors* too heavy?"

"They weren't too heavy. I just didn't think about it."

"Did you have any other weapon?"

"Just the colors."

"That wasn't really a weapon, was it? You ran to the enemy without any means of fighting back. You *charged* the enemy. You're a hero."

"I never said I was."

He picked at a hole in the knee of his pant leg.

"You dropped your weapons, picked up a pole with some cloth attached to it, and ran at men who were shooting at you. That's heroic."

"Maybe you're right."

I wasn't right. I knew I wasn't right. There was something I was missing.

"What did you do when you got to the Yankees?"

"I got up on top of their bulwarks and waved the colors before they dragged me down."

"They dragged you down. But they didn't kill you. Why?"

"I wish I knew. I begged them to."

He begged to be killed. He had begged me to let him die, too, and I had ignored him.

"They killed many of the men in your company, right?"

"Almost all of them, from what I been able to figure out."

"But not you."

"Right."

"What was special about you?"

"There's never been anything special about me."

There is something so terribly special about you, I thought.

"No, there was one thing. There were many men charging up that hill, but you were the only one who was unarmed and carrying the colors. You were very conspicuously unarmed."

"That didn't help the other two color-bearers. They got shot dead. I don't see what this has got to do with anything."

He knew very well what it meant. He was flashing little smiles and rolling his eyes when he answered me, as if he was having fun. He was deriving some joy from this.

"So they got shot dead. Do you think that if they'd been carrying a rifle, they'd have been spared?"

"Hard to say."

"Let's assume that they would have been treated as any other Confederate charging the Yankees. They would have been shot, more than likely."

"Probably."

"But when they were carrying the colors, they were distinguished from everyone else. They were unarmed."

"Yes."

"But it didn't help them."

"No."

"Did it help you?"

We sat silently looking at the floor between us for a good long time. I felt regret for having pushed the conversation so far beyond the point of return, for having changed the nature of our—*(our what?)*—friendship so radically and irrevocably. Whatever Zachariah said now, he would be a different man for it, and the thing that made me afraid and regretful was the uncertainty. What kind of man?

"I'm not dead."

"Did you kill anyone that day?"

"I don't rightly know."

"When you stood on the Yankee trench and waved the flag, what were you doing?"

"I was rallying the men, raising them up, giving them some guts maybe."

"Who stood below you?"

"Yankees."

"And what did you do to them?"

"Nothing."

He rubbed the stump of his right leg, as if for good luck.

"Did you forget why you were there?"

"No."

"So why didn't you jump into the ditch?"

"I don't know. Anyway, they pulled me into the ditch quicker'n shit."

"And you begged them to kill you."

"Yes."

"You ran at them unarmed and then begged them to kill you."

"Yes."

"You wanted to become a suicide."

"I don't know."

"Has anyone ever asked you to kill them?"

"A couple of times. Some who were dying real poorly, a lot of pain. I did what they asked."

"But you weren't dying."

"No."

"If I asked you to kill me, would you?"

"No."

"I've thought about it often, you know. I've wanted to die many times. I lost my children, and when that happened, I would have put my pain against any one of those boys you killed for mercy's sake. What about mercy upon me?"

"You could still live. Things could change."

"Nothing could change the fact that my children are dead. That is an absolute fact."

"But you can change. It will pass. I wouldn't kill you because you don't need to die."

"Yes, I suppose. Did you need to die?"

"I don't know."

"But you asked to die. Unarmed, unhurt, you asked to die."

"Yes."

"Did you know they would refuse you?"

Zachariah looked away from me. I could imagine him a boy in Arkansas with too much to think about. He looked relieved.

"I yelled at them, and the louder I yelled, the more I knew they weren't going to kill me. I don't know how I knew. I'd seen the other men with the colors get cut down, but I knew the colors were the only chance for me. I was just another man with a rifle otherwise. I didn't expect to live. I expected to die. I'd taught myself to expect that, and not life."

"But what we expect and what we want are not always the same."

"Never are."

"You wanted to live."

"Yes."

"You've always wanted to live."

"Yes."

"You knew how to stay alive."

"I had an idea."

"The colors."

"Yes."

He quit talking to me. He didn't ignore me—it would have been impossible to ignore each other in that little cave with the dancing shadows and the vestiges of my household strewn about. There wasn't enough room. But he didn't talk, and I thought that perhaps he didn't think he *needed* to talk. An understanding had been struck, and the air around us no longer seemed to vibrate. It was just air. I watched Zachariah relax and absentmindedly stroke the stump of his leg again, as if he was gaining comfort from it. I think he was.

I had discovered why I had been drawn to him, the unusual thing that had distinguished him. He was a living thing, not a dying one. He lived at the very edge of the border with death and had learned how to live by courting death and then tricking it. In that bedroom where I'd first seen him he was one of many men. Most of them were dying, and many had more immediate need of the surgeon. But he'd succeeded in drawing my attention by protesting it. He had some innate understanding of human nature that I was only beginning to understand. He had turned his dread of being left behind, which I had seen raw the night before, into a strategy for living. He knew I would take care of him, and the more he protested, the more extraordinary my efforts would become. I felt a surge of anger that quickly subsided. I had been tricked, and yet I had also been needed by a man, a person, who had wanted to live. I couldn't be angry at him. Furthermore, I thought him even more heroic for having learned how to live when everyone around him was falling. An odd sort of war hero, but a war hero nonetheless.

Zachariah had closed his eyes and did not see me crawl across to him on my hands and knees, feeling at every moment that my arms would collapse under me, they were shaking so. I could hear his breath, which suddenly sounded loud. So did the sound of my skirts dragging in the dirt behind me, leaving behind a trail. I came upon him and crawled over his legs, or what was left of them, until my head had almost bumped his chest. I arched my back so that my body fit into his without touching and brought my face up to his. His bottom lip was thick. *I have never noticed that. Why have I not noticed that?* As he breathed, his rough lips moved slightly and the muscles in his jaw flexed and his chest rose intolerably close to mine, and so I did the only thing possible: I closed the gap between us and pressed my mouth hard against his. The blood rushed to my face. His lips received mine, and I felt him kiss me back, pressing his hand against the small of my back. *His hand is so big.* I kept my eyes open so that I could see his face, so I could see him kissing me. He never opened his eyes, and just when I thought that I was lost, he pulled away. He had both of his hands on my shoulders, holding me up.

He opened his eyes and looked at my face. He looked at the hair falling into my eyes, the flush in my cheeks, the swell of my numb lips, the trace of my chin. I realized my chin was trembling. There was wet on my cheek. I wasn't crying. I looked at him and saw the trace leading from the corner of his eye to the edge of his jaw, so obvious on his dusty face. I began to push forward again, ready to abandon everything, and he held me back. He smiled. I sat kneeling before him, the blood pounding in my ears. Soon the pounding subsided, and when I looked at him, I saw that he had closed his eyes again. I backed away from him slowly and came to rest against the wall again, bereft and relieved and grateful.

I could not bear the thought of the Union soldiers taking Zachariah away. I knew he couldn't stay, not forever, but I wasn't done with him. I had more to learn. I didn't know what John would think, but I would not let Zachariah be removed from my care. I dozed, and when I awoke, I watched Zachariah slap at pill bugs with his left hand, childishly intent on them. He was whispering, *Curl up, curl up like a baby*, while he flicked them around like tiny marbles. I did care what John thought. I had not cared for some time, but now I did. I wanted to tell him what I'd discovered and to show him that the years of my convalescence had not ended in vain, that my illness had not been the fruit of a morbid fascination with the beyond, but a desire. To live? That was too simple, too simpleminded. What I knew was that I was more like Zachariah than anyone else I'd ever known, even Mariah. Surely John would see that I needed to learn as much from this odd man before he went on, to God knows where.

I had been drawn to Zachariah Cashwell as an idea. I wanted to tell him these things, to explain how his strange and foreign presence had released me. I wanted to tell him what I had learned. I wanted him to be proud of me, to be impressed by me. It didn't matter what I said, I realized, just so long as he saw me with new eyes, so long as I could not be forgotten. I had been drawn to him as an idea, but I had come to love him as a man. I had come to love him as a woman loves a man whom she can never have. An impossible man. An unreachable man. A man of infinite possibility. I hadn't known that was what it felt like.

And when I knew this, I heard the voices above us.

30

ZACHARIAH CASHWELL

It was true that I had never wanted to die. I thought my desire to live had been something I'd just recently picked up, right here at this godforsaken hospital. I had felt my gumption slip away and my blood thin, and I'd become just another beggar of life, just another survivor, but at least I'd once been a hero, a fearless man. Down in that hole, I began to doubt the whole goddamn story. My story.

That one day, the last day I saw my mother, I thought I would die and I prayed I wouldn't. I remembered that now. I reckon it's possible to remember things even when you don't think much about them anymore or even think about them at all. Sneaky thoughts that lie around in your head, pulling on strings and making things happen, and you don't even have the first thing to say about it because you don't even feel it.

I thought I was ready to die many times. I thought that was how I had become strong. I thought pretty damn much of myself because of my willingness to take a bullet. I looked at the men around me and saw weakness. Even the men who were bigger than me, even that hog-necked loudmouth who picked up the colors before me—I reckoned even *he* was weak, at least weaker than me. Who would care about what the band was playing, and who would talk so damned much, and who would have so much fun poking and pushing at the little men around him, if he didn't love life more than anything? I was stronger than that, I thought. I knew some of the old-timers thought the same way. It had crossed my mind that many of us who were old-timers were the ones who weren't afeared of death, who didn't care. I just hadn't thought about how strange it was that us death-eaters—because that's what I thought of myself—were the same bastards who had lived through the fighting year after year, and it was usually the new kid full of piss and life who took a bullet in his head. Well, that's not true. I *had* thought about it, but I reckoned it meant that all of this was just a son of a bitch. At least that's what I said when we were sitting around smoking and talking. But maybe it meant something else.

There is something beautiful about war, you can't deny that. If you look at it the right way, even the killing has got its beautiful side. Once you get used to the sight of a whole line of men cut down in an open field, you can even start to appreciate the scene like it was a rare painting, something you ain't ever going to see again, something perfect and absolute. There was also a lot of things complicated about war, which sounds like I'm saying something anybody with a brain would know, but it ain't. A squad of men rushing a trench looks simple enough, I guess, but when you're in the middle of them and you're moving, there's a lot that happens that you wouldn't see if you weren't paying attention. The squad tightens up one second and stretches out the other because of the hills, or because the bullets are flying through like a packed wedge of hornets, or because an artillery shell just exploded off to the side. The squad stretches and contracts like a spring, and it also shuffles itself up, and sometimes that means there's a man right ahead of you looking and moving in the same direction as you. Sometimes, if you were tired enough or drunk enough, you'd think he *was* you, only he was a second or two ahead. When he took the bullet, sometimes you could almost feel the pain, and then you'd be happier than shit because it *wasn't* you, like when you get waked by a bad dream. *But for the grace of God go I.*

But maybe it weren't only the grace of God.

My soldiering life was over, I knew that sitting in that hole with Carrie, listening to her puzzle over me like I wasn't really there, like I was something in one of her books. I can't say I wanted to have that conversation, but I reckon that I was going to have it sooner or later, so why not have it while scrabbling around like a rat in the earth?

When she kissed me, I had a thought. *This is what I've been waiting for.* And she was so soft and warm, and the way she'd come crawling at me like a cat, well, I will never forget that. When I felt her heart against my chest, I knew I couldn't never break it, which is the flip side of love the way I saw it. But I'd seen her come to me while faking sleep, and I'd felt her against me, and I knowed that she would have left everything behind. All that was much more than I had any right to expect. That kiss would last me for many years. I was never all alone after that.

31

CARNTON

John hadn't known what to say to Carrie when he and Mariah rode up to the house, and so he had said very little.

He had walked the horse up to the edge of the back steps, where Carrie waited for them. Carrie's skirts were smeared with red dirt, and she was slowly clapping dirt off her palms.

"Will Baylor is dead," he said. "Just seen Mrs. Baylor. Died on the battlefield, I understand."

Lord, I sound like a gossiping aunt. If she only knew.

Theopolis had gone to get Carrie when he saw the horse and riders from quite some distance, coming through the grove from the pike; he'd thought they might be the first of the Union men on the way to take over the house and imprison Cashwell and the others.

The others. Later she would admit to John that she had forgotten about the others, the lamest of the lame, the six destroyed men who remained in her hospital. Then she heard a couple of them scrabbling at the window behind her. They were trying to see who was coming. The men who could haul themselves up to the window were the least lame of the most wretched, their bodies twisted, carved, and shrunk into new forms.

These were the men who would never be ignored again in their lives, and that realization had just begun to dawn on them: on the man with no jaw or tongue, the other with only an arm left, the third missing an eye and a nose and most of his left side. These were the three who pulled themselves up to the window, the three Carrie turned around and saw while awaiting John's approach. With some dread, they had wanted to see who would be the one to take them away, the first of the innumerable, the endless parade of people who would gasp and stare at them as long as they lived.

But it was Carrie who was the first to stare. She had spent the better part of a week among them, and never once had she stared. They had only been the sum of their wounds, a collection of tasks and duties. Perhaps it was the different perspective, seeing them through the window rather than lying at her feet. The window framed them like a perverse painting, and she saw them truly as men. They knocked and scratched at the sill, and they could see the horror pass across her face: they were creatures, lolling and bug-eyed ghouls, who had been made by God and unmade by man. The man with no jaw, who could not talk, let tears build and drop down his cheek because he knew no other way of telling her to stop staring.

The fact that it was Carrie McGavock who was the first to stare and recoil, the woman who had bathed their wounds and sung to them at night, who had smiled at them, and who wrote out the letters they dictated to their families—this was the hardest cut of all. Much later they became used to the stares, the unsolicited charity, the years of infantile conversation shaped by the common assumption that their brains had been somehow diminished by their wounds. But in that moment, staring back at the woman staring at them, the future seemed mightily oppressive and unbearable, and they would have given the rest of their bodies for the possibility of anonymity. Carrie had, in a moment, made them aware of themselves, and they would never lose that awareness. Through the years they would meet with other veterans at reunions and holiday parades, and at those times they'd refer to Carrie as an angel, telling expansive stories about her kindness and her care. Even so, they never quite forgot that it was Carrie who had given them that first glimpse of themselves.

It was a misunderstanding, but as no words passed between them, it could not be put right. Carrie was horrified not *by* them, but by the fact that she had *forgotten* them in her desire to know a man who, truth be told, didn't need her. What they saw was shame.

No one ever came to look for John. *What was one more murder in a town of dead people?* John thought. He never told Carrie about the incident at the smokehouse. That's how he would always think about it. *The incident.* Always *the incident.*

The next morning a short man in a worn blue uniform rode up to the house, dismounted, climbed the steps, and knocked on the back door. From the yard, John could see the men at the window, craning around to get a look at the visitor. When no one answered, he turned around and took his campaign hat off to scratch his head. A few strands of hair flowed over the slick dome of his head. He pulled at a lopsided mustache and finally spotted the burial party. None of them had called out or thought to call out. Nor had they thought to hide.

"Where's Sergeant Cashwell?" John asked Carrie.

"In the house, John. He'll be fine."

Carrie plucked at a few hard clods of cold, crumbling dirt. She didn't look up, but she didn't sound frightened, either.

"What do you mean, 'fine'?" John said. "Why did he spend the night in that hole, then?"

"The worst of them passed on by in the night, the men who would have taken things into their own hands, for revenge. They passed right on by, and I assume that this man is someone official. I'm not afraid of the officials."

John wasn't as certain of things, but he looked at Mariah and she seemed equally calm. He watched the man approach on foot, having tied his horse to the porch rail. He got within thirty feet before hailing them.

"Is this the McGavocks'?"

"I am John McGavock."

The man stopped and scratched his head again.

"Where are all the rebels?"

"Dead or gone. Except for the few, the worst off. This was a hospital."

The man looked at John with relief, and John knew that here was a man uncomfortable with his role. He looked like he'd spent the war behind a desk, transcribing messages for far more important men, men he feared and despised. He was pale and baggy, slightly gin-blossomed, and he wore his uniform stiffly in the way of men who could not forget what they were wearing. Such men wrote out the orders, saw to their delivery, kept the casualty lists, composed the triumphant white lies telegraphed back to headquarters, and ensured that the men who told those lies were always comfortable and well nourished. John knew men like the one standing in front of him, scratching his head and adjusting his collar. He knew that they were the men who made the war work. Not the ones who waged the war, but the ones who made it easier. There were such men on both sides. He wondered if he would have been such a man had he gone off to battle. He felt some measure of sadness for the man, knowing how he must have spent the war: unappreciated and resentful, perhaps even remorseful. He was not a happy man.

"So there are only a few prisoners?"

"We think of them as patients, although the doctors ran off days ago. Not prisoners. Certainly not *our* prisoners."

The man let slip a little smile and a glimpse of unusually small and white teeth. He had very few opportunities to assert himself, John reckoned, and he was happy for this one.

"They are most certainly prisoners, by order of General John Schofield, U.S. Army. All Confederate soldiers who cannot be moved for health and general brokenness—and I have been appointed the judge of that, sir—shall be prisoners in effect, if not in fact. And at such time that the prisoner regains his health and mobility, he shall be remanded to our custody to be transported to prison."

John thought, *He must have memorized that, or his English has been corrupted by his work.*

"I am Major Jonathan Van der Broeck, and I will be acting as garrison commander of the wounded, under the direct commission of General Schofield himself. I will need an accounting of each of the men under your care, to include their name, rank, unit, and state of origin. My assistant, Sergeant Allston, will be along to pick up the list and to make a preliminary inspection of the premises. Once a week I will be arriving to inspect the condition of each of your patients and to determine their ability to travel."

"That seems like a lot of fuss for so few men, Major Van der Broeck."

A pained look broke through the officiousness. Van der Broeck shook his head.

"There are wounded men all over this town, in every church and parlor big enough to hold them. Hundreds, maybe thousands. Didn't you notice? I believe I may have the largest command of any major in the army, even if most of them are rebels. Not that I would keep track of such things."

He nodded to Carrie, who had come to stand beside John, and turned on his heel. John could sense the burden of things lifting off all of them and dissipating. He imagined them all floating off. Carrie broke his reverie, as she was wont to do. He loved that she wasn't floating away but standing on the ground behind him.

"So they're not taking him anywhere?"

"Them."

"All of them. They're staying?"

"It appears so. For the moment."

If he looked at it from the right angle, John could imagine that nothing had happened and nothing had changed. The town was back in the control of the Union, and his house was a hospital again. The war had subsided around them, and if he stayed out of town, he wouldn't have to reckon with the changes it had wrought. Even the piles of men and uniforms and gear that had ringed his house were gone, carted off without John noticing.

"Nothing will be the same again," Carrie said. She was reading his mind but drawing the wrong conclusion.

"It will be better," he said.

"For whom?"

John turned around and faced her, and could see Mariah and Theopolis gathering up their things.

"You think it will be better for Mariah and Theopolis, John?"

John looked down at Carrie. She looked at him without sadness or judgment, just curiosity. Sadness and judgment were such familiar expressions it took him a second to register this new one.

"For those two?"

"Them. And the rest of them."

"I don't know. It is better that the war has gone away, no matter what else happens."

"I'm not as sure of that. I can't see into the future."

"Perhaps you should ask Mariah, then."

"What would she know, John? What are you suggesting?"

"Only that she knows things, you've said so yourself. I'm not saying anything more about that."

"She knows things? You believe that now? I thought you didn't believe in such superstitions."

Mariah had stopped tidying up the cemetery and stood waiting for them, looking straight at John. Nothing had changed about her except the wrinkles of her brow, which had smoothed out and relaxed, as if she had nothing to fear or worry about. He could see that she would never be his slave again, no matter what he chose to call her. Theopolis, standing behind her but avoiding his eye, still acted like a slave, but John could see that this would change also. He had lost his power, not only over them but over his wife, too. And probably his children? Yes, them, too. It was a relief.

"Oh, just ask her, Carrie."

He drew her close and embraced her briefly and chastely, like a sister. He goosed her side, and she slapped at his hand. That would change, too, he thought. His feelings for her. Passion. It would change. The Lord giveth, and the Lord taketh away.

#

ZACHARIAH CASHWELL

One morning after my night in the hole I woke up to see Mr. John McGavock sitting in a cane-back chair at the end of my bed, his head hung down between his shoulders like a man carrying a great weight without any hope of letting it go. I had noticed he didn't often talk to Carrie. He looked like he was in trouble, like he was a boy just been blessed out. I was starting to feel like a prisoner *and* a geek in a carnival, everyone gawking at me. I wondered what business he had with me, what I could possibly tell *him*. I spoke up anyway, seemed polite.

"I'm Zachariah Cashwell."

"I know. I've seen you. Around the house. I notice things."

Then I saw him pull a thin knife from his coat pocket, the kind of thing you might use to bone a chicken. *Oh boy*, I thought, *the man of the house has a knife, and here I am*. I didn't like the way he said "notice," as if I'd done something with his wife, but I didn't think it was the right time to square the record. He looked like a rich man who had become tired of owning things.

"Now that you're awake, Mr. Cashwell, did you know your head is bleeding?"

I could feel a drop of blood run down behind my ear.

"Thank you."

"For what, may I ask?"

"For telling me about my head."

"I thought you might have meant something else."

"I don't know what else. Thanks for letting me stay here in this room at knifepoint?"

"This knife isn't for you."

"You going to fight off the Union boys all by yourself with that knife?"

"Not Union."

"Who? Niggers?"

"Confederates. Your people. My people."

Now, that was something I hadn't been expecting. It hadn't crossed my mind that he might be a sympathizer, a Union man. He looked like all of the men who ever came to the train depots to make speeches about our courage and sacrifice and honor and the rest of that mess. He looked like a politician, sideburns and all. He'd allowed his house to be overrun by us, and his wife to tend us. He couldn't be one of them.

"Why are you afraid of them?"

"That's my business."

"Suppose it is."

I wondered if every member of the McGavock family was going to take their turn sitting across from me and staring. McGavock looked at me not like he hated me, but like he had no use for me, which didn't make me feel any safer in his care. I figured I'd have to take care of myself if it came to that. But he just kept looking and looking at me. There wasn't much else to look at, I'll admit to that, but it didn't seem very polite.

"You and my wife get along well."

"I wouldn't say that, Mr. McGavock. I think she'd as soon beat me over the head as listen to me, truth be told."

"She wants you to stay here. Very much."

"She's a kind lady, Mr. McGavock, and I reckon she don't think I'm healthy yet."

"I don't think that's it. I should be jealous, shouldn't I?"

"No cause, sir. Please believe me about that."

"I don't know you, and therefore I have no reason to trust you on such a matter. I should throw you out. I should beat you down for trifling with my wife. That's what most men would do, hmm?"

"I haven't trifled with her, sir."

"No, I don't believe you have. Any other woman, I'd think that you *had*, but not with my wife. Carrie would not let herself be trifled with, I know that much. And so, although I don't know what kind of person you are, I know that she is fond of you, and I will not come between her and a new friend, even if he is most unsuitable. I've learned that I have not the standing to intervene, I have much damage to undo. And she's had so few friends. This does not mean that you and I are friends, although I will be as charitable and assume you are an honorable man worthy of my respect. I trust my wife in this matter."

I didn't have anything to say about any of that. I had never heard a man talk of his woman that way, but what he said seemed right. I just hadn't decided what it was that Carrie wanted from me, exactly, and I could see that he didn't know, either. McGavock turned his head and spit. There was a little blood in it, and I looked at him and realized that his face looked sour because he was chewing on his cheek pretty damned hard. He was nervous. He pulled out a flask and took a long pull, the kind of drink a man takes when he's getting ready to drink and keep drinking. He offered it to me, and we drank together.

"You killed men. Correct, Mr. Cashwell?"

"Yes, sir. I didn't ever stick around to check to make sure they were dead, but I had a good notion about it."

"But you killed men up close?"

"Sometimes. Most of the time it wasn't exactly a *close* thing, with bayonets and knives and all that. Just shooting at lines of men who were shooting at you, mostly."

"Have you ever examined your work?"

"I don't understand."

"Did you ever have the opportunity to quietly contemplate the killing of a man and then to see it done just as you imagined?"

"Never quietly, and it was never like I imagined. It was worse."

"I see. Pity."

"Reckon I don't see it that way."

"Forgive me. What I mean, Mr. Cashwell, is that what you're describing sounds so uncivil. Chaotic."

"That hasn't been much of a problem in my life. Being civil or not, I mean. Nobody expected it of me, one way or the other."

McGavock spit again. The walls began to fade. I realized I wasn't blinking. Something had happened to that poor son of a bitch. Or he'd done something I didn't want to hear about. I distracted myself by stretching out my leg and yawning.

"You've been with whores, though, Mr. Cashwell?"

"I've known some, yes."

"Known how?"

"Some of my aunt's friends. My aunt and uncle owned a saloon back home. She was a religious lady who thought she was called to take care of the women who worked out of the bedrooms upstairs. She was their friend. My uncle took some of their money, but they were happy to give it because my aunt was so kind. She never let me upstairs."

McGavock raised his eyebrows, and then he laughed.

"You grew up in a whorehouse."

"A saloon."

"Yes, of course."

He fell to thinking, and running his hand through his hair. He stopped chewing the inside of his cheek.

"What is your opinion of the whore?"

"Which one?"

"As a group. All of them."

"I don't know all of them."

McGavock began to laugh, and then he stopped. He had been all set to laugh at me because I was so goddamned dumb. I knew this, because I was trying to be dumb. I'd found that if they thought you were dumb, they'd quit talking to you after a while. But his laugh stopped before he could get off a good smile, and his face twisted back down until it was serious again. Only his eyes were big as supper plates.

"You don't know all of them. That's right. That's right. You don't. No one does. That's exactly right."

Then he *did* smile, but it was a kind smile. He smiled and he patted his knees. *Pat. Pat. Pat.* Real slow, like he had just thought of something but he couldn't remember what it was.

"You'll have to stay with us. You're in no condition to be captured and taken away."

"I suppose not, Mr. McGavock. Thank you."

He told me his whole story then. It took hours, back to when he was a young man. I listened close. There were sounds come from outside the room every once in a while, and one time I thought I heard soldiers arguing with themselves, but no one ever found us. His story made me very happy, which sounds wrong. But I was looking at a man who was just a man. Not a special man, just a man, and that meant I could be a man like him someday, with a house and a family like his. And a wife like his.

33

CARRIE MCGAVOCK

Becky did not stay away from the house for very long, even after I sent her and her brother away for their own safety. I hadn't really expected her to stay away after watching her tend the men, always appearing to be looking for someone who never appeared. A day or so later she was back, already changing bandages and water when I awoke and went into the sickrooms. I suppose she thought they might still be bringing wounded to the house and that one of them might be the man she was looking for or someone who had news of him. If she was disappointed to discover that no one had arrived in her absence, she didn't show it. No one had arrived since the second day, although many had departed this house and this world. She kept working, which I understood to be her way of maintaining her dignity and guarding her heart. I had known women like her but older, poor, sharp-faced women who would not acknowledge having anything to do other than to work until they died, and for whom boundless labor guarded them against the perils of unreasonable hopes and foolish dreams. Dreams of love, for instance. I prayed that she would find this man, that he would help free her, and that they would indeed love each other unreasonably and foolishly. *And what do you know of love, Carrie McGavock?* I thought. Perhaps not very much, but I was learning.

I didn't say anything to her when I saw her again, and she said nothing to me. I just walked over and helped her tie off the bandage on the stump of a man with long, hairy arms and a soft, lively red face. He looked kind. *Could you love him instead?* I thought, but knew better than to say anything.

Becky was standing in the house with the others, the ravaged and maimed, when John rode up and told me that Will Baylor had been killed, that he had been to see Mrs. Baylor. My first thought was that he was one of thousands, and so why was *that* news? But then I remembered that Will Baylor had been my favorite among the Baylors, the most intelligent and witty and thoughtful of the bunch. The prettiest, too. I said a silent prayer and didn't think much more about it right then.

When I went back into the house, I found Becky standing stock-still and mute, her arms rigid at her sides and her fingers splayed apart, palms forward. She was not looking at me, she was looking up into the ceiling. I could tell she was trying to see up through it, into the sky, and on to whatever it was that ruled above us, because I had made that very same gesture too often to forget. It was the posture of a woman frozen by her pain and hatred.

I knew then that Will Baylor had been her beau. *Damn him, damn him,* I thought. *What was he doing toying with a girl like that? That wasn't fair, that was damned awful of him.* I felt shame immediately. I knew nothing about them. I barely understood myself in these matters. I thought of Cashwell off in his room.

Of course, I went to Becky and took her in my arms, and she sobbed and sobbed, always wiping the tears from her face before they could run onto my dress, but I just hugged her harder. Then I brought her into the parlor to sit down.

She said nothing for a while and just struggled mightily to take back her tears. Eventually she stood up and said she had work to do, that it was nothing, that it was the strain of the war that had toyed with her head but that she was all right now.

"Sit," I said.

She sat down, and the tension seemed to run out of her. I thought she might faint. She sat on the chair with both feet planted before her and rested her chin on her chest.

"Will Baylor. That's the man."

The lights were low, and I could barely see her face, but nevertheless, I knew she was shocked to hear me say his name.

"What do you mean?"

"Your beau. He was Will Baylor, wasn't he?"

I could see the tears glistening in the dim light thrown off by the lamps. She only nodded her head. I was about to say something, extend some condolence or something equally useless, but she spoke first.

"I loved him. And he loved me. He's the only boy who ever did. We been sneaking around on account of his father."

Baylor. I understood without her saying anything about it.

"He come to visit me whenever he had a chance, and before the war I would meet him up by the river and we'd spend days just walking in the shallows and all, getting our feet wet, stirring up the frogs and the shiners. I reckoned we'd always be doing such things."

There was nothing I could say. I had learned, by hard lessons, how pitiful the words of comfort could be. There was nothing that could possibly be said, not even *I'm sorry,* that accomplishes anything, at least not at first. The only truth that could be said is that there's never enough time: love always snatches itself away before you're ready. And why would I say such a thing to a girl so broken and alone?

"I thought we would be married. Silly, reckon."

"That wasn't silly."

"It was silly to ever think anything good could come of getting above myself like that, with a boy like that."

"The river was good, or am I wrong? When you were with him, *that* was good, right?"

"It's not enough. I won't never be enough. I made a mistake."

She got up, and I knew she was going to be leaving for good. Then she kneeled on the floor, and before I knew what I was doing, I knelt down with her, feeling the hard wood under my knee and the rough, scratchy homespun under the hand I laid upon her shoulder. She prayed.

"Dear Lord, I pray that You spared Will the pain and the lonesomeness I got on me right now. I pray that You took him quick and that he knows that I miss him more than any other thing under Your sun. Tell my dear mama to go find him and hold on to him, because I'll be coming one day and I expect him to be there waiting on me. There ain't nothing more I want from You, Lord. I don't need nothing else except that. In Jesus' name, amen."

Then she shrugged off my hand and stood up. She looked at me with hard eyes, not out of hate, but out of determination, I believe. She was determined to get about the rest of her life like all those other sharp-faced, work-worn women keeping their hopes and dreams screwed down like preserves in a jar. She didn't want me to stop her or to hug her again. I gathered her in my arms anyway, and I felt her relax again. I felt the sobs coming up from deep in her chest. I thought if I could just hold her, I could persuade her to stay, and perhaps convince her that the life she had imagined was not over. But she stood up straight again, gently pushed me away, and looked at me with kinder eyes this time.

"He loved me, you know. A girl like me, I can be loved, too. It ain't impossible."

She walked out of the house, down the steps, and out into the driveway, kicking up a dirt cloud around her feet. The dust made her appear to be drifting away from me, until finally she disappeared beyond the bend and into the wood.

34

CARRIE MCGAVOCK

After the Union officer left, Mariah and I spent some time calming the men who remained in the house. We tended to their various complaints and their certainty about being captured and sent to some Yankee prison and their anger about not being able to fight back and resist.

The man with no jaw, whose name was Hunt, waved at me with his scrap piece of paper and wrote madly: *I want a rifle.*

"I don't have a rifle to give you, Hunt. What would you do with it?"

Kill the Yankee bastards who did this to me.

"The chances are, those Yankees are dead, Hunt. You're alive, so you've won."

It don't work like that.

I wiped the spittle from his neck and tried to get him to lean back against the pile of pillows and linens that served as his back-rest against the wall of our downstairs parlor. He was in a foul mood and wouldn't be settled. He remained sitting in the middle of the floor, bent over his paper.

You'll give me up, all of us. Got to protect us. I'm the only one who can hold a rifle still.

"I won't give you a rifle, and I won't have you fighting. There's been enough fighting."

I am not a child.

"I didn't say you were a child, Hunt."

Quit treating me like one. Quit calling me Hunt. He looked up and licked the end of his pencil thoughtfully. *Captain Hunter.*

"That's you?"

Yes. I saw how you looked at us, and I don't want to hear Hunt anymore. Captain Hunter.

"All right, Captain Hunter."

Don't say it like you're kidding.

"Yes, Captain Hunter. But I can't give you a rifle."

All right.

Mariah was much more apt to spar with the soldiers, and she argued with them about what was going to happen to them all. Sometimes I would stop and listen to her in the hallway, and although she kept talking to them, I got the strange feeling that she was working out things for herself and that the men knew this and were temporarily turned from their own complaints by the fascination of thinking about what would happen to her, a Negro, now that the war was almost over. Everyone knew the war was almost over. It was something that didn't have to be discussed.

Mariah could never—or would never—talk about her plans and thoughts directly, and so they seemed to adopt a sort of code. One of them might ask, "Where am I going to go?" and Mariah would say, "Wherever you happiest. You got to be where you happy and on top of things, whoever you are." Or they'd say, "Everything's going to be different," and Mariah would say, "That *is* the truth. You a smart one."

That was an odd thing for a Negro to say to a white man, and yet not one of the men said a word about it. They were enthusiastic about whatever she said, and avid listeners. They listened to her as one would listen to a bearer of immense wisdom, and although I knew that Mariah was no more wise than I was, it was the thing she was wise *about* that caught the attention of those men in the room. They imagined their lives newly bound by their injuries, constricted and controlled by the charity and whim of others. They saw a future in which certain prerogatives of a free man were denied by their wounds, and in this they must have seen a glimpse, a piece, of Mariah's life. This struck me hard. She was the old-timer, the one who had gone before them down that road, and they were the newcomers thirsty for word from that world.

Mariah, bless her, gave them solace. At least she talked as if happiness was a possibility. I felt relieved, but not for the soldiers. It occurred to me that I had never considered whether Mariah was happy or not and that this question would soon be the only question of any significance in my life. It occurred to me that I could lose her, as I had lost John Randal and Mary Elizabeth and Martha.

Later I finally went upstairs to the room above the entryway, where I had once rocked away most of my time, and where I had once thought I could hear the voices of my children. Had *they* been happy? Had Mary Elizabeth found happiness in her six years? Was that happiness I had seen, watching her bounce along through the wheat field across the driveway, just a mess of brown curls bobbing along above the stalks, searching for the field mice with the ridiculously large ears, before she became too weak to walk and then to talk? Had that been happiness, and did she know it? Did Hattie and Winder know what happiness was? I wasn't sure it mattered. Perhaps that's the blessing of childhood, that happiness needn't be named or even recognized. When does the mania for naming things come on? I wondered. Probably when the thing named has been lost. Would Hattie and Winder leave me then, when they could put a name to the happiness they had lost? I wouldn't be able to bear it.

I sat still and looked out the window across the property and listened for the voices of real men crossing it.

What had conspired to make Zachariah a wounded but living fugitive and to make revered leaders of the dead generals I had laid out on my porch? What separated them but luck? I stood up from the rocking chair. I had never feared Zachariah, but I had felt a tremor of fear within me while I covered the faces of those generals. I had heard it called *the invisible hand:* the possibility that they knew who or what was in charge, had been granted an audience with whatever power that was, while the rest of us suffered for our ignorance. This was the thing that frightened me. Those generals had been acquainted with whatever *thing* had sent men at each other bearing guns and knives. I wished one of them had lived, to tell me if this was true.

Theopolis repaired the roof, which had been stripped of some planks for firewood when the yard was filled with men in camp. The yard looked wide and empty without them, and even though the charred black circles of their fires remained, and the grass was bent where they had lain, it was their absence that was most noticeable. The yard had forever changed, and I quickly considered asking John to preserve the fire rings as a remembrance. *Something to mark the spot.*

I abandoned the thought. No one would forget what had happened here, no one would need reminding. I went into the house.

A month passed. Then another. Spring arrived, and the soldiers came to take the lingering wounded away, even Zachariah. Off to prison, we all knew, but we didn't speak of it.

Zachariah and I spent those intervening days playing backgammon. We didn't talk a lot, but I didn't need that from him anymore. I was content to watch him grow stronger and to watch him stare out the window between games. I had decided that people talk an awful lot, perhaps too much, and that sitting silent was the greatest of luxuries.

Every day the color came back to Zachariah's face, shade by shade, until his face flushed and blanched like the rest of us. He became adept with his crutches, and I noticed his shoulders grow full and round. He was no longer gaunt, and this was most evident in his face. Where there had been lines and hollows of slack skin, there was flesh. His face was softer, younger. I could see the boy in him, the boy who had never been far from the surface anyway.

In March, Hattie and Winder returned from visiting relatives in

Louisiana. It was safe then. Their presence made things seem safer, as if two children playing in the dirt of the yard, or shouting and running into the cool grass to feel the morning wet on their skin, were the Lord's guarantee of order. There was no one left to threaten them, and even if there was, I thought I would know how to take care of them if there was a problem. Their shouts and their rollicking around the house made everything seem a little lighter, a little less consequential. It was difficult to continue worrying about the future when Winder was eating dirt and making pig noises in the yard for the amusement of the remaining wounded, an act he kept putting on until they had all been taken away. I was surprised that he was not more frightened of the disfigured men who lived in our house, but I suppose disfigurement would never be uncommon again, and I've heard that children get used to things quicker than most people.

What Zachariah didn't know about me he had already guessed, so I rarely spoke up except to protest the way he'd cheat by upsetting the board and blaming it on the missing leg that had left him unbalanced. He was an enthusiastic cheat, but not a good one, and I knew that if he ever met up with a real sharp, he'd lose everything. I prayed he would fall in with good people when he left me.

He told me an odd story, though. It was about his mother and his father. The story was disconnected, full of gaps, as if he was trying to tell it without revealing the worst parts. His father had died, and his mother had gone off with a preacher. This I had already known, and although it was sordid, I didn't think it at all unusual for people of his kind. That was a terribly arrogant thought to have, but it was indisputably true. I had learned enough as a child about the people who moved up and down the great trace—lawless, poor, violent, and damned, every one—to be able to imagine life in Zachariah's Arkansas, among the kind of people who couldn't ever stand still, who always had to be moving on, for whom neighbors were an oppression. But Zachariah added a detail to the story that I couldn't quite reconcile. He said the thing he remembered most about the day his mother left was the smell of the dirt on his father's grave. *That dirt smelled real fresh, like it hadn't ever been in the light before. And I guess it hadn't.* The dirt was fresh on his father's grave when his mother left. *She rode off and I— I couldn't move, see? I just could watch.* He hadn't run after his mother, he had just stayed behind and smelled the dirt. How could that be? The more I pondered the question, the more hideous the scene became. I had to force myself to quit thinking about it for fear of losing what sanity I had won back.

I had my suspicions about what had happened that day when Zachariah was a boy, a boy whose face I could picture with greater clarity since Zachariah had recovered his health. I believe he meant for me to have those suspicions, but he didn't want to confirm them aloud. He was, to the end, a source of endless mystery to me. There was always a new puzzle about him to solve. He was everything we—John and I—were not, and in his mysteries lay a certain kind of knowledge about the world that was both liberating and terrifying. I believe Zachariah knew this and was content to let these matters remain unspoken so that I would not be overcome by fear. I was grateful to him for this, even if I was indescribably anguished by my growing understanding of him.

The day they came for him, the sun beat down upon the house and the grounds until the early morning mist had been dissipated and the ground became hot beneath our feet. It was too hot for April.

Almost every week, that Union officer came to take away another of my charges. I could not understand why it was necessary to remove to prison men who not only could not fight but had told me separately and in their own way that they had no desire to threaten anyone anymore, despite their bluster. The last thing they could threaten would be the Union army, which had routed our Confederates with such dispatch those last five months. We all knew the war would soon be over, and yet here he came, that porcine little man in his Union blues, to explain why this one or that one needed to come with him to prison. I understood that he was only following orders—he didn't seem the sort of man who would do anything without direction—and that he took no pleasure in his task. When he arrived on a morning, he would have two other soldiers with him, hard men with sunburned faces who looked like they wanted to be somewhere else, doing something other than hauling men off to prison. In my dreams I still remember those two men, whose faces are not terribly distinct anymore—I believe one had a red mustache—but who were eloquent in their exhaustion. They were as tired as I was, as the men lying in my parlor were, as my husband was, as Zachariah was. Exhaustion could not be transformed by victory, I saw. This gave me some comfort.

All of the men who were taken away did their best to remain dignified despite their terror. Those that could walk did not resist, and walked out the door between the two guards without looking back at us once. Those who could not walk allowed themselves to be carried between the two guards. They would apologize for the awkward load they made, and thanked the men for assisting them. They would not look back, either.

I know, of course, that the little Union officer had sensed my attachment to Zachariah and avoided taking him from the house even though he was as fit as he would ever become, even though he could walk off under his own power without any assistance at all. I believe Zachariah was spared capture so that I might be assuaged and more cooperative with the little officer as he went about his duties. In this he was right, and although I was not grateful to him for his shrewd assessment of the situation and my character, I was happy to have Zachariah with us as long as possible. I wanted him to know my children, I wanted him to imagine what *I* had lost while looking into their eyes. He gave no sign of any recognition, but only carved little toys for Hattie and Winder—a lean, ridge-backed hog for Winder and a little sway-backed horse for Hattie. He told them not to lose them, that there was something special about the little toys and that bad luck would come to them if they were lost. The children, of course, became afraid of their toys and put them away in drawers for safekeeping and never took them out again. Zachariah, I knew, would never have his own children if he could help it.

The Union man could not put off the capture of Zachariah forever. I knew I had to prepare for his departure after my strange, beautiful companion had become the last of the wounded left in

the house, practically a new member of the family, and even a con-
fidant of John, with whom he played cards late into the night.

Nothing had ever lasted. This is how I pitied myself, by
thinking it over and over again: *Nothing had ever lasted. Nothing ever
lasts.* The fragile wonders such as love and children disappeared
with abandon. Did I love Zachariah Cashwell? Yes, yes, yes. It was
impossible, but yes. I imagined a day when he would pick me up
and carry me off, and I would hold on to him by his arms, sensing
heat in his ropy muscles, praying it was the same heat I felt in my
scalp, my cheeks, my belly. How could I love such a man? He was
a strange man from a stranger world, so foreign in every possible
way. He knew nothing of running a household or a plantation or a
business. My house did not impress him, nor our land, nor our few
remaining fine things. What did he care for china or silver or
French wallpaper? Perhaps that's why I was drawn to him: he
didn't care, and I was shocked and excited by the idea that such
things weren't worth caring about, that the most beautiful objects
were still objects and therefore dead. He was alive, and he had
lived for reasons other than propriety and position. He had lived
for its own sake, to breathe and to ride and to see what he could
see. This thrilled me. *He* thrilled me.

O Lord, I would have followed him had You let me, but You did
not give me the strength to become a fallen woman. I was and
have always been Carrie McGavock, mother of children and the
wife of a good man. I cared what the world thought of me, and perhaps this was the truly foreign thing about Zachariah Cashwell—
he didn't care at all. I could only pray and hope that he cared for
me, that my feelings weren't silly and girlish fantasies, but that
they were the response of a woman to a man who desired her.
That was all I needed to know, that's all I needed to sustain me.
That I was the object of *desire*.

On that hot April morning the little officer came to the door
without his guards and knocked. I knew that it was Zachariah's
time, and after opening the door and exchanging a few words, I
hurried to his room. When I burst through the door of the extra
bedroom in the wing, he was leaning on his crutch and looking out

the window. He had seen the man ride up, too. I stood still, silent and bereft. He shuffled around on his crutch to face me, and I did not see the fear in his face that I felt for him. He let the corner of his mouth turn up, like he was about to smile but thought it wasn't appropriate. He cocked his head, and—for the life of me this is true—he looked the charming rake. A rogue. It made me smile, even as I stomped my foot on the floor to get his attention and let him know I was serious. It wasn't until he reached over and brushed my cheek that I felt the chill of my tears.

"Might I borrow a comb from you, Mrs. McGavock?"

A *comb?* Had he nothing to say to me? I straightened myself and wiped my face and pointed.

"There's one in the top drawer of that bureau."

He walked over to the bureau and pulled the drawer open. There was an old bone comb in there, one that I had used to untangle Winder's curls. Zachariah looked at his hand, looked up at me, smiled, and then began to apply spit to his long black hair. He pulled the comb through it, again and again, and I watched the rats' nest become a smooth stream of black. He put the comb down and hobbled over to the chest where Mariah had placed his folded and clean uniform. I turned and began to walk out of the room, out of modesty and confusion and sadness.

"Please. I need some help."

When I turned around, he had dropped the coveralls I'd given him, which I had modified to accommodate his stump, and stood balanced before me in his long johns. I saw his eyes then. I discovered it was possible to look into a person's eyes for months at a time and still not know his every shape and expression. I was surprised by how dark they seemed in that moment and how they turned down at the corners as if he would have to fight to make them turn up again. They were so unrelievedly sad. I waited for him to hop over and hold me and tell me he didn't want to ever leave me, that he would take me with him. I wanted to smell his neck and feel his chest against mine. But he just stood there, looking at me through those weary green eyes, indulging for the moment whatever thoughts were passing behind those eyes, before blinking and trying to smile again.

He was able to open the chest at the foot of the bed, but he couldn't stoop down far enough to reach into it. I stepped forward and removed the uniform, placing it on the bed. I could hear his breath, so shallow, when I drew near. That was the last sign I ever saw of his anxiety.

He picked up his uniform blouse, which looked far too torn and patched to ever wear again, and tugged it on. I watched his fingers work the buttons and was surprised at how graceful they were; I'd become so used to watching him lurch around on his crutch that I'd forgotten he might still possess some grace. Then he sat down on the bed with his trousers in his hand, and I understood that I was to help him put them on.

I tugged at the pant legs, first by standing in front of him, then by kneeling behind with my arms around him. He had never allowed me to do this for him before.

When his pants were most of the way on, I went back to standing in front of him and helped him to arrange the pant legs so that they were straight. The remainder of his missing leg had withered so. Touching his two legs was like touching two different men entirely, or catching two glimpses of the man's future: to shrink and to falter, or to grow strong. I had no inkling what would happen to him, one way or the other.

He finally stood again, and I will admit that he startled me. You'd think I wouldn't have forgotten that he was *Sergeant* Cashwell, but I had. And there he was, those stripes on his arm. He saw me looking at them.

"I'd rip these off and give them to you, but I might be able to get some money for 'em someday, them being collector's items. I reckon I might not be seeing much money for a while, so please forgive me."

"I wouldn't want those dirty old things."

"I don't really want 'em, either, truth be told."

Zachariah looked over my head, and I turned to see John leaning in the doorway, and I blushed. He didn't notice, fiddling with the loops on his trousers before he looked up.

"Do you need anything, Sergeant Cashwell? Do you need money?"

"I don't reckon they'll let me have money, Mr. McGavock."

"I suppose you're right."

They both looked at each other, nodding their heads like heavy branches in a slow wind. I have since noticed that men communicate in this fashion, although I'm not sure how. What I knew was that they looked ridiculous, and yet I was happy that John had apparently come to see Zachariah off.

We walked down the hall and into the main house, through the dining room and past the wallpaper with its scenes of exotic lands at the edge of my imagination. We turned left in the central passage, and at the door stood the little officer and Mariah, who had kept him waiting in the hall.

I took Zachariah's hand, warm and rough, and he gripped my hand tightly. Mariah and John were watching me, but I didn't care. *I didn't care.* When he walked toward the little officer, I went with him. When he stood before the man and surrendered himself as a prisoner, I held on to him. And when he walked out of the house and down the steps, his fingers loosened and pulled along my palm to the ends of my fingers.

Then they were gone, and the fast-fading feeling of his callused skin on my fingertips was the only thing he'd left behind.

From the Diary of
Major Jonathan Van der Broeck, U.S.A.

He was under a sort of parole of honor, without being guarded. He had substantially recovered from his wounds at the time our regiment arrived at Franklin. On our arrival the colonel had handed me an order which directed me to keep track of the Confederates at McGavocks' and to haul in those who were able to move. I would take a detail of two men, with two ambulances, and go to McGavocks' every once in a while and take some of the men who were there and bring them to Franklin, for the purpose of being sent to Nashville and thence to the North to some military prison. Due to what I called a clerical oversight, for which I received a good drubbing, one sergeant enjoyed the hospitality at McGavocks' far longer than any other. When the colonel found out, he ordered me to go immediately and take the man into custody, and so I took an ambulance myself and rode out there. I could have taken some men, but I didn't think I needed them.

I went into the house, met the lady of the establishment, and inquired of her for the sergeant, and was informed that he was in another room. I requested the lady to round up the sergeant and to tell him that I desired to see him. She disappeared, and after a little while the sergeant walked into the room on one crutch.

He was a man of medium stature, thin and rangy, black hair, piercing green eyes that glistened, and looked to be about thirty years old. He was a splendid-looking soldier, even in his battle-torn rags. I stepped forward and briefly and courteously told him of my business. "All right," he answered, "I reckon I'm ready."

We left the house. He moved well on the crutch, and he asked to sit up next to me in the cart, rather than down below. I allowed him this, but warned him that he would have to get into the bed when we approached town for appearance's sake. When we were up, and I had just taken the reins in my hands, he asked me if I wouldn't mind waiting a moment. He turned in the seat and looked toward the open front door, which was at some considerable distance and so dark that it was impossible to see anyone inside. Still, he looked and looked. I slapped the reins, and we bumped away along the driveway.

Before we were out of sight he asked me to stop the cart, and I obliged him. I turned to follow his gaze.

Everyone had gone back inside—everyone except the lady, who still stood on that high front porch, watching us.

I slapped the reins. The horses moved off, but he kept watching that house until we rounded the bend in the driveway and all you could see was part of the upper porch.

Even without a leg he looked a capable man. If he could survive prison, he'd be better off than most men, I thought. Two days later he disappeared from the custody of the prison detail. One night he was there, the next morning he was gone. I got a good drubbing for that, too.

BOOK III

35

THE GRIFFIN HOMESTEAD

Becky Griffin grew bigger so slowly that her brother and her father didn't notice until she was just a month or so from delivering. *She* had noticed, of course, and hadn't cared to hide her condition. She had wanted to grow large quickly so that she would have to spend the spring and the summer answering the questions. *I loved a boy and a boy loved me,* she planned to say, and that's all she planned to say. She had wanted to declare this much to the world, but the world didn't notice. Only her father and her brother noticed, and by that time she could barely speak for the pain shooting through her back and the disorientation of her dizzy spells.

She never told her father the name of the boy. Eli would have recognized him, but she knew he would never be able to give him any name other than Cotton Gin, and that would be guard enough against the revelation of Will's identity. Now that Will was dead, she had no intention of sharing her child with the Baylors, or even allowing them to know of its existence. She would possess a living part of Will they could never share, and this pleased her. When she wasn't too light-headed to think, she realized that the Baylors would probably say it was just as well, that the child of trash like

her could never be the child of their Will. She knew what would
happen if she told her father or her brother about Will Baylor.
Soon enough her father would go see Mr. Baylor to ask for help
supporting a child the Griffins could ill afford, and Mr. Baylor
would likely treat him as a common beggar. She would not, not
ever, allow her father to be humiliated like that. He would do it for
her, she knew, setting aside whatever pride he had left to help her.
She wouldn't have it. And anyway, she reasoned, they wouldn't
help however hard her father begged.

Mr. Griffin said no more about the circumstances of her pregnancy after it was clear she would never reveal the name of the
father. He said nothing about her morals or her character or her
foolishness. She had saved the family when their mother, his wife,
had died. How would they have eaten? How would they have
stayed together? He owed her these few months of happiness, and
he owed her those faint smiles he saw steal across her face when
she rubbed her belly.

Eli couldn't quit thinking about the man he had met at the
farm, the one who called himself Cotton. Instead of considering
what he owed Becky, he considered what this Cotton owed *them.*
He minded his father and didn't badger Becky about it, but in the
hot, heavy months of July and August, Eli stole out of the house
in just his coveralls and a hat, as if he were going swimming in the
creek, and hiked around the countryside and the town trying to
catch a glimpse of the man who had done this to his sister. What
he would do when he found him, he hadn't a notion. He knew
only that he was angry that his sister and the baby had been left to
fend for themselves by that tall, puzzling Confederate with the
ridiculous name. He knew his sister had been in love with the
man, and perhaps he should have left it at that. But what the hell
was love if it meant being used up and left behind? What kind of
man in love would do such a thing? Eli soured on the idea of love
that summer. He loved his dead mother, his father, and his sister.
Only them. All others had best not cross him. Someday he would
find this Cotton. In the meantime he watched Becky carefully.

Becky knew in August there was something gravely wrong. Her
back spasmed constantly. She could not stand up for more than a

minute without fainting, and her fingers and toes felt tingly and odd. She prayed that God would take her and spare her child and said nothing to Eli or her father. They could do nothing for her, she knew, and she wanted no charity from anyone else. She wanted to deliver this child herself, as her mother had done and her grandmother before. If she could not do that, how could she deserve a child? If she had been in her right mind, she might have asked for help, but the pain had made her stubborn and single-minded. What help she would have would be the help of her family, as bedraggled as it was.

The baby decided to come into the world on August 29, 1865, whether the Griffins were ready or not. Becky was ready, but knew nothing but pain and more pain. Eli and his father had thought they were ready, but as Eli would write to Carrie much later, what did they know?

> *Pa had birthed cattle, and he reckoned it weren't much different, but it was a hell of a lot different, yes, it was. That baby wouldn't come out for hours, and the whole damned time Becky was losing blood. For hours she was screaming, and I said to Pa, "Who can help us?" and he said there was nobody. Becky would faint from the pain, and I'd wake her up by splashing water on her, and then she'd push and groan and scream some more, and still that baby wouldn't come out. And so I tried to think on it for myself. Where could I go for help? And I thought of you, Miss Carrie, but Becky weren't hearing of it. "Don't you go bothering her," she said, again and again. But other than you, there weren't no one. At least there weren't no one who would help us.*
>
> *Right about that time, just after the war was done with, folks started moving out of this place, going other places where the war hadn't turned everything to shit. Please pardon my language, but I can't rightly think of a better word for what this place was like. My best friend, my only friend, Ab, he left. The neighbors on every side of us were gone. There weren't anyone for miles. I didn't no more care one damn about that war, or who won it or who lost it or any other damn thing about it. That war had cleared the place out. Don't you remember how*

empty it got? I remember looking at all the unworked fields surrounding us for miles, like we was an island in an ocean of scraggly brush and thistle, and thinking that it all looked like someone had died. It looked like death itself out there. It was all around us, and there weren't no getting out from under it, and all we had was that cabin and those candles and that sister of mine screaming and pleading to God, and there weren't anything I could do to help her.

I couldn't take it no longer after watching my sister for most of a day, and that's when I left the house and went running for help from you, all the time my sister screaming and cursing and damning me for leaving her. "This is my *baby!" she kept on saying, over and over again. So that's how I came to be standing up there on your porch, crying and trying to put words to the things I'd seen back in our cabin. You didn't need me to say much, 'cause I could see you understood right when I said the word* baby. *Next thing I knew, you and me and Mariah were in your cart running your horse hard for our place. I remember you said, "I don't know what I can do," and so I said without thinking that she was as wounded as any of the damned soldiers you'd tended the winter before, and you'd been able to help* them, *so of course you could help Becky unless you got something about helping poor folk and not Confederates. You slapped me good then.*

You remember that it was Mariah what got down on her knees before my sister, like she was praying to her, and tried to turn that baby. I remember seeing her look into my sister's eyes all fierce and tough, like she was trying to see into that part of Becky that was also fierce and tough. Reckon she didn't find it, or that part of my sister was all wored out by then.

You know most of the rest. Mariah delivered that baby with the greasy blue cord around its neck. The boy was already dead when it entered the world, blue as a berry. My daddy cut the cord and laid the boy down on the kitchen table and wrapped him up in some blankets, so that Becky could see him one last time, but she was already screaming again and couldn't see anything with her eyes pinched so hard shut. Then the blood came, and I could tell by watching you and Mariah do your best to stop her blood that there wasn't any hope. She didn't quit bleeding for hours, and by the time she did quit she was white and clammy and talking gibberish. Hot as hell, too. You and Mariah laid wet rags on her forehead while my pa and I watched, but there was no cooling her off. You held her hand while she got hotter and hotter and thrashed around in her bed, and you kept holding her hand long after she'd quit thrashing and had passed from this world.

It makes me feel better that you and Mariah were there with her when she passed. She talked about you two a lot.

The thing you don't know is that all the rest of what happened years later, at least my part of it, started that night. We was riding in the cart—you and me and Mariah and Pa—carrying Becky and her baby back to Carnton to be laid out proper. I was sitting between you and Mariah, and Pa was in the back of the cart holding on to Becky and not listening to anything or noticing anything around him. We was coming up around the bend in your driveway when you said this: "Damn him. Damn you right to hell, Will Baylor." You said it under your breath, I guess thinking that no one was listening to you, but I was listening to you close right after I heard you say "him."

You probably didn't realize that Becky had never told me or Pa the name of her beau. She was prideful in that way, I guess. I thought we'd never get justice after Becky passed, that the man who had killed my sister would never face a reckoning. Then you said those words, and everything became clear to me.

It didn't take me long to figure out that Will Baylor had died in the battle. It's possible he wouldn't have abandoned my sister had he been alive, but it's hard to know. He was dead anyway, and so I didn't have no more business with him. But I watched them Baylors close. I watched them in their fancy clothes and their gleaming carriages pulled by strong and beautiful horses. I watched them get richer, and I watched other people get poorer and more violent and more lonely, and I especially watched that old man, the man who I reckoned had been the one to scare my sister and Will into hiding. I watched him special close, but I didn't do nothing. What was there to do?

Then come your unpleasantness with the man, and you know the rest.

36

ZACHARIAH CASHWELL

I should have knowed it would come my time eventually; it seemed I'd been running for years. I'd become good at it, a master of escape. Ought to have found a carnival and shipped out with them to perform escape tricks for money, but the kinds of escapes I'd mastered weren't exactly the kind that could be done under the lights, and they weren't all that exciting, either. Darkness was everything, and waiting for the right opportunity. That opportunity always came along, and I'd learned to count on it these last years. I come to count on it so much that I'd become sloppier and sloppier about staying the hell out of trouble. What did I care? I'd slipped right out from under that fat little Yankee officer's watch back there without even a scratch. Just up and walked out the unlocked door of the old store in town, the little officer's jail, while he and his other charges snored and farted around me dreaming their boring little dreams. I came to think I was being watched over, that I could do and say what I want without suffering for any of it.

* * *

If you got to hobble and limp everywhere with a dull ache of a wooden leg, working for the railroad is the kind of thing to make a man forget that there's a thing wrong with him. You catch a ride on one of them engines with the cowcatchers, perched up there ahead of the fireman and off to the side of the engineer, just laying your head out the window and smelling that sweet, pulpy smell of summer on the fields, and you can very easily forget a whole lot of things. But I didn't get to ride much. Not enough for my taste leastways.

It was something to watch what happened to the country when the railroad came through. I don't mean *the country*, like the kind of thing you had to swear your allegiance to and vote about and all the rest of it. I mean the country, the place where we all from, at least those of us who didn't have much before the war and didn't have much to show for it after. I don't mind saying that it was a great relief, maybe on all of us to one measure or another, to come through the country to build something for once, and not burning or digging or chopping or shooting. Not sitting in the cold rain and swallowing your fear, looking out at old fields full of unharvested cotton and wondering what you could have done with the money from that harvest if you'd just had the chance; but sitting in a saloon made of thick pine railroad ties and waxed canvas with a couple of aces on the flop and cash money on the table. Men *brought* us whiskey and women and money. They didn't avoid us no more, they didn't pull the shutters closed on their little cottages marooned in abandoned fields, they didn't douse their lights when we passed.

I was working the Memphis & Selma Railroad, which weren't much of a railroad then, and never got finished. Just tracks to nowhere that stopped where the last man sunk the last spike. It was the company of old General Nathan Bedford Forrest, who the Federals never got up the gumption to arrest after the war. A lot of the men got all fired up about being part of "Forrest's company," like they were back in the war riding with the man, but for my own self I didn't care one damn who paid me at the end of the week. I'd take money from big Abe himself, if he were around to give it out. I knew the money weren't going to last long, though, no matter who was paying wages. We was always running out of money at our camp, and I heard the other camps along the line down around Columbus and Selma were running out of money, too. I reckoned Forrest found railroading a right bit harder than running around on horses and shooting every damned thing he saw. He didn't look like no Wizard of the Saddle no more, that's for sure. He looked like a skinny, gray old man who had got over his head with this railroad thing.

In those years there were railroad camps like ours all over the South, and I did my time in plenty of them. There was thousands of miles of track to repair and thousands more to be laid afresh. There were men, men with money, who came through and got up on stumps and told us we were new men in a new South, forging by our sweat the means for the South to rise and take its share of the money and business we was owed, that we weren't to be backward no more. Sounded like a bit of bullshit, truly, and I hadn't never thought of myself as backward, exactly, but if I got to wear me one of them nice fob watches on a chain and dark striped vests like those fellers wore, well, I was all in favor of being dragged out of my backwardness.

So we laid track from Charleston to Little Rock, from Mobile to Nashville. We made our own towns temporary, outside the real towns, and we didn't have no law except the law that the company made for us and the law that got sorted out between men at the point of a knife. After a while, that came to seem like plenty of law.

I had traveled around a little after getting away from those Union boys up in Franklin. I'd learned how to walk on my wooden leg so that it looked like I only had a little limp, and I'd learned to ride a horse even if I was a little unbalanced. I don't mind saying that I got to looking pretty damned good when I was riding, and it was a shame I couldn't ride except when I could pinch a horse out of a tenant man's yard in the late night, to ease my travel. I ain't no horse thief, I didn't *keep* those horses. I'd ride 'em awhile and then send them back to where they come from, and I reckon a good many of 'em made it back to where they belonged. I reckoned I'd given my damned leg for people like them farmers, they could give me a ride on their nags every once in awhile.

Jerrod, my old friend from Carnton, had been the one to find me in a saloon in a new town—Birmingham—and told me about the job on Forrest's railroad. His hair was as black and as greasy and as long as ever. It still hung over his face like he didn't want no one to ever see him. He'd taken to wearing all black duds, too, and so he had the look of an undertaker or a devil, depending on your point of view. But I knew him to be a sweet boy, and he still was, when I met up with him in Birmingham, even though I come to find out he'd learned to shoot pretty good with just that one eye of his and that he'd got into a career as a private detective, which meant he was a gun for hire.

Our camp was a few miles south of Memphis, and we was a rough crowd. The more we thought of ourselves that way, the rougher we got. You don't know how depraved a man can be until you let him do just what the hell he wants, and most of us—I'd bet that included most all of the men who'd worn gray at one time or another—were of a mind, in those years after the war was over, to do whatever the hell we wanted.

Some of the men'd clear brush and sweet gum and poplars during the day and watch the track men come through the cut, amidst the buzzing of flies and humming of mosquitoes, laying down crushed rock and pounding down crossties. The evening sun never wanted to go down, seemed like, and in the last minutes of its trip across the hazy white sky the light would shoot through the crowns of the trees, right on through the leaves and the veins of the leaves, and make them glow just at the edges, and that's how you knew it was about time for someone to go on down to the creek and pull out whatever whiskey or liquor was on hand. Whiskey ain't best served cold, but that really weren't a consideration for men who leaked out enough water in the Tennessee heat to fill a dozen troughs each himself. Once they were in the liquor, there weren't no telling what kind of man would pop out of that jug when it'd been tipped up and emptied and licked dry of every drop. Some men you just didn't want to know, and they didn't care if you knew them or not.

I felt much at home.

There were always people running away from a railroad camp.

The same things that would draw you in—money and liquor and women—could be your downfall if you weren't careful. If you was running, it was because you done something you oughtn't have and it was your own damned fault. It weren't like war, when everything you had in the world, even your life, was likely to be taken from you without any explaining or reasoning. Now there were *reasons* for being whumped on, even if those reasons didn't make no sense. Men carried pistols and Bibles and liquor, and there wasn't no trying to piece out what didn't belong, because it all belonged. I wasn't anything special in that camp, and the ladies were ready to take me on for a piece of silver, if I'd had the inkling. I hadn't the inkling, but I did like the whiskey and the gambling and the way the lamps sent off wavy, glassy beads of light that slapped against the sides of the tents, beads that would slip and slide over the beams and poles and canvas as the wind blew or as I got drunker.

I had the title *Exchequer of Camp, Memphis & Selma Railroad*, but everybody knew I was the clerk. The money man. The man who had his ear to the wall, who knew the people who knew the people who could get a man what he wanted. I was important, if not indispensable, although the supervisor used to call me that. I was most definitely dispensable, though, as things turned out. Dispensable was a mighty polite word for it.

My escape began the week old Forrest decided to show up and pore over the books I'd been keeping, looking to see if there weren't someplace he could save some money, to see if he could find some money hidden somewhere. That was the week Twist Fitzhugh, who ran the log tavern we all drank at, decided to catch him a nigger and chain the fella to a post in the backyard of his saloon. Twist was a fat little bastard with a red shiny head and a face like a slab of rock. He owned some acres on either side of the tracks, but Twist was not the kind of man who liked to work up a sweat, and so his land remained uncleared. He tried like hell to get some of the men to jump ship and spend a couple months chopping down trees in exchange for free liquor, but when you consider that it was out of goodwill that any of us actually paid for

Twist's nasty swill, his proposition didn't seem like such a bargain. His land lay unused, and it drove that little schemer crazy, and he'd stand behind that pinewood bar picking at splinters, scratching his hairy belly through the gaps between the buttons of his shirt, and yammering about "work ethics" and the way men used to pitch in and help each other, and a whole lot of other bullshit that none of us paid much attention to.

Then he got his nigger. Don't know how Twist got up the energy to catch one, but one night we came by the tavern and there was this Negro sitting with his back against Twist's chicken coop. He had a collar around his neck and a heavy chain attached to it. He was a tall and young Negro, kind of yellow with a sharp nose and deep black eyes. He'd look at you if he raised his head while you were out pissing behind the tavern, and his face was the face of a man who could take anything and still figure out a way to keep going on. He'd have been a powerful enough man if he weren't so damned underfed. Twist said he'd caught the nigger trying to steal a chicken, which I knew to be a lie because Twist didn't actually *have* chickens, unless that was the word you used for the women who roosted in his coop with their tricks. Back then, though, if you had any story to justify whipping a Negro, it was a good enough story for most people.

Twist kept his Negro chained up at night, but during the day, when the tavern was closed, he'd take him off the chain and make him clear brush. Twist had a cross-eyed son named Gypsum, who we all called the Gyp. The Gyp was thirteen years old, and dumb as a board, but he could handle a rifle, and so the two of them would accompany the nigger into the woods, where Twist would whip him into working harder and faster, while the Gyp stood by to make sure their new friend didn't run. That's what they called him: *our new friend.* People didn't have *slaves* no more, understand.

The first couple days of the Negro's captivity, I went along with it like the rest. Didn't want to say anything likely to get me in trouble. I know there were some other men who were sickened by the sight of that Negro's neck, which was hatching sores where the collar rubbed him wrong. There were a couple whispers about letting the Negro go, but as bad as the whiskey was at Twist's, it wasn't bad enough to be cut off entirely, which Twist would do if he found out who let his prize go. And you couldn't predict what that demon child, the Gyp, would do.

So I kept silent. I didn't like it much, but I reckoned that the nigger had done something to get himself in trouble, and I had learned that there was some rough justice out here. It weren't right to chain a man up like that, Negro or not. I'd never known many Negroes except for the ones at Carnton, Mariah and Theopolis, and they were all right. As for others, I didn't have much to say about 'em one way or another. But I could see pain in the man's face, and some smarts, too, and it was impossible for me to think of the Negro out back on the chain as just another animal. I had been spoiled my knowing that Mariah nigra. Not enough to do anything about it, but enough to feel guilty about letting things go on.

I didn't much respect myself then, truth be told. Didn't like the man I was, not much anyway.

Things changed the night before Forrest's arrival at the camp. We didn't reckon we could be ass drunk while he was on the premises, so Jerrod and me and some others decided to get ass drunk *before* he was on the premises. Toward the end of the night, after swaying between the tables made of trestles and boards and knocking over some glasses, I made my way out the back door and down the three steps to the yard, where I intended to relieve myself. Instead, I tripped over the nigger's chain and fell to the ground. The way I remember it, though, I looked down and I was sinking *into* the ground, and soon I could barely see anything above the tips of the grass looming so high above me. I must have passed out. That night I had the only dream that had ever scared me, which was also the only dream I ever had since leaving Carnton.

The preacher man took my mama. I saw her go. I heard her go. I heard her say, "Good-bye, my love."

An angel came to me with a message. He said, "Deeper, saith the Lord." And so I thought and I thought, and then I remembered. The angel took me roughly by the hand, and I was surprised by the calluses on his palm. He asked me to stand by the door. I'd forgotten that door. He said, "Wait,

wait," and then "Now!" and he pushed it open. He walked quickly into the room, where my father sat with his back turned and his face in his hands. I could see the brown hills through the window over his head, and I noticed that there were no trees. Just hill after hill of brown grass rolling away. The angel glided toward my father and pulled something from beneath his wing. A gun. A little pistol. My father turned and said, "I saw you in the window," and then the angel put him down with that little pistol. My father's head came to rest on the windowsill. His eyes were open, and he seemed to be looking up. He hadn't shaved that week, and I saw my father's gray hair for the first time. The long, deep wrinkles on his cheeks, like trenches, had disappeared. His faded coveralls showed the growing stain. I wondered, Had he seen me in the window? I wanted to tell him that there was no use looking up like that, weren't nothing up there, the angel was standing right there in front of him. But my mother appeared behind me and covered my mouth with her hand. Her hand was sweaty, and she smelled sour. She had been gone for days, and she was wearing the same frock she'd left in. She was shaking, but I wasn't sure who scared her the most—the angel or me.

Then she walked into the room, and I knew it was me. She and the preacher held their arms around each other and whispered for days, until they both turned to me. The preacher smiled. He was small and wore glasses. He was pale like he hadn't ever been outside, and when he came toward me, his glasses quit reflecting the light and his eyes looked dark, almost black. He smiled and wiped his brow and stood in front of me. I was almost his height, but not quite. He told me to turn around, and so I did, but not before looking at my father one more time. My mother stood over him, closing his eyes tenderly with one hand while she pulled something out of his pocket. After I turned away I saw nothing.

But I heard the angel again, and the angel had another message. He said, "A fornicator, or covetous, or an idolator, or a railer, or a drunkard, or an extortioner: with such a one, no, not to eat." And then he said, "But if there be no resurrection of the dead, then is Christ not risen?" I heard the scrape of a shovel and saw my mother throwing dirt on the face of my father, who was lying in a hole. The yellow dirt filled his eyes and the wrinkles of his face until he was only something shaped like a man, and then he was nothing at all. The preacher stood by my mother and read from a book.

I felt ropes on my wrists and legs, and I could see the preacher and my mother, when the wind wasn't blowing and blinding me with dust. I heard a voice, and I didn't much care whose it was. "For he that eateth and drinketh unworthily, eateth and drinketh damnation to himself, not discerning the Lord's body. For this cause many are weak and sickly among you, and many sleep. For if we would judge ourselves, we should not be judged. But when we are judged, we are chastened of the Lord, that we should not be condemned with the world."

I watched them ride away. My mother said, "Good-bye, my love," and I thought I heard her laugh. I slept for a long time, maybe days. Then another angel came and untied me. He told me he was only a messenger and could not explain. Or else he said, "I don't understand. What the hell has happened here, goddammit?" That part is never very clear in my dream. The last thing he says to me, after untying the ropes that bound me and kept me from getting up, is that I should go find my aunt and live with her.

That's when I wake up. My aunt, I remember, never asked me why I'd come to her.

The next morning I awoke behind the tavern with my cheek resting on the ground, staring into the face of the Negro not ten feet away. In his sleep he looked younger, like a boy. The sight of his collar and his chain made me want to throw up, and I stumbled off to the edge of the woods and retched. I walked back and looked down on him. I had a simple thought that came to me quickly and which I could not ignore. I would not let anyone, even a Negro, be bound in my presence. Where was this Negro's mama? His daddy? Who did he have? He'd been abandoned. I ain't weak-minded enough to think he *was* me, but I knew he was enough like the boy I'd been that I couldn't let it go like that.

The mistake I made was thinking I could sort things out all rational-like. I should have broken that chain right then. I was a fool.

Forrest arrived that next morning and created a stir. Some of the men shouted cheers and stamped their feet and called for a speech. I'd seen the man a couple of times and knew that he was no spontaneous speechifier. After a few moments, as Forrest dismounted and tied his black horse to the rail in front of the camp office, the shouts and talking died down. The men were seeing him truly for the first time, and I knew he weren't what they expected. He got down slowly, and the only thing that came out of his mouth was a few loud, painful, wet coughs. He was skinny and completely gray. He was a tall man, but he looked short because he was so bent and twisted up. His eyes were red and watery, but there was still a little fierce in them, and so I knew better than to help him put up his horse. I was waiting for him at the doorway and stepped aside when he shuffled in.

That day we spent going over the books, papers everywhere. I had good handwriting, which was about the only useful thing I'd ever picked up as far as education, and I'd got taught pretty good by the previous clerk how to fill in the numbers and line 'em up. I didn't know much, but I knowed about money. There weren't much, and I could have told him that at the beginning and saved him the trouble, but he wanted to see everything for hisself. Wanted to see what every man was paid, wanted to see every dime we'd spent on timber and rails and spikes and tools. We toured the camp so he could see these things for himself, to make sure no one was stealing nothing. All day I waited for a moment to ask him my question, the one I'd begun to think up that morning out back of Twist's place. When we returned to the office, he sat down and pulled out a flask and rummaged around for a tin cup. He did not invite me to join him, and he didn't invite me to talk to him, either.

There was a ruckus outside. I went to the window and looked out toward the tavern and saw a crowd of the men standing around the nigger while the Gyp ran around him, poking him with a stick always just out of reach of the prisoner's grasp. Forrest was watching me.

"What's that sound? Ain't they working?"

"They got a nigger chained up behind the tavern, General."

"They do? Hmm."

He went back to his flask and picked up the books again.

"General Forrest?"

He didn't say anything. I think he knew what I was going to say and didn't want to hear it, but I said it anyway.

"It ain't right, General."

"You damned right about that. This railroad should be *making* me money."

"I mean that nigger."

Silence.

"General, it ain't right to have him chained up like that. It's illegal. That boy ain't done nothing."

"He ain't done nothing? Nothing?"

"They say he tried to steal a chicken."

"Well, then."

"But there ain't no chickens."

He put the book down and took a swig. He stared up at the ceiling for a while, cocked back in the chair, and let his legs stretch out in front of him. Then he fixed those red eyes on me.

"I don't got the time to be worrying what every damned fool does with a Negro. If they happy, and they do my work for me, then I'm happy. I ain't fooling with that."

I was losing my chance. I knew he didn't want no problems with Negroes on his railroad. Everyone knew he'd got hisself mixed up with the Ku Klux. I'd read the newspapers, and I knew he was doing everything he could to try to get people to forget that he was the wizard, or some such shit. I knew he didn't care whether that nigger lived or died, but I also knew that his reputation had been bad for business. Folks didn't really mind niggers getting their due for getting above themselves, as they said, but the rich ones and the politicians who gave out the money for railroads didn't want to be the one to dirty their hands at it, or to be doing business with those who did. People were almost as afraid of the Ku Kluxers as they were of free Negroes roaming the country. That's what the paper said. So I took a chance.

"What's gone to happen when folks find out we got a nigger chained up like a dog at one of the Memphis & Selma camps?"

Now he stood up, and this time he weren't bent over like an old man, and I could see why men had followed him. I'd have been too scared not to.

"All right, then."

I didn't know what he meant, but I followed him outside, down the steps, and over to the tavern where the Gyp was still running around like a fool with that stick. Forrest walked right through the middle of the crowd, which parted like a stream around a rock. He stood in the middle of the circle, and the Gyp stopped running and stood stock-still. Even the Negro paused and waited to hear what the man would say.

"Mr. Cashwell has told me that he wants this here nigger freed. I myself don't care much about it one way or the other, but I *do* know that if the fool who chained this sumbitch up gets me in trouble for it, I gone to come back and put a bullet in that fool's goddamn head. Seeing as how that would make a mess out of my railroad camp, and seeing how Mr. Cashwell has volunteered to solve my problem by freeing this nigger to go run off to wherever his people run off to, I'm gone to deputize Mr. Cashwell to free this nigger if he sees fit. And that's the end of my problem."

Well, the crowd didn't like that much, I could tell, but only one of 'em would say anything about it. Twist stepped out of the crowd.

"That there nigger stole one of my chickens. I want my compensation."

Forrest got a coughing fit right then, and he bent over and hacked out a gob between his feet. When he stood back up, he took a second to get his bearings again.

"You shut the hell up, little man. Don't ever talk back to me."

Then he walked right back through that crowd, got onto his horse, and rode away toward Memphis.

Well, that wasn't the end of *my* problem. I knew I had only a few seconds to do what needed doing, before the men could fix themselves on me, so I walked forward as quickly as I could on my aching stump and unhooked that collar.

"Run like hell," I whispered.

The other men didn't know what to do first, there was too much going on. Some were watching Forrest ride off, others were watching the nigger run into the woods, and I hoped that I could get back to the office without getting stopped. But Twist jumped in my path, just as I got clear of the crowd.

"Where the hell do you think you're going, nigger lover? You done fucked up bad."

The other men started to close around me, and I could smell their sweat and feel the heat of a hard day on the tracks drifting off 'em. I saw the Gyp go for his rifle, which was leaning against the chicken coop.

"Put that rifle down, boy, and the rest of you step back. You heard the general. The man had permission."

Jerrod had his pistols out, one pointed at the Gyp and the other in the general direction of the crowd. He stood between me and the office. Thank God I'd made one friend at least.

"You all get back in that saloon and drink and forget all this shit. I been known to use these pistols. And I don't even like any of you-all."

Twist wasn't giving up that easily.

"To hell with you, Jerrod. Cashwell is a nigger lover, and he owes me. He has disgraced me."

Jerrod strode up to the little saloonkeeper and put one of his pistols to the man's head.

"And I'll disgrace your brains all over this ground if you don't get back in that swill shop of yours."

I didn't stick around to hear the rest of it. I went as fast as I could toward the office, went inside, and barred the door behind me. *What the hell am I going to do now?* I looked around for my things, and I realized I didn't have much except for a blanket and a Bible. I was wrapping them up together when I heard a knock on the door. I didn't have a weapon except for an old axe in the corner, and I grabbed it.

"It's me—Jerrod."

I let him in. He took his broad-brimmed hat off his head, pushed his greasy black strands from in front of his face, and put it back on. He fixed on me with a queer look.

"You're going to need more than that axe. Goddamn you're a fool. Why the hell did you do that? Weren't none of your business. What you care for a nigger anyway? You made a mess, boy. They in the tavern getting liquored up now, but that won't hold 'em long. They gone to come for you. You got to run."

"I know."

"Then, git. I'll stay behind for an hour or so, guard the road and make sure no one come after you. Then I'll catch up. I'm sick of this railroad shit anyway. Which way you gone to head?"

"I don't know. East, reckon. Toward Franklin."

"Franklin?"

It just came up in my head like that, without thinking. But as soon as I said it, I knew that was the only place I would go.

"You deaf?" I said.

"Least I ain't a gimp like you. Franklin it is."

"Where'll I meet you?"

"I'll find you."

Jerrod rode out of camp with me for about a mile or so, glowering at anyone who dared look at us. Then he pulled up, went into the woods to set up an ambush, and waved me on.

The next day Jerrod caught up to me while I was breaking camp and dousing my fire. He looked tired and happy.

"Shot me one of them bastards, but only winged him. They turned back after that. They had a noose, looked about your size."

I thanked him and stoked the fire again. I'd caught a couple brim in a creek nearby and was going to save the other for the road, but I roasted it up by wrapping it in wet grass and burying it in the coals. Jerrod's face went dark after he was done eating.

"You made an awful mess, Zachariah. I didn't like what they were doing no more than you did, not that I'm a nigger lover, but I also knew better than to do *that*. What the hell did you think was going to happen?"

"I don't know."

He spit on the coals.

"They killed the nigger, you know. I heard one of 'em talking about it while I tracked them up the road. Put a railroad clamp around his neck and threw him in the river. They were looking for you and found him hiding in the woods not half a mile from camp. Didn't know where to go or how to get there, I reckon."

That's when I knew I'd never go back to living like that. I had tried to make order of it all, and out of my order had come the killing of a man I had meant to save. There isn't no pain like knowing that, picturing a man at the bottom of a river paying for my mistake. Jerrod was right. I had been stupid to think I could interfere in the doings of men like that.

I wasn't like any of them men, and I don't know how I got that way. But it was true. I didn't know what kind of man I could be if I was not one of them, but I knew that there had been one time— *one* time—when I'd been showed a different man in myself, and that was when I was with Carrie McGavock. She would know what I should do. What I *wanted* to do was to take her away and love her like I knew I could. That's what I'd always wanted. That's what I'd never stopped thinking about, sitting in all those saloons and work camps in all those little forgotten places. *She* was always there. I stayed away because I knew I didn't deserve her. But now I needed her, and that was something real powerful.

Didn't know where to go or how to get there. At least I knew that much now.

Much later I read that Forrest bragged about setting free a Negro who had been unlawfully imprisoned at one of his railroad camps. By then his company had failed and he hisself was almost dead, so I didn't grudge him trying to make something more of hisself with that story. He didn't mean nothing to me. Let him believe what he wanted. I knew he was what he was, and men like that don't change.

37

CARRIE MCGAVOCK

I was wrong about the breeze in Tennessee, that it couldn't compare to the cooling wind off the water surrounding my papa's plantation. I learned how to find a spot on the back gallery that perfectly intercepted whatever wind or puff had decided to kick up during those heavy, sun-flooded days of summer, and in my rocker I could achieve a modicum of cool and comfort. Inside, it was impossible to find a cool spot except in the evenings, but on the back gallery it was possible to look out over our yard and watch the children and think that there wasn't a place anywhere more suited to me. This was necessary on those days I spent out there, writing letters to the families of the dead. It was good to know I was planted somewhere pleasant.

> *June 12, 1866*
> *Dear Mr. Robertson,*
> *Please forgive my tardiness with this letter. I have been inexcusably remiss in my correspondence, which is a doubly contemptible state of affairs considering your loss*

and the kindness of your letter, dated May the 22nd. I will endeavor to tell you all I know about your son, Randolph, in the hopes that it might ease your burden for even a moment. I cannot imagine the despair of a father such as yourself.

But, of course, I could.

Your son was a strong young man who spent his days praying to his Lord Jesus Christ that he would be delivered unto Him, and that He would guard and protect those he loved, who I took to be you and your family.

I had no earthly idea if Ran Robertson, who died on my best parlor floor from an infection and loss of blood from his stomach, had any warm feelings about his family or that he cared that they would be protected. I did not know whether he was a believer or that his father was a believer or that his father would take word of his son's prayer as comfort. I only knew that writing such a thing to this man, even if he was no believer, was the best way I knew to convey my own sorrow for him and his son. In my experience I'd learned that even those undisposed to pray would take solace from the knowledge that others had prayed for them. And if such a prayer had not been offered to the Lord from Ran Robertson's lips, I thought, so what? I was writing a letter to the living, not the dead; what did the dead care? The white lie soothed the pain of a man who had written to me, *I dohn know what becaim of me son, and I wished I did. I sorely do.* My lies were justified.

He was with us for a few days, but I always think he knew that he would pass on. He was strong-minded and not afraid. He was a comfort to the other men around him, who were facing the same prospect of quitting this life earlier than they had ever expected, and for that I am grateful that your son, whom we called Ran, was with us even for those few short days.

The men did indeed take solace from men like Ran and the others who were slipping away. They were not alone in the room. It didn't matter whether Ran had stoically borne his pain and his destiny or had screamed and cried the whole way to his final rest—it was his presence alone that would have been a comfort. So I had no qualm presenting Ran as a strong and resigned man, even if he hadn't been. He might as well have been. I was writing to the living.

His death was peaceful, quiet, and quick.

It had not been peaceful—few if any of their deaths had been peaceful. To what I know war rarely makes peaceful deaths, but that was something that I thought a man like Ran had a right to carry to his grave. Everything was over now.

I received many letters, and in the years after that battle I spent much of my time on the back gallery, rocking slowly and trying to keep my stationery steady in my lap. I did not like to compose those letters while sitting inside, even when it was cold, because there was too much about the house to remind me of what it had actually been like to have those boys there. I didn't want the truth slipping unbidden into the letters.

They wrote to me because they heard from survivors of the battle who returned home, wherever home was, that our house was the last place many of the missing had been seen. Some of the men told stories about us, tales that made us into angels who had gone to extraordinary lengths to save not just a few men, but all that was left of the entire Confederacy, and that we—well, they meant *me*, of course; Mariah and the others were never mentioned—were bright polestars of Southern womanhood. These families—fathers, mothers, brothers, aunts—wrote to me to find out what had become of their men. And so I told them.

After I finished my letter to Mr. Robertson and set it aside for Mariah to deliver to the postal clerk in town, I looked out over the yard and watched Winder and Eli returning from the creek. It surprised me to see how tall Winder had become, but it always surprised me. He was just this side of becoming that little man he had always longed to be. Eli, who *had* become a man, was barely taller than my little boy, whose bones seemed to rattle around in his skin, so gangly. They sauntered up to the porch like they were old gunslingers.

"No fish, Winder?"

"No fish, Mama. I think we got 'em all a few weeks ago. Ain't none left."

"There *are none* left."

"Yes, ma'am."

Eli stood beside him, smiling his toothy grin, knowing it was his fault my son sometimes talked like he didn't have any education. Eli was my new son. He was Winder's hero, leader, instigator, comrade in arms in battle against the fish of our creek. He was an orphan, and even when he smiled, I could see that he still didn't think he had a right to be happy for a second. I could understand why he felt that way, and it pained me to see a boy, even one about to be seventeen, torn against himself like that. In all of the history books and newspaper articles that would be written about the war, who would write or even remember the people like Eli?

Becky had died, more than a year ago, in the summer after the battle while giving birth to a baby boy. This had changed Eli, and Lord knows he had good reason.

There was a hardness in his way of speaking, an edge, that made him seem angry. At what, I didn't know for quite some time. He always volunteered to run into town to get provisions at Baylor's store, and I had been told by some of the ladies in town that he could be seen wandering the streets of Franklin regularly, a package of groceries under his arm, looking into windows and peeking around the corners of houses, watching men work. One day Josh Harper, the blacksmith, caught Eli spying through the window of the Baylor house, trussed him up like a Christmas turkey, and deposited him on our front porch with a note explaining Eli's perversity. I knew there was something more wrong with the boy than the loss of his family. But when John and I looked at him sitting on the edge of the old Jackson rocker in the office, rubbing the rope burns on his wrists and awaiting his punishment, we knew that whatever it was, it wasn't a perversity. He was persevering in something, some idea of his, regardless of the consequences. John made him dig potatoes for two days straight as punishment, but neither of us had any hope that he would stop searching for that thing that was missing, whatever it was.

After Becky's death Eli had lived with his father in their little cabin down the pike. Winder went to see him every once in a while, and he'd come back with tales of how dirty the house had become, how the kitchen always smelled of rotted meat, and how all the neighbors had moved away, leaving Eli with no friends other than Winder. Even that little fat boy had left, the brave little soul who had brought Eli to me the night of the battle. I started sending food—smoked ham, eggs, a loaf of bread—with Winder, but he'd always bring it back untouched, with word that Eli's father wanted no charity. *He doesn't want to be human*, is what I thought, but I didn't say it to Winder.

Then, in that winter, almost on the first anniversary of the battle, Eli again appeared on our doorstep, bearing a note.

> *Dear Mrs. M,*
>
> *I cannot raise this boy. I am tore up with Becky's passing, and I miss her as bad as I miss my poor wife, who I think about every day. I got to get away, to start something new. I want to change, I don't want to be this here man no more. I want to be a different man. I will send for the boy when I'm right.*

He didn't bother to sign it, and I never heard from him again. I never asked John if we could take the boy in as our own son. He never asked me, either. John just showed him upstairs to Winder's room—now *the boys'* room—and that was that. The boy was dead tired and dirty. The cuffs of his overalls dragged long white threads behind. I didn't bother ordering him into the bath that night.

Somehow Eli was able to stay dirty. It was the dirt of a clean creek, though, not the dirt and refuse of despair and resignation. I had been able to scrub that off him, I hoped.

No fish. We'd have to eat ham again.

"Do you need for me to go on down the cellar, Mrs. McGavock?"

"No, Eli, I think we'll do fine with what we have tonight. Go see Mariah about what she needs for the kitchen."

"Yes, ma'am."

Winder was about to bounce along after Eli when I stopped him by grabbing onto the back of his short pants and holding on. He practically dragged me out of my chair and down the steps before he realized I'd hooked him.

"Mama?"

"Sit next to me for a second, Winder."

I went back to my chair, packed up my paper and pens, and looked down at Winder sitting next to me on the porch, his scratched and bloody knees—there were short hawthorns down by the creek—drawn up to his chest. How could he be so young but so grown up?

"Did y'all catch fish?"

"No, ma'am."

I loved Winder with all of my heart. He was so loyal and kind. I hoped someday he'd know what deserved that loyalty and kindness.

"Answer me straight, Winder."

He put his head on his knees and peered down between his legs. He let a little wad of drool slide out of his mouth and stretch itself to the floor.

"Stop that, Winder. Did you catch fish?"

"Yes, ma'am."

"Why didn't you bring them home?"

"We put them back. Got 'em off the hooks and slipped 'em back down into the water. Mostly bream, a couple of suckerfish. Maybe one bass, but we weren't sure."

"Why did you do that?"

"It was Eli's idea."

I had suspected as much. They'd spent a lot of time down there at the creek, and I knew a boy as country as Eli would know how to catch fish, and yet they only brought home fish every once in a while, and always the littlest, most pathetic fish you ever saw.

"What was his idea?"

"Not to kill the fish. He said he don't ever want to kill anything, and he makes me kill the fish when he decides we ought to bring some up to you. He says he didn't want you suspicious. He even gets mad at me when I kill spiders. I think he likes to see the fish, he likes to feel them and hold them in his hand and look at them in the sunlight, but he almost always takes the hook out and slips 'em back into the water."

"Does he make you return your fish to the water?"

"No, but I never catch fish. I'm not very good at it."

"I see."

What would I have written to Eli's father if Eli had died on that battlefield?

> *Dear Sir,*
>   *Your son Eli was a gentle boy trapped in the body of*
> *a man.*

It was too hard to write about someone you loved, or liked, or even knew briefly.

> *He hated killing, and would not kill. This is probably*
> *why he died.*

All this death and dying. How is it possible to tell the story of one's life entirely with reference to death? It must surely be impossible to describe life in death, and yet I felt then—and feel now—that there is no possible way to tell the story of my life without recounting these morbid years. There is no possible way to tell the story of my farm, my town, my state, this whole damnable Southern Confederacy we were so sure of, without recounting the deaths. I have heard men in the town square talk about the lingering shame of defeat, and they are welcome to spend their days ticking off the bill of particulars against their honor and dignity sealed that last day at the Appomattox Court-house. That is their story. I saw absence instead. Not the absence of honor and dignity, but of people. How awfully empty this country seemed in those years.

I didn't feel the shame of defeat, but I felt the horror in the empty farmhouses, the lonely roads, the untended land. We would occasionally ride up to Nashville on social business, John and I, past mile after mile of weed-choked fields quickly succumbing to the surrounding forests, past farmhouses turned gray from neglect, curtainless windows like empty eyes. No light ever came from within these houses, these dozens and dozens of houses that had once been home to *someone*. How I regretted that I had never bothered to stop in to speak with these people, to know them. They had been no more a part of my life than the landscape. But then their men had died, or had disappeared, countless thousands and thousands of men, and the dying broke through the bounds of the battlefield and came to embrace the countryside and our towns. All those young boys. We were a new country, that was cer-tainly true. A new country of old men and angry, stubborn men. There were moments when I could look out from our carriage and think that there wasn't anything this country couldn't become, which was not at all a comforting thought.

I thought of Eli as one of the lucky ones, although I do not believe he thought of himself that way.

> *Eli was ever in pain, sir, and never quite understood what had happened to him. None of us did, truth be told. He was brave only in the way a mule is brave, stubbornly moving on without thought despite very good reasons for stopping. He did not embrace his fate so much as he walked right into it. I do not recall that he prayed at the end, although how would I know? I am not so pious as to believe that I know when a person is speaking to God, nor am I so falsely pious that I would*

venture a guess, at least not in Eli's case. If Eli was
praying, that was his business, I believe.

It would have been simply impossible to write such a letter, and
I thanked God (without an ounce of self-piety) that it had not
been necessary. It was so much easier to ease the minds of
strangers about the children I had barely known, to tell them lies.
I felt *good* telling them. I remembered a letter I'd sent to my mother
years ago about the death of Martha. I'd felt so right, so righteous,
in telling her every detail about her awful death, covering up
nothing. I thought I'd done her a service, a tribute, a vengeance
against death, and perhaps I did accomplish those things. But
what had I done to my poor old mother? I would never know.
Misery charts its own course, popping up here and there unintended. Perhaps there were some things best left unsaid about
death, things that ought to be taken to the grave as the property of
the dead. There would be plenty of time for all of us to suffer
without suffering the death of others over and over again. I had
learned to lie about some things and to leave other things unsaid.
Oh, I had finally become such a proper lady!

I would never write such a letter for Eli, however sorely tempted I might be. I would never write such a letter for Winder or
Hattie or John or Mariah or Theopolis. If I were to write a letter
for any of them, I would always say that they went to their grave
peacefully with the name of the Lord upon their lips, and pray
that someday I would believe it.

I *would not,* however, tolerate the lies about fish. Eli and I would
have to talk about that. Or perhaps John would talk to him. I
rested in the chair and closed my eyes, feeling the breeze and
blessing the dressmakers of New York and Paris for their aban-
doning of the corset. I was positively cool sitting there in my new
crinoline dress, the first dress I'd bought in years. Black, of course,
and just the kind of dress I could alter and mend as I saw fit, and
thus the sort of dress I could wear forever. I intended to wear it
forever. I was cool, perhaps for the first time in decades. Bless the
porch, the gallery, the wind. If there was another war, I vowed, I
would remain in this spot to defend the porch, with its view of the

grove leading down to the creek, and my precious garden, which had been newly reborn. The rudbeckia again swayed and genuflected in the borders, which I could spy through the balusters at the end of the porch. Hattie had become quite a gardener. She had her hair up in a lazy chignon, and her work dress—indigo, like an old slave!—pinned up around her knees. The peas were coming to fruit, and the roses needed trimming, and the lamb's ear needed culling, and there she was making sure it was all in order. She had turned brown in the sun, and when she stood up and looked off toward the sun, gauging its progress and angle, she looked like an Indian. I would have to tell her not to bare her legs so often. She was becoming a woman, and I suspected I knew what men might think of her. *I* knew she was still just a girl, and I aimed to keep it that way.

These were my days, writing letters, watching my children, and waiting for John to return from one of his missions to town. We had lost so much of our land that I'd been tempted to ask him why he bothered to appeal to the better natures of the moneylenders, Mr. Baylor chief among them, but I knew that it was the effort that kept him happy. We both somehow knew that this place, Carnton, would remain a shell of itself forever, that it had long since failed as a plantation and was in the process of collapsing into itself, with this old house the only thing left of the McGavock family's ambition. The grove would move in on us, too. I didn't mind.

John had vowed that he could support us without the plantation, and I had faith he could. But his ideas—turning Franklin into a railroad town, creating a wood-milling center, building a textile factory—gained no supporters and therefore no money. There were those in town who thought that life would naturally return to the way it had been before the war, and it was these men who had the money to make John's ideas reality. I could not help being surprised at the persistence of John's conviction: that *he* would have to be the man to drag Franklin into the modern world, or the town would die. This was not the man I had married, the haunted and timid heir to his family's farm. I liked the new man even as he failed. I was especially surprised that his failures did not send him spiraling into anger, as they would have before the war. Now I had come to love those moments with him, in his office sipping sherry, when he laughed disparagingly at the men in town and their lack of imagination. *If they want to live like primitives, watching the world go by, that's their business,* he'd say, raising a toast to my glass. *I've done my best, and I'll keep doing it until they're all dead and gone and we can sweep away the dead wood and start anew around here.*

I was awaiting his return that day on the porch and looking forward to just such a tête-à-tête in his office. I was only thinking of the comfortable chairs and the fine sherry when I spied him astride his horse, coming up the driveway. I saw no reason we could not continue like that indefinitely. It was pleasant enough.

I wish I could have looked closer at the man riding toward me, because then I might have been prepared. Later I would say to Mariah of that day, *The sherry had to run out sometime,* but that was the least of it.

38

CARNTON

Every clank, thump, rattle, and crash of the cookware angered Mariah just that much more, made her just that much more uncertain that she was right. She was not the cook. She wasn't supposed to be cooking. They'd *had* a cook, they'd had half a dozen cooks since the war, all Negroes, and every one of them had left. The last had left telling Mariah she was still a slave. *I ain't livin' like this, cooking and cleaning up after white folk. It's like it ain't changed, and I reckon there got to be something else in the world for a body to do. So I'll be movin' on, Mariah.* Oh, she was going to move on? To where? To do what? Could she read? No, she couldn't. *Mariah* could read, and so could her son, and yet cooking wasn't below *her*. No, she was a *slave* still. She hadn't broken the chains—wasn't that what one of them had told her, laughing in her face?

Mariah assumed there would be no fish—she knew Eli's game, he was no mystery to her—so she'd already been soaking the ham, and boiling grits, and cooking down mustard greens. Greens. How she hated everything to do with greens. Poor man's food, and yet the McGavocks liked that green slop. They had the luxury of liking it and could eat it when they wanted. They didn't *have* to eat it. That was the difference.

"You making greens again. Damn, I hate them greens."

"Don't you swear in my kitchen, Eli."

Eli walked in with a happy grin and a big man's swagger, rolling his shoulders around in their sockets like he was too big for the room. He was a funny boy becoming a funny man, Mariah thought. He sat down on the preacher's bench in front of the fireplace and began to pick his fingernails with a thin, sharp piece of shale he carried in his pocket.

"I know you hate greens, too, Mariah, so I *know* you making something else for yourself. What is it? I want some of that."

"I would have liked to have had some fish, Mr. Eli. Don't suppose you got some fish this time."

"Can't say I do. Did. I mean, we didn't catch any fish."

"Just once, Eli, you could bring me one of them fish to fry up."

"Talk to the fish, Mariah."

"You don't think I can?"

"I know you can."

Now that Theopolis had gone off and made himself a life in town, Eli was the closest thing Mariah had to kin out at the house. He felt like kin, or at least like someone who knew better what her life was like because he'd come up hard, too. Even if he was a white boy. She knew he might someday be riding around slapping at her people and running his mouth, *nigger, nigger, nigger*. For all she knew, he was already picking up that kind of talk down there at the store, from that cracker storekeeper. She doubted it, because she admired the boy's intelligence and had faith that it would win out, but you just never knew. She did know that he always visited Theopolis at his cobbler's shop, and that was also good. She hadn't talked to her son in a couple weeks. She was happy to have Eli around.

While Eli picked at his fingers, Mariah clanged at the stovetop and muttered under her breath. Eli looked up and brushed his raggedy brown hair from his eyes.

"What you saying now, Mariah?"

"Mind your own business."

She'd been wondering about what Theopolis had said to her when he told her he was moving to town for good. He wasn't mean about it, like the cooks had been. She was his mother, and besides, he could read just like her. He didn't resent her. *That's what they were, just jealous. They don't got nothing to go to, and they mad because I can do whatever I want.* She thought about that lie for a moment. She couldn't do whatever she wanted, but the reasons weren't that she was just an old slave, like the parade of cooks had told her. And they weren't what Theopolis thought they were. *You just can't see it, see what your life could be like. It's not your fault. You'll change.* He'd been kind, but he'd also been firm, even as she begged him not to leave. He'd smiled and stroked her hair and looked every bit the businessman and pillar of the community he hoped to become. But she hadn't cared a lick about being left alone, and her reasons for staying had nothing to do with her lack of sight. She had plenty of sight, too much sight. Even Eli knew this, but Theopolis had never believed it. He was afraid that believing in her, or the warnings of Miss Eloisa, would mark him for an ignorant Negro the rest of his life. He was afraid of that worse than he was afraid of anything else, and *that's* what scared Mariah. She could see, all right. She could see a future much more frightening than the one that Theopolis imagined. *Where do all those folk think they're going to go?* she said to herself again. *What do they know but cooking and cleaning and picking cotton and eating greens and sleeping on hay ticking?*

"Mariah, I got some news for you. About Theopolis."

"What about him?"

"He's making shoes for Mr. Baylor's store now, got himself ten new orders and more where that came from. Work boots and oxfords and all sorts of things I ain't ever heard of. Mr. Baylor thinks Theopolis has a lot of something. I forget what, but it was good, I reckon."

"What, boy?"

"*Promise.* He said he had promise. Reckon that? He telling a Negro he got promise? What you think he promised, a white man like that, like Mr. Baylor? What you think Mr. Baylor don't got that Theopolis got, and that he could make himself a promise about? What's it, Mariah? You mad?"

"No, Mr. Eli. And don't you go thinking I am, either. I just wish my boy could tell me such things hisself."

She sniffed, and in her nose she caught the scent of the ham bone she was boiling with the greens. She had sometimes searched for a word to describe the smell of a ham bone in a pot of greens, at the very moment when the bone loses its flavor and the greens take over, bright and pungent. The word was *decayed*, she realized. It smelled like something decaying, going back to the earth.

What promise did Theopolis have? There was much the boy had to offer. The question was what that dried-up old man Baylor wanted with her boy. That was the question.

"You know, Mariah, I believe Theopolis would want to tell you hisself, only he's so busy and you never go to visit. I believe he'd like you to visit."

He's nice enough for a white boy, she thought.

While Mariah sat and thought, she let Eli mess around with the food on the stove, stirring the greens and flipping the ham steaks frying slow in the deep iron skillet. He yelped when the fat sprayed up onto his arm, but he stuck with it. He kept looking over his shoulder at Mariah, to see if she was all right. Or maybe it was to see whether *he* was all right, whether he was doing things right, whether he was pleasing her with his cooking. Mariah watched him dance and shuffle from pot to pot, flicking his face around to sneak a peek at her, and she thought that it would be his constant worrying about what other people were doing that would upend the boy someday, if he weren't made to grow up quick and become his own man. She would see about that, take charge of it. He was a nice boy.

Her own boy was a nice boy. A nice and kind man who, of course, wouldn't see anything wrong with Mr. Baylor bringing him into his circle. She hadn't talked to Theopolis, but she knew how he'd be feeling: surprised, flattered, and especially vindicated in his decision to move to town. She could hear him rehearsing his speech to her. *Well, ain't that something? Just a country Negro without nothing, and what you know? I might just start up a shoe factory, things*

*keep a-goin' like this right here. This Negro's got promise, Mama. I been
told so. I understand why you'd want to stay out here with these people.
You ain't known nothing else. But I got to make my way, make a new way,
'cause I'm young and ain't no one going to take care of folk like me no
more. Got to take care of your own self.*

She wondered if they made him come through the back door of
the store to deliver his shoes. She wondered how he explained
that. He'd think of something, she was sure. She wondered how
he explained the young Negro they'd found downriver, burned
and drowned, with a plow collar around his neck weighing him
down. He was from Pulaski, and word upriver was that *he* had had
promise, too.

White men had another word for "promise" in a Negro. They
had many words. *Uppity. Coon. Unnatural. Traitor.* There were lots
of words for what Theopolis had.

She prayed that Theopolis would know how to stay out of
trouble. He would be right about one thing—there weren't no one
to help him. Mr. John might have helped him. *Mr. McGavock.* But
he could barely help himself lately, or the family, so what good
could he do Theopolis? As long as Theopolis didn't get any more
mixed up with that Baylor man, as long as he didn't take a notion
to stick his head up too far, as long as he didn't covet too much of
the white man's world. She knew that there wasn't anything to
covet that a good, God-fearing man like Theopolis didn't already
have, but she also knew that her prayer for Theopolis was nigh to
hopeless. He would need her help, too.

Eli was tapping on the pots with her good wooden spoons, but
she sat and listened for a moment. It was no tune she could recognize, but it was lively and smooth and a welcome noise. He was
concentrating so hard on the sounds.

"Take the ham bone out the greens."

"Aww, it ain't right. I like the pork in my greens. Ought to have
ten ham bones in the greens, I were making 'em. Only thing that
saves it."

"Take it out. It's ready."

39

ZACHARIAH CASHWELL

We didn't go to Franklin right away. We told ourselves that we were circling around the country, covering our tracks just in case one of them boys from the camp decided to catch up with us. It was likely that some word was getting passed around the railroad circuit about us, but it wasn't real likely they were actually chasing us. We'd have to watch what we said to people, 'cause folks didn't really like wandering strangers around, and you were liable to get in trouble quicker than shit if folks didn't know you. But we were smart about it. What Jerrod was really doing was enjoying a little freedom, and what I was really doing was working up the courage to go back to Carnton. So we wandered around Tennessee, headed mostly east but taking detours north and south as the spirit moved us, or when we caught word of something interesting to see, usually a tavern.

The first thing to know about being on the run, which was a thing I had learned after much experience, was that you had to know how to explain every single damned thing you had with you, and every step you'd taken since practically the day you were born, and if you couldn't do it, you were risking getting collared and dragged into the authorities, or robbed or shot. You had to know what to say no matter what some nosy jackass asked you. Sometimes you could tell 'em to mind their own damned business, but that never held people off for very long. You had to know what to say, and every word out of your mouth had to be true, just not true about *you.*

My saddle? Why, I got that special made in Memphis. Who made it? Well, Jimmy Blackstone over on Market Street, of course. I ain't riding just any saddle around, friend. Got to take care of my backside, and I like a saddle smooth like glove leather. Ain't ever had nice gloves, course, but you understand. Sure, run your hand over it, I don't mind. Blackstone likes to work them special tools and carve up all kinds of curlicues and every pretty little thing he can think of when he ain't drunk. It really ain't my style, but, hell, I didn't want to break old Jimmy's heart, now, did I? No, sir, I can't trade you for it. Won't sell, either. Like I said, I'm mighty particular about my ass. It chaps pretty easy, if you get me. This here? Well, those are my custom-plated Colts. No problem, no problem at all, friend. You have a good ride, now.

It weren't even close to being the softest saddle I'd ever ridden. I had boils and sores all up and down my backside, and I couldn't stand to sit down at the end of the day. And if those pistols of Jerrod's were custom-plated, they were custom-plated with tarnish and sweat and road dirt, and looked like hell. But you had to have a story, especially 'cause Jerrod had really started to look like death. Not like he was going to die, but like Death itself. His hair was so black it looked *heavy,* and that eye of his had become brighter and brighter as he'd become used to the loss of the other one. He was self-conscious about the hole where his eye should have been, and so he didn't like to go about during the day. We traveled at night.

Jerrod was still bent on making his way, eventually, as a gun for hire and all-around tough man, and that meant practice, he said. I caught him one morning off in the woods shooting at my little Bible from a good seventy-five feet. I cuffed him and gave him hell, but not before noticing that he'd put a bullet right smack in the middle of the book, which had stopped the bullet.

My daddy gave me that book. I'd carried it everywhere ever since, even into battle, and it ain't once got a bullet hole in it, or even a stain, until Jerrod went and had to play outlaw on the damned thing. He stomped off saying he was going to go find some whiskey. *Must be a moonshiner around here someplace,* he said. *They a whole lot nicer than you, that's for damned sure, even if you got you a Bible and know how to talk out of it.* I went back over to the fire and flipped the two little bass fish I was roasting.

The hole in the book stopped at Second Samuel. I already knew those verses.

> And Absalom met the servants of David. And Absalom rode upon a mule, and the mule went under the thick boughs of a great oak, and his head caught hold of the oak, and he was taken up between the heaven and the earth; and the mule that was under him went away.

I read on, where the pages were only a little torn by the bullet:

> And a certain man saw it, and told Joab, and said, Behold, I saw Absalom hanged in an oak.
>
> And Joab said unto the man that told him, And, behold, thou sawest him, and why didst thou not smite him there to the ground? and I would have given thee ten shekels of silver, and a girdle.
>
> And the man said unto Joab, Though I should receive a thousand shekels of silver in mine hand, yet would I not put forth mine hand against the king's son: for in our hearing the king charged thee and Abishai and Ittai, saying, Beware that none touch the young man Absalom.
>
> Otherwise I should have wrought falsehood against mine own life: for there is no matter hid from the king, and thou thyself wouldest have set thyself against me.
>
> Then said Joab, I may not tarry thus with thee. And he took three darts in his hand, and thrust them through the heart of Absalom, while he was yet alive in the midst of the oak.

Ain't that the way of the betrayer, that old rascal Absalom? Seducer of Israel, caught up in an oak, abandoned by a ornery mule, killed where he hung. Mama used to say that if there'd been an oak somewhere around the house, which there weren't, she'd have had it chopped down right quick to avoid temptation. I don't even now know who would have been the tempted one. I remember that my father didn't have much use for Absalom, though.

I kept reading and thinking about that book. I had thought about being a preacher once. Even thought I had heard the call. But I was little, and that was before I began dreaming of the angels and before I went to live with my aunt. After that, I hadn't so much as gone to hear a preacher, not ever. Even so, I was sad about the hole in my book, and it made me think about what might have happened had I been a preacher.

This here book, I said out loud, *has on it the mark of the devil. There is a bullet hole here, friend, and it stops right here in Second Samuel. Now, why? I tell you, friends, I was waylaid by the lowest of the low, the meanest and dirtiest man you seen, and he were the devil's own soldier.*

A preacher got license with the truth, I knew that much. Got to keep people in their seats.

And he went to rob me, and I held the Good Book up because I'd been reading it as I rode. Do I always read while I ride? By the Lord, yes! The Word of the Lord is good for any time, even if it ain't the most comfortable time. And that bullet traveled through the book I held with love, and it turned that bullet away from my heart, and I thought I heard the Lord say, "I will not let this one, most humble of my dirty-faced and sinful children, be smited." He stopped that bullet right here, right where Absalom gets hisself hung up in that tree. And I reckon Absalom stopped that bullet for me, and although I don't dole out the forgiveness in this life, if I get a chance, I'll be putting a good word in for old Absalom up in heaven.

And so that is how I come to have a Bible with a bullet hole in it, and I come to you today to spread the good news of this here book's loyalty under fire.

Well, I sounded like a preacher, and that made me laugh right out. But then I picked at that fish and thought a little more about it. I could be a preacher. I knew enough about preaching, I'd seen it high and low. I'd do anything to get my daddy back, but if I had to steal a few ideas from that goddamn snake who come into our house and stole everything, that *reverend*, well, that seemed like it was right and just. Maybe that's the new man I was to be.

"You a preacher now?"

Jerrod stood in the clearing with a jar of whiskey. If you've got a nose for where men make their whiskey, like we did, a trip across the country is just moving from one still to another. We'd look along the little creeks, in the cool dark places where the shiners keep their stills and the centipedes lie around waiting to fall on your neck when you ain't looking. I'd always make a lot of noise to announce myself, and act real grateful that they'd sell me their rotgut for far more than its worth. Jerrod liked to sneak up on 'em. He thought that was funny.

"Preacher. That's good cover. Good thinking. I just heard you from over there in the woods. Guess you practicing. Guess you preacher fellas gots to practice, although it seem a little funny you got to practice the Word of the Lord. Ain't that the sort of thing that just comes to you right there slap on the spot, like you got the fire in your belly and it just got put there by the Lord Hisself? But what the fuck do I know, I'm as bad a sinner as they come. Where's my fish?"

I looked at the little hunk of black on the spit and then back at him. It always surprised me how much he could eat, being so skinny and all. I watched him bite through the fish, skin and all, and damned if he didn't find a whole lot of white flesh in that burned-up mess. I reckoned he knew some things that I didn't, could see things I couldn't.

"What you think we should call our gang?"

"We don't got a gang, Jerrod."

Jerrod got a thoughtful look on his face, which made him look a little queasy. Then he smiled.

"All right, then. Can't blame a man for trying. I done heard about a job. Heard it from an old boy living out in the woods a few miles or so over those hills, moonshiner. Something about digging up Indian bones. Big-deal Yankee project, but they hiring. And I like anything to do with the injuns, seen a couple when I was little."

"Indian bones."

"That what the man said. Here's the thing, too. It's in Franklin. I reckon it's time to get on, if that's where we going and we ain't going to have a gang."

I hadn't really thought I'd find a job, or even a good reason to go to Franklin besides *her*. And what was I going to do when I found her? Something, but I still didn't know.

"They digging *in* Franklin?"

"Somewhere south of there, I think. Where they got those weird-looking hills off the side of the road. I remember them from when we was marching up in there. What do you know, turns out they ain't hills at all, but *burial mounds*. Reckon they a lot of people all heaped up in there. Savages."

I thought, *Too many bones already in Franklin*, which made digging up Indian bones seem right stupid. Then I noticed something odd about Jerrod. He had drawn one of his pistols and was staring at it, like it was going to talk to him.

"Jerrod?"

He was just wiping his mouth and swallowing his last bite of that burned fish. He was having a hard time swallowing.

"Yeah?"

"Where'd you get that moonshine?"

He didn't answer right away.

"You just come across a moonshiner in the woods?"

"Yeah."

"Snuck up on him."

"Like usual."

"Then what?"

"He had a fright, but we got to talking. Told me about the job. Sold me this whiskey."

"And?"

"I took his money. Reckoned we needed it. We got nothing, Zachariah."

"And?"

"And I killed him."

I should have known that, and I shouldn't have asked it. No matter how much you think you know a man, if he's a killer, it's hard to sleep or eat. Men like Jerrod, even a man who was my friend and who had saved my life, were hard to trust. I was afraid of Jerrod, truthfully, but I was also happy to have some company. I sat silent for a while.

"Zachariah?"

"Yeah?"

"I'm sorry I killed him. I didn't need to kill him. I wish I hadn't. I know you wouldn't have killed him, and it makes me a little ashamed to admit it to you. You'd have never done something like that, would you?"

I didn't say nothing.

"Zachariah?"

"What?"

"You a good man."

For a few nights, at least, I slept comfortable on that. And then I prayed for Jerrod's soul, something I hadn't done for anyone since I was a boy.

40

CARRIE MCGAVOCK

There was one man in our little town who was not a backward-looking primitive, as John had called them. I was very sure that I wished he *were* a backward-looking primitive. Then his motives could have been ascertained, his intentions predicted. If only this man had been stupid like the rest of them.

But Baylor was not a stupid man. He was a bitter, hard man who had never once made a secret of his disdain for Confederate leaders during the war. On the Confederacy itself, who knew what he thought? He was not a man for abstractions, and he was certainly no sentimentalist. His contempt was for Confederate leaders, every one of which he had made a point of calling a fool at one time or another. *If the Confederacy is its leaders, I have little hope for the whole experiment,* he'd say. His contempt had only deepened since the war. He'd lost a son, Will, on the battlefield at Franklin, and I believe that this very fact caused him to gain a certain sense of provenance not only over his home and his fields but over the whole town. His son had gone and given himself to the cause in his blood, and from what I can tell, this made Baylor think he'd given more than any other man in Franklin and that they owed him something. Whether or not he got along with his son, a matter of some debate, was hopelessly beside the point. His son was dead and gone, led to his death by men that old man Baylor reviled.

Was Zachariah Cashwell, even though he wasn't much of a leader, one of those men he would have hated so? I could not fathom it, although I knew it would be true. This is how I knew the depths of Baylor's hatred. I had been made stronger and wiser by the knowledge that a man like Zachariah could love me, that I could be loved by so unlikely a man. On the rare occasion that I went to town and saw the way our town had gone on in no particularly remarkable way, I could not help but wonder if God had meant for Zachariah to lose his leg so that we could go on as ever. It seemed wrong, and I believed God had meant Zachariah for something far greater, which I had never quite understood. I wondered about this while walking in my garden and asking myself if Zachariah would enjoy the flowers Hattie had made to grow in fulsome waves again. I wondered about it while tending the graves of my children, and I wondered about it when I bathed myself and when I drifted off to sleep late into the night. I wondered, Lord help me, if the Lord had intended *me* for him. And then I fell into dreamless slumber.

John had gone to see Baylor yet again. He had long since given up on getting back the many acres of land Baylor and the trust company had taken into their possession when we defaulted on John's loans. There was no question of getting any of our land back, since most of it was already in the process of being divided and let out to any number of poor young soldiers and their younger brides and their skinny hollow-eyed children, all of whom worked the land themselves and gave up part of their takings to Baylor. Every fourth Saturday you'd see a parade of men on mules or in homemade carts plodding toward town, toward Baylor's store, where they'd settle accounts and buy more equipment and seed. A never-ending cycle. One of the little farms abutted the edge of our property at the railroad track, and sometimes I'd pass by and watch the little, dark, and nervous wife next door tend her beans and pick her squash. She never said hello, and neither did I. I think perhaps I frightened her.

The thing John wanted Baylor to understand was that he was a man of ideas, that despite the poor decision he'd made in buying uniforms and equipment for the Confederate company from Franklin, and paying for it with a loan secured by his family's land, he could still be counted on to develop profitable ideas that would make them both money if only Baylor would unclench his fist and make the investment. This never happened. I don't think it was because Baylor could not see that change was coming to Franklin. I believe Baylor simply didn't want to share the future with a partner. The future was his. The Confederacy owed him.

John rode up to the porch that day, and I could see he was heavy with a burden he didn't know how to lift off himself. The lines along the outside of his mouth, which had begun to form jowls, were deep and black. He would not look at me, just busied himself with hitching the horse to the balustrade. Finally he looked up, and it was as if his whole face were being pulled from some unknowable force below his feet. He was a sorry sight.

To this day I can't fathom how he understood that the news he brought from town would send me into a fury. And yet there he stood in his black suit and well-shined boots, rubbing at his baby jowls and looking up at me with watery eyes, like he was a child about to be beaten. Many years later I would appreciate this prescience of his and what it said about his love for me.

"Seen Baylor."

"Did he decide to take the house, too?"

"He doesn't want the house."

"What does he want?"

"He doesn't want anything. At least not from us."

I had come to feel like some sort of princess holding court up there on the porch, a sovereign in black sitting tall on her rocking throne while the blue paint of the ceiling boards flaked and the floorboards creaked. This was not how I wanted to act with John, not anymore. I gathered my skirts about me and stood up, still hoping that this conversation could be salvaged and that soon the two of us would be laughing over tales in his office.

"John, let's go into your office. It's cooler."

John looked relieved for a moment, and the lines around his mouth softened. He removed his short hat and wiped the dirty grime from his brow.

"I'll join you after I've put up the horse. Might take a while."

"I have all the time in the world."

In the office I paced. I knew John had some dreadful thing to tell me. I thumbed through his collection of *Harper's Weekly*s, neatly stacked on the bookshelf, flounced down in the old Jackson rocker, got back up, and finally stretched out upon the small couch, under an old map of Tennessee. The dust rose up when I sat down, and I watched it fill the sun streaks flowing through the tops of the windowpanes and between the slats of the blinds.

John finally came in, having knocked the mud off his boots, and took his seat in the rocker across from me. I expected that he would reach for the decanter on the side table, but he did not. I sighed.

He slipped down like a little boy, until the back of his head rested against the top of the chair. He let his arms flop off the chair arms, and he looked at me with a squint.

"Baylor took me aside and told me he was fixing to plow up his south field and put it back into production, probably more cotton."

I was not impressed by this revelation.

"So Mr. Baylor will actually do some farming for himself? Bravo for him. I suppose he's worn out all his tenants by now."

"In the field between his old gin and the pike."

"Yes."

"You understand which field I'm speaking of?"

"I do not."

John wiped some dust off the knees of his trousers and, with what seemed like great reluctance, finally did reach for the sherry decanter, pouring himself a deep glass. He looked at me and I shook my head. I feared sherry if not taken in just the right mood. I wasn't in that mood.

He sipped his drink.

"That's the old Union trench line, Carrie."

What did I care for a Union or Confederate trench line, or any other scar of those years? What did I care what Baylor did with his piece of the battlefield? I thought to myself, *The sooner it's covered in white bolls, the easier it will be for us all to forget that it once ran with another color, a horrifying, tawdry, final color.*

"Well, good for Mr. Baylor again."

John stood up and walked over to one of the windows, rubbing his finger along the edge of the glass until it moaned and squeaked. He was looking at an old map of Tennessee while he spoke.

"Do you ever wonder what became of all the dead?"

They were taken from here. Taken away in carts and wagons and piled upon makeshift sleds that slipped almost silently over the cold winter mud. I assumed that most of them had been taken home, where the dead had their proper place. Of course, we had enough of our own dead lying in the grove across the yard, and there were those that had been buried in the trench through Baylor's field. I suppose I believed that the dead would all make their way to similar little cemeteries, in similar groves, sons next to fathers next to mothers. The dead, the incontrovertible proof of failure, had mocked our efforts in those days after the battle. The truth is, I had sometimes stood by and watched the piles of men hauled off, and wished them a safe journey to the end of the earth. I hadn't thought all of that through, not then.

"I assume most were taken home."

John put his finger on the glass of the framed map and traced the meandering of the Mississippi.

"Many were."

"Many."

"Some."

My breathing came harder and my face flushed, as it always did when I began to feel unmoored, or upon the discovery that there was yet another thing under the sun that I had not understood. Or both. John continued.

"A negligible number, really, from what I understand. The

Union got their dead out of town, but they didn't take them very far, just as far as the new cemeteries in Nashville and Murfrees-boro."

"That is a shame."

"What kind of shame?"

"That they didn't see fit to send those boys back to their homes."

"How would they have done that?"

"By rail, horse, boat. There would have been so many ways. And why are we talking about this?"

John snorted out his nose and kept touching his precious map. He was beginning to irritate me.

"You know what bodies smell like after a few days? You can't drag it wherever it came from without packing it in salt and coal, at least, and even then it's a mighty queer affair. But I can assure you, no one went to that kind of trouble for our dead or their dead. No one ever did that, not during the entire war. Men stayed where they dropped, most of them."

"So where are they? Where are all those men they hauled from here?"

My mind drifted. I imagined the dead beneath my feet, under the floorboards, in Hattie's garden. Where were they hiding? I looked out the window past John's shoulder and imagined that every tree protected a man lying at its feet, every hill a hill of bones. They could be anywhere.

"There were many more dead than were taken away from our house, Carrie. Thousands more. You saw only a few, the ones who had been able to leave the battlefield with breath in them. You never met the men who never left the field."

It is possible to know something without ever understanding it. I had known that many more had died than had died here, because I had heard the numbers. *Five thousand dead, six thousand dead, countless dead.* Had I bothered to spend much time with those numbers, to divine their meaning, I would have understood the full cost of that November day. But I had not bothered until just then, with John's back to me and a forest of trees waving at me through the window, each tree grasping and reaching toward me.

Thousands more. It was incomprehensible. John turned back to me, and my face must have flushed, because he went over to the sideboard and poured me a little whiskey. Stronger medicine.

"Are you all right?" he asked as he handed me the glass.

"I am taken aback by my own ignorance."

"Good. So you understand the problem."

"I understand that my little part was so small and insignificant as to be almost worthless."

"That isn't what I meant, and it isn't true. I won't have you pouting."

"I don't pout."

"The thing you have to understand is that those men, the thousands of men who died here in Franklin, they're still here. Dead, but still here. And most of them, including the ones who died here, are lying under a couple of feet of dirt in Baylor's field, Carrie, and he's planning to plow it under."

I imagined the plow going through those bones, crunching them up and turning them into fertilizer. I got up and poured another glass of whiskey and kept my hand on the center table, steadying myself. *These boys.*

"The thing is, it isn't going to go over well, this plan of his. No, sir. There are people in this town who won't let that happen, and they aren't the sort to send a negotiating party out to the Baylors' to parlay. There could be a fight. The way some of those men are, what they talk about, *down in Baylor's own damned store.* It isn't possible that he could do it without stirring up the snakes."

"Who buried them?"

"Oh God, Carrie, would you stay with me for one moment? That doesn't matter."

"Matters to me."

I finished my whiskey.

"What matters is that I don't know why, but I think that Baylor is stirring things up on purpose. He don't need that field. He's got something else going, and I can't figure it out."

John went back to his seat, and we sat watching each other. I seemed to be getting drunk, which was a relatively rare experience for me. The air seemed slow and old, and I wished John had opened the window when he was standing by it. The house seemed unimaginably ancient right then, and me along with it. I watched John's Adam's apple as he swallowed his sherry. He switched to the whiskey, too, and then sat back down where I could watch him some more. The war was over, what were we doing worrying over the men who had died in it? They had no worries, surely.

And yet I could not shake the feeling that all that we had done in this house in those days—the healing and the comforting and the cleaning and the death watches—that they weren't real, that they'd been figments of imagination, and that the only solid evidence of what we had done was lying in that field, rebuking me for failing them. I had already failed them, so they would not expect me to save them from Baylor's plow.

Save them from the plow. It was ridiculous and none of my business.

"How were they buried?"

"How should I know? It's not important."

I had been resting my feet on a little footstool that Martha had decorated. I pulled them off and placed them firmly on the ground and leaned forward. Very unladylike. John was scratching at his ear. He had lost interest in me for the moment. I could almost see his nose getting liquor red, second by second.

"It's the most important thing, John."

It still amuses me to remember the look of alarm on his face. It was his own fault, I have to say.

That evening, an hour or so before sunset, I took Mariah down to the pike. We rode in the horse cart and took the long way out to the road so that John wouldn't be awakened from his nap. I didn't tell Mariah why we were going, but I suspect she knew before I even asked her. This is how she had always been since we were little girls, aware of things before anyone else.

It didn't take us long to travel up the pike and then strike out across the field, until we were in a low spot a few hundred yards across from Baylor's old gin. Grasshoppers flew into the air away from us. I noticed how their wings glowed in the waning light; and the farther they receded, the more they seemed just small points of light until finally they were doused in the taller grass far away. We sat still, and when the grasshoppers ended their flights, it was as if they'd never been there at all.

Mariah wasn't watching. She was staring straight ahead, and in my shadow her face seemed unnaturally dark. She knew why we were there, and she had no interest in any of it. I felt sad for her, and not because I was going to make her do something she'd rather not do. I felt no compunction about *that*. I felt sad for her because I knew she was thinking of her son.

"He'll be all right, Mariah."

"Ma'am?"

"Theopolis. He'll be all right."

"You don't know that."

"I believe it."

"Well, I don't believe it."

"Chances are, he'll stay right where he is and make his shoes, and that will be the end of it."

"I don't see that. Don't see that at all. I see much worse."

"You're a pessimist."

She turned toward me. She had hate upon her face, and it scared me.

"All I know is, you-all fighting that same war over and over and over again. One white man think he ought to do one thing, and another think he ought to do some other thing, and they all gone to make life hell for everyone else. You tell me how the sense in any of that."

"There isn't. I see that."

"We here because that old man gone to plow up this field, and you can't stand it. Can't *stand* it. So you drag the nigger along to help you and protect you and tell you what you want to know."

"Don't talk to me like that."

"Oh hell. Whip me, then. We gone on too long, Miss Carrie, for you to tell me my place. I known my place since I was a little girl. More than you knew."

"Stop it."

"We here because you gone fight with a man over what he want to do with his own land, where there buried hundreds of white men who ain't done one damned thing for me or mine *ever*. If they'd had their way, my son wouldn't have no cobbler shop. But you got to have everything *just so*, and you can't stand that you didn't save every one of them boys, that you didn't come close even. Truth is, you just like all the rest of the white folk: you think everything what happens is because you did or didn't do something. That Mr. Baylor, he think the same thing. He think he got to meddle and get people stirred up, elsewise the town ain't going to be the town he wants. He wants power, like all you-all, and don't tell me that coming down here to visit these dead men ain't about power. Who got the power to do what they want with them bones? You been sitting up there on that porch for two years, thinking you done right and good, and then along come this man with his plow, and you got to do it all over again, and you got to drag me along with you. But you *did* do right; you don't got to do right again. Who says it ain't God's plan for these dead boys to stay here in this field and get plowed over and ground to dust? You got that much power, Miss Carrie? You that rich? You know what God wants?"

I could think of nothing to say to that outburst except something silly and beside the point.

"We're not rich."

"You don't have money, don't mean you ain't rich still."

She misunderstood me, but I couldn't help that. I moved the cart forward a little to watch the grasshoppers fly again. They disappeared like little memories.

I *did* want to have everything set right, but I thought I knew something about men she didn't know. I knew that if a man like Baylor plowed that field, it would never be forgiven by others. Itself an act of violence, the plowing would breed more violence. It would be a challenge, and the men who would rise to Baylor's challenge were the more terrifying. They were the defeated and the bitter, and there were so many of them. Mariah was right that we fought that war over and over and over again. I just didn't see why I ought to sit by and let another skirmish erupt when I could stop it. I did not know how I would stop it. That was my dilemma.

"I don't know what to do, Mariah."

"Let's ride home, Miss Carrie."

"We can't do that."

"Why not?"

"Because I know these men. I've read about them, in my letters. They are not strangers to me. I just need to know what they want."

Mariah reached up and felt my forehead for fever. She sat back in her seat and chuckled. I'd heard that chuckle before. She thought I was crazy.

"They ain't got much to say, Miss Carrie."

"Then let's just walk around the field a little bit and hear what they're not saying."

She knew what I was asking. She'd known it all along, and she'd been trying to postpone it. She always tried to postpone it, ever since she was a little girl and I found out about her sight. Could she see the dead? I never knew. I only knew that she took the dead more seriously than anyone I'd ever known, and what she thought she saw when in their presence was real to her. Perhaps these were only the wispy last bits of the fog I imagined souls to be, a fog that dissipated with time. Like memory, only more vivid.

"I could say no."

"You won't. You're as curious as I am. Ornery but curious."

I got down from the cart and went over to her side, where I waited. She sat with her arms crossed, as if trying to hold herself back. Then she said, "Damn," and climbed down next to me.

We didn't talk for some time. I took her arm, and we walked slowly through the field, a few dozen yards from a long pile of old dead Osage orange trees that ran parallel with the base of a hill, below Baylor's place. Our skirts whispered against the grass and against each other. The ground was lumpy and uneven, and we often stumbled. After I nearly fell headfirst to the ground, my boot heel stuck in a hidden hole in the grass, Mariah held me up and then held me still. She quit walking.

"What is it?"

"Just a feeling. I'm seeing faces going by and into the distance until they real little, and then circling back and going by again.

They got no expressions. They just going round and round. I almost think they going to go so far they can't come back, but they come back."

We walked on, found more solid ground, and I stroked Mariah's hair while she looked down at her feet and cursed me under her breath.

When the cursing stopped, I spoke again.

"What now?"

"There a big bird, real white, like the ones we had back in Terrebonne. He stepping around in the shallows of a big water. And there a man rowing a boat along the shore, rowing and rowing. He singing something. I can tell because he moving like there's music and I can see his mouth moving. Every so often he stops and pulls in a long line with a big net attached to the back of it, and he dumps all kind of little fish into a big bucket he got at the front of his boat. Then he just go on again. His boat say 'Bait.' Funny name. He look happy. He just keep doing it over and over again, happy as anything. Don't look like he want to stop, ever. The sun is pretty on the water, but he don't look like he sweating a lick."

I tried to bring Mariah along, but she pulled back.

"They all alone. I see a lot of men. That one playing the piano, this one eating fried chicken, that one preaching in the pulpit and smiling up at the Lord Jesus upon the cross. I see a man drinking whiskey, and another man riding his horse faster than I ever seen a horse move. But there ain't nobody else with them. That man eating chicken alone."

I was starting to think that I didn't want to hear any more, but Mariah was frantic.

"They gots what they want. They all gots what they want. They just don't got anybody to share it with, I guess. I feel that. I feel lonely. I feel cold, real cold."

I had never in my life tried to interpret the things Mariah saw, and I didn't this time, either. But I imagined the man in the boat, turning his circles and catching his fish, over and over and over again. His heart's desire, certainly, but only to be had without rest or relief. It was a horror I had not imagined, that one could hardly imagine. It was enough to make a body question paradise itself.

We rode back to the house in the dark, this time with Mariah driving the horses. I knew John would be upset, but I didn't care. I knew those men in the field, and now Mariah knew them, too, and there wasn't any way to ignore them any longer. Bones are bones, but not when they are married to life and memory, whether in the letters of the living or in the vision of a woman trembling at dusk in an unwelcoming field. After that, they're something more than bones.

41

FRANKLIN

It was too late in the year for blueberry flowers, so Mariah went after roots from the grove—forest peas, which were just flowering. If she could dry up some of those, maybe she could get Eli to slip some pieces into her boy's clothes. The Indians said that the root of the forest pea would carry a soul through difficulty unharmed. That would be a start.

She hitched her skirt up and felt the summer sun beating down on the back of her legs and neck. She liked that feeling, the feeling of absorbing the sun. It made her feel larger. She did not enjoy the thorny vines scratching white lines across her legs, but that couldn't be helped—the forest pea, an almost invisible purple ghost among wildflowers, had to be stalked. She followed the McGavocks' creek until she was off the property and far away to the south. The forest floor was dry and smelled like a neglected attic except when the breeze kicked up and the trees hushed at each other, and suddenly she could smell the creek and the little black locust trees angling for a space at the water.

She couldn't concentrate—her head was too full—and finally

she quit looking. The forest pea was not a plant that could be stumbled upon. It had to be sought with an empty mind. But she couldn't empty her mind; there was too much to think about. So she waded into the creek and watched the minnows poking at her toes. For the moment she was content to stand there and feel the water and watch the treetops. This was the kind of happiness she had hoped for her son. Modest, quiet, unseen, inalienable. She admitted, finally, that there were times, very rare ones, when she did go walking for its own sake. Or her own sake, more accurately.

She made for the edge of the forest and the pike, which would take her home. She broke through the wild hedge of little poplars that ringed the older trees and emerged into the wide sunlight, where she stopped short. She dropped her skirts until they hung properly. She straightened her dress. She wiped the dirt from her cheeks and tucked her hair behind her ears.

Where did all the white men come from?

Somehow she'd become twisted in the woods and had ended up in the middle of one of the cities of the dead. This old burial mound was one of a few around Franklin. Most were located along the Harpeth River, where they were part of that chain of mounds and subsumed ancient cities that ran down along the Natchez Trace. Mariah had never much wondered about them, only occasionally marveling at the odd shape of the hills, small, grass-covered pyramids whose peaks had been worn and rounded by the elements. She had never thought much about what might be contained in such a hill, and she had no idea who might have built them. They were, in fact, the remnants of a disappeared civilization, forgotten even to the few local Indians who still remained when the whites first brought slaves here.

White men in broad, thick mustaches, sleeves rolled above their elbows, crawled over the hill like termites. They carried shovels with them and had carved an indentation in the side of the mound. It looked like someone had taken a bite out of it.

Mariah backed herself back into the woods. They were pulling things out of the ground and carrying them down to a set of large tables, where men worked with brushes. A procession of men bore long bones like bundles of kindling upon their shoulders. The skulls they treated with some daintiness and, perhaps, respect.

A man with a broad black hat watched from the top of the hill. He stopped one of the workers, took a bone from him, hefted it in his hands, and then placed it along his own upper thigh, as if to measure himself against the other man who, Mariah guessed, must have been dead a million years. The dead man had been much taller, that was clear. The man in the hat laughed and handed the bone back to the worker, who took it down to the tables, where other workers began to brush the dirt away. She watched the man in the black hat and thought he looked like a nice man. His face was fat and red, but he looked strong and healthy, and he didn't do much except to scratch his ear and nod at the men carrying bones away. Mariah wondered why he wanted those old bones and whether he knew whose souls those bones had once contained. He didn't look much like an Indian.

Before she retreated entirely into the forest to find a different way back to the house, she felt her head begin to throb. She slumped down against a black oak and waited for the spell to pass. She hoped there would be no visions, no voices, because she was afraid of what might emerge from an open grave and enter her head. But she closed her eyes against the pain.

Then she saw the living, not the dead. She saw little boys chasing after their mothers, and old feists that by rights *should* have been dead. There were cook fires going here and there and tall, leathery men sitting on their haunches and smoking while they waited for their food. They all worked and cooked and smoked in the shadow of the hill behind them. It was early morning, and the sun had not risen off the horizon much. No one looked at Mariah except one old man off to the side, who pounded out tools on a large, flat, granite rock. He had his eye on her. Next to him a pile of arrowheads grew. Mariah's head throbbed again, and the other people became streaks of light that glowed and dazzled and dimmed. *Shhhhhhh.* That's all she heard. It was like an exhalation. Peace. Silence. They were gone.

42

ZACHARIAH CASHWELL

By the time we arrived in Franklin and I walked into that nigger's shoe store looking for a new boot for my wood leg, I'd almost begun believing that I was traveling toward my true home.

The nigger was Mrs. McGavock's, I knew that straightaway. He'd been the one to shove me down in that hole. I didn't hold that against him, but I remember his mistrust of me, and *that* I held against him. But from the looks of the other boots lining the shelves of his workshop, it seemed like he made a good boot, so I was willing to forget all about the past.

Jerrod and I had got all turned around on our way to Franklin, and we'd ended up coming through town from the north. Our journey had taken us past fields that were just being reclaimed again, past old men clearing little cedars and hip-high poplars from old cotton fields, and past young women cradling new babies on their hips, maybe fathered by them same old men in the fields. I didn't see no other men except for the niggers. I'd long since got used to the niggers running their own places. What did I care? But *they* hadn't got used to it yet, and sometimes I could tell they didn't know whether to doff their hats or shoot me in the head. The countryside had changed.

As we got closer to Franklin, though, some of the hills were familiar, rolling around into the distance or eaten up by a stand of trees. My eyes showed me other hills that seemed familiar, too, their curve and height and whatnot, even if I'd never seen them before. My mind was playing tricks on me, reckon, since it knew I was heading toward Franklin and that soon I would be up on a hill I knew all too well. Or maybe God was playing that trick with me. Same thing.

I didn't know whether Tennessee was emptier and quieter than it had been those years before, but that's just how it seemed. I reckon I'd changed, or my memories had grown and twisted and shifted over time. Tennessee had been filled with noise and smoke, and now it was getting back its fields, and all you could hear was the sparrows and the mockingbirds chasing crows. Sometimes you could hear one of them young brides calling to her husband. I saw signs of the war here and there—the stumps of felled and burned trees, bullet holes in the sides of barns—but it was also possible to look around and imagine that it had never happened, that it was 1860 again and people were just going on with they lives like always, only the Negroes were going on with their lives a little more openly than normal. The closer we came to Franklin, the more it shocked me that the war weren't on the lips of every single man, woman, and child we met. It wasn't, but it was all I could think about. The war, Carnton, and her.

So Jerrod and I rode into town, and before long we were standing in front of a tin-roofed cottage with a little porch from which swung a sign with a shoe on it. And inside this house was that Negro of hers. I could see him from the street because he was so light he almost shined in the dark of that little room. I turned to Jerrod.

"Reckon I need a boot."

Jerrod leaned up against the porch post and spit into the dirt.

"I never understood why you need a boot for a foot that don't exist."

"I got my reasons."

"I mean, you could have anything at the end of that thing. You could have a hoof, and we could take you over to the smith's. Or you could have a paw or a ball or something. You ain't creative, I'll say that."

"I got a foot, and it needs a boot. Let me go in here and talk to this nigger about a boot. Maybe you could find the animals some water, too."

"Ought to sell your horse, if you settling down here."

"I ain't settling down."

"You'll stay."

He gave me a look, as if he was wanting to say more, but he didn't. He knew me well enough not to say her name to me.

"I ain't staying."

I walked into the cobbler's shop and stood in the doorway, looking down at the man cutting leather from a pattern. He was big, but his fingers were thin, and they moved faster than I could track them. I didn't remember delicate fingers.

"Howdy."

He looked up quickly. He hadn't noticed I'd come in. He was about to say something but choked it off. He looked at me some more, and I saw him recognize me. A man's eyes set just so when they got you pegged, and he'd got me pegged. Didn't know how to play it, though, I reckon, so he chose to act like we was strangers.

"May I help you, sir?"

"You may. I need a boot."

"One pair of boots."

"One boot."

I stomped my wood leg on his floor, and the echo gave him the idea.

"I see."

"For the wood leg, not the good one."

"Yes, sir."

"I was thinking they ought to match, though. Same kind of leather and all. Got to keep up my appearances."

I knew I looked like hell, and I could see him trying to reckon what appearances, exactly, I was trying to keep up. And why.

"How quick can you work?"

"I've got a week's worth of work already."

"How much to jump ahead of the line a little?"

"Well, I can't—"

"What if it was Mrs. McGavock done bring you one of her husband John's shoes?"

That wasn't exactly the right thing to say right then. He and I both knew he'd do up Mr. John's shoes right quick, but if he were to admit that, it'd make him seem like not much more than the McGavocks' house nigger still. He was one of the other kind of Negro, the kind that couldn't stand to be reminded of that past. The kind who would think about shooting your head off before doffing their hat.

"I thought I knew you, mister."

"You can call me Mr. Cashwell."

"Zachariah Cashwell."

"Mr. Cashwell."

"Yes, sir, Mr. Cashwell."

"So you ain't answered my question. How much?"

He stood up, and I realized again how tall he was and how distinguished he looked for a Negro. This fellow never let a thread slip out of place, I could tell. I had been trash to him once before, and I reckoned I was still trash to him. White, but trash even so. He stretched the fingers of his hands and cracked them, and yanked down on his vest until it lined up with the bottom of his belt, just proper-like.

"For a cripple I'll do it right away. Got to be right with the least of His creation, however they come. And to answer you other question, I would not have to fix John McGavock's shoes."

"Why is that?"

"Because he has someone to fix his shoes already in his employ."

I'd heard Negroes try to talk like educated men before, but this one was one of the first that sounded natural about it.

"Would that be your mama?"

"Ain't your business, is it, sir?"

It wasn't, and I let his rudeness slide. I was suddenly interested in making peace because he was part of my memory of the McGavocks, a piece of the story that ran through my head about Carrie. And as I'd come closer to Franklin, that story had got so it didn't let up. It was all I could think about. *Carrie McGavock, Carrie, Mrs. McGavock, Carrie.* I'd played around with him enough.

"I'd be very grateful to you if you'd fix me up a boot for my wood leg here. Thank you."

"You're welcome."

He gestured to a chair against the wall of the cottage, next to the door, where he wanted me to sit down. I did, and took off my leg, which I held up to him.

"This is going to take an hour or so. Will you wait?"

"I can't go anywhere else without that leg, so I reckon so."

"All right."

He swept his work aside and stood my leg up on his table. It was carved of cedar so it wouldn't rot or get insects chewing at it. It looked sunburned, mostly red with some white stripes in it. I could smell it from across the room. It still smelled good.

The man who made it had been a railroad hand who liked to think hisself an artist, and so every useless little toe had also been carved into the leg, and there was even the rounds and lines of some muscles on the back side of the calf. *No sense in not being accurate,* he'd said. I hadn't complained, but now—standing there where that Negro could stare at it—I felt self-conscious about it. It was foolish, and it looked naked. But this Negro, who had carried me into a hole and protected me, much against his will, and had every right to be amused by the sculpture, he didn't laugh. He stroked the leg with his big hands, feeling the grooves between the toes, the line of ligament up the heel, those two muscles at the back, and the sharp ridge of the shin. He looked at me again, and the look in his eyes was curious and sad. He looked at my stump and up at my face and then back at the wood thing in his grip.

"Sorry about your leg."

"So it was you cut it off back there at McGavock's. Bastard." I smiled.

"I just carried off them old legs, I didn't cut 'em off. That was for those white men and their saws. Can't blame me."

"Even so, you stay the hell away from this other leg."

Theopolis smiled. "All right, then."

We settled into a comfortable silence for a long time after that. All I could hear was the snipping of shears and the pop of his long, thick needles pressing through leather. He traced the outline of that wood foot, took its measurements, and fit the leather around it with care, like he was making a boot for a regular foot that might blister and scrape.

"What's your name again?"

"Theopolis."

After a while I hopped out the door and into the sun on the porch. I had got damned sick of dark, low-ceilinged little rooms over the years and preferred to be out in the light. I didn't know how anyone could live like that, although I had surely lived like that once. Put two people in a room like that, and you can't avoid the other, you got to talk and carry on. I was happy not to have to talk and carry on for a little time.

I leaned back into one of Theopolis's wood porch chairs and rested my head against the unpainted shingles of the wall. They were warm in the sun, and I fell asleep.

When I woke up, an old man with hard eyes and white hair was stomping his way toward the shop from the street, where he'd left his horse. He scratched his crotch and walked bowlegged for a few steps until he caught sight of me and straightened up. He looked at me like he thought it would be better for everyone if I would dry up and blow away.

"Who are you?" he said.

"My name is the Reverend Thomas Jefferson Purefoy, mister."

Don't know where I came up with that name. Never used it again.

"What the hell you doing here?"

I thought that was a mighty rude way of talking to a reverend. I thought he might have seen through my story, and I was fixing to give him an earful of Ecclesiastes just to keep him honest, when I caught him staring at my stump.

"Where's your leg?"

"I don't really know, sir. Reckon it's somewhere around here."

I felt around for one of the Colts, but they weren't there. I remembered they was in Jerrod's saddlebags. I puffed myself up some anyway, to throw the old man off. I'd bite him until he screamed for his mama if he kept talking to me like I was shit.

"Did you just cut off your leg for the hell of it, or did you get it blown off?"

"It was cut off by surgeons because of an injury I got during the war. Right around here, matter of fact."

By this time Theopolis had heard me and had come out to investigate.

"Theopolis, who is this man?"

"He's a customer, Mr. Baylor."

"You got customers? *I'm* your customer. This man could be any damned cracker. Get in there."

That man rubbed me raw, that's the truth.

43

CARRIE MCGAVOCK

We never used to go to those town parties, those of us who lived out on plantations and ran our households. I'm talking about the women, the mistresses, the plantation ladies. Town parties were for town men and, often, our husbands. We lived in an isolation that ensured that we, at least, would embody whatever it was that made Southerners different and purer and more correct than any other race upon the earth. That is, we were like creatures in a zoological garden, examples of our race, preserved and contained within the bars of the well-turned balustrades. Meanwhile, the rest of the Southern nation ran around as if unleashed, free from the very moral binds that we, the women, preserved and then tied around our wrists. Men drank in public and cavorted with certain other women who wore the latest from Paris. They all went to parties together, even our own men.

The war changed much, not least the invitation lists for parties in town. This was my least favorite change, even if it meant I no longer stored myself away at Carnton like a keepsake. The women who had invited me to their houses in the daytime, the same women I had avoided these many years, now expected me to attend their nighttime bacchanals as part of the entity called *Colonel McGavock*. I attended out of sympathy for my husband, who felt obliged to attend as a matter of business strategy: he would strategize while the men around him became drunk, until they were no longer able to understand anything he suggested except that whatever it was would cost them money, and the easy and obvious answer to that was *no*. I loved to observe him from a corner in the hostess's parlor and watch his shadow against the looming ceilings gesticulate madly while the corpulent and red-faced men of our town bobbed and swayed around him trying to stay upright. There is a kind of loveliness to be seen in a man who pursues a doomed cause not out of ignorance, which would be ugly, but in the full knowledge that he is bound to fail.

The night after I found out about Mr. Baylor's plans for his field, we were invited to attend a dance in celebration of the engagement of Judge and Mrs. McEwen's daughter, the judge having returned from the war healthy and good-natured, as if he'd spent it on vacation. He had been out of touch with his wife for most of the time, and he had never been very clear about where he had fought. He simply returned one day, still fat, hung his gun back over the fireplace, and sat back down in his library chair to catch up on the old newspapers. If ever I regretted my time in the country, I had only to look at Mrs. McEwen to know that I was far better suited to country life than town life. The opium had turned her skin to rice paper, crinkled and white and about to disintegrate at any moment. It was a marvel that she was able to raise any child to marriageable age. When I saw her in her home that night, she looked oddly like a woman betrayed, like a woman who could not look at her husband without contempt. John had told me about encountering her in town just after the battle, standing on her porch with two friends and staring at nothing. *They all wore thin dresses, too thin for the weather or for propriety. None of them seemed to be blinking, but their eyes glowed and were wet. Cecilia McEwen was smiling as if she'd just seen something naughty. I exchanged meaningless niceties, but I was as fascinated by those women as I had been as a boy when I'd gone to the carnival to see the bearded lady and a shrunken head from the Congo. They were human, only more so for being oddities that were both real and not real, embodying the difference. Ghosts really, and clearly insane.* John steered far clear of her during the evening. Her dress was tasteful and well sewn, and it seemed to choke her.

I was busy fending off the servant thrusting trays of canapés while I decided how I would approach Mr. Baylor when he arrived. I did not know what I would say to him, but I could not quit thinking about the idea of those dead men unearthed by sharp iron and exposed again to the light of day. What would I ask?

He arrived flustered and angry, as he usually did, towing his dim-witted wife along behind him. She could not put a stop to his plans for the battlefield because *she* was surely unaware of them and, perhaps, even unaware that such a thing as a plow existed upon the earth. And even if she were able to understand her husband's plans, what did she care for the bones of dead boys she didn't know? I could not imagine her mustering any outrage for anything greater than a table improperly set or an untidy house. Bones in the field, if they meant anything to her, would mean *untidiness.* She would be of no use to me.

Baylor took a whiskey, and I watched him stride into the parlor and steer toward the knot of men that John had gathered to hear of his plans for reviving the railroad. Baylor was no fool. He knew the men in that room had reason to be wary of him, and perhaps angry, because of what he planned for his field. But he also knew that men—many men—were weak and that they could be charmed into abeyance for the moment by a charismatic and powerful man like him. The face he typically displayed for women and his inferiors—children, Negroes, farmers—would not be welcome in such a gathering, and so I watched how, with every step across the room, the architecture of his face shifted and his skin re-formed itself until he was transformed into the image of the benevolent man of business, offensive to no one. This was the most awful face of all, I decided.

After a few minutes, talking with his thumbs in the loops of his pants and shifting around like his suit afflicted him, like he was just plain folks, I could tell that he had easily outmaneuvered John and had taken control of the group. I leaned against the bookcase in my corner, my head resting on a long row of Sir Walter Scott's Waverley Novels.

I was thinking about what Zachariah Cashwell would say about what I was seeing, which was something I often wondered, when Mrs. McEwen grabbed me by the elbow and gently pulled me along with her toward a little group of women who were watching their men and speaking inanities about the sorrowful state of their households and the intricacies and significance of a bustle's angle. They were intelligent creatures, some of them, without a thing to talk about. I looked at Mrs. McEwen's face, and she was rapt with fascination at their talk, as if it was in the language of alien invaders. She said nothing, and only stared at them in amusement until all of them, uncomfortable under her gaze, politely excused themselves. I wondered why she had found me. Perhaps she thought I would be as amused as she was. I knew that the laudanum had withered and finally killed whatever concern she might have had for them and their opinions, and I might have found a friend in her if she hadn't been mad. She scared me, but I was happy to be guided along. After the women had drifted off, we posted ourselves on the other side of the mantel. We watched each other and didn't speak. I stroked the glass on a bell jar encasing an old carving of a gnatcatcher.

"Have you any medicine?"

Her voice startled me. It was gravelly and soft.

"No, I don't."

"Have you seen the doctor? Any doctor?"

"No."

"I see."

We stared off at the group of men. John had detached himself to admire the books in the bookcases, and Baylor seemed to be wrapping up whatever business he had been conducting with the judge and his fellows. Mrs. McEwen spoke again.

"This is all mine, you know."

"Of course."

"I am the heiress of all you see, and all that transpires within those borders. I have seen plenty that you have not seen, that you *cannot* see, but which explains everything and makes me quite happy with my little inheritance."

I wondered whether I would have said such things, whether my mind would have also melted, had I taken all that laudanum they gave me. I was desperate to leave her, and yet some latent sense of propriety bound me to the spot. I stared at the gnatcatcher as I listened, praying that John would come over and give me an excuse to leave. Even so, I felt something for Mrs. McEwen, some distant connection to something she had just said, and so I spoke.

"What have you seen?"

Her eyes grew wide, and she cocked her head at me, like the bird under the bell jar.

"I have seen the war, oh yes, of course, but I have also seen other wars, and I have seen mad horses rushing from one war to another, carrying the same poor souls into the fray again and again until they are exhausted from the endless cycle of body and spirit, body and spirit, and they cry out for relief and they are given that relief. *Please, have you any medicine?* The cleverness of God's plan to beat the will out of men amuses me. That is what's needed in this world."

I decided not to wait any longer, and with a nod I turned my back on her and went to collect John before Baylor could leave. I'd had an idea, which Mrs. McEwen's raving had reinforced. But she was not done with me and whispered loudly at my back, and I stopped briefly.

"You, on the other hand, succumb to that will of men and fortify it with your ministrations upon their bodies, in living and in death. Yes, I know what you are thinking, I see you eyeing Mr. Baylor. All will love you for your sacrifice, but it will only postpone the inevitable."

I heard her sigh and slump down into a parlor chair. I didn't turn around.

"If I had the energy, I would stop you, but I suppose I will applaud you like the rest. Brava, St. Carrie!"

I moved off quickly, wanting to never hear the woman's voice again. Ladies brushed past me in their muslin and silk, moving from one seat to another, on the couches in the parlor and on the hard chairs in the library, and I couldn't tell sometimes whether the whispers I heard were the sound of them talking or the sound of their skirts brushing against each other. It was time for us to leave, that was certain.

I saw Mrs. Baylor, who had been stuffing her face with brittle over by the dining room doorway, look up and see Mr. Baylor marching across the room to retrieve her. She dusted off her hands like she'd been sanding wood, took his arm, and they swept out into the entranceway, out of sight. John had seen me looking frantic, I'm sure, so he came and collected me by the arm.

"What's the matter, Carrie? Should we go?"

"Yes. But there's a man outside I need to see."

I dragged John outside, and we caught up to Baylor and his wife just as he was putting the reins to his team.

"Mr. Baylor?"

He must have thought he would make an uninterrupted departure, but I had determined that he would not stir the hornets and let others take the stings.

"Yes, Mrs. McGavock?"

"I wanted to talk to you about your field."

"I am in a great hurry, Mrs. McGavock. Perhaps we could talk about your agricultural interests some other time? Please come call on us."

"I have no interest in agriculture."

He knew what I was talking about.

"What could interest you about my field, then?"

"The men who are buried there. They interest me."

When he crossed his arms and leaned toward me, his chest seemed to fill up my vision. John stood silent at my elbow. I suppose he knew it would be no good trying to interrupt me, that I would just keep talking. Perhaps he was glad of this.

"Mrs. McGavock, they do not interest me in the slightest. People may think I'm rich, but even I can't afford to let acres of good land lie fallow because it contains the bodies of men who fought an idiotic battle in an ill-considered, stupid war, whose souls have long departed, and whose fellows never bothered to come back for them. So much for the honor of the Confederacy."

I didn't have an answer. If I had been someone like Baylor, if I'd owned land and had such intractable opinions about the worth of others, I might have found his argument persuasive. But I was not that kind of person.

"It is already out of your hands, Mr. Baylor. It is already a grave-yard. All it is missing are the headstones."

"By that standard, Mrs. McGavock, the whole earth is a grave-yard of one sort or another. Perhaps we should never plow a field again. Perhaps we should starve for the sins of the deceased, for every unacknowledged and unmarked death."

"I am not asking that. I am asking only that you spare *this* field, in *this* place. I do not expect you to do this out of kindness or sen-timentality. In exchange for sparing it, I expect we could raise money to compensate you."

The new moon was just breaking through the clouds low on the horizon, and Baylor's face was momentarily lit in gray light, like a ghost. Everything about him and his cart gleamed, from the hal-ters on his horses to the spokes on his wheels. His teeth gleamed when he smiled at me. He mustered a look that seemed almost kind at first, until it melted into righteous pity.

"I'm sure, Mrs. McGavock, that there isn't enough money in this town to compensate me for that field, what took place on it, and what is contained above and below it. Where would *you* find such money?"

He was looking past me to John when he said this last bit, and his condescension cut me to the quick. My voice grew louder, shriller, and I didn't seem able to control it.

"There are other people in this town who won't want to see that field plowed, *Mister* Baylor. And if they can't come up with the money, they'll come up with other means."

"Are you threatening me?"

"I am not. I am trying to prevent the threats. I am trying to get you to see reason, so that those who would threaten you will have no cause. I am appealing to your common decency."

"I have decency, Mrs. McGavock, but it is not the common sort to which you are referring. And I will not have you interfering with my business, and the fate of that field is surely my business."

John finally spoke, no doubt tongue-tied by my audacity and vehemence.

"That's enough, Baylor."

Baylor suddenly looked more comfortable, as if he'd been hoping for John to step in.

"Then take some control of your woman, McGavock. Explain to her about how *business* works and how she oughtn't meddle in the *business* of others."

"Oh, but I don't disagree with her. You're being a fool, Baylor. That field isn't worth the agitation, and you know it."

"Oh, let the petty sentimentalists bring their grievances against me. Let them try to threaten me. I am ready. My soul is rested and clean. I have nothing to fear."

He put the reins to his team and clucked his tongue.

"And now I am going."

John and I stood and watched Mr. and Mrs. Baylor go, two black silhouettes against the brightening night sky. I took John's arm, and we walked out to our own carriage. We rode in silence for some time, each caught in dark thoughts. Finally John spoke, and his words surprised me, for I thought he would chastise me for my discussion with Baylor.

"You know, these streets are nothing like they were that day."

"That day?"

"Well, in those days. The week after the battle. These streets are proper, normal. They've been graded and cleaned, and the trees that were shot through with lead have been removed. The men were like toys left out by children. There were soldiers left behind to bury them all, and a more miserable job I cannot imagine. This town and that battlefield looked like nothing human. I lost my mind for days, exploring that hellscape. Surely you knew I was not right in those days?"

"I was busy, John."

"Yes, you were."

"I'm sorry."

"You have nothing to be sorry about. You were doing right."

Silence. It was a quiet ride toward the moon.

"But these streets, they were paths through a different world, and all of those dead men created that world."

There was guilt in his voice. It was powerful, and it made his body tremble. I put my hand on his, and he allowed this for a moment and then shrugged me off. I thought of that night he'd appeared below my window when I was a girl and how wracked he had been then with some sort of misery that I had found irresistible. He was that man again. I understood why he felt this way. He had walked among the dead, unable to provide succor or to ease their passage. At Carnton the misery and the dying had been orderly, at least, and all those who did die were prepared. I saw to that as best I could.

"All their faces, Carrie. I couldn't look at them and not wonder what they had been thinking. So many looked as if they wanted to say one more thing. Now I imagine them under the weeds of Baylor's field still with those damned looks on their faces, still trying to say whatever it was they had meant to say. Now I can't help thinking that the only meaning of all that killing was that it made it possible for Theopolis to open a cobbler's shop. Such a simple thing."

"They wouldn't have thought of it that way."

"How do you know? That's what we think, but how do we know? Forgive me, but these memories are almost too much for me. It was impossible for me to look out over that battlefield and the gray and blue backs and not wonder about God."

In that moment I had a vision of that field, and these streets, and what they must have been like. Carnton had for so long been the center of everything that I hadn't been able to see how insignificant my heroism had been. I had indeed begun to think of myself as a heroine, not least because of those letters that continued to come to me singing my praises. There had been a battle, yes, but most important, there had been the hospital, a place to heal, one way or another. I had not paid attention, really, when people spoke of the other hospitals in town, of the sacrifices of other women. There was only Carnton. I felt I was flying above the battlefield, and I could see the field and the town. I knew the magnitude of what had been lost. Baylor's field looked like a quilt from up there, a patchwork of men in wool who had died before anyone could help them. Our great heroics at Carnton were as nothing to the thousands. Oh Lord, I hated John then, just for an instant.

What was John guilty of? What was I guilty of? We were alive, we'd survived. Was that not God's wish for us? Certainly it must have been, and yet who could believe that any human had been intended by God to die so miserably and so suddenly? Had they gone down before God could attend to them? Was that blasphemy? Whatever carried me above the battlefield glided down and down and down until I was the size of an ant and riding a magic carpet over and around mountains of knees and elbows and backs, forests of mustaches and beards and matted hair, chasms of mouths frozen open in wonder, a whole wilderness now disappeared beneath the red soil of Baylor's field. What would those men say if they could finish those sentences John had seen on their lips? I prayed they would not speak to me, that I would not hear them.

As we came around the bend in our driveway, the moon seemed to be sitting just on top of the house and threatening to crush it.

When we went up to our room, I found another bundle of mail at the foot of my bed. I was so keyed up and distracted I first didn't notice it; and then when I did, I bent over to put it in with the others: so many other bundles lay in the bottom of my wardrobe, unopened.

I had never read more than a few of the letters that came from the families of the missing and the dead, and then usually only those that had been penned and addressed properly, on good stationery with good ink. I knew, I suppose, that by reading only the letters of women like me, I would be spared any loose revelation of pain or anger, as such sentiments would never slip into the letters of ladies raised as I had been, to be circumspect with strangers. The letters that came scrawled on packing paper in pencil, riddled with misspellings—these were objects of much greater mystery, and I feared what they contained. So many letters came to me, I told myself, I *had* to have a way to sift through them. This had been my way. A year and more had passed, and already the words *Carnton, Franklin, Tennessee* had come to mean something to those who heard of it. It was not the address of the warmongers and their plotters and strategists. Carnton was the address of the war itself. It was the place to send letters asking impossible questions.

I lay in bed next to John, staring out into a room that seemed, in the moonlight, mysterious and terrible. The wardrobe's door gaped like an eye or a wound.

John at last fell asleep, but still I lay there as if listening. Finally I rose and pulled out the bundles and went into my little room above the stairs and piled the letters next to my chair. It took five trips to carry all of them.

I lit a candle and began to read.

All of them.

It was far worse than I had imagined. The courtly letters had only hinted at what I now discovered in the scrawlings and erasures of those letters written by, or for, the mothers and fathers who had never had much more than their children and didn't realize how much they had needed them until they were gone. Anger and hope and grief and hatred and loneliness were not separate emotions, experienced in turn, but irrelevant names for the constituent parts of one inescapable experience of the world without pity or memory: no memory of the prayers, kindnesses, and promises that had been made to the Lord, or to their children, all of which had not been lies, but *had* been uttered with a hope that was revealed to them as ignorance by the deaths of their children. If they were to hope for anything again, and quite a few expressed versions of hope in their letters, it was tentative and qualified. It was simply the hope that the memory of their children would not also die.

These letters carried great weight, unbearable weight. Their children had not died so much as disappeared into a mist at the edges of the discernible world. They had no idea where Franklin was or what it was. Their memories had no place to rest except in those letters. They contained the intimate details of lives that might as well have been myth to me.

caught a fish
loved to make biscuits
had a pig named George
loved his daughter, who looks just like him, but that
don't mean nothing to her cause she don't know what he
looked like, never saw him not once not ever, and I got to
put her out cause we don't got the money for her no more,
and I hope she don't come out bad.

I absorbed all this. I wanted to send them the portrait across from my bed, the portrait of my three dead angels, to tell them that they weren't the only ones who knew this weight and that they ought to leave me alone. And yet I took it in, and by the end I was seeing things and imagining a portrait of a thousand angels looking down on me in horror as I wept silently in my bed.

Well on toward dawn, Hattie came in, and she said nothing. She'd become such an unusual young woman. She was quiet. She made things grow, obsessively, and never bothered about the dirt beneath her fingernails. She was something of an eccentric, but a harmless one who could be adored for her oddity. She put her head in my lap, and I stroked seeds from her hair. We read the rest of the letters together, and she never said a word. I believe that she had already known what would be found in those letters, and their mysteries were no surprise to her. I touched her brown face and smoothed the wrinkles in her nightgown. She looked up at me when we finished with the last, this one from a father in Greenville, Alabama, who had hoped his son would follow him in his law practice. Hattie looked at me as if to say, *What are you going to do now?*

What would I do?

What could anyone, any one woman, do?

44

ZACHARIAH CASHWELL

The boot Theopolis made me was just about as perfect a piece of leather as I'd ever seen. Coffee-colored, soft where it needed to be soft, stiff where it needed to be stiff, and at the back, just above the short heel, he'd stamped a simple *T,* his mark.

When Jerrod and I left the shop, there was still a couple of hours of daylight left, and I wanted to get out to the Indian dig as soon as possible, before all the jobs were gone. I wasn't exactly sure what it was I could do out there, but I thought that maybe they might be able to use a clerk. Hell, I'd count them savage bones if they needed it. Jerrod said he'd dig or polish skulls. I just wanted to disappear into someplace where the railroad company weren't likely to come looking for me. An Indian cemetery seemed pretty unlikely to me.

We rode through the town, which looked nothing like it did that night I'd spent there years before. There weren't nobody running or bleeding or stealing tobacco off me. Just a little town again. I thought the town had no right to go back to normal, but I thought that about every town. New oaks had been planted, fences rebuilt, the road graded, the shutters on the windows repainted in black and green and blue. We rode east with the sun at our back, and I could understand why someone would build a town right there on that rise. The land east cooled to various shades of yellow and gold while we rode, and here and there the fields were cut through by creeks lined with sycamores and beeches, and from a distance it looked like the land had veins, like it were alive. Even atop the horse, I could see the killdeer flitting from haystack to haystack, and the sparrows picking among the leavings at the base of trees, and the red-tailed hawk gliding quick from one field to another, always landing high up in a tree that hid him good, until suddenly there was flapping and commotion and what all, and out of it came that hawk gliding smooth as anything again to another treetop in another field.

I didn't recognize the battlefield until we had fairly well passed it by. It was overgrown with grass and hawthorn and wildflowers that bloomed gaudy and swayed in the slightest breeze. *Good soil down in there now*, I thought. My mama had always told me that blood made plants grow strong, and she had never let waste a single drop of chicken blood when she killed a hen for dinner. I looked down from my horse on a beautiful, wild field that seemed like it could never be tamed again. I tried to find the tree where my squad had formed up for the charge, but so much had grown in the years, including my own memories, that it was impossible for me to say for sure which tree was which.

"Why we stopping?" Jerrod said.

"Don't you want to see this place again?"

"Not ever, if you don't mind, Mr. Preacher Man."

I gave a light heel to my horse, and we started walking again. I was afraid we weren't going to make it to the site before they knocked off work, but it wasn't as far as I thought, and soon I could see their fires over the next hill.

I tried to avoid looking, but I couldn't help watching over on my right for the big house to appear between the trees, and soon it did. I recognized the porch on the back, and those big windows, and that old garden where we'd piled all of those who passed on.

The place looked empty, but when I squinted, I could see a small person rooting around in that garden and tossing weeds over her shoulder in a shower of dirt clods. *They got white folk doing their work for 'em now.* I rode on, and quit watching the house. There wasn't a place for me there no more. I wondered what would happen if I just appeared on their doorstep and knocked. What would I tell her? Would she take me in again? Did she still think of me? A part of me craved an answer, and another part didn't want to risk hearing the wrong answer. Not yet. We rode on.

By the time we got down into the camp I was feeling, for no good reason, pretty good about my prospects. Who wouldn't hire a one-legged man accompanied by a thug with a strong back? Don't reckon I know why, but this sounded reasonable to me. The men looked beat-down tired, covered in red dirt and mud that they didn't bother to wipe from their hands as they sat down to eat at a long table lined up outside their long tent. Suppertime, I decided, was a good time to introduce myself.

I got off my horse and tied him to a tent spike. I pulled out my Bible and walked with Jerrod toward the men. I held up my hand in greeting.

"Who's in charge here?"

They were almost all bearded, and every one of them looked like he'd been digging his whole life. They were substantial men, and they didn't talk much. One jerked his head toward the tent, and when I looked over toward it, I saw the flap moving, as if someone had been watching us a moment before. I looked back to the table and saw that they were eating well, better than I would have expected. Biscuits, country ham, and big jars of milk. I was going to get hired on to that outfit or die trying.

I went into the tent first. Jerrod backed into it behind me, his eyes still on those country ham steaks, so he didn't notice that I stopped stock-still when I saw who was sitting at the trestle desk at the end of the tent. Jerrod kept backing up, no doubt drooling down his chin, until he knocked us both down into the damned dirt. I had to climb on top of him to get some purchase on the ground with my wood leg and raise myself to standing again.

The man sitting at the table at the end of the tent was that Union lieutenant who saved my life right there in Franklin. He was short and balding, and he looked nothing like a soldier, but everything like the kind of man who would fiddle with old bones for a living. He wore spectacles on the end of his nose, but they couldn't hide his eyes. Those eyes still carried in them the contempt and anger and pity I'd remembered from what now seemed a lifetime ago, looking down at me in the Union ditch. It was true that we'd just entered his tent like two clowns, but I couldn't shake the feeling that he knew who I was and that the way he was staring was reserved only for *me*. This changed my plan entirely.

Did I owe that man something? There had been a time when I didn't think I owed him a damned thing except a bullet in the head. He'd saved me for the surgeons' torture table, and how could he be forgiven that? He was the enemy. He and his men had cut down the men in my squad without a care or a second thought, and that same goddamn field I'd just ridden past was the evidence of his butchering. What had sparing me done? Left me alive to think about those dead boys and to see the flowers sprouting on top of roots no doubt sunk deep into the bodies of my friends; to hobble along on the wooden sculpture of a half-assed artist who was more interested in making the thing look real than making it comfortable; to range across the territory without a single goddamn idea what I was supposed to do, without the luxury of, say, deciding to waste my time brushing off the bones of dead savages and examining them with one of the big magnifying glasses he had lined up on his desk. If I'd died on that battlefield, I wouldn't have had to live all that shit, and there were times when living it was a burden. I noticed too much now, I saw too much. If I'd cared to, I could have hated the man sitting in front of me, and if I'd been of the right mind, I could have pulled out that .45 and shot him dead.

But, hell, I had long ago been convinced that I wanted to be alive. I'd changed my mind about that, or more truthfully, Carrie McGavock had changed it for me.

This man had saved me even when I didn't know that I wanted to be saved. He would have been commended for stabbing me through the heart and letting me bleed to death in the bottom of his ditch, among the other dead boys, but he hadn't done that. Now I was glad.

What do you say to a man like that? I began to hate him just because I didn't know what to say to him. It was all too turned around and twisted just to introduce myself and say *thank you*. Those two words couldn't say what I meant. The only way I could properly acknowledge what he'd done would be to recount it, and to tell him how I'd lived since, so he could know all of what he done for me, not just that little part in that one little moment at the top of that hill.

And so I began to talk without being asked to talk, and I told him all about that day of the battle and how we'd prepared and how I was sure I'd die going up that hill, so sure that I wasn't frightened by it, and how I'd noticed the ants and the blades of grass each time I threw myself to the ground and how I'd taken the colors and rushed his position and how he'd looked down at me in his ditch and refused to kill me. I told him about being a prisoner and an invalid and a degenerate gambler. I confessed my sins to him, is what I did, and I think I even shocked Jerrod a little. I must have talked for the better part of an hour, and not once did the man interrupt me. He sat in his chair, still as a rock, with his elbows on the desk and his fingers drumming each other over and over again. Finally I begged him for forgiveness. Not for attacking him, which had been my duty, but for doing so little with what he'd spared for me.

I ran out of things to say. I stood quiet in front of him, aware that my days as a preacher were over but hoping that he would take me on anyway. He leaned back in his chair.

"I have no earthly idea what you're talking about, sir."

"The ditch. I was in the ditch. I had the colors. Right here in Franklin."

"I remember the ditch. I remember the battle. I remember watching a number of color-bearers fall before our fusillade. I do not remember taking pity on one of them and sparing his life. You have me confused with someone else, this is most clear. I gave no quarter that day, and as much as I've prayed to God to show me something worthwhile I did that day, He's seen fit to show me nothing. I am not the man you think I am."

"You are. I don't have you mixed up. I know who you are."

"Then you have lost your proper memory of the battle, mister."

"Call me Zachariah. Zachariah Cashwell."

"Zachariah, then. In any case, I wish to hear no more about what you think I did during the war. In fact, I would like to hear no more about that war, or that battle. It is a trial to be here in this place, but my work at the college has brought me here, and so I must remain until I have completed this excavation. Perhaps it is my penance, an irony of God's."

I was mad now. Mad in every sense, including the crazy, foaming-at-the-mouth sense. Weren't nobody going to tell me that I didn't have my memories of that day crystal clear, because those memories had explained everything to me during the years since the war ended. How I came to be there, standing in that tent, could not be explained without that moment in the ditch when that man told me I was his prisoner and would not die that day. I knew that man's face, and it was the face staring up at me now. I could not stand the idea that I didn't remember everything perfectly; otherwise, what else had I gotten mixed up? I had memories of friends who had died. Had they existed? Did they look like I remembered? I did not want to spend the rest of my life wondering about such things. I would prove to this man that he had saved me, but I realized it couldn't be done right away. I needed to lay low, work on him slowly. I also needed some ham steak.

"Well, I reckon that's possible. God's penance is blessed, but it can be terrible, too."

"That, Mr. Cashwell, is the truest thing you've said since walking into my tent with your companion here."

I'd forgotten about Jerrod. I looked down at him, and he was just staring at me all squinty, like he wasn't sure who he was standing beside.

"We'd like jobs, mister."

"Professor Stiles. You can call me Professor. We've got jobs, but only your man here . . ."

"You can call me Jerrod."

"Only Jerrod has the qualifications, which are that he can walk on two real legs and lift heavy things. I'm not sure what to do with a one-legged man."

"Well . . ."

"But I'll find something for you. It's the least I can do for someone whose life I held in my hands and didn't crush out. Perhaps you can catalog bones. Can you write?"

He was confusing me.

"So you believe me now?"

"No, but it's a fiction that I'd dearly like to believe. If I believe in it hard enough, perhaps it will come true."

He raised his hat off his head, and I saw dust motes rise up off it in the last beams of dusk coming through a tear in the tent. He was bald and shiny under that old hat. He wasn't as young as I remembered. Not as young, and not nearly as pure as I'd imagined him. He'd had a hard few years, too.

"Yes, I can write."

Hours later only a few of us were left around the cook fire, none of us saying much. I wanted to know what the hell the man from the tent, who they called the professor, and his crew were doing here, but I didn't know how to start the question without being insulting. I said to him:

"You got a nice operation going here."

Professor Stiles puffed on a pipe and looked at me through the haze of smoke. Jerrod kept edging toward him, trying to catch a snort.

"I actually don't really know what I'm doing. Not really."

That wasn't the kind of thing I expected to hear. I was more used to hearing men boast about things there weren't no way they could have done. Men were bound to have done or said bigger and more impressive things now more than they ever had years ago, when the things we done and said had actually been impressive. Now it was just a way of talking. But the professor was a Yankee.

"You look like you know what you're doing."

"I got sent down here by the college to supervise this excavation only because I'm a professor of antiquities, and they decided that these burial mounds qualified as antiquities. But I'm a Greek and Roman scholar, I don't know a thing about Indians, and I don't recognize or understand much of what I've seen come out of this burial place. But I have to do it, or lose my job, so there you are."

He might as well have come from across the ocean speaking gibberish for all I understood of what he said. I could not imagine this college, those antiquities. He came from a place I would never see, where he spent his time doing things I couldn't see the use of doing. It impressed me some, to think that men like him could waste their time in uncountable ways, collecting and sorting things that were forgotten and thrown out long ago, and *still* they had time to come down here and whup our asses. Mighty impressive.

"Why not just leave them alone? What you get out of taking them bones and jars and boxes out of the ground like that?"

"For preservation. They need to be preserved, for posterity."

"How long you reckon they been there?"

"Oh, I'd say at least a thousand years, maybe more. Hard to tell. There's only a little documentation of these cultures."

"A thousand years in that hill?"

"Yes."

"Sounds preserved to me."

His pipe had gone out, and he fumbled around looking for a match to relight it. I half expected Jerrod to leap up and light it with a burning coal just to earn him some tobacco, but he'd already slunk off to find a dry place for sleeping. It was just the two of us.

"That's a good point, I suppose. They were preserved where they were, as they were intended to be preserved."

"Right."

"But no one could see them, these treasures, these antiquities."

"I could have lived without seeing a mess of Indian skulls lined up on your shelves."

"But there's knowledge there, things to learn about those skulls and the urns and jewelry they were buried wearing. And, anyway, what if someone comes along and is sick of this hill and tears it down? Then everything is lost."

"So you got to take 'em up out of the ground to preserve them."

"Right."

"You going to bury them again? Around here?"

"No, I think I'll return to the college with them, and perhaps some of the items will find their way to museums."

I didn't much care about dead Indians. I'd never much thought about them, really. It just seemed funny that they had to dig into the graves to save them and that the dead would end up scattered around the country, anywhere but where they'd started. In the dark I could still see into the side of the hill, where the workers had dug their tunnels. It was a twisty maze in there, and I reckoned there might be thousands of Indians buried in that clay. I got scared for a second thinking about the twisting little paths beneath the earth that led the way to things I weren't ever supposed to see. It made me think of everything else that I had never seen and wasn't supposed to see. Here was a village of the dead beneath my feet, and a mile or so away lay the war below, everything preserved in place.

CARRIE McGAVOCK

Truly he was an awful man, so awful he fascinated me and made me want to stay near him and observe his every hand gesture, his every facial expression, his every foul idea snaking out of his mouth. How such a man had become a success was not in doubt. The strong always win, for a time. The mystery was how he could have become *prominent* in our town and not reviled. Perhaps that was the fear that kept him in the good graces of society. It was one more reason for me to eschew society, that was for certain.

John and I sat in the Baylors' parlor, to the right of the staircase. There was an ancient harpsichord inside which looked as if it hadn't been opened in years. Dust clogged the filigreed decoration on its legs and case, making the scenes that had once lived within them look as if they were fading and eroding to nothing.

Baylor was an old man, like so many others. His white hair, combed back, seemed placed upon his skull, a strand here, a strand there. Soon it would be all gone, and all that would be left would be the brown sphere and, perhaps, the tufts of hair poking up off his round ears. He had a small mouth but a sharp chin, and this he stroked incessantly. He wore a cotton suit, well pressed, and narrow black boots. His power was not in his body, but in his eyes, which were bright and unblinking, and in the insistence of his voice. It was a low, rattling voice that he let fill the air between us, absorbing whatever we said until we were left just to listen.

Again and again John and I implored him to leave the graves alone. Offer to sell the land to the town, John told him; perhaps the town could sign a note to make the full purchase price payable in five years, by which time the worst effects of this dreadful war would have passed us.

Instead, Baylor talked: about the skyrocketing prices of corn and beans, about the huge need for tilled fields, about his own empty pocketbook.

I sat watching Mr. Baylor talk on about the new situation in Franklin and how he couldn't see any way of avoiding the plowing of his field, seeing how the economy was. But after the night before, with those letters, all I was thinking was, *I will lift the burden of memory and place it somewhere else, and if I don't, I will die. I will save those men in that field.*

John had become used to my years of strength and optimism, but not so used to it that he didn't remember the years of my melancholy. I must have looked a sight to him, gray-faced and silent. He had been worrying over me all morning, and even now he kept looking at me. I felt faint, and yet my anger kept rising.

Finally I said, losing all patience, "It is difficult for me to listen to these words, Mr. Baylor. I'm thinking of your boy."

"My boy?"

"Will."

"Leave him out of this."

"He died right in here, didn't he? Oh no, I'm sorry, he died outside, didn't he? You wouldn't even let your blessed son in this house. Young Will."

"Get out."

"We're going," John said.

John had me by the arm and was pulling me to the door before

I could object. Baylor walked behind us, swinging that cane of his as if about to use it on us, like an overseer.

"Stay out of this house."

John yanked at the door.

"He ignored you all the way to the grave, didn't he?" I persisted. "And where is that grave? Not in the family plot, I believe. Did you put him in a pauper's grave, or did you at least find him a decent place and mark it?"

Mr. Baylor's face gained color while I watched, from gray to pink to red. He began to thump the floor in front of him with that cane he didn't need and never used, but which he carried around at times.

"You dare to mention Will's name?"

John could take no more.

"Should she call him Cotton? That's what he called himself, right? When he wrote those newspaper columns? Cotton Gin."

"What do you know of sacrifice, McGavock? Either of you. You talk to me of my son, and yet you couldn't possibly understand what it meant to me to see him dead on that bed."

"My wife and I have lost three children, Baylor. I know something of that pain."

"No, you don't. *No, you don't.* If God took your children—and God bless them—then you have only to pray about it. But I lost my son to the cause of mountebanks and losers and cranks, whose fine talk and wayward sense of the truth led my son down the path to damnation, and me along with it. I lost my son for stupidity's sake, and not his own, either. Oh, he was stupid, but stupid like an enthusiastic and credulous young man. His wasn't the stupidity of the self-deceivers and the sentimentalists who ran that goddamn war, or the trash who started it in the first place. Let your child be wasted on purpose, with someone else's blessing and approval, and then talk to me of your sacrifice. I will not let those men who ran that war, and those of you who stood by and let it go until it was too late to stop, escape into this new age without *penalty*. I *want* to see the humiliation and the anger and the pain on your faces. I *have* to see it. You owe me this, all of you owe me this. My *son,* my loving and beautiful son, was sacrificed upon the altar of your insanity and your evil. I loved him, but I will not commemorate his actions, or the actions of any of those other boys, any more than I would celebrate a suicide. I've given you your sacrifice, ask no more of me."

Sacrifice, I thought. Is that what Martha was, and Mary Elizabeth, and John Randal? *Sacrifice?* They didn't seem like sacrifices to me. They seemed like children. I remembered, separate and yet joined, the distinct moments of their birth: the swirls of wet black hair on their heads; my arms, reaching out, asking, *Is she healthy?* Or, when John Randal was born: *Is he alive?*

"We've all lost so much," I said. "Why can you not see that the destruction of the graves will only do more?"

"My mind is settled on the matter, Mrs. McGavock. Please do not trouble me again."

He turned his stare on John.

"You're lucky I didn't take your whole damned property, by the way. You're as much of a loser as the rest of them. You'll never have a damned thing, John McGavock, and when you die, there will be no one to remember you."

We were down the stairs of the front porch and into the yard before he said this, and I could not leave it be. I wrenched my arm from John and turned back to Baylor. I wished and prayed at that moment that lightning would strike his house and that fire would erupt and that the whole place would burn to the ground and that nothing would ever emerge upon it again, like a salted ground. He looked down on me.

"Is memory so important?"

"What?"

"To be remembered when you die. Memory."

He rolled his eyes.

"Must we debate the obvious?"

"So it's yes. Yes, it's important."

"I suppose."

"Then what shall you do about the dead in your field? They would require something to stoke the memory, would they not? They could not stand plowing."

John was already in the cart and calling for me. Mr. Baylor was leaning against his porch post, looking at me as if I might leap up at him. *I* was floating above it all, anchored only by the weight of those letters, and I could see how odd I must have seemed to him at that moment. I'm not sure that Mr. Baylor even understood what I was talking about or what I was suggesting.

"I'm putting that back into corn and beans. I've already given you my answer."

"No."

"What do you mean *no?*"

I did not really know what I meant, but I knew I had to keep asking. I was making a fool of myself, but I didn't care.

"I mean no, you won't be plowing those men under. Those *boys.* It will not happen."

He laughed. Perhaps he thought me a lunatic. He squinted out at John, hoping, I suppose, that my husband would ride over and sweep me up and take me and my insanity away with him. If I had been standing there on his porch, talking with such a woman standing in my yard, I might have run into the house and locked the door. I saw myself standing there, looking as pale as I used to look when I was willing myself to travel the border between the living and wherever my children had gone. I imagined I might look a little terrifying to a man who, at his age, must have thought of his own mortality. Could the Reaper come as a woman? It might have seemed so.

"That is impossible."

"I don't think it is."

"Not for those men. I will not go out of my way for those men. They made their choice, and their choice dropped them right there, and that's what they deserve. I will not help them."

"You will."

"Good day, Mrs. McGavock."

He turned and walked slowly into his house. He looked over his shoulder at me once before he shut the door, and I saw pity in his crinkled, yellowing eyes. *I could do a lot with that pity,* I thought.

I called out once more, to his closed door, before turning and joining John in the carriage:

"You will, Mr. Baylor."

We rode off.

"What have you done, Carrie?"

"We'll see."

A few days later I heard from Mariah, who had heard from Theopolis, that Zachariah Cashwell had returned to Franklin. She mentioned it casually, in passing, an afterthought, as I was retreating to my room to write my endless letters.

"Returned to Franklin?" I said to her as pleasantly as I could, but I know that I did not deceive her. My heart beat hard in my throat.

She told me that he'd found work in that Union officer's archaeological excavations, south of town.

I wondered, as I went up the stairs and sat down to pen the next letter, if he would come to see me. Or when I would go to him.

> *Dear Mrs. Lloyd Pritchard,*
>
> *I do not remember your son. It is quite possible that I never met him, and it is quite possible that he never came here to Carnton. It is most likely, in fact, that he died a soldier's death on the battlefield and that he lies there to this day. I do not know where he is, but I intend to find out. I intend to find them all. You will hear from me again, very soon.*

Zachariah. It was Zachariah, first and perhaps foremost, who showed me that there were people in the world who could abide the chaos and the brutality and even, sometimes, put it right.

Oh Lord, he could have been an omen of any number of things, a vision sent by God to tell me something that I couldn't augur. Or he could have been the flesh-and-blood man I could not stop thinking about, who had decided to come back to me.

46

CARNTON

From the moment Mariah saw them unburying the dead, she planned to return. Several times, in her hunt for wild roots and herbs, she would watch from the shadow of the trees not too far from the burial mounds, just close enough to see and hear the chink of the picks in earth and rock, but too distant to hear what the men were saying.

A week passed, and she wanted to know the man who would take those folks back up out of the ground, the man in the hat that was too big for him. She wanted to know more about the bones. *Reckon I can bring 'em something to eat. Must be something I can do.* She'd rarely had any interest in the doings of white men, but something, in the ending of the war and the beginning of a new life, had changed. *I done caught that bug Theopolis caught. Freedom. Should have stayed back in the kitchen. What use do I have for that world?*

Next day she brought biscuits to the men digging at the Indian bones, and some coffee beans for the black-hatted supervisor, a Yankee college professor, she learned, and she sat in the shade of a locust watching the men work.

They just like termites, them white ants, she thought. She'd spent hours as a child searching out termite nests and exposing them, just to watch the little white creatures scurry about futilely. She had watched them disappear into the depths of their tunnels, just as these men were doing, and emerge with bits of building material to begin rebuilding, an impossible task. After a while she'd break the nest apart to get to the center, where she'd find the huge, fat queen, whose massive egg sac made her look like a fat worm with the head of a termite. Her children stood by to defend her, rushing Mariah as she reached her hand into the royal chamber, and Mariah would usually come away with a few hanging on to her fingers by their jaws. These she would brush away, knowing they would soon die, that all of them would die once she'd taken their mama.

Mariah's own mother had uses for termite queens: dried up, pulverized, taken in a drink. Mariah was never told what these uses were. She was too young to know such things, her mother had said. She had noticed that it was the other men in the cabins who coveted the termite queen concoctions, but had been too young to understand why. *That's an old charm, older than black folk,* her mother had said.

Now, as they dug in the sun, backs brown and glistening, Mariah wondered what these new men would do when they found the queen. She shook her head. *They ain't termites. And those just dead bones.*

The professor walked over and peered down at her from under his brim. Then he doffed his hat, and she saw how white his head was. He was a man who hardly ever got outside, and he knew better than to tempt the sun.

"Thank you, Mariah, for the coffee. You've been kind to me and my men."

"Just something Mrs. McGavock wanted me to do for you, Mr. Stiles."

This was a lie, but it was a lie she had to tell for propriety's sake.

"Well, tell your mistress thank you. And you don't have to bring anything to come visit, either. I've seen how interested you are in our doings. You're welcome to come and watch as my guest. We're almost through here, anyway, so if you want a tour, you got to ask soon. We'll be going to some of those other mounds north of here, along the river, before long."

He looked expectantly at her, and it made Mariah uncomfortable. She nodded and stood up.

When a few days later Zachariah Cashwell arrived, she knew him in an instant, and he knew her, but they did not talk. He did not speak to her, and she knew better than to greet a white man first. She would have liked him to have spoken to her. It seemed that they had washed up at Franklin like piles of driftwood or seaweed set down by a particularly terrible wave; but the next wave had come, and the next, and the sticks and seaweed dispersed, each floating out into its own pool or patch of ocean—still visible to one another, but drifting in different directions. She watched him as he hobbled around the camp, carrying bones or tools or other items, and he soon faded in significance, paling beneath the bright intrigue of the objects he carried.

So at first she was surprised when Carrie asked her, the next morning at breakfast, if Mariah would be taking luncheon to the excavation the following day—surprised at Carrie's interest in such matters. Then she remembered Zachariah and was surprised no longer.

47

CARRIE McGAVOCK

Mariah led me down through the woods to the excavation. She had suggested we take the road, but since I had many reasons for keeping my visit secret, I declined. I told her to take me the way that she would go, and so we slowly picked our way through the underbrush and over creeks. I noticed there were plenty of fish in the creeks that Eli and Winder had claimed were so empty.

Soon we were staring from the edge of the woods at a work site teeming with shirtless, brown, and sweaty men hauling loads on their backs and in barrows. They looked like ants, the way they worked without having to be told. They called to each other from time to time, but it was a remarkably silent place. I believed it was reverence, even for the long dead of a strange people. They did not look like naturally reverent men, but I suppose that reverence was the natural state of men in the presence of a grave, no matter how hard and unfeeling they were. We all die, we all have it in common. It is an awesome and fearsome thing.

Just before I went marching into that camp with vague ideas of seeing Zachariah and somehow solving my problems at the same time, I pulled back into the woods and hid behind an old blackberry bush.

"What you doing, Miss Carrie?"

"I don't know, exactly, why I'm here."

"I was wondering the same thing."

I could smell the biscuits in the basket I was carrying, and I knew they'd soon grow cold, and it was for that reason I plunged ahead into camp without a plan. Sometimes it's just a little thing that's needed to set things in motion.

Of course, two women parading through a work site like that is bound to cause a little commotion, and soon enough, the head of the excavation, a little bald man with regal carriage, came out of his tent. Then he was followed by a man I recognized from Carnton, with a patch over his eye and two pistols stuck in his coat pockets. And then came Zachariah.

He looked confused at first, like I was the last person he'd have expected. He walked smoothly on what I knew was a wood leg and a new boot that had all of Theopolis's custom flourishes. He'd filled out some, and I noticed how thick his broad shoulders were. He'd been working some, during these years. He wore a pair of dungarees and a white shirt with buttons down the front, and he looked like he took pride in that white shirt. It was spotless. He was spotless. Everything about my first glimpse of him since he left Carnton was spotless, unblemished, perfect, and burned into my memory from that moment forward.

He smiled, dug his hands into his pockets, and walked over to me. Mariah took my basket and walked it over to the head of the excavation, who called over some of his men. The man with the black eye patch grabbed two biscuits, like a child, and ducked back into the tent before anyone noticed.

Zachariah stood before me, not a foot away, and it was all I could do not to reach out and hold on to his shirt, to pull myself closer. His eyes were still bright and clear, so lively he seemed almost to be laughing at me.

"Meant to come see you up at the house, but we was right busy here, and I didn't have nothing nice to wear anyway."

"You look just fine, Zachariah."

"You look more beautiful."

I blushed and turned my head. This was no accident, no coincidence. Zachariah had come here on purpose, I could tell by the way he looked at me. For what? I did not know what he wanted from me, but I suddenly knew what I had wanted to know all along, ever since he left me that day in the possession of those Union officers: I knew that he was alive, that he would not forget me, and that we were forever two people who could not be sundered by distance or time. Ours was not a romance that could be made holy or by official union, but it was nonetheless permanent. I remembered how we used to talk to each other, so direct and blunt.

"Why did you come back, Zachariah?"

"Needed a job."

"Why are you *here*, though? Here, with us? With me?"

He didn't know what to say to me, so he fidgeted. I watched his eyes, and behind them I could see his mind turning over any number of options, perhaps explanations he'd worked out, words he had wanted to say to me, and nothing seemed to be satisfying him. He shook his head.

"Just happened."

"Nothing just happens."

He laughed and seemed to relax. He could see he knew the answer to my question now.

"Things *do* just happen, Carrie. You ain't learned a thing yet, have you?"

My hands were trembling, and I grasped them behind my back to keep them hidden. I felt like I was talking to some other part of myself when I talked to Zachariah, some part of me that had been absent for a long time but had returned briefly, only to disappear again for years. I would lose this part of me again when he went away, and I prayed that would not happen for a long time. I had visions of him settling in Franklin, of him picking up a trade and living in town and *always being around me*. I knew immediately this was not fair. I began to cry, little tears that dried in the heat. Zachariah put his hand on my shoulder.

"There's never been someone like you, Carrie. No one like you or your kind of people ever once treated me like you treated me. Respectful, like I had something to say, like I was worth keeping in your house. Not even my own kin would have stuck up for me like you did. I've never known anyone like you. It's hard to forget that feeling. You don't get to have it again, but you can't quit thinking you might."

"What was it, Zachariah? The feeling?"

"Don't know. Never had it before."

And neither had I.

We stood in the heat, listening to the insects whirring in the trees and the men murmuring to each other over Mariah's biscuits. What we had together was impossible and wonderful and fleeting, and so we both enjoyed standing close for as long as we could. I looked out over the camp, watched the men, and wondered if they could really help me. I knew there was one man in that camp who would do this thing I was going to ask of them, but I needed more.

"I've come for help. For your help and for help from these men."

Zachariah stepped back from me for a moment, and I suddenly was terrified that he thought this was the reason I'd come to see him—to get something out of him. But he only looked puzzled and a little amused.

"What could we possibly do for you? We ain't farmhands, me least of all of 'em."

"I need some men who can dig and also be gentle while they're digging."

"Well, they are sure enough diggers. What you need to dig?"

"I need to show you."

For days after the confrontation John and I had with Baylor, nothing changed. The dead stayed in the ground, the townsfolk in Franklin muttered unkindly about Mr. Baylor and his plans for the field, and some of the men in town who had fought with some of the soldiers who now lay buried a few hundred feet away promised retribution the moment he put his plow to the soil. Still, it is one thing to be outraged and quite another to find a solution. Talk of purchasing the land was silly, for who had the kind of money in those years to turn Baylor's head and soften his heart? One of our farmers, bless him forever, Lord, offered to trade his own land for the cemetery field. Baylor waived him off.

Two thoughts, call them epiphanies or divine interventions, both arrived unbidden in those few days and made clear to me what I was meant to do. The first came as we rode back from Baylor's house, and John told me more about the battlefield as he'd seen it during his days of roaming the town. The magnitude of it all was suddenly apparent to me. My mind darkened, his words having wormed their way inside me without my noticing, and in that moment I had a vision of that field and those streets, and what they must have been like.

The second epiphany was much simpler. I simply remembered what Mariah had said about the dead in that field: *They all alone. I see a lot of men.* That was my sign from God. *I am alone on this earth.* How often had I thought that very same thing, rocking in my room above the entryway, imagining that I had been abandoned by my own children? On my knees in angry prayer I had said those words as both a statement of fact and an accusation. But I knew now I was not alone on this earth. It hadn't come to me in a rush, there were no angels involved. I had just kept living, and living had shown me that there were other things in the world, like a one-legged sergeant who listened to me like I was the most exotic thing in the world, like a boy who could die on the floor of my house thinking only of how to get word to his mother, like a husband who would do anything for me even if it meant angering the man who held his debts, and so many other things I had observed just by sitting and living and keeping my eyes open.

I was not alone. I was surrounded by the living and the dead. I had always been that way, and it was a relief to finally know it truly. I knew I had always inhabited that gray and foggy space between living and dying, perhaps more than most people. I could not see the dead, as perhaps Mariah had been able to do, but I could *feel* them. I knew there was no preserving them in Baylor's field, that there would never be any rest for them as long as they lay outside my protection, and that there would be no rest for much of the *living*, either. Those men were the chains that bound the living. They were the missing whose absence shackled the survivors in place, people afraid to move on for fear of being gone for their sudden return. They drew the living back to the war, back to that batttlefield over and over and over again, reenacting its rituals and its skirmishes until they all would be dead. Baylor could not—*he would not*—act out his revenge with the casual desecration of those dead, whoever they were. He bore the broken heart of a man who loved his son, but he had allowed it to twist him into a monster. I would save him from that, too.

When I realized this, I walked out to where the grove had once stood—a forest of ancient cedars and oaks, walnuts and tulip poplars the Union army had cut down a few years before. Set in the center of what had been that grove, the gravestones of my children stuck up out of the ground and seemed to glow. I stood there, looking first at the names of my children etched into the rock, and then behind me, where the ground sloped gently downward. We would need only to put a gate in at the far side of the wrought-iron fence that circled my children and my ancestors, and this small plot of sacred ground could be joined to a much larger one.

They will have to come to Carnton. They'll be safe there. I will mourn them if no one else will.

The idea was so simple, and yet I could hardly breathe thinking about it. Could I bring the dead to me without losing my mind again, without sinking into the boggy depths? Yes, I could. They would not be alone, not as long as I was alive.

Zachariah and I agreed that he would ride up to the house that evening after he had finished working so that he and I could ride the battlefield and I could tell him about my larger problem with Baylor. Perhaps he had a solution—I had learned not to doubt his resourcefulness. I thought that John had done all he could do but that Zachariah could somehow find a way to get through to the man in some way we hadn't thought of. His companion appeared to be a gunfighter, after all.

That was the plan, at least.

Had I been paying attention to a certain young boy on the cusp of becoming a man, perhaps that's how it would have happened.

48

FRANKLIN

Eli always knew what was happening at Carnton, and when John and Carrie decided to ride off to see Mr. Baylor about something having to do with the battlefield, he knew all about it and was halfway to the Baylor house before they'd even finished hitching up their trap for the ride. He knew they would never take him, and so he didn't bother to ask. He didn't tell Winder about it, either, even though the boy followed Eli around like a loyal dog.

Eli had been watching Baylor and his family for months, trying to puzzle out the story of the man and his brood from snatches of conversation heard through open windows, and by observing those who went to see Baylor and those who crossed the street to avoid him. He had even followed the man to his son Will's grave, which was in a public cemetery but in a very fine spot, and he had watched him spill tears on the grass in front of the stone that read simply "Will Baylor, 1840–1864." He knew he should have felt something for the man, but his mourning, something Eli felt that Baylor tried to hide from everyone, made him despise the man even more. *Where are the tears for my sister's grave? Even though they dead, you still running around like you don't want no one to know you loved your son, all just because he was a rebel and you don't like them. Well, hell, what would you think of my sister, then? I'm sure you would not have even shed a tear.* He hated the man even more when the man was at his most vulnerable and pathetic.

He had a hiding spot around the corner of the old smokehouse, which still had hundreds of bullet holes in it. While he was waiting to hear something from the Baylor house, he would count the holes, and almost always he'd be about done with the counting when someone would yell something or come out of the house, and he'd lose track.

That's where he was when he heard the tail end of the McGavocks' conversation with Baylor, when he heard that bent-up old devil talk to the two people who had ever done anything for him, Eli, when he had been abandoned. How could he talk to Miss Carrie that way? He would not allow it. *This* was the woman who had come to their cabin to save his sister, dying while trying to bring into life another Baylor boy. She and Mariah had helped, they'd been *kind*, and they weren't kin to him at all. And here was Baylor, the secret mourner, treating the McGavocks like they were dirt, or worse—like Miss Carrie was crazy—to be worrying about dead soldiers. It really didn't matter what their conversation had been about; it was the disdain Baylor had for people he loved, which for the first time Eli witnessed with his own eyes on that day, that gave him resolve. He knew what he had to do now. He would not allow a man to speak to Miss Carrie that way. Not any man, and especially not *that* man.

His hate and obsession were the tinder, but it took an outrage against the living, someone he could defend before it was too late, to spark the fire. He had to bide his time, though. He couldn't follow through with his plan right away. He needed to do it just right. He planned to do it at night, and in his head he made a checklist of all he would need. He already knew where to find the most important items, perhaps the only items he would need. He just needed all of the McGavocks and Mariah to be out of the house. And when Carrie and Mariah went off to visit the Indian mound, and Mr. McGavock went off to look at one of his raggedy fields, Eli had his chance.

Eli knew one thing about Carnton that he shouldn't have known, and that was where John McGavock kept a small set of dueling pistols. They were up high on a shelf in his wardrobe, pushed back behind his sets of braces and cuffs. They weren't much to look at, rusted after not being used for years. They'd only been shot three times, each time by Eli himself. It was one of his most important secrets, the other being what he knew about his sister and her beau. These were secrets he shared with no one.

On three occasions Eli had cleaned up the barrel and chamber and hammer of one, just enough so that it would fire without looking like it *could* fire. Each time he'd taken it deep into the woods loaded with one round from the case, and each time he'd put a hole in an old cedar stump from ten feet. He had no love of the gun or of firing it. It just seemed like something he ought to know how to do.

Now he took down the pistol and shoved it deep in his pocket. In his other pocket he put the five remaining bullets and caps. He would load it later, on the way.

He would do it that night. He had only one night, because he didn't know how often Mr. McGavock checked his guns, and he would never lie to the McGavocks, even if they asked him if he knew where the guns were. He'd have to do it before they had a chance to ask. He waited until nightfall. Miss Carrie, expecting a guest, was too distracted to notice when he slipped off.

But Winder noticed. He'd seen the whole thing. Eli had underestimated Winder's resourcefulness; he had been watching *him* over the years as closely as Eli had watched Baylor. He knew about how Eli followed Baylor around and how he would sometimes mumble in his sleep about his sister and a man and angels and how he took his father's dueling pistol out into the woods to shoot. Winder was no dummy, although it served his purpose to have Eli think it—it made it easier to follow him without getting caught.

That night he watched Eli take the pistol and run out of the house. Winder had an idea where he was going. He couldn't decide whether Eli's actions were wrong or not, but he figured to let Eli make that decision. He trusted Eli, and he would not break their bond of loyalty, even if Eli didn't know it existed. So he went to his room and pulled out his collection of dead grasshoppers, which he counted again and again, but after about a half an hour of debating with himself, he went to Carrie to tell her what had happened. Zachariah Cashwell, the man with one leg who had lived with them, had just arrived. *That's odd*, he thought.

His mother screamed when Winder told her the story, and his father came running. The three adults stood in the foyer talking quickly. Then the one-legged man got back into his saddle with some difficulty and went riding hard toward town. Winder's father came next, followed by his mother, whom he had never seen ride a horse. *Eli's already there*, he thought. *You won't catch him.*

It was a long run from the woods to the steps of Mr. Baylor's front porch. It had not taken Eli much shouting to get the old man to come out of the house and down the steps to meet him. He had not given a second thought to raising his precious pistol and firing.

He had not aimed to kill, and the bullet lodged in the old man's left leg. He went down awkwardly, and Eli thought he heard the snap of a bone as Baylor twisted and screamed and tried to back away as he fell.

The old man did not know who he was, didn't recognize him, and that suited Eli just fine. Baylor hadn't known who his sister was, either.

Eli wanted to look into the man's face before he killed him, and so he walked carefully around the figure on the ground, always out of reach. He watched the blood pool and run in a strong rivulet down the slope of the man's dirt yard, toward the pike. Eli reckoned he had only a few minutes before the sound of his pistol would attract others. He'd have to finish it fast. He hadn't thought he could kill someone. *Reckon it matters who that someone is.* He could kill Baylor, that was certain, and he intended to do it. He got around to the man's head and looked and saw eyes that stared up unseeing, pleading with something beyond Eli, something more important than Eli, and Eli felt slighted. Here he was, bringing death, and the man was ignoring him as if he weren't even there. He raised the pistol.

When the others arrived, Eli had already shot Baylor and had his pistol up to the man's head. What were they going to do? John and Zachariah shouted at Eli to put down his pistol, but he only shook them off. They couldn't shoot the boy, although Zachariah had one of his Colts and John had his hunting rifle. They raised the weapons, but it was apparent in Eli's eyes that he was going to do what he was going to do, whether he died or not. And anyway, why *would* they shoot the boy? For the sake of Baylor? Eventually they went quiet and lowered their weapons, unsure what would happen next.

Carrie watched the boy confront the old man, and she watched the old man bleeding on the ground, refusing to beg for his life, refusing to do anything but to treat Eli like he was trash. She thought to shout out, but she didn't know what to say, and she felt suddenly afraid. Then she felt anger—at Eli? Baylor? Herself? She did not know, but welcomed it. *Good,* she thought, and then she cringed at the horror of that thought. *Good, good, good.* This hadn't been her plan, but *good.* She longed to be settled back in the safety and confinement of her little room at Carnton, far from the complication of towns and men. She wondered where the rest of the Baylors were. It was just Mrs. Baylor and a daughter, she remembered. They were probably hiding, hoping we'd do something. *I'd be hiding, too.*

She watched the boy approach the head of the old man and study him for a moment. Carrie knew she should speak, knew she should stop what had begun, but the words would not come out of her throat. There were no words, actually, just vague sounds and thoughts muddling around in her head.

Then Carrie heard the boy speak, clear as if she were standing beside him in the light thrown by the quarter-moon.

Eli was yelling about the boy Cotton. He said he knew Will's name but that he would always know him as Cotton. He told Baylor about how Cotton had courted Becky in secret because the old man would never have allowed it. He told him how he had learned that Cotton died on the battlefield right there on his own farm, leaving Becky to bear his child. It was the secrecy that enraged him, he said. His own sister had never revealed Cotton's real name, not even when she was dying.

Carrie could see that the old man was losing blood, but she could also see that he was getting some fight back into him. He raised himself up on his elbows and leaned back with his head up, gritting his teeth in pain but listening directly to the boy.

"Son, I'm dying here. I'm sorry about your sister, but you got no cause to come here with that pistol, and you'll hang for it."

"I ain't your son, and I ain't hanging for nothing."

"I need a doctor."

The boy ignored the old man, and Carrie wondered if it was God's intention for her to ride in and save the old man from the boy. She waited for some kind of sign.

"Not once, Mr. Baylor, not once did my sister say the real name of your boy."

"How does this concern me?"

"I've been thinking about how I might have been able to save her if I'd just known Cotton's name. I knew Cotton came from money and that he probably came from town. But I didn't know which son of a bitch owed my family help. A doctor, a place to rest, some medicine. I didn't know which one of you had an obligation to my sister, and so she died. I wish I'd gone to Mrs. McGavock sooner, but back then I didn't know what she thought of us, either. I didn't know what any of y'all thought of us."

Carrie cringed in shame. Baylor began to say something, but the boy cut him off.

"What I did know was that my sister died, and her son died, all because everybody was afraid of you, whoever you were, and what you would say about what they done, or who they were. I am alone now; I ain't got no one. That's your doing. I am alone on this earth, and that's also your doing. I'm here because I been thinking for years that if I ever figured you out, I would find you and show you that I weren't afraid of you or of crossing you or of killing you."

"Boy . . ."

"And you about to be killed now."

I am alone on this earth. Carrie had again received her sign from God.

"Don't do that, Eli."

Carrie's voice startled Eli, and he stepped back from Baylor as if the man were talking to him in two different voices and could throw one of them around and make it sound like a woman's. Carrie's horse seemed to understand the task at hand and began to walk forward into Baylor's yard.

"Don't kill that man, Eli."

Eli looked at her uncomfortably, as if he was possessed. But he stood up straight and faced her.

"I will kill him. I got my reasons."

Carrie lifted herself down from her horse and walked toward him. She stared into his eyes so intensely that he looked away.

"Step aside, Eli. I have business with this man. Lower that gun."

Eli did as he was told. She felt wild and angry and tough as hell. She knew that Eli wouldn't dare to cross her, even though, moments before, he was prepared to kill a man.

She stood over Baylor, who blessed her for interceding. She didn't speak, but picked up a small, sharp rock and made a tear a few inches from the bottom of her dress. Then she ripped it until it detached as one long, wide piece of cotton. A bandage.

She examined the wound with an expert's eye. The metal had torn through the fleshy part of Baylor's leg, leaving a jagged hole in his trousers. She took the rock and ripped his trouser leg at the bullet hole and then tore it off as she'd torn off the bandage. His leg was blue-veined and ghostly white except where the blood coursed down in steady, heavy streams. *He might die here anyway*, Carrie thought. She told Eli to fetch her a short, thick stick, which she then used to tighten the bandage above the wound, shutting off the blood.

"I believe you don't have much time to get to a doctor before that leg dies, Mr. Baylor."

She stood up again and looked down upon the man in the dirt, who had seemed to shrink before her eyes. He was an old man clinging to life, as primal as every other man. He let his hair gather dirt as he scrabbled at the ground, grimacing. One side of his face had turned clay red. And yet he was still the same man he had been minutes before, perhaps even more so. He croaked when he tried to talk.

"Have that boy arrested."

"I will not. He is not my business."

"Then I shall."

He tried to get to his feet but only managed a few moments before slumping heavily back down, panting.

"Mr. Baylor, I want to remove the dead from your field and bury them properly on our land."

He looked up at her, and she saw panic in his face.

"I am dying here, and you are talking about my field? You have no shame. You set this young boy upon me, who probably doesn't know any better . . ."

"The hell I don't," Eli said.

". . . so you could get those bones out of my *field*? And I'm supposed to just give up like that, bend to your crime? You would have me *shot* for those bones? You are insane."

"You weren't listening to the boy. His trouble with you is his own. You were listening, weren't you?"

"Yes." He went quiet for a moment. "Yes, I was. But I can't bring that boy's sister back, or her baby, or my boy. I can't bring any damned one of them back. The only thing that can be done is to go forward, and that does *not* include getting misty-eyed over dead who died so foolishly."

He called out to the house for his wife but received no response. We were the only people in the whole world right then.

"Just foolish, dead soldiers, that's what you think?"

"You must get me help, Mrs. McGavock. Please have pity."

"Those men in your field are no different from this boy here. Alone, without options, watching death come for them and those close to them. *Look at him!*"

Even Eli seemed to jump at her words.

"Do you see him? He's the boy who's dead in the field. Thousands of boys with no other option but, as you say, *to go forward*, straight into the fire. Do you think they marched themselves there on their own decision? Do you think they looked at your field and said to themselves, *This is a mighty fine place to die*? Your quarrel is with them? Is it?"

Baylor had propped himself up on his elbows again.

"I have learned, Mr. Baylor. I have learned from a man ten times more courageous than you that it was life and not death that those men, like this boy here, sought from this place. It's a paradox, but it's true nonetheless. I have learned from that man of the cruelty in the strategies of men, powerful men, men not unlike yourself. I have learned from him that there could have been no worse fate than to have died on your field, and yet there had been no choice. *Who would help them?* You were listening to the boy. Who? Who would help them, with their few choices, with no way out?"

Silence.

"No one. And it is alongside those men and boys that your own son fell, and surely you don't *hate* your own son. A stupid battle, yes. A brutal and cruel war, yes. But are those the men you hate? Are those the men with whom you have a quarrel?"

More silence.

"They aren't, no more than this boy. Any more than your own son. *Your own son!*"

Carrie could see she was running out of time. Baylor's eyes drooped and popped open intermittently, flashing and then slowly dousing themselves.

"We will leave now. I've told you what I want from you, but I will not threaten you for it. Neither will this boy. I will send for help, and I will not say one more word to you about this."

She bent over the old man with her hands on her hips and brought her face close to his. She could smell the tobacco in his hair.

"The bitterness will kill you quicker than that bullet, Mr. Baylor."

Carrie stepped back from the man, breathed deep, and put her hand tenderly on the top of Eli's head. She was relieved, and she relaxed and heard the cicadas buzzing in her ears for the first time.

She tried to figure out how they were going to get the boy and make an escape, as that was the most immediate thing that boy was going to need. *He has greater concerns than my interest in that field. He needs to run.*

She prayed to God that if He let the lonely, abandoned, sad boy get away and become happy again, if he'd ever actually *been* happy, she would not let Him or Eli down. She would give the men in that field a proper place to spend eternity. She would not shy away from the task. She would be about God's chores.

Eli pointed the pistol down at Baylor and set his thumb, ready to cock it. Carrie went toward him, and he waved her off with the pistol. The old man did not plead and cry for his life, as he had before. He stared straight into the barrel.

"I didn't hear you give Mrs. McGavock an answer, old man."

Baylor ignored the boy and turned his head toward Carrie. "Yes," he said.

Eli kept the gun pointed at Baylor. "Yes what?"

Baylor turned back to his attacker. "You can put that gun down. I've already decided to let Mrs. McGavock have her way."

"Or I'll shoot you, understand?"

"No, go ahead and shoot me. I'm going to die anyway. You'll learn someday, if you live long after this, that there are things about you, boy, that are more persuasive than that pistol of yours."

Eli cocked the hammer. It seemed he had taken Carrie's words to heart; he had his own business with the old man.

At that very moment Eli seemed to turn his scared and shining face straight toward Zachariah Cashwell. Cashwell could see the boy was begging for someone to relieve him of a burden he couldn't remove himself, an obligation he would have to meet unless someone stopped him. He was scared but ready to pull that trigger. Zachariah had been listening to every word Carrie had said and watching every gesture she'd made, and in her words he had found something of what he had come to find—a vision of himself as a different, better man. *I have learned from a man ten times more courageous than you that it was life and not death that those men, like this boy here, sought from this place.* He was proud to think of himself as courageous, but her words stirred up something else in him. He had not saved a single boy that terrible day in that place, and yet he knew what she said was true: every one of them had wanted to live, and there had been no good deaths on that field. *He* had been saved that day, but he had done no saving. No boy left that battlefield intact because he, Zachariah Cashwell, had made it possible.

He had one more chance to tell Carrie that he had missed her terribly and that he could never love someone as he loved her. He knew he couldn't have her ever, and her husband was sitting right there with a rifle, but he would have said it. He knew he had one more chance to thank her for saving his life when he didn't know he wanted it saved. He knew he had one more chance to tell her he had never known a woman like her and that he might not have ended up as he had if he'd known earlier there were women like her who saved lives instead of taking them, who could take in stray boys and love them without making them feel dirty and an imposition. He almost spoke of these things, right in front of Eli and Baylor and John, but he kept his mouth shut. She had already given him his gift. They would have to wait for another day, if there ever was one, to talk about the rest of it.

Having already committed a hanging crime, the boy stood over the old man. Baylor sat there, steadfast and unmoved by the boy and his weapon, as if welcoming his death. He was bleeding a little below the tourniquet. He'd need the doctor right quick, Zachariah thought.

Zachariah saw a boy who, if he was ever to grow to be a man, would have to live on the run, maybe forever. He looked over at Carrie, who stood a few feet from Eli, frozen. Zachariah would not accept that there was to be no other future for Eli except a hanging. Especially not if the hanging was for the crime of shooting a goddamn meddling, rich old fool who deserved at least a bullet in the leg and probably much more. Zachariah had no doubt that the justice that would be done, as much as it would make Zachariah sick to see it, would be proper and right and legal and that Carrie and John would accept it, even if it destroyed them. This was part of what Zachariah loved about all of them.

Proper and right. They were good at *proper and right,* and it was this that distinguished him from the McGavocks. That had not changed. Someday he hoped to be proper and right himself, but not quite yet.

He spurred his horse across the yard, snatched Eli up, and rode off past the house, around the new stable, down the hill, over a stream that seemed awfully familiar, and kept on going for years.

That best part of me has left again, and who knows when I will know it once more? Carrie thought, riding slowly back to Carnton next to the other man she loved. *We had so little time.* The tears, she lied to John, were tears of joy.

49

CARRIE McGAVOCK

The day I began retrieving the dead was impossibly, incongruously beautiful. It was a day that might have been held over from before the war, from my childhood back in Terrebonne when the sky was deep blue and cloudless and the wind carried the scent of the woods and fields. It was innocent.

The professor who had been excavating the Indian mound stood next to me, and we looked out across the field. He'd closed up the dig and resigned his position at whatever college had sent him. He had convinced five men to stay with him, including Jerrod, whom I remembered from his days with us at Carnton. The rest walked or rode off north somewhere. I was glad to have these six men who had so much experience handling remains. I'd decided on this course long before I'd ever considered what it actually meant.

Professor Stiles had warned me away. He told me the sight of the recently uncovered men would be too much for some of his men to take, let alone a woman. I told him that I was meant to be there and that if I fainted, then I was intended to faint. But I would not shy from the remains of these men or pretend that what I was doing wasn't itself a horrible solution to a more horrible proposition. I would not pretend that their movement from abandonment to discovery to final rest was an unremarkable journey. They would be exposed, the professor told me, and the stench would billow up, and some of them would be reduced to bones, and others would have mummified faces like leather. There would be hair and clothing everywhere. Their teeth would be bared and snarling. He did not think I should see such things. I said I thought I must see such things, that such things were the wages of war and it was only our own weakness as sinners, including my own, that required these last near 1,500 men to make the sacrifice that left them alone under a couple feet of Tennessee topsoil.

I believe that the professor was a man of faith, although he did not say it, and that he had no more use for war than I did. He told me, reluctantly, that he had been at the Battle of Franklin and that many of the men he would be digging up would be men he had helped to kill. I told him it was good that he could be there to do penance for that, and he nodded his head and wiped the sweat from the rim under his big black hat. *Penance. Don't know that I've made penance even once since then*, he said. *A man of faith*, I thought.

Mr. Baylor had not complained about giving us access to his field. He could not walk for a while after his encounter with Eli, but he kept his leg, and I suppose that was something he appreciated. He was a man of his word, and I suppose I should have never doubted that. He had been a schemer, but not ever a liar, and although I don't think he was happy about my plan for his field, he did not complain about it. He didn't give us much time, only three weeks, but he did not interfere. *Take on that nasty work if you must*, he told me. He watched us from the remains of his gin, sitting on a chair under the lean-to attached to the side of the ruin. He watched us every day, as if he were standing vigil over something. Once I looked up at him as his daughter tried to bring him back to the house toward suppertime, and he fended her off. He would not leave until we had left, and sometimes I think he stayed there until it was too dark to see.

Thanks to John's few remaining acquaintances among veterans of the army, we'd been able to acquire the notes of many of the original gravediggers, enough so that we could map out the field with some accuracy. *Arkansas by that redbud, Mississippi by the old hedge, Missouri in the middle right there, along with Texas and Tennessee. Alabama at the edge of the pike . . .*

We knew enough to begin digging, and that's how I found myself on the prettiest day I could remember, waiting for the first man to put the first shovel in the ground. John had command of a line of five large oxen carts waiting behind us, which we would use to shuttle the dead back and forth to the old grove right next to our family cemetery, where I had once walked and admired the complexity of the trees and of creation.

"Are you ready, Mrs. McGavock?"

Professor Stiles was sweating under his hat and in his coat. I thought he looked every bit an undertaker, and I smiled at the thought. He took that as a sign I was ready.

As they dug, I pulled out a bound book of blank pages, in which I intended to record the names and final resting places of the men. I had not brought a chair and had nowhere to sit, so I knelt a few yards away from the diggers and propped the book upon my lap.

It wasn't very long before they found the first grave, and as they scraped the dirt away, they exposed man after man, a dozen or more in a row, each facing up. They looked so much alike in death staring up at the sky out of sightless skulls. I cried out at the shame of it, that these men who had lived as individuals would be reduced to so many identical parts of some larger whole. The professor and John rushed over, thinking, I suppose, I'd been overcome by the gore of it all, but I waved them off.

Upon the chests of each of the men lay a piece of wood on which the gravediggers had done their best to scrawl a name and unit. Who knew how they'd discovered these names? I suppose they'd known many of the dead and that the others had something to identify them. A letter from home or enlistment papers or a name sewn in their uniform. I was grateful there were names, at least.

Each man was laid in a cart in the same order he was buried, and assigned a number, which was attached to the body and recorded in my book next to the name. Out of respect we did not pile the dead upon each other. This made John's task that much more difficult, but he did not complain. He just mounted up and dragged cart after cart back across the fields toward Lewisburg Pike and down the pike to the tollhouse and then down our lane, where two of the professor's men were waiting with fresh graves and wooden markers on which they scratched the initials and numbers I had assigned. John did not complain even when people began to line the road back to Carnton, watching him and craning their necks to get a good look at his cargo. I believe that he, too, had lost all interest in the good opinion of anyone around us and didn't give a hoot what they did or thought or saw.

The professor's description of the dead had been accurate. What I hadn't imagined was the magnitude of the task, which became apparent after the first dozen men were laid bare of dirt, and I considered how many similar rows of men must stretch out in every direction under my feet. *Fifteen hundred.* The entire plot must be filled with these men, I thought. We would have to work all day, every day, and I wasn't sure we would be able to rescue even half the men before Baylor's time limit expired.

As the days wore on, I considered walking up to the gin and begging Baylor for an extension of time. I would have done it, but soon another group of strangers began to appear. They weren't gawkers. These were the dirt farmers who lived perpetually in hock to the store, who worked much of what had been our land on behalf of Mr. Baylor himself. I'd forgotten them, and the fact that so many had been in the war themselves. They were stalk-thin and hollow-eyed, they had the yellow pallor of the perpetually undernourished, and they wore only threadbare clothes, but each brought with him a shovel and a cart and the promise of his time. Along with their labor, time was all they had to offer, I realized. I considered that it might be some kind of tribute to fallen comrades, but it was more likely the urge that some people have to pitch in and work when they see that work needs to be done. Every day a few more of these men showed up, until John had ten

looked up at me curiously, squinting through the deep crimping at the corners of her eyes. When I looked back, she was busily at work at the book, paying me no mind. *Good*, I thought.

In the little room over the entryway there was a small chest. In that small chest was a drawer, and in that drawer was a mourning veil. I put it on and walked into Martha's room to look in her mirror and make sure it fit. It looked old, but it would do.

The violence would not end, but I still had my role to play. Someone had to do it, to be that person. I was the woman they wrote the letters to; this house was the last address of the war. Now it was the final resting place of the dead, or at least almost 1,500 of them, and they could not be left alone. I had resolved to be the designated mourner, to be the woman who would remember so others could forget. In the forgetting, I prayed, would be some relief, some respite from the violence and bitterness and vengeance. Did I have hope? It did not really matter, but I had little. Still, there are things we are called to do that we cannot refuse, as futile as they seem, because to refuse them would mean to lose faith. Not just faith in God so much as faith in man, which I suppose amounted to the same thing.

When I returned to Mariah, I was carrying my own stool, and I sat down upon it and put my hands on my knees, just as she did. She looked up from the book and studied me.

"That veil need some work, Miss Carrie."

"I've plenty of time to mend it."

"I reckon you do. Yes, ma'am, you do."

The two of us wore those stools out over the years, but John always made us new ones.

CARNTON

1894

They walked slowly toward the house, back down the rows of the dead. Mariah followed behind, and little Paul scampered ahead. Three times Zachariah stopped to cough an evil, wracking cough, and three times Carrie helped him wipe his mouth and stand up. Those coughs told her all she needed to know. She thought it odd that the man who had taught her how to live in a world without sense was dying of a cause easily knowable and even *predictable*. Consumption. *The cough.*

"I don't want to be buried with Arkansas, if you don't mind. I know you got that book and all, and you don't like things not being exactly right and whatnot, but I'd just as soon be buried with Tennessee."

"I can do that."

"Seems like everything important happened here, so I might as well be buried with the Tennesseans."

"Anywhere you like. But you won't die."

"I don't need to be lied to."

"I know, but I do."

He coughed and spit, and Carrie could tell that his ribs would need tending.

She helped him up the steps of the back porch, which hadn't been painted in years. The balustrade had been wrapped up in wild vines and pokeberry, the wild world creeping in.

Cashwell turned at the top of the steps and looked out over the yard and the cemetery, the remains of the grove and the hills that hid the town beyond.

"I guess you couldn't leave once you got them in the ground over there."

"No, I don't think I could have, even after John died. Too much to do here."

"Like weeding."

Mariah harrumphed but let the insult slide. She could allow him that one, she thought.

"You done good, Carrie."

"I don't know about that."

"Well, you did something. More than most people can say."

He looked over at Mariah.

"You, too, Mariah. You done good. Don't know why you stayed around this place so long, but you done good."

Mariah leaned against the top baluster and twiddled a piece of grass in her fingers.

"Don't know nothing about *good*. Stayed around, at least. Too much work to do."

Zachariah was too overcome by the urge to cough and didn't reply. Carrie took him by the arm as if to lead him into the house, and he nodded.

As they crossed into the house, Zachariah spoke once more, just to Carrie.

"Eli's got three girls who call me Granddaddy."

"I know. He writes me from time to time."

Then he let Carrie guide him toward clean sheets and cool water. After she had laid him down to nap, she walked over to her sewing box and pulled out her scissors, which she used to clip a lock of Zachariah's gray hair, which she tied with a black ribbon and put in her pocket. Then she went to her wardrobe, and from the back of the bottom drawer she pulled an old and tattered flag, folded neatly into a triangle. She walked back to Zachariah's room, where he had almost drifted off.

"I believe this is yours. Professor Stiles gave it to me. He said he had kept it with him since the day of the battle. He said he's sorry he lied to you, but that you would understand him trying to forget. This is your property, he said."

Zachariah nodded, and closed his eyes. She turned to go, but then she heard him whisper.

"I knew that sumbitch was lying. My memory weren't ever *that* bad."

Then he fell asleep, and she walked softly down the stairs, pausing only to listen to him sigh as he settled in, comfortable at last.

EPILOGUE

Had the Battle of Franklin ever really ended? Carrie walked her cemetery, and around her the wounds closed up and scarred over, but only in that way that an oak struck by lightning heals itself by twisting and bending around the wound: it is still recognizably a tree, it still lives as a tree, it still puts out its leaves and acorns, but its center, hidden deep within the curtain of green, remains empty and splintered where it hasn't been grotesquely scarred over. We are happy the tree hasn't died, and from the proper angle we can look on it and suppose that it is the same tree as it ever was, but it is not and never will be.

The widow at Carnton embodied a hope that the tree would remain standing. No one with any sense would have looked upon the old fields and the abandoned farms of the once so proud and haughty South and not seen that things had been changed irrevocably and forever. Railroads began to unfurl again like spiderwebs across the Southern lands, killing off towns outside the turns and bends of the rails, creating others out of nothing more than proximity to the belching, screeching, clunking engines and their cargo. Men made and lost fortunes in those years and decades. A whole new kind of Southerner emerged, one for whom the customs and traditions of the old ways were nothing if not impediments to the acquisition and exploitation of wealth. They came to despise the old aristocrats and their thousand-acre plantations as forcefully, if not for the same reasons, as the abolitionists. But every transformation comes with the price of a whole new collection of frustrations and ennui born of rootlessness. Men transformed themselves and the South, and around Carnton fields were grown over with cedars and poplars while other old forests were cleared, the physical shape of middle Tennessee and the rest of the South shifting and recombining to correspond with the successes and failures of men. Once a cool grove of limbed-up old forest trees, now a golf course. Transformation carries with it the creeping awareness of the infinite possibility of change, the infinite *likelihood* of change, and at some point the whole thing becomes frightening and unmooring. One longs to know that some things don't change, that some of us will not be forgotten, that our perambulations upon the earth are *not* without point or destination.

Carrie McGavock, a transformed woman herself, remained at Carnton in those years. That she would stay there with her cemetery, marking its depth and breadth with her daily walks and her constant care, was, ironically, a counter to the transformation. From her little grove radiated another web, only this one offered the possibility of relief, that at least some things, some people, would not be forgotten, that all was not a race to an anonymous vanishing. Who has not witnessed the businessman, the politician, or the artist in their occasional moments of melancholy, wracked by desire for something solid to stand on, something they suspect they might have known were they living in a distant time, one they might not have ever known? Carrie McGavock witnessed it, thousands of times, every time someone came to visit her cemetery and realized that, at least for some, the sacrifice of living meant a sort of immortality so long as the handsome woman in the long, well-worn black bombazine kept her eye on her boys.

In death we are cleansed of our sins and our willfulness and the full complication of our life. Carrie knew this. She had read the letters of the families year after year and watched as their memories of the dead shifted and changed, becoming more wistful and simple as those memories receded in time, until all the dead were heroes. This would happen to her in time; she knew this and she dreaded it. Simple heroes are already forgotten, barely recognizable as flesh and blood. The thing she wanted most was to be remembered as she was. *No hope for that, I suppose, Mariah.*

A few years after she had reburied her dead, a family from Georgia arrived at Carnton, coming from Liberty County, where they lived with few neighbors in the country west of Hinesville, along a stream full of bass where they grew corn and kept to themselves. A man, his wife, his adult son, and his son's teenage boys. They were called the Winns, and they arrived in a wagon. Months earlier, they had asked the man at the store if he would write a letter for them to the woman they'd heard about in Franklin, Tennessee. *We are farmers, and all we gots corn to pay you for your time, but we would be awful obliged if you could tell us what come of our son, James Wilson Winn.* Carrie consulted her book, found their son, who was known in the cemetery as only *JWW,* and wrote to tell them that he had been found and that he lay in her cemetery among men he had known, that his story had ended but he was remembered. She didn't hear from them again, and she folded the letter in with the others. There had been so many letters during all those years.

Almost a year later they arrived at Carnton. They were thin and dusty and big-eyed, looking at her standing on her porch wrapped in honeysuckle and clematis and creeper vines, intimidating in her black but welcoming, in the way she stood and smiled at them. They told her they'd been traveling for more than a month, that they had been lost, and that they had almost turned home two days before, but they had taken the harvest moon that night as a sign. They wished to see their son, James, and to take him home to be buried at their place, in the soil that had held him up and fed him so many years before. Carrie wondered when they had last eaten a real meal. She also wondered what they were doing traveling in the summer away from their farm and their crops and garden, but she had heard of the drought and knew better than to ask. She asked if they would like to eat, and they said no.

She took them out to the cemetery, down the grassy aisle that separated one side from the other, state from state, until she arrived at Georgia. In the middle of one of the aisles, with his initials now carved upon the stone above his head, lay their son. *JWW.*

One of the boys turned and headed back to the cart for the shovels they'd brought with them, but Mr. Winn held him back. He held on to his grandson's arm and looked around the cemetery, all the while gripping the boy's arm tighter. He was not a terribly old man, but he seemed so from the dirt and dryness and days that had not varied for decades. He was bald and brown, and his forehead was carved through with lines that arched in the center and tailed off at the ends. Stoop-shouldered and ropy strong, he held on to his grandson, who could look and know exactly how he would look when he was old, and his grandson made no sound of protest. The man's eyes registered row upon row of young men who had been lost but were finally found, and the neatly clipped grass, and the iron fence that now kept them all in and separate from a world that had gone on without them, and he saw the beauty of the Tennessee hills that stretched away into the remains of the grove and beyond, toward the river. He looked down where James lay, the son he had not watched grow older, the son who had not married or had children, the son who had liked to fish in that bass stream, unlike his brother. Mr. Winn had fished alone for so long he had forgotten that. His son had died for something he had not understood, something that his father had known to be yet another of man's trespasses against paradise, man's unwillingness to leave things be. And yet his son was at rest among those he had known and with whom he had left the world behind.

He let go of his grandson. He shook his head and held his chin hard against his chest, not looking up. Carrie almost stepped forward to comfort him, but the man's wife had already done that. They didn't need her, she knew, and she stepped back. The man whispered to his family, and then they walked back to their wagon. Carrie caught up with them just as they were about to leave.

"Please, have supper with me. And you're welcome to stay."

Mr. Winn looked down at her, the reins limp in his hands, and smiled sadly.

"You done all you needed to do, Mrs. McGavock. We got to get back."

He ignored her pleading, but Mrs. Winn reached down and held her hand for a moment before the wagon lurched off.

Almost exactly a year later the Winns returned, this time with their wagon full of dirt. Again Carrie met them at the edge of her porch, and again she led them out to their son.

Mr. Winn looked over the cemetery again. His grandsons were just a little bigger, but he had become just a little smaller. He nodded his head.

"I'd like to rebury my son, if you don't mind, Mrs. McGavock."

Carrie was momentarily confused.

"Where do you wish to take him?"

"Don't want to take him anywhere. We want to bury him right there, but with his dirt we brung from the farm. Seems right, to end up in the soil you were supposed to end up in. It ain't been much good to us down in the field, thought James might use it better."

Then the man's whole family went to get their shovels and to pull the dirt wagon around to the grave.

While they worked, Carrie went down to Theopolis's old tool-shed, down by the cabin where she had hid Cashwell, and inside among the spiders and the secretive crickets, she found an old rusty shovel. She used the shovel as a cane to brace her on the long trip back up the hill, trying to hold her skirt up so she wouldn't trip, past the kitchen where she could see Mariah bent over the stove like she'd never ever left it, into the cemetery, and to the side of James's grave.

This time, she thought to herself as she took her place graveside and dug deep, *they're not leaving without supper.*

AUTHOR'S NOTE

If God was watching that Indian summer afternoon of November 30, 1864 (and some have argued that He was not, another explanation of events), He would have been looking here: on the continent of North America; in the southeastern section of what had once been and would again be called the United States; in the central part of a state they called Tennessee; between the mountains and the great river; among the burial mounds of an ancient Stone Age culture that had known nothing of firearms and artillery; in the bend of a small river at the convergence of three bright white macadam roads, where brilliant streaks of light rose and fell along a gentle undulation of hills washed in the dun and yellow and red of autumn.

At that place there was a town called Franklin. And in this town, if He did have the power of foreknowledge, as we have been taught, He would have known that in a few hours 9,200 men would fall dead, or mangled so badly they would sometimes wish they were dead. He would have known that a fragile young woman with cares of her own would watch her house be invaded by a horror she would never forget, that Franklin boys would watch their families disappear, that old men would watch their sons die for something they could not understand, and that the events of the day would rattle around Franklin as memories or ghosts for years and decades and centuries to come. It might have occurred to Him to wonder at the vagary of His own Creation, that this would happen in Franklin by virtue of nothing other than its misfortune in being on the route between Atlanta and Nashville. But that is war.

Many consider the battle to be the bloodiest five hours of the Civil War. In the waning afternoon light, a crimson cast fell over Franklin. The smoke from the guns—so thick that troops couldn't tell enemy from ally—glowed a thick, dull red. Running toward it, many soldiers later remembered the light as an ominous sign, but still they kept running. It was one of the greatest massed-infantry assaults ever seen in North America—more than double Pickett's similarly ill-fated charge at Gettysburg a year earlier.

Federal troops had already occupied Franklin for almost two years before Major General John Schofield and his Union army arrived on the morning of Wednesday, November 30. By then the entire town had been fortified, encircled by a series of trenches, breastworks, and forts. That fatal afternoon, Confederate General John Bell Hood—over the protests of Generals Cleburne, Cheatham, and Forrest—marched his Army of Tennessee down Winstead Hill, just to the south of Franklin, and assaulted up the next hill through nearly two miles of open fields toward the well-fortified Union lines. Wave after wave of Confederate soldiers sprinted down Columbia and Lewisburg Pikes, converging past a plantation house called Carnton, and up toward the fortified town—only to be struck down, again and again.

Through the late afternoon and into the evening, there were more casualties those five hours at Franklin than in the nineteen hours of D-Day—and more than twice as many casualties as at Pearl Harbor. There were moments so bloody and overwhelming that even the enemy wept. When a fourteen-year-old Missouri drummer boy—a mascot of Cockrell's Brigade—charged up to a loaded and primed Ohio cannon and shoved a fence rail into its mouth, witnesses said the child turned into what was described as the "mist of a ripe tomato."

Most of the fighting was over by nine o'clock, both sides depleted. That night—or very early in the morning—as General Hood prepared to resume battle the following day, General Schofield withdrew his Federal troops to the Union stronghold of Nashville.

Those who were left—the ragged rebel army and the townspeople—had to wait until the early morning light before they could see and begin to understand the horror of the battle. The dead covered the ground. Rivulets of blood ran across the fields and pooled shoe-deep in the trenches, where men were stacked like cordwood: The body of Col. F. S. S. Stafford, of the 31st Tennessee, was found dead standing upright, wedged up to his waist in corpses.

The Battle of Franklin occurred on the edge of a small, isolated town of 2,500. Think of it: 2,500 men and women, trying to bury or heal more than three times their number in dead, dying, and wounded men, on one of the smallest battlefields in the United States. The Union had suffered 2,500 and the Confederates almost 6,700 casualties in "Bloody Franklin," as it came to be called. A full third of the Confederate infantry had disappeared in the smoke of the battle. Generals Patrick Cleburne, John Adams, "States Rights" Gist, Otho F. Strahl, Hiram B. Granbury, and John C. Carter were all killed, eight others were wounded, and one captured: the largest number of American generals ever lost in battle. Eleven enlisted men received the Congressional Medal of Honor.

Not long after, General Hood resigned, and the negotiations at Appomattox Courthouse brought an end to the war, but its outcome had already been decided. As General Issac R. Sherwood, a lieutenant colonel in the 111th Ohio Infantry who was himself wounded at Franklin and was one of the last veterans of the war to serve in Congress, put it in his *Memories of the War*:

The battle of Franklin . . . was the most destructive of
human life, in proportion to the number engaged, of any
battle in the four years war. Franklin dug the grave of the
Confederacy. . . . When the true story of the war is written,
the valley of the Harpeth River and the Brentwood Hills,
south of Nashville, will become the valor-crowned fields
where the destiny of the Southern Confederacy was settled. The final day was Appomattox, four months after
Franklin; but Appomattox was not a battle. It was an event,
surrender. Four months before Appomattox the black curtain of destiny had fallen on the vast stage of human grief
and woe amid the lurid lights of flashing guns. The epochal
date was April 1865, but the forces that made that day possible were marshaled on the green hills around the Harpeth
River. At midnight on the battlefield of Franklin, the
finger of destiny was lifted, pointing the open road to
Appomattox.

The "Big House" at Carnton stood at the edge of the eastern
flank of the battlefield. Some fighting took place within a few
hundred yards of the house itself, while many more men fought
each other on the plantation fields, stretching away toward the
town of Franklin.

The name "Carnton" derives from an old Gaelic word, *cairn,*
which is sometimes translated as "city of the dead." Randal
McGavock, John's father, had named the property after his
father's birthplace, "Carntown," a house built on top of an
ancient cemetery near Glenarm Bay in County Antrim, Ireland.
The wealthy McGavock family owned between twenty and forty
slaves, who worked a diverse farming operation: a large orchard;
fields of corn, beans, sweet potatoes, wheat, oats, hay, and potatoes; and herds of fine thoroughbred horses, sheep, cattle, and
hogs. The plantation produced nearly everything the family
needed. Blacksmiths, coopers, weavers, carpenters, and tanners
all lived on the property, providing all essentials except for
luxury items for the house and family.

The Battle of Franklin transformed Carnton into a makeshift

The back porch of Carnton with the McGavock family, c. 1904.
Forty years earlier, on the morning of December 1, 1864, the bodies of
four Confederate generals had been laid out on this same porch
after being carried from the battlefield.

field hospital for the hundreds of wounded and dying soldiers brought from the battlefield along the Columbia Pike south of Franklin. They filled up the house, the outbuildings, and the grounds.

Colonel W. D. Gale, from General Stewart's staff, wrote in a letter to his wife:

> [Mrs. McGavock's] house . . . was the rear of our line. The house is one of the large old-fashioned houses of the better class in Tennessee, two stories high, with many rooms. . . . This was taken as a hospital, and the wounded, in hundreds, were brought to it during the battle, and all the night after. Every room was filled, every bed had two poor, bleeding fellows, every spare space, niche, and corner under the stairs, in the hall, everywhere—but one room for

her own family. And when the noble old house could hold no more, the yard was appropriated until the wounded and the dead filled that, and all were not yet provided for.

Our doctors were deficient in bandages, and [Mrs. McGavock] began by giving her old linen, then her towels and napkins, then her sheets and tablecloths, then her husband's shirts and her own undergarments. During all this time the surgeons plied their dreadful work amid the sighs and moans and death rattles. Yet, amid it all, the noble woman . . . was very active and constantly at work. During all the night neither she nor any of the household slept, but dispensed tea and coffee and such stimulants as she had, and that, too, with her own hands.

Following the war, in 1866, the McGavocks designated nearly two acres of land abutting their family cemetery for the reburial of close to 1,500 Confederates. The original shallow graves, dug

The McGavock Cemetery, c. 1866, with the original whitewashed wooden markers, surrounded by its new, still unpainted, wooden fence.

immediately after the battle, had been difficult to protect, and the family that owned the land decided to plow it over and put it into cultivation. Carrie McGavock's rescue of the dead was an extraordinary feat. Today the cemetery serves as the final resting place for 1,481 Confederate soldiers killed at Franklin, plus fifteen veterans of the battle and one civilian who died while helping the McGavocks to rebury the dead. The cemetery is today maintained by the United Daughters of the Confederacy.

In the mid-1980s, the nonprofit organization founded to restore Carnton asked me to join their board. As I learned more about the story of Carnton and met the McGavock descendants, I realized there was a *reason* one of the largest private military cemeteries was in the backyard. I began to ask questions. Eventually, as some of the descendants let me look at the scrapbooks they'd saved of articles and obituaries, I came to realize the extraordinary history of this place. From the Battle of Franklin—in the present day so often forgotten, even in Franklin—to Carrie McGavock herself, I knew there was an important, bigger story that needed to be told and remembered.

To understand what happened, I have tried to fill in the blanks and empty spaces, always studying the historical details to help create a novel, not a history. My hope was to use the tools of fiction to divine a greater truth about the war, about the sacrifices of women like Carrie, and about the world she inhabited. There are far better historians of both this battle and the Civil War generally, and I've included their work in the bibliography. I hope you'll read them.

My one true interest as a writer has always been in Carrie, and in the people who moved in her orbit. Why Carrie, particularly? As William Thackeray once wrote, "Good or bad, handsome or ugly, rich or poor, they are all equal now." But I believe that some remain more equal than others, and that some are more deserving of our praise and our remembrance. If I've accomplished nothing else with this novel, I hope I've remained faithful to Carrie's memory—and that she lives on these pages as someone worth remembering.

Caroline Elizabeth Winder was born near Natchez, Missis-sippi, on September 9, 1829. Her mother, Martha Anne Grundy, was the daughter of the Hon. Felix Grundy, the great lawyer and senator from Tennessee. Her father, Van P. Winder, owned a plantation southwest of New Orleans among the bayous. This is where Carrie—she hated to be called "Caroline"—grew up. As *The Confederate Veteran* wrote in her obituary, "She received the best intellectual and moral training according to the ideals and standards of the Presbyterian Church, of which the family were members." Although she has left little surviving written testi-mony of her life, there are a few stories that have been passed down over the years.

One of my favorites deals with her portrait by Washington Bogart Cooper, the leading society painter in Nashville during the two decades before the war. As a teenager, she was sent from her home in Louisiana to spend the summer with her mother's parents in Tennessee—probably to reconnect with her cousin and future husband, John McGavock. While Carrie was there, an argument arose over the color of the dress she intended to wear for her portrait. Cooper wrote to Carrie's mother, in Louisiana, for guidance: Carrie was insisting on being painted in black, which was completely inappropriate for a young unmarried girl. Mrs. Winder's response was both brief and to the point: "I have tried to guide my oldest child in appropriate and godly behavior all her days. I sent her to Nashville with fourteen dresses. Good luck, Mr. Cooper."

Carrie and John were married on December 8, 1848. The couple had five children, three of whom had died before the Battle of Franklin: Martha W. (1849–1862), Mary E. (1851–1858), and John Randal (June–September 1854). She had a portrait painted of these three "angels," as she called them, and hung it on the wall across from her bed. Two children, Harriet "Hattie" Young (1855–1932) and Winder (1857–1909), grew into adulthood and survived their mother.

After the war, Carrie devoted herself to tending her cemetery and caring for orphans, as the Reverend Robert Gray wrote in his privately printed *The McGavock Family*:

Caroline (Carrie) Elizabeth Winder at nineteen, by Washington Bogart Cooper.

Colonel John McGavock, by Washington Bogart Cooper.

The Lost Children, *by William Browning Cooper:* (left to right) *Mary Elizabeth, Martha, and John Randal.*

Daguerreotype of Martha (left) *and Mary Elizabeth McGavock.*

It has been her habit for years to take to her house from two to three orphans, generally from the asylum in New Orleans, to act as household servants; at the same time educating them, giving special attention to their religious training, and when they are of age paying the outfit agreed upon, and finding them suitable homes and employment. We have seen the fatherless and motherless little ones as happy as larks, and as gentlemanly and ladylike in their deportment as the most fastidious could desire.

In time, Carrie McGavock was transformed into a living martyr and curiosity. The story is often told that when Oscar Wilde made his infamous tour of America in 1882, he told his hosts that his itinerary should include a visit to "sunny Tennessee to meet the Widow McGavock, the high priestess of the temple of dead boys." She became famous without ever leaving her farm, renowned for her daily wanderings in the cemetery, for her mourning clothing, for her letters to the families of the bereaved, and, most of all, for her constancy. From the day the last of the dead was buried in her backyard, she rarely left her post in the cemetery, continuously checking her book of the dead.

This is not speculation. Carrie McGavock became a national embodiment of the grief that civil war had laid upon the whole nation. Cemeteries grew and sprouted as if a plague had swept the country. So many cemeteries were built by governments and laid out in perfect regimentation, with much pomp and ornament; it was modesty that distinguished the cemetery at Carnton, which for years didn't even have stone markers or a fence. All that the cemetery at Carnton had was Carrie, who had not shrunk from the war, who had not ignored it, who carefully preserved the inscriptions on the grave markers in her *Cemetery Record Book*. She had brought the war home, and she grieved every day of her life for the row upon row of men she had never known. As we might take comfort to know that there are mothers and monks and nuns praying around the clock for the relief of our sins, men and women of this country took comfort and even pride from knowing that Carrie was there at her post, day after day. She was a Southerner who had become an American by her persistent sacrifice. Her genius was that she had known all along that this would happen to her, that this was her purpose.

So much changed in the aftermath of war. The plantation class grew old and died, as John did in 1893, and it was unclear who would take their place. Violence and lawlessness marked those years following the war, and still Carrie stayed put. By the thousands, as country people became town folks and her house became an old pile—older, grayer, and more rickety—still Carrie would not move. The world changed around her, but she remained a rock in the stream, letting the flow of time rush past.

Carrie McGavock, c. 1894, the Widow of the South.

When she died twelve years after her husband, her obituaries—which appeared in Franklin and Nashville, Richmond and Jackson, Chicago and New York—sought again and again to describe her. A paper in Mississippi compared her to Boadicea, queen of the ancient Britons, and another to Joan of Arc. My favorite begins simply: "The last Rebel was buried at Carnton yesterday." Her little patch of dirt had become so famous that there needed to be no explanation of what or where Carnton was. Her story was now part of our story. "Those of us who recall how she ceased to care for herself as she cared for the dying and how she spent her remaining years caring over the dead, we and all generations after us will rise up and call her blessed," the Reverend John Hanna said at her funeral. But Hanna and the rest of the eulogizers were wrong: Generations did not rise up and call her blessed; most soon forgot her name, and the memory of all she had done began to fade into nothingness.

* * *

Winder and his heirs made "good marriages." His descendants have become educators, doctors, adventurers, businessmen, and public servants; Hattie married the Irish immigrant George Cowan, who had ridden with Nathan Bedford Forrest.

John and Carrie McGavock were buried in the McGavock family cemetery, next to their three lost children—and within feet of the 1,500 soldiers whom Carrie watched over for so long.

While I make no claim that I know any of the real characters who populate this book, I have concluded that Mariah may well have been the most complete human of them all. Rarely does she seem altered by her circumstance. Mariah had been given to Carrie when both were girls, and the two remained together, whether living at Carnton or in town, throughout Carrie's life. Of Carrie, Mariah was reported to have said that "no woman ever had a better friend." She died on December 16, 1922, at ninety years old. She retained, her obituary says, "her mental faculties and her devotion to her friends until the last." I would have expected nothing less.

Mariah Otey Reddick, with Carrie's grand-daughter and name-sake, Carrie Winder Cowan, January 6, 1885.

* * *

I submit my sincerest apologies, to those who require it, for meandering from the history in the interest of telling a story. Other than Carrie and her immediate family and slaves, most of the other characters are either composites of historical figures from Franklin's past or were born in my imagination.

There remains so much that I do not know, which I now realize I will never know. All I can know for sure is that there was once a battle here, and it forever changed everything.

—ROBERT HICKS
Franklin, Tennessee

McGavock Confederate Cemetery, with the small limestone markers that replaced the original wooden markers; the larger stones were placed by individual families. The iron fence that now encloses the cemetery was added in the late nineteenth century. (Photo Credit: Robin Hood)

BIBLIOGRAPHY

Ayers, Edward L., *The Promise of the New South: Life After Reconstruction* (1992)

Ayers, Edward L., *Vengeance and Justice: Crime and Punishment in the Nineteenth-Century American South* (1984)

Beale, Howard K., *The Critical Year: A Study of Andrew Johnson and Reconstruction* (1930)

Carman, Jack B., *Wildflowers of Tennessee* (2001)

Cash, W.J., *The Mind of the South* (1941)

Chesnut, Mary Boykin, *A Diary from Dixie* (1949)

Cimprich, John, *Slavery's End in Tennessee* (1986)

Clinton, Catherine, *The Plantation Mistress* (1982)

Clinton, Catherine, and Nina Silber, eds., *Divided Houses: Gender and the Civil War* (1992)

Cox, Jacob D., *The March to the Sea: Franklin and Nashville (Campaigns of the Civil War* X) (1882)

DeForest, John William, *Miss Ravenel's Conversion from Secession to Loyalty* (1867)

Donald, David, *The Politics of Reconstruction, 1863–1867* (1965)

DuBois, W.E.B., *Black Reconstruction in America* (1935)

Faust, Drew Gilpin, *Mothers of Invention: Women in the Slaveholding South in the American Civil War* (1996)

Foner, Eric, *Reconstruction: America's Unfinished Revolution, 1863–1877* (1988)

Foote, Shelby, *The Civil War, A Narrative: Red River to Appomattox* (1974)

Foster, Helen Bradley, *New Raiments of Self: African American Clothing in the Antebellum South* (1997)

Fox-Genovese, Elizabeth, *Within the Plantation Household: Black and White Women of the Old South* (1988)

Friedman, Jean E., *The Enclosed Garden: Women and Community in the Evangelical South, 1830–1900* (1985)

Gay, Mary, *Life in Dixie During the War* (1897)

Gower, Herschel, and Jack Allen, eds., *Pen and Sword: The Life and Journals of Randal W. McGavock* (1960)

Hill, Samuel S., ed., *Varieties of Southern Religious Experience* (1988)

Hurst, Jack, *Nathan Bedford Forrest: A Biography* (1993)

Jaynes, Gerald D., *Branches Without Roots: Genesis of the Black Working Class in the American South, 1862–1882* (1986)

Kousser, J. Morgan, and James M. McPherson, eds., *Region, Race and Reconstruction: Essays in Honor of C. Vann Woodward* (1982)

Lamon, Lester C., *Blacks in Tennessee, 1791–1970* (1981)

Litwack, Leon, *Been in the Storm So Long: The Aftermath of Slavery* (1979)

Logsdon, David, ed., *Eyewitnesses at the Battle of Franklin* (1988)

Lorenz, Konrad, *On Aggression* (1966)

Lytle, Andrew Nelson, *Bedford Forrest and His Critter Company* (1931)

McDonough, James Lee, *Five Tragic Hours: The Battle of Franklin* (1983)

McKitrick, Eric L., *Andrew Johnson and Reconstruction* (1960)

McPherson, James M., *Battle Cry of Freedom* (1988)

Milton, George F., *The Age of Hate: Andrew Johnson and the Radicals* (1930)

Morgan, Marshall, *The Battle of Franklin* (1931)

Osofsky, Gilbert, ed., *Puttin' on Ole Massa: Slave Narratives of Henry Bibb, William Wells Brown and Solomon Northrop* (1969)

Ownby, Ted. *Subduing Satan: Religion, Recreation, and Manhood in the Rural South, 1865–1920* (1990)

Rable, George, *Civil Wars: Women and the Crisis of Southern Nationalism* (1989)

Roark, James L., *Masters Without Slaves: Southern Planters in the Civil War and Reconstruction* (1977)

Robateau, Albert, *Slave Religion: The Invisible Institution in the Antebellum South* (1978)

Saxon, Lyle, *Fabulous New Orleans* (1928)

Scaife, William R., *Hood's Campaign for Tennessee* (1986)

Scofield, Levi T., *The Retreat from Pulaski to Nashville, Tenn.: Battle of Franklin, Tennessee, November 30, 1864* (1909)

Scott, Anne Firor, *The Southern Lady: From Pedestal to Politics, 1830–1930* (1970)

Stover, John F., *The Railroads of the South, 1865–1979* (1983)

Sword, Wiley, *The Confederacy's Last Hurrah: Spring Hill, Franklin and Nashville* (1992)

Sword, Wiley, *Southern Invincibility* (1999)

Trelease, Allen W., *White Terror: The Ku Klux Klan Conspiracy and Southern Reconstruction* (1971)

Warwick, Rick, ed., *Williamson County: In Black and White* (2000)

Watkins, Sam R., *Co. Aytch* (1881)

Winkler, Gail Caskey, and Roger W. Moss, *Victorian Interior Decoration: American Interiors, 1830–1900* (1986)

Woodward, C. Vann, *Origins of the New South, 1877–1913* (1951)

Wyatt-Brown, Bertram, *Southern Honor* (1982)

WITH GRATITUDE

While my list of acknowledgments is long, it will never be complete. There are so many folks who told me stories and opened windows to the past; who supported, rallied, and encouraged me through this process. That said, I would truly be amiss if I didn't thank the following:

My parents, both gone now, are the foundation of it all. My dad was filled with stories—about growing up in the South a century ago, a place with one foot in the past and one foot in the present. Though the Civil War had been over for forty years when he arrived, so much of it, both good and bad, permeated the world in which he grew up. That fading world was passed on to us with his stories. I will forever remember my mother, while not near the storyteller, for her overwhelming capacity to love, and for her wisdom and the belief—which she shared with my dad—that all things are possible.

Then there is my brother, Marcus Sanders, and his wife, Candy Allen, who continue to remind me, through their own passion for life, how very lucky I am to call them my family.

That first conversation with Jeff Kleinman, my agent, was probably the single most important event in the process that led me here. Under his care, every step of the way, a story came to life as he reeled me in again and again.

I was fortunate to find an extraordinary freelance editor in Duncan Murrell, without whose creativity and vision this idea would never have gone very far, and without whose hard work and insight this book would never have been finished. What he does is an art, and as I and many other authors will attest, he is one of that art's finest practitioners. He gave me the confidence that I really could be a writer.

Then there are the amazing folks at Warner Books, who believed in this book when it was little more than a handful of pages and a very big dream. First and foremost Amy Einhorn, editor extraordinaire, for working so very hard with such amazing sensitivity, honesty, and care. Any author would be so lucky to have her bringing all the pieces together. I feel as if I won the lottery with Amy. Todd Doughty is simply, without a doubt, the very best publicist anyone could ever ask for. And thanks are of course due to Jamie Raab, Larry Kirshbaum, Maureen Egen, Emi Battaglia, Ivan Held, Martha Otis, Karen Torres, Bob Castillo, Rebecca Oliver, Nancy Wiese, Bruce Paonessa, Anne Twomey, Tom Whatley, Harvey-Jane Kowal, Ann Schwartz, Huy Duong, Toni Marotta, Blanca Aulet, Flamur Tonuzi, Oscar Stern, Janice Wilkins, Brad Negbaur, and last but not least Jim Schiff. Special thanks are also extended to Giorgetta and Leo McRee, who designed the book.

Hunter Kay, my business partner on the project, amazingly, against all odds and despite the pitfalls of any working partnership, has remained my friend through the years.

Kay and Curt Jones and Caroline and George Ducas literally supported me toward the end as I pushed to the finish. Without their help, I would have been lost.

Justin Stelter—a sounding board, my hardest critic, a good friend, a supporter of all good things, a young writer in the making.

Mary Springs and Stephane Couteaud, Hazel Smith, Constance and Gordon Gee.

Pete Donaldson and Jay Sanders.

My good friend Rick Warwick and all the other real historians and scholars who tried their darnedest to keep me on track. I would be completely amiss if I didn't mention our beloved county historian, Virginia McDaniel Bowman; James Redford, Gail Winkler and Roger Moss, Angela Calhoun, Margie Thessin, Lee Miller, and all the folks at Carnton, Paul McCoy, David Fraley, Ed Bearss, Wiley Sword, Carroll Van West, and James Lee McDonough, who first told me the story of the Battle of Franklin some thirty-five years ago.

Then there is Thomas Cartwright. With regard to the Battle of Franklin, there has never been anyone who has ever touched me with more passion than Thomas. He has been my resource for understanding and detail, again and again. Luckily for me, he is a friend.

The McGavock family—Kay and Roderick Heller, Mary and Winder Heller, and Patty and Hanes Heller, friends and encouragers of the book, battlefield recoverers at Franklin, Carnton, and so much more—and all the rest of their tribe.

My fellow travelers in Franklin's Charge, some of whom have been with me from that very first spring day on the back porch at Carnton when I laid out a pipe dream of preserving those last fragments of the battlefield. Through your tireless efforts, that pipe dream has been given life: Danny Anderson, Ernie Bacon, Warner Bass, Julian Bibb, Dorie Bolze, Mary and Hank Brockman, Angela Calhoun, Jim Campi, Thomas Cartwright, Amy Grant and Vince Gill, Sam Huffman, Rudy and Peter Jordan, Jim Lighthizer and everyone at CWPT, Stacey McRight, Tommy Murdic, Jeanie Nelson, George Patton, Mary Pearce, Damon Rogers, Cindy Sargent, and Joe Smyth. Future generations may well forget all that you have done for them, but your good work will go before you. If we really are eternal, as we've been taught, please know that you have my eternal thanks.

The loved ones who were ignored and stood by as I ate up their time with Jeff (Pete Verloop and Corinne), Duncan (Sherri and Caroline), and Amy (Matt, Ashley Rae, and Tess).

And, finally, there are Catherine Anderson, Michel Arnaud,

Michael Balliet, Bo Bills, John Bohlinger, Gertrude and Ben Caldwell, Dub Cornet, P.J. Dempsey, L.D., Steve Emley, Diana and Gary Fisketjon, Valerie Ellis Fleming, Andrew Glasgow, Rob Hodge, Linda and Doug Howard, Chad Huie, Monte Isom, Jay Jones, Eric Levin, Evan Lowenstein, Mary Ruth Martin, Matt McGregor, T.M., Dave Pelton, Tommy Peters, Ellen Pryor, Charles Salzberg, Tamara Saviano, Michael Sherrill, Toby Standefer, Lynn and Ghislain Vander Elst, and Tim Young. Your care, wisdom, and encouragement over the years are not forgotten.